Lady Baltimore

Southern Classics Series
M. E. Bradford, Editor

Southern Classics Series
M. E. Bradford, Series Editor

Lady Baltimore

OWEN WISTER

illustrations by
Vernon Howe Bailey and Lester Ralph

with a preface by Thomas Fleming

J. S. Sanders & Company

NASHVILLE

Library of Congress Catalog Card Number:
92-089830

ISBN: 1-879941-13-9

Published in the United States by
J. S. Sanders & Company
P. O. Box 50331
Nashville, Tennessee 37205

Distributed to the trade by
National Book Network
4720-A Boston Way
Lanham, Maryland 20706

1992 printing
Manufactured in the United States of America

To

S. Weir Mitchell

with the affection and memories of all my life

TO THE READER

You know the great text in Burns, I am sure, where he wishes he could see himself as others see him. Well, here lies the hitch in many a work of art: if its maker — poet, painter, or novelist — could but have become its audience too, for a single day, before he launched it irrevocably upon the uncertain ocean of publicity, how much better his boat would often sail! How many little touches to the rigging he would give, how many little drops of oil to the engines here and there, the need of which he had never suspected, but for that trial trip! That's where the ship-builders and dramatists have the advantage over us others: they can dock their productions, and tinker at them. Even to the musician comes this useful chance, and Schumann can reform the proclamation which opens his B-flat Symphony.

Still, to publish a story in weekly numbers previously to its appearance as a book does sometimes give to the watchful author an opportunity to learn, before it is too late, where he has failed in clearness; and it brings him also, through the mails, some few questions that are pleasant and proper to answer when his story sets forth united upon its journey of adventure among gentle readers.

How came my hero by his name?

If you will open a book more valuable than any I dare hope to write, and more entertaining too, *The Life of Paul Jones*, by Mr. Buell, you will find the real ancestor of this imaginary boy, and fall in love with John Mayrant the First, as did his immortal captain of the *Bon Homme Richard*. He came from South Carolina; and believing his seed and name were perished there to-day, I gave him a descendant. I have learned that the name, until recently, was in existence; I trust it will not seem taken in vain in these pages.

Whence came such a person as Augustus?

Our happier cities produce many Augustuses, and may they long continue to do so! If Augustus displeases any one, so much the worse for that one, not for Augustus. To be sure, he doesn't admire over heartily the parvenus of steel or oil, whose too sudden money takes them to the divorce court; he calls them the 'yellow rich'; do you object to that? Nor does he think that those Americans who prefer their pockets to their patriotism, are good citizens. He says of such people that 'eternal vigilance cannot watch liberty and the ticker at the same time.' Do you object to that? Why, the young man would be perfect, did he but attend his primaries and vote more regularly,— and who wants a perfect young man?

What would John Mayrant have done if Hortense had not challenged him as she did?

I have never known, and I fear we might have had a tragedy.

Would the old ladies really have spoken to Augustus about the love difficulties of John Mayrant?

I must plead guilty. The old ladies of Kings Port, like American gentlefolk everywhere, keep family matters sacredly inside the family circle. But you see, had they not told Augustus, how in the world could I have told — however, I plead guilty.

Certain passages have been interpreted most surprisingly to signify a feeling against the colored race, that is by no means mine. My only wish regarding these people, to whom we owe an immeasurable responsibility, is to see the best that is in them prevail. Discord over this seems on the wane, and sane views gaining. The issue sits on all our shoulders, but local variations call for a sliding scale of policy. So admirably dispassionate a novel as *The Elder Brother*, by Mr. Jervey, forwards the understanding of Northerners unfamiliar with the South, and also that friendliness between the two places, which is retarded chiefly by tactless newspapers.

Ah, tact should have been one of the cardinal virtues; and if I didn't possess a spice of it myself, I should here thank by name certain two members of the St. Michael family of Kings Port for their patience with this comedy, before ever it saw the light. Tact bids us away from many pleasures; but it can never efface the memory of kindness.

Table of Contents

Full-Page Illustrations

Preface

Lady Baltimore was written forty years after the conclusion of the war that had divided the United States into two nations. Reunited by force and in law, they were still two nations at the opening of the Twentieth Century. Federal occupation had not ended in South Carolina until the election of 1876, and in Charleston, a city which even many Southerners blamed for starting the war, the humiliation of Reconstruction was still an enflamed wound that could not be assuaged by July Fourth speeches or crusades against the remnants of the Spanish colonial empire.

Charleston was a subtropical fairyland, brooding on the past and nursing resentments, when the Philadelphian Owen Wister paid his first visit in 1898. It was the first stage of a honeymoon trip—the Wisters were married on the very day that war broke out with Spain—and the groom declared in a letter to his mother, "Charleston is simply delicious . . . precisely what we hoped, only a great deal more so. Of all the American towns I've come into as a stranger, it's incomparably the most charming."

Charleston people were—and are—proverbial for their courtesy, but not for the welcome they give complete strangers. Owen Wister, however, had advantages that few visitors enjoy. His Western stories had already made him one of America's most popular writers, and, what is of greater significance, he was the great-grandson of Pierce Butler, a South Carolina delegate to the Federal Convention who had married a Middleton. Outside of South Carolina and Virginia, such distant connections might mean next to nothing; in Charleston they were everything, and the novelist was received in the best homes of the city. With Mrs. Wister's appointment as Pennsylvania's commissioner at the Charleston Exposition of 1901, the couple had an excuse for a prolonged visit.

Owen Wister was a very unlikely man to write a book that, in Jay Hubbell's words, "shows keener insight into Southern life than any other novel from a Northern pen." If he was the great-grandson of Major Butler, he was also the grandson of Fanny Kemble, the actress whose *Journal of a Residence on a Georgia Plantation in 1838 and 1839* had helped to arouse European hostility against the Confederacy. Despite his Harvard education (college and law school) and his interest in music (he had played his own composition for Liszt!), Wister was best known as an outdoorsman, an Easterner who, like his friend Theodore Roosevelt, had made himself a rugged man of the West. It was this rare combination of extremes, as Walker Percy noted in his essay, "Decline of the Western," that enabled Wister to write *The Virginian*: "Any man who can speak idiomatic French to Liszt and hunt big game with Corporal Skindin and Dean Duke—who were 'incarnations' . . . of his Virginian—is no ordinary dude."

What Wister loved about Wyoming was not so much the beauty of landscape as the natural aristocracy of the men. The East had lapsed into commercialism and decadence, and it was his hope that a new American civilization could be realized in the unspoiled wilderness. He was soon disappointed, as he saw the spreading evidence of crassness and cupidity in the towns that sprang up in Wyoming, and the time he spent in Charleston was enough to convince him that a real American civilization still lingered on in some parts of the South.

Wister conceived a novel that would not just be set in Charleston but would be about Charleston, which he describes at the beginning of chapter two as "the most appealing, the most lovely, the most wistful town in America." Henry James talked the author into changing Charleston to Kings Port, King Street to Royal Street, but no one who has spent time in the city and its environs will have any difficulty identifying the places described in the book. It is the city, not young John Mayrant, that is in a real sense the hero of *Lady Baltimore*, and it is Charleston that has the last word, after all the human characters have been disposed of as neatly as in a Da Ponte libretto. "And so my portrait of Kings Port is finished," begins the last paragraph in which the author begs the indulgence of his Charleston friends. Most Southerners, even his prickly friends in Charleston, could not fail to be pleased by a novel that is the most generous tribute that any American city has received from a stranger.

The Virginian, Wister's first novel, was written originally as a series of stories, but it was in Charleston that he cut and pasted them together into a coherent tale. It is easy to dismiss the love story that serves as *The Virginian*'s plot as mere window-dressing to attract women readers who might otherwise be appalled by the coarseness of his subject, but it is hard not to see an allegory in the story of the fun-loving Southerner-turned-Westerner who falls in love with a Vermont schoolmarm. The best qualities of North and South are merged in the union of the Virginian and his Yankee bride.

The emerging theme of so much American fiction (and later, film) was the reconciliation of North and South. Wister's first attempt at this subject was also his most influential. *The Virginian* is the archetypal Western novel, and it inspired several generations of writers and film-makers to find the resolution of America's sectional conflict in the West. It is the theme of John Ford's greatest films: *She Wore a Yellow Ribbon*, *Rio Grande*, and even *The Searchers*, to say nothing of Clint Eastwood's *The Outlaw Josey Wales* (based on Forrest Carter's novel *Gone to Texas*). The myth of American unity, as expressed in our literature and popular culture, was forged in the West by Wister and his friends, Theodore Roosevelt and Frederick Remington.

By the time he finished *The Virginian*, Wister had not only despaired of the West, but he had begun to share the widespread alarm over the effects of massive immigration. In *Lady Baltimore* he would attempt to find American unity not among the sturdy plainsmen but in a reconciliation of the best people of North and South against the nouveaux riches and foreign elements that were, in his view, taking over the country.

Wister refuses to frame his argument in a simple antithesis of
North and South or even Old v. New. Instead, he sketches out,
through the vehicle of his characters, an interlocking set of oppo-
sitions. His narrator, Augustus, is sent by his formidable aunt
Carola to Kings Port in search of genealogical information. They
are, like the author, of distinguished northern stock and have
ancient connections with Charleston families. What Augustus
finds in the South is a people who still retain the civilization that is
being lost in the North. Unhappily, slavery and war have divided
the best Americans. As he explains to his friend John Mayrant:

> Of course we had a family quarrel. But we *were* a family once,
> and a fine one, too! We knew each other, we visited each other,
> we wrote letters, sent presents, kept up relations. . . . And these
> ladies of yours—well, they have made me homesick for a
> national and social past which I never saw, but which my old
> people knew. They're like legends, still living, still warm and
> with us.

The remarkable Charleston ladies in question, Mrs. St. Michael
and Mrs. Gregory, serve throughout the book as a kind of tragic
chorus, commenting on the action and establishing the moral and
cultural context in which the characters and events are evaluated.
Augustus holds up their faces as a mirror of the world gone by
and comments, "Such quiet faces are gone now in the breathless,
competing North: ground into oblivion between the clashing
trades of the competing men and the clashing jewels and chandeliers of the competing wives."

In this respect, the contrast is not so much between regions as
between the character of the leading classes. While the South is
still ruled by an aristocracy that has not forgotten its obligations,
the North is dominated by the people Augustus calls "the yellow
rich," the "lower classes that have boiled up from the bottom
with their millions." His northern friend, Beverly Rodgers, who
has learned how to hold his nose long enough to swallow their
champagne, bows to the inevitable. Although Rodgers names
them "the replacers," he is determined not to be among the

losers: "If you don't want to see yourself jolly well replaced, you must fall in with the replacers."

The replacers enter upon the scene, appropriately enough, in an automobile. In one of only two or three dramatic scenes in the novel, the car strikes and kills a young girl's dog. "Charley, a five or ten spot is what her feelings need," comments one of the travellers. The girl, Eliza La Heu, is too grief-stricken to be aware of the offer, but young John Mayrant snatches the bill out of Charley's hand and throws it in his face. Thus the old world of loyalty and courage confronts the new world of wealth and influence.

Charley and his party of travellers are the new world of finance. Of uncertain origins—his accent is "that New York downtown foreign, of the second generation, which stamps so many of our bankers." In the eyes of his sister and friends, it is John Mayrant who has been boorish. He is conspicuous, he is romantic, he is unreliable. Even the accomplished Beverly Rodgers complains: "melodrama was the correct ticket and all that in 1840, but we've outgrown it."

The two worlds cannot penetrate each other. Charley's partner after examining the churches and houses of old Charleston, makes his only observation in the book: "This town's worse than Sunday," and no matter where they are or whom they meet, the New Yorkers can only talk of business deals. Touring the old Huguenot church, we overhear Charley gloating over a rival's defeat: "I guess they know they got a gold brick."

The plot of the novel, such as it is, concerns a wedding cake that is ordered for a wedding that is not to take place. The young man of old Charleston, John Mayrant, has foolishly engaged himself to a Southern woman of doubtful connections, who has thrown her lot in with the yellow rich of Newport. She is a liberated woman, who smokes, drinks cocktails, and flirts somewhat too openly. Augustus, who takes his lunch at the Woman's Exchange, strikes up a bantering acquaintance with Eliza La Heu, who serves him his daily slice of Lady Baltimore Cake. Although she can never quite bring herself to trust a Yankee, Eliza does speak candidly with him, and their conversations have the air of a flirtation manque. When they are not talking of John Mayrant's difficulties, they discuss the historic antagonisms of their peoples. Augustus attempts to explain to her that he harbors no resentment against the South. "If I ever have children, they shall know 'Dixie' and 'Yankee Doodle' by heart and never know the difference."

Eliza La Heu is one of the most attractive women characters in American fiction. Far from being a haughty Charlestonian, she is a "plantation girl" with a mocking sense of humor, a warm affection, and a sense of honor that would cause her to refuse John Mayrant, if he wavered in loyalty toward his fiancee. Young Mayrant, on the other hand, realizes he has been a fool but would rather die than break his engagement. If John Mayrant and Eliza La Heu stand for everything that is real and true in the postwar South, Hortense Rieppe and her father, a cowardly general who disgraced himself in the war, are the New South: boastful about an ancestry and patrimony that no one can verify, they have learned to play the role of professional Southerners for the amusement of New York *arrivistes* who cannot tell the difference between gold and a gold brick.

In Wister's eyes the entire North is infected with falseness. Augustus's friend Beverly Rodgers, with all the instincts and background of a gentleman, can recognize the great lady in Eliza La Heu riding away on a negro's cart with her dead dog, but he cannot see through Hortense Rieppe, whom he mistakes for a well-born Charleston lady. Augustus's aunt Carola, despite her birth and breeding, is tricked into joining a bogus genealogical organization, the Selected Salic Scions, that can prove the royal descent of all its members. Augustus, who is ashamed to admit how much of Carola's snobbery he shares, tells Miss La Heu how much he admires John Mayrant's ancestors—"There's not a name in South Carolina that I'd rather have for my own." He is surprised by her tart rejoinder: "Oh, you mustn't accept us because of our ancestors."

Augustus may be half in love with Miss La Heu, but she is reserved for John Mayrant. In the contrast of the two weddings, of Charley and Hortense, John and Eliza, Wister makes his point more tellingly than in his tirades against the yellow rich. The New York wedding is written up in the newspapers with a glowing account of the participants as "up to date and distinque." The groom's speech is the high point of the ceremony. Noticing the combined forces of Oil, Sugar, Beef, Steel, and Union Pacific in the bridal party, Charley shares his philosophy of life: "Poets . . . say that happiness cannot be bought with money. Well, I guess a poet never does learn how to make a dollar do a dollar's work." Supposing that he and his friends are rich enough to "organize a corner on happiness," he generously promises to let his friends in on the deal.

The wedding of John and Eliza is not written up in the papers. It was, however, "solemnized" in a house where "the long linked chain of births and deaths . . . has not been broken." The American past is summed up and recapitulated in this house, and "the assembled essence of kinship." When Augustus attends the christening of John Mayrant, Jr., he asks the child's mother if she will teach him both "Dixie" and "Yankee Doodle." We are reminded not only of his conversations with Eliza but of the nationalist creed he had espoused to her at the Woman's Exchange. He declared himself "no more a Southerner than a Northerner." His "sacred trust," he explained, was to be simply "an American."

Wister's Americanism led him to be a jingoist critic of Woodrow Wilson's tardiness in dragging his country into the Great War, and near the end of his life he was almost arrested for organizing a meeting to protest Franklin Roosevelt's attempt to pack the Supreme Court. As he foresaw in *Lady Baltimore*, America had come of age in the Spanish-American War, but everything depended on how the nation would exercise its maturity. The freedom-loving farmer still survived in the hinterlands, "but the great cities grow like a creeping paralysis over freedom. . . . We're all thinking a deal too much about our pockets nowadays. Eternal vigilance cannot watch liberty and the ticker at the same time."

It was the most somber observation of a somber book, and his friend from Harvard, Theodore Roosevelt, would have none of it, neither the praise of the South nor the denigration of capitalism. In retrospect, unfortunately, we can now see that it was the novelist, and not the statesman, who grasped the practical realities of the Twentieth Century.

Rockford, Illinois   THOMAS FLEMING

"The young girl realized his intention and straightened stiffly"

LADY BALTIMORE

I

L IKE Adam, our first conspicuous ancestor, I must begin, and lay the blame upon a woman; I am glad to recognize that I differ from the father of my sex in no important particular, being as manlike as most of his sons. Therefore it is the woman, my Aunt Carola, who must bear the whole reproach of the folly which I shall forthwith confess to you, since she it was who put it into my head; and, as it was only to make Eve happy that her husband ever consented to eat the disastrous apple, so I, save to please my relative, had never aspired to become a Selected Salic Scion. I rejoice now that I did so, that I yielded to her temptation. Ours is a wide country, and most of us know but our own corner of it, while, thanks to my Aunt, I have been able to add another corner. This, among many other enlightenments of travel and education, do I owe her; she stands on the threshold of all that is to come; therefore it were lacking in deference did I pass her and the Scions by without due mention,—employing no English but such as fits a theme so stately. Although she never left the threshold, nor went to Kings Port with me, nor saw the boy, or the girl, or any part of what befell them, she knew quite well who the boy was. When I wrote her about him, she remembered one of his grandmothers whom she had visited during her own girlhood, long before the war, both in Kings Port and at the family plantation; and this old memory led her to express a kindly interest in him. How odd and far away that interest seems, now that it has been turned to cold displeasure!

Some other day, perhaps, I may try to tell you much more than I can tell you here about Aunt Carola and her Colonial Society — that apple which Eve, in the form of my Aunt, held out to me. Never had I expected to feel rise in me the appetite for this particular fruit, though I had known such hunger to exist in some of my neighbors. Once a worthy dame of my town, at whose dinner-table young men and maidens of fashion sit constantly, asked me with much sentiment if I was aware that she was descended from Boadicea. Why had she never (I asked her) revealed this to me before? And upon her informing me that she had learned it only that very day, I exclaimed that it was a great distance to have descended so suddenly. To this, after a look at me, she assented, adding that she had the good news from the office of *The American Almanach de Gotha*, Union Square, New York; and she recommended that publication to me. There was but a slight fee to pay, a matter of fifty dollars or upwards, and for this trifling sum you were furnished with your rightful coat-of-arms and with papers clearly tracing your family to the Druids, the Vestal Virgins, and all the best people in the world. Therefore I felicitated the Boadicean lady upon the illustrious progenitrix with whom the Almanach de Gotha had provided her for so small a consideration, and observed that for myself I supposed I should continue to rest content with the thought that in our enlightened Republic every American was himself a sovereign. But that, said the lady, after giving me another look, is so different from Boadicea! And to this I perfectly agreed. Later I had the pleasure to hear in a roundabout way that she had pronounced me one of the most agreeable young men in society, though sophisticated. I have not cherished this against her; my gift of humor puzzles many who can see only my refinement and my scrupulous attention to dress.

Yes, indeed, I counted myself proof against all Boadiceas. But you have noticed — have you not? — how, whenever a few people gather together and style themselves something, and choose a president, and eight or nine vice-presidents, and a secretary and a treasurer, and a committee on elections, and then let it be known that almost nobody else is qualified to belong to it, that there springs up immediately in hundreds and thousands of breasts a fiery craving to get into that body? You may try this experiment in science, law, medicine, art, letters, society, farming, I care not what, but you will set the same craving afire in doctors, academicians, and dog breeders all over the earth. Thus, when my Aunt — the president, herself, mind you! — said to me one day that she thought, if I proved my qualifications, my name might be favorably considered by the Selected

Salic Scions — I say no more; I blush, though
you cannot see me; when I am tempted, I seem
to be human, after all.

At first, to be sure, I met Aunt Carola's suggestion in the way that I am too ready to meet
many of her remarks; for you must know she
once, with sincere simplicity and good-will, told
my Uncle Andrew (her husband; she is only my
Aunt by marriage) that she had married beneath
her; and she seemed unprepared for his reception
of this candid statement: Uncle Andrew was un-
affectedly merry over it. Ever since then all of
us wait hopefully every day for what she may do
or say next.

She is from old New York, oldest New York;
the family manor is still habitable, near Cold
Spring; she was, in her youth, handsome, I am
assured by those whose word I have always
trusted; her appearance even to-day causes people
to turn and look; she is not tall in feet and
inches — I have to stoop considerably when she
commands from me the familiarity of a kiss; but
in the quality which we call force, in moral stature,
she must be full eight feet high. When rebuking
me, she can pronounce a single word, my name,
"Augustus!" in a tone that renders further remark needless; and you should see her eye when
she says of certain newcomers in our society, "I
don't know them." She can make her curtsy as
appalling as a natural law; she knows also how
to "take umbrage," which is something that I
never knew any one else to take outside of a
book; she is a highly pronounced Christian, holding all Unitarians wicked and all Methodists vul-

gar; and once, when she was talking (as she does frequently) about King James and the English religion and the English Bible, and I reminded her that the Jews wrote it, she said with displeasure that she made no doubt King James had — "well, seen to it that all foreign matter was expunged" — I give you her own words. Unless you have moved in our best American society (and by this I do not at all mean the lower classes with dollars and no grandfathers, who live in palaces at Newport, and look forward to everything and back to nothing, but those Americans with grandfathers and no dollars, who live in boarding-houses, and look forward to nothing and back to everything) — unless you have known this haughty and improving *milieu*, you have never seen anything like my Aunt Carola. Of course, with Uncle Andrew's money, she does not live in a boarding-house; and I shall finish this brief attempt to place her before you by adding that she can be very kind, very loyal, very public-spirited, and that I am truly attached to her.

"Upon your mother's side of the family," she said, "of course."

"Me!" I did not have to feign amazement.

My Aunt was silent.

"Me descended from a king?"

My Aunt nodded with an indulgent stateliness. "There seems to be the possibility of it."

"Royal blood in my veins, Aunt?"

"I have said so, Augustus. Why make me repeat it?"

It was now, I fear, that I met Aunt Carola in that unfitting spirit, that volatile mood, which, as

I have said already, her remarks often rouse in me.

"And from what sovereign may I hope that I — ?"

"If you will consult a recent admirable compilation, entitled *The American Almanach de Gotha*, you will find that Henry the Seventh — "

"Aunt, I am so much relieved! For I think that I might have hesitated to trace it back had you said — well — Charles the Second, for example, or Elizabeth."

At this point I should have been wise to notice my Aunt's eye; but I did not, and I continued imprudently: —

"Though why hesitate? I have never heard that there was anybody present to marry Adam and Eve, and so why should we all make such a to-do about — "

"Augustus!"

She uttered my name in that quiet but prodigious tone to which I have alluded above.

It was I who was now silent.

"Augustus, if you purpose trifling, you may leave the room."

"Oh, Aunt, I beg your pardon. I never meant — "

"I cannot understand what impels you to adopt such a manner to me, when I am trying to do something for you."

I hastened to strengthen my apologies with a manner becoming the possible descendant of a king toward a lady of distinction, and my Aunt was pleased to pass over my recent lapse from respect. She now broached her favorite topic,

which I need scarcely tell you is genealogy, beginning with her own.

"If your title to royal blood," she said, "were as
plain as mine (through Admiral Bombo, you know),
you would not need any careful research."

She told me a great deal of genealogy, which I
spare you; it was not one family tree, it was a
forest of them. It gradually appeared that a
grandmother of my mother's grandfather had been
a Fanning, and there were sundry kinds of Fannings, right ones and wrong ones; the point for
me was, what kind had mine been? No family
record showed this. If it was Fanning of the Bon
Homme Richard variety, or Fanning of the Alamance, then I was no king's descendant.

"Worthy New England people, I understand,"
said my Aunt with her nod of indulgent stateliness, referring to the Bon Homme Richard species,
"but of entirely bourgeois extraction — Paul Jones
himself, you know, was a mere gardener's son —
while the Alamance Fanning was one of those
infamous regulators who opposed Governor
Tryon. Not through any such cattle could you
be one of us," said my Aunt.

But a dim, distant, hitherto uncharted Henry
Tudor Fanning had fought in some of the early
Indian wars, and the last of his known blood was
reported to have fallen while fighting bravely at
the battle of Cowpens. In him my hope lay.
Records of Tarleton, records of Marion's men,
these were what I must search, and for these I
had best go to Kings Port. If I returned with
kinship proven, then I might be a Selected Salic
Scion, a chosen vessel, a royal seed, one in the

most exalted circle of men and women upon our
coasts. The other qualifications were already
mine: ancestors colonial and bellicose upon land
and sea —

"— besides having acquired," my Aunt was
so good as to say, "sufficient personal present-
ability since your life in Paris, of which I had
rather not know too much, Augustus. It is a pity,"
she repeated, "that you will have so much research.
With my family it was all so satisfactorily clear
through Kill-devil Bombo — Admiral Bombo's
spirited, reckless son."

You will readily conceive that I did not venture
to betray my ignorance of these Bombos; I
worked my eyebrows to express a silent and time-
worn familiarity.

"Go to Kings Port. You need a holiday, at
any rate. And I," my Aunt handsomely finished,
"will make the journey a present to you."

This generosity made me at once, and sincerely,
repentant for my flippancy concerning Charles the
Second and Elizabeth. And so, partly from being
tempted by this apple of Eve, and partly because
recent overwork had tired me, but chiefly for her
sake, and not to thwart at the outset her kindly-
meant ambitions for me, I kissed the hand of my
Aunt Carola and set forth to Kings Port.

"Come back one of us," was her parting benediction.

II

THUS it was that I came to sojourn in the most appealing, the most lovely, the most wistful town in America; whose visible sadness and distinction seem also to speak audibly, speak in the sound of the quiet waves that ripple round her Southern front, speak in the church-bells on Sunday morning, and breathe not only in the soft salt air, but in the perfume of every gentle, old-fashioned rose that blooms behind the high garden walls of falling mellow-tinted plaster: Kings Port the retrospective, Kings Port the belated, who from her pensive porticoes looks over her two rivers to the marshes and the trees beyond, the live-oaks, veiled in gray moss, brooding with memories! Were she my city, how I should love her!

But though my city she cannot be, the enchanting image of her is mine to keep, to carry with me wheresoever I may go; for who, having seen her, could forget her? Therefore I thank Aunt Carola for this gift, and for what must always go with it in my mind, the quiet and strange romance which I saw happen, and came finally to share in. Why it is that my Aunt no longer wishes to know either the boy or the girl, or even to hear their names mentioned, you shall learn at

the end, when I have finished with the wedding;
for this happy story of love ends with a wedding,
and begins in the Woman's Exchange, which the

Kings Port the retrospective

ladies of Kings Port have established, and (I trust)
lucratively conduct, in Royal Street.

Royal Street! There's a relevance in this
name, a fitness to my errand; but that is pure
accident.

The Woman's Exchange happened to be there,
a decorous resort for those who became hungry,
as I did, at the hour of noon each day. In my
very pleasant boarding-house, where, to be sure,
there was one dreadful boarder, a tall lady, whom
I soon secretly called Juno — but let unpleasant
things wait — in the very pleasant house where I
boarded (I had left my hotel after one night) our
breakfast was at eight, and our dinner not until
three : sacred meal hours in Kings Port, as invio-
lable, I fancy, as the Declaration of Independence, but a gap quite beyond the stretch of my
Northern vitals.   Therefore, at twelve, it was my
habit to leave my Fanning researches for a while,
and lunch at the Exchange upon chocolate and
sandwiches most delicate in savor.   As, one day,
I was luxuriously biting one of these, I heard his
voice and what he was saying.   Both the voice
and the interesting order he was giving caused
me, at my small table, in the dim back of the
room, to stop and watch him where he stood in
the light at the counter to the right of the entrance
door.   Young he was, very young, twenty-two or
three at the most, and as he stood, with hat in
hand, speaking to the pretty girl behind the
counter, his head and side-face were of a romantic
and high-strung look.   It was a cake that he
desired made, a cake for a wedding ; and I directly
found myself curious to know whose wedding.
Even a dull wedding interests me more than
other dull events, because it can arouse so much
surmise and so much prophecy ; but in this wedding I instantly, because of his strange and winning embarrassment, became quite absorbed.   How

came it he was ordering the cake for it? Blushing like the boy that he was entirely, he spoke in
a most engaging voice: " No, not charged; and
as you don't know me, I had better pay for it now."

Self-possession in his speech he almost had;
but the blood in his cheeks and forehead was
beyond his control.

A reply came from behind the counter: " We
don't expect payment until delivery."

" But — a — but on that morning I shall be
rather particularly engaged." His tones sank
almost away on these words.

" We should prefer to wait, then. You will leave
your address. In half-pound boxes, I suppose? "

" Boxes? Oh, yes — I hadn't thought — no —
just a big, round one. Like this, you know!"
His arms embraced a circular space of air. " With
plenty of icing."

I do not think that there was any smile on the
other side of the counter; there was, at any rate,
no hint of one in the voice. " And how many
pounds? "

He was again staggered. " Why — a — I never
ordered one before. I want plenty — and the very
best, the very best. Each person would eat a
pound, wouldn't they? Or would two be nearer?
I think I had better leave it all to you. About
like this, you know." Once more his arms embraced a circular space of air.

Before this I had never heard the young lady
behind the counter enter into any conversation
with a customer. She would talk at length about
all sorts of Kings Port affairs with the older ladies
connected with the Exchange, who were frequently

to be found there; but with a customer, never.
She always took my orders, and my money, and
served me, with a silence and a propriety that
have become, with ordinary shopkeepers, a lost
art. *They* talk to one indeed! But this slim girl
was a lady, and consequently did the right thing,
marking and keeping a distance between herself
and the public. To-day, however, she evidently
felt it her official duty to guide the hapless young
man amid his errors. He now appeared to be
committing a grave one.

"Are you quite sure you want that?" the girl
was asking.

"Lady Baltimore? Yes, that is what I want."

"Because," she began to explain, then hesitated,
and looked at him. Perhaps it was in his face;
perhaps it was that she remembered at this point
the serious difference between the price of Lady
Baltimore (by my small bill-of-fare I was now made
acquainted with its price) and the cost of that
rich article which convention has prescribed as
the cake for weddings; at any rate, swift, sudden
delicacy of feeling prevented her explaining any
more to him, for she saw how it was: his means
were too humble for the approved kind of wedding cake! She was too young, too unskilled
yet in the world's ways, to rise above her embarrassment; and so she stood blushing at him behind the counter, while he stood blushing at her
in front of it.

At length he succeeded in speaking. "That's
all, I believe. Good-morning."

At his hastily departing back she, too, murmured: "Good-morning."

Before I knew it I had screamed out loudly from my table: " But he hasn't told you the day he wants it for! "

Before she knew it she had flown to the door — my cry had set her going, as if I had touched a spring — and there he was at the door himself, rushing back. He, too, had remembered. It was almost a collision, and nothing but their good Southern breeding, the way they took it, saved it from being like a rowdy farce.

" I know," he said simply and immediately. " I am sorry to be so careless. It's for the twenty-seventh."

She was writing it down in the order-book. " Very well. That is Wednesday of next week. You have. given us more time than we need." She put complete, impersonal business into her tone; and this time he marched off in good order, leaving peace in the Woman's Exchange.

No, not peace; quiet, merely; the girl at the counter now proceeded to grow indignant with me. We were alone together, we two; no young man, or any other business, occupied her or protected me. But if you suppose that she made war, or expressed rage by speaking, that is not it at all. From her counter in front to my table at the back she made her displeasure felt; she was inaudibly crushing; she did not do it even with her eye, she managed it — well, with her neck, somehow, and by the way she made her nose look in profile. Aunt Carola would have embraced her — and I should have liked to do so myself. She could not stand the idea of my having, after all these days of official reserve that she had placed

" It was almost a collision "

between us, startled her into that rush to the door,
annihilated her dignity at a blow. So did I finish
my sandwiches beneath her invisible but eloquent
ire. What affair of mine was the cake? And
what sort of impertinent, meddlesome person was
I, shrieking out my suggestions to people with
whom I had no acquaintance? These were the
things that her nose and her neck said to me the
whole length of the Exchange. I had nothing
but my own weakness to thank; it was my interest in weddings that did it, made me forget my
decorum, the public place, myself, everything, and
plunge in. And I became more and more delighted over it as the girl continued to crush me.
My day had been dull, my researches had not
brought me a whit nearer royal blood; I looked at
my little bill-of-fare, and then I stepped forward
to the counter, adventurous, but polite.

"I should like a slice, if you please, of Lady
Baltimore," I said with extreme formality.

I thought she was going to burst; but after an
interesting second she replied, "Certainly," in her
regular Exchange tone; only, I thought it trembled a little.

I returned to the table and she brought me the
cake, and I had my first felicitous meeting with
Lady Baltimore. Oh, my goodness! Did you
ever taste it? It's all soft, and it's in layers, and
it has nuts — but I can't write any more about it;
my mouth waters too much.

Delighted surprise caused me once more to
speak aloud, and with my mouth full. "But, dear
me, this is delicious!"

A choking ripple of laughter came from the

counter. "It's I who make them," said the girl.
"I thank you for the unintentional compliment."
Then she walked straight back to my table. "I
can't help it," she said, laughing still, and her delightful, insolent nose well up; "how can I behave
myself when a man goes on as you do?" A nice
white curly dog followed her, and she stroked his
ears.

"Your behavior is very agreeable to me," I
remarked.

"You'll allow me to say that you're not invited
to criticise it. I was decidedly put out with you
for making me ridiculous. But you have admired
my cake with such enthusiasm that you are forgiven. And — may I hope that you are getting
on famously with the battle of Cowpens?"

I stared. "I'm frankly very much astonished
that you should know about that!"

"Oh, you're just known all about in Kings
Port."

I wish that our miserable alphabet could in
some way render the soft Southern accent which
she gave to her words. But it cannot. I could
easily misspell, if I chose; but how, even then,
could I, for instance, make you hear her way of
saying "about"? "Aboot" would magnify it;
and besides, I decline to make ugly to the eye
her quite special English, that was so charming
to the ear.

"Kings Port just knows all about you," she repeated with a sweet and mocking laugh.

"Do you mind telling me how?"

She explained at once. "This place is death
to all incognitos."

The explanation, however, did not, on the instant, enlighten me. "This? The Woman's Exchange, you mean?"

"Why, to be sure! Have you not heard ladies talking together here?"

I blankly repeated her words. "Ladies talking?"

She nodded.

"Oh!" I cried. "How dull of me! Ladies talking! Of course!"

She continued. "It was therefore widely known that you were consulting our South Carolina archives at the library—and then that notebook you bring marked you out the very first day. Why, two hours after your first lunch we just knew all about you!"

"Dear me!" said I.

"Kings Port is ever ready to discuss strangers," she further explained. "The Exchange has been going on five years, and the resident families have discussed each other so thoroughly here that everything is known; therefore a stranger is a perfect boon." Her gayety for a moment interrupted her, before she continued, always mocking and always sweet: "Kings Port cannot boast intelligence offices for servants; but if you want to know the character and occupation of your friends, come to the Exchange!" How I wish I could give you the raciness, the contagion, of her laughter! Who would have dreamed that behind her primness all this frolic lay in ambush? "Why," she said, "I'm only a plantation girl; it's my first week here, and I know every wicked deed everybody has done since 1812!"

She went back to her counter. It had been very merry; and as I was settling the small debt for my lunch I asked: " Since this is the proper place for information, will you kindly tell me whose wedding that cake is for? "

She was astonished. " You don't know? And I thought you were quite a clever Ya — I beg your pardon — Northerner."

" Please tell me, since I know you're quite a clever Reb — I beg your pardon — Southerner."

" Why, it's his own! Couldn't you see that from his bashfulness? "

" Ordering his own wedding cake? " Amazement held me. But the door opened, one of the elderly ladies entered, the girl behind the counter stiffened to primness in a flash, and I went out into Royal Street as the curly dog's tail wagged his greeting to the newcomer.

III

KINGS PORT TALKS

OF course I had at once left the letters of introduction which Aunt Carola had given me; but in my ignorance of Kings Port hours I had found everybody at dinner when I made my first round of calls between half-past three and five — an experience particularly regrettable, since I had hurried my own dinner on purpose, not then aware that the hours at my boarding-house were the custom of the whole town.[1] Upon an afternoon some days later, having seen in the extra looking-glass, which I had been obliged to provide for myself, that the part in my back hair was perfect, I set forth again, better informed.

As I rang the first doorbell, another visitor came up the steps, a beautiful old lady in widow's dress, a cardcase in her hand.

" Have you rung, sir ? " said she, in a manner at once gentle and voluminous.

" Yes, madam."

Nevertheless she pulled it again. " It doesn't always ring," she explained, "unless one is accustomed to it, which you are not."

She addressed me with authority, exactly like Aunt Carola, and with even greater precision in

---

[1] These hours, even since my visit to Kings Port, are beginning, alas, to change. But such backsliding is much condemned.

her good English and good enunciation. Unlike
the girl at the Exchange, she had no accent; her
language was simply the perfection of educated
utterance; it also was racy with the free censori-
ousness which civilized people of consequence are
apt to exercise the world over. " I was sorry to
miss your visit," she began (she knew me, you see,
perfectly); "you will please to come again soon,
and console me for my disappointment. I am
Mrs. Gregory St. Michael, and my house is in
Le Mairé Street,[1] as you have been so civil as to
find out. And how does your Aunt Carola do in
these contemptible times ? You can tell her from
me that vulgarization is descending, even upon
Kings Port."

" I cannot imagine that! " I exclaimed.

" You cannot imagine it because you don't
know anything about it, young gentleman! The
manners of some of our own young people will
soon be as dishevelled as those in New York.
Have you seen our town yet, or is it all books
with you? You should not leave without a look
at what is still left of us. I shall be happy if you
will sit in my pew on Sunday morning. Your
Northern shells did their best in the bombardment
— did you say that you rang? I think you had
better pull it again; all the way out; yes, like
that — in the bombardment, but we have our old
church still, in spite of you. Do you see the
crack in that wall ? The earthquake did it.
You're spared earthquakes in the North, as you
seem to be spared pretty much everything disastrous — except the prosperity that's going to

[1] Pronounced in Kings Port, Lammarr*ee*.

ruin you all. We're better off with our poverty than you. Just ring the bell once more, and then

"Shabby enough now, to be sure."

we'll go. I fancy Julia — I fancy Mrs. Weguelin St. Michael — has run out to stare at the Northern steam yacht in the harbor. It would be just like her. This house is historic itself. Shabby enough now, to be sure! The great-aunt of my cousin, John Mayrant (who is going to be married next Wednesday, to such a brute of a girl, poor boy!), lived here in 1840, and made an answer to the Earl of Mainridge that put him in his place. She was our famous Kings Port wit, and at the reception which her father (my mother's uncle) gave the English visitor, he conducted himself as so many Englishmen seem to think they can in this country. Miss Beaufain [1] (as she was then) asked the Earl how he liked America; and he replied, very well, except for the people, who were so vulgar. 'What can you expect?' said Miss Beaufain; 'we're descended from the English.' Mrs. St. Michael is out, and the servant has gone home. Slide this card under the door, with your own, and come away."

She took me with her, moving through the quiet South Place with a leisurely grace and dignity at which my spirit rejoiced; she was so beautiful, and so easy, and afraid of nothing and nobody! [2]

In the North, everybody is afraid of something: afraid of the legislature, afraid of the trusts, afraid of the strikes, afraid of what the papers will say, of what the neighbors will say, of what the cook will say; and most of all, and worst of all, afraid to be different from the general pattern, afraid to take a step or speak a syllable that shall

---

[1] Pronounced in Kings Port, Bow*fayne*.
[2] This must be modified. I came later to suspect that they all stood in some dread of their own immediate families.

cause them to be thought unlike the monotonous millions of their fellow-citizens; the land of the

In quiet South Place

free living in ceaseless fear! Well, I was already afraid of Mrs. Gregory St. Michael. As **we**

walked and she talked, I made one or two attempts
at conversation, and speedily found that no such
thing was the lady's intention: I was there to
listen; and truly I could wish nothing more
agreeable, in spite of my desire to hear further
about next Wednesday's wedding and the brute
of a girl. But to this subject Mrs. St. Michael
did not return. We crossed Worship Street and
Chancel Street, and were nearing the East Place
where a cannon was being shown me, a cannon
with a history and an inscription concerning the
" war for Southern independence, which I presume
your prejudice calls the Rebellion," said my guide.
" There's Mrs. St. Michael now, coming round
the corner. Well, Julia, could you read the yacht's
name with your naked eye? And what's the
name of the gambler who owns it? He's a gambler, or he couldn't own a yacht — unless his
wife's a gambler's daughter."

" How well you're feeling to-day, Maria!" said
the other lady, with a gentle smile.

"Certainly. I have been talking for twenty
minutes." I was now presented to Mrs. Weguelin
St. Michael, also old, also charming, in widow's
dress no less in the bloom of age than Mrs.
Gregory, but whiter and very diminutive. She
shyly welcomed me to Kings Port. " Take him
home with you, Julia. We pulled your bell three
times, and it's too damp for you to be out. Don't
forget," Mrs. Gregory said to me, " that you haven't
told me a word about your Aunt Carola, and that
I shall expect you to come and do it." She went
slowly away from us, up the East Place, tall, graceful, sweeping into the distance like a ship. No

haste about her dignified movement, no swinging
of elbows, nothing of the present hour!

"What a beautiful girl she must have been!"
I murmured aloud, unconsciously.

"No, she was not a beauty in her youth," said
my new guide in her shy voice, "but always
fluent, always a wit. Kings Port has at times
thought her tongue too downright. We think
that wit runs in her family, for young John Mayrant has it; and her first-cousin-once-removed put
the Earl of Mainridge in his place at her father's
ball in 1840. Miss Beaufain (as she was then)
asked the Earl how he liked America; and he
replied, very well, except for the people, who were
so vulgar. 'What can you expect?' said Miss
Beaufain; 'we're descended from the English.' I
am very sorry for Maria — for Mrs. St. Michael
— just at present. Her young cousin, John Mayrant, is making an alliance deeply vexatious to
her. Do you happen to know Miss Hortense
Rieppe?"

I had never heard of her.

"No? She has been North lately. I thought
you might have met her. Her father takes her
North, I believe, whenever any one will invite
them. They have sometimes managed to make
it extend through an unbroken year. Newport, I
am credibly informed, greatly admires her. We
in Kings Port have never (except John Mayrant,
apparently) seen anything in her beauty, which
Northerners find so exceptional."

"What is her type?" I inquired.

"I consider that she looks like a steel wasp.
And she has the assurance to call herself a Kings

Port girl. Her father calls himself a general, and it is repeated that he ran away at the battle of Chattanooga. I hope you will come to see me another day, when you can spare time from the battle of Cowpens. I am Mrs. Weguelin St. Michael, the other lady is Mrs. Gregory St. Michael. I wonder if you will keep us all straight?" And smiling, the little lady, whose shy manner and voice I had found to veil as much spirit as her predecessor's, dismissed me and went up her steps, letting herself into her own house.

The boy in question, the boy of the cake, John Mayrant, was coming out of the gate at which I next rang. The appearance of his boyish figure and well-carried head struck me anew, as it had at first; from his whole person one got at once a strangely romantic impression. He looked at me, made as if he would speak, but passed on. Probably he had been hearing as much about me as I had been hearing about him. At this house the black servant had not gone home for the night, and if the mistress had been out to take a look at the steam yacht, she had returned.

"My sister," she said, presenting me to a supremely fine-looking old lady, more chiselled, more august, than even herself. I did not catch this lady's name, and she confined herself to a distant, though perhaps not unfriendly, greeting. She was sitting by a work-table, and she resumed some embroidery of exquisite appearance, while my hostess talked to me.

Both wore their hair in a simple fashion to suit their years, which must have been seventy or more; both were dressed with the dignity that such years call for; and I may mention here that so were all the ladies above a certain age in this town of admirable old-fashioned propriety. In New York, in Boston, in Philadelphia, ladies of seventy won't be old ladies any more; they're unwilling to wear their years avowedly, in quiet dignity by their firesides; they bare their bosoms and gallop egregiously to the ball-rooms of the young; and so we lose a particular graciousness that Kings Port retains, a *perspective* of generations. We happen all at once, with no background, in a swirl of haste and similarity.

One of the many things which came home to me during the conversation that now began (so many more things came home than I can tell you!) was that Mrs. Gregory St. Michael's tongue was assuredly "downright" for Kings Port. This I had not at all taken in while she talked to me, and her friend's reference to it had left me somewhat at a loss. That better precision and choice of words which I have mentioned, and the manner in which she announced her opinions, had put me in mind of several fine ladies whom I had known in other parts of the world; but hers was an individual manner, I was soon to find, and by no means the Kings Port convention. This convention permitted, indeed, condemnations of one's neighbor no less sweeping, but it conveyed them in a phraseology far more restrained.

"I cannot regret your coming to Kings Port," said my hostess, after we had talked for a little while, and I had complimented the balmy March weather and the wealth of blooming flowers;

"but I fear that Fanning is not a name that you will find here. It belongs to North Carolina."

I smiled and explained that North Carolina Fannings were useless to me. " And, if I may be so bold, how well you are acquainted with my errand!"

I cannot say that my hostess smiled, that would be too definite; but I can say that she did not permit herself to smile, and that she let me see this repression. "Yes," she said, "we are acquainted with your errand, though not with its motive."

I sat silent, thinking of the Exchange.

My hostess now gave me her own account of why all things were known to all people in this town. "The distances in your Northern cities are greater, and their population is much greater. There are but few of us in Kings Port." In these last words she plainly told me that those "few" desired no others. She next added: "My nephew, John Mayrant, has spoken of you at some length."

I bowed. "I had the pleasure to see and hear him order a wedding cake."

"Yes. From Eliza La Heu,[1] my niece; he is my nephew, she is my niece on the other side. My niece is a beginner at the Exchange. We hope that she will fulfil her duties there in a worthy manner. She comes from a family which is schooled to meet responsibilities."

I bowed again; again it seemed fitting. "I had not, until now, known the charming girl's name," I murmured.

[1] Pronounced *Lay*hew.

My hostess now bowed slightly. " I am glad that you find her charming."

" Indeed, yes! " I exclaimed.

" We, also, are pleased with her. She is of good family — for the up-country."

Once again our alphabet fails me. The peculiar shade of kindness, of recognition, of patronage, which my agreeable hostess (and all Kings Port ladies, I soon noticed) imparted to the word "up-country" cannot be conveyed except by the human voice — and only a Kings Port voice at that. It is a much lighter damnation than what they make of the phrase "from Georgia," which I was soon to hear uttered by the lips of the lady. "And so you know about his wedding cake? "

" My dear madam, I feel that I shall know about everything."

Her gray eyes looked at me quietly for a moment. "That is possible. But although we may talk of ourselves to you, we scarcely expect you to talk of ourselves to us."

Well, my pertness had brought me this quite properly! And I received it properly. " I should never dream — " I hastened to say ; "even without your warning. I find I'm expected to have seen the young lady of his choice," I now threw out. My accidental words proved as miraculous as the staff which once smote the rock. It was a stream, indeed, which now broke forth from her stony discretion. She began easily. " It is evident that you have not seen Miss Rieppe by the manner in which you allude to her — although of course, in comparison with my age, she is a

young girl." I think that this caused me to open
my mouth.

"The disparity between her years and my
nephew's is variously stated," continued the old
lady. "But since John's engagement we have all
of us realized that love is truly blind."

I did not open my mouth any more; but my
mind's mouth was wide open.

My hostess kept it so. "Since John Mayrant
was fifteen he has had many loves; and for myself,
knowing him and believing in him as I do, I feel
confident that he will make no connection distasteful to the family when he really comes to
marry."

This time I gasped outright. "But — the cake!
— next Wednesday!"

She made, with her small white hand, a slight
and slighting gesture. "The cake is not baked
yet, and we shall see what we shall see." From
this onward until the end a pinkness mounted in
her pale, delicate cheeks, and deep, strong resentment burned beneath her discreetly expressed
indiscretions. "The cake is not baked, and I, at
least, am not solicitous. I tell my cousin, Mrs.
Gregory St. Michael, that she must not forget it
was merely his phosphates. That girl would
never have looked at John Mayrant had it not
been for the rumor of his phosphates. I suppose
some one has explained to you her pretensions of
birth. Away from Kings Port she may pass for
a native of this place, but they come from Georgia.
It cannot be said that she has met with encour-
agement from us; she, however, easily recovers
from such things. The present generation of

"'Although we may talk of ourselves to you, we scarcely expect
you to talk of ourselves to us'"

young people in Kings Port has little enough to
remind us of what we stood for in manners and
customs, but we are not accountable for her, nor
for her father. I believe that he is called a general. His conduct at Chattanooga was conspicuous for personal prudence. Both of them are
skilful in never knowing poor people — but the
Northerners they consort with must really be at
a loss how to bestow their money. Of course,
such Northerners cannot realize the difference
between Kings Port and Georgia, and consequently they make much of her. Her features do
undoubtedly possess beauty. A Newport woman
— the new kind — has even taken her to Worth!
And yet, after all, she has remained for John. We
heard a great deal of her men, too. She took
care of that, of course. John Mayrant actually
followed her to Newport."

"But," I couldn't help crying out, "I thought
he was so poor!"

"The phosphates," my hostess explained.
"They had been discovered on his. land. And
none of her New York men had come forward.
So John rushed back happy." At this point a
very singular look came over the face of my
hostess, and she continued: "There have been
many false reports (and false hopes in consequence) based upon the phosphate discoveries.
It was I who had to break it to him — what
further investigation had revealed. Poor John!"

"He has, then, nothing?" I inquired.

"His position in the Custom House, and a
penny or two from his mother's fortune."

"But the cake?" I now once again reminded
her.

My hostess lifted her delicate hand and let it fall. Her resentment at the would-be intruder by marriage still mounted. "Not even from that pair would I have believed such a thing possible!" she exclaimed; and she went into a long, low, contemplative laugh, looking not at me, but at the fire. Our silent companion continued to embroider. "That girl," my hostess resumed, "and her discreditable father played on my nephew's youth and chivalry to the tune of — well, you have heard the tune."

"You mean — you mean —?" I couldn't quite take it in.

"Yes. They rattled their poverty at him until he offered and they accepted."

I must have stared grotesquely now. "That — that — the cake — and that sort of thing — at his expense?"

"My dear sir, I shall be glad if you can find me anything that they have ever done at their own expense!"

I doubt if she would ever have permitted her speech such freedom had not the Rieppes been "from Georgia"; I am sure that it was anger — family anger, race anger — which had broken forth; and I think that her silent, severe sister scarcely approved of such breaking forth to me, a stranger. But indignation had worn her reticence thin, and I had happened to press upon the weak place. After my burst of exclamation I came back to it. "So you think Miss Rieppe will get out of it?"

"It is my nephew who will 'get out of it,' as you express it."

I totally misunderstood her. "Oh!" I protested stupidly. "He doesn't look like that. And it takes all meaning from the cake."

"Do not say cake to me again!" said the lady, smiling at last. "And — will you allow me to tell you that I do not need to have my nephew, John Mayrant, explained to me by any one? I merely meant to say that he, and not she, is the person who will make the lucky escape. Of course, he is honorable — a great deal too much so for his own good. It is a misfortune, nowadays, to be born a gentleman in America. But, as I told you, I am not solicitous. What she is counting on — because she thinks she understands true Kings Port honor, and does not in the least — is his renouncing her on account of the phosphates — the bad news, I mean. They could live on what he has — not at all in her way, though — and besides, after once offering his genuine, ardent, foolish love — for it was genuine enough at the time — John would never —"

She stopped; but I took her up. "Did I understand you to say that his love was genuine *at the time?*"

"Oh, he thinks it is now — insists it is now! That is just precisely what would make him — do you not see? — stick to his colors all the closer."

"Goodness!" I murmured. "What a predicament!"

But my hostess nodded easily. "Oh, no. You will see. They will all see."

I rose to take my leave; my visit, indeed, had been, for very interest, prolonged beyond the

limits of formality — my hostess had attended
quite thoroughly to my being entertained. And
at this point the other, the more severe and elderly
lady, made her contribution to my entertainment.
She had kept silence, I now felt sure, because
gossip was neither her habit nor to her liking.
Possibly she may have also felt that her displeasure had been too manifest; at any rate, she spoke
out of her silence in cold, yet rich, symmetrical
tones.

"This, I understand, is your first visit to Kings
Port?"

I told her that it was.

She laid down her exquisite embroidery. "It
has been thought a place worth seeing. There is
no town of such historic interest at the North."

Standing by my chair, I assured her that I did
not think there could be.

"I heard you allude to my half-sister-in-law,
Mrs. Weguelin St. Michael. It was at the house
where she now lives that the famous Miss Beaufain (as she was then) put the Earl of Mainridge
in his place, at the reception which her father
gave the English visitor in 1840. The Earl conducted himself as so many Englishmen seem to
think they can in this country; and on her asking
him how he liked America, he replied, very well,
except for the people, who were so vulgar.

"'What can you expect?' said Miss Beaufain;
'we're descended from the English.'

"But I suppose you will tell me that your
Northern beauties can easily outmatch such wit."

I hastened to disclaim any such pretension;
and having expressed my appreciation of the anec-

dote, I moved to the door as the stately lady resumed her embroidery.

My hostess had a last word for me. " Do not let the cake worry you."

Outside the handsome old iron gate I looked at my watch and found that for this day I could spend no more time upon visiting.

IV

THE GIRL BEHIND THE COUNTER — I

I FEAR — no; to say one "fears" that one has stepped aside from the narrow path of duty, when one knows perfectly well that one has done so, is a ridiculous half-dodging of the truth; let me dismiss from my service such a cowardly circumlocution, and squarely say that I neglected the Cowpens during certain days which now followed. Nay, more; I totally deserted them. Although I feel quite sure that to discover one is a real king's descendant must bring an exultation of no mean order to the heart, there's no exultation whatever in failing to discover this, day after day. Mine is a nature which demands results, or at any rate signs of results coming sooner or later. Even the most abandoned fisherman requires a bite now and then; but my fishing for Fannings had not yet brought me one single nibble — and I gave up the sad sport for a while. The beautiful weather took me out of doors over the land, and also over the water, for I am a great lover of sailing; and I found a little cat-boat and a little negro, both of which suited me very well. I spent many delightful hours in their company among the deeps and shallows of these fair Southern waters.

And indoors, also, I made most agreeable use

of my time, in spite of one disappointment. When, on the day following my visit to the ladies, I returned full of expectancy to lunch at the Woman's Exchange, the girl behind the counter was not there. I found in her stead, it is true, a most polite lady, who provided me with chocolate and sandwiches that were just as good as their predecessors; but she was of advanced years, and little inclined to light conversation. Beyond telling me that Miss Eliza La Heu was indisposed, but not gravely so, and that she was not likely to be long away from her post of duty, this lady furnished me with scant information.

Now I desired a great deal of information. To learn of an imminent wedding where the bridegroom attends to the cake, and is suspected of diminished eagerness for the bride, who is a steel wasp — that is not enough to learn of such nuptials. Therefore I fear — I mean, I know — that it was not wholly for the sake of telling Mrs. Gregory St. Michael about Aunt Carola that I repaired again to Le Mairé Street and rang Mrs. St. Michael's door-bell.

She was at home, to be sure, but with her sat another visitor, the tall, severe lady who had embroidered and had not liked the freedom with which her sister had spoken to me about the wedding. There was not a bit of freedom to-day; the severe lady took care of that.

When, after some utterly unprofitable conversation, I managed to say in a casual voice, which I thought very well tuned for the purpose, " What part of Georgia did you say that General Rieppe came from? " the severe lady responded : —

"I do not think that I mentioned him at all."

"Georgia?" said Mrs. Gregory St. Michael. "I never heard that they came from Georgia."

And this revived my hopes. But the severe lady at once remarked to her: —

"I have received a most agreeable letter from my sister in Paris."

This stopped Mrs. Gregory St. Michael, and dashed my hopes to earth.

The severe lady continued to me: —

"My sister writes of witnessing a performance of the opera *Lohengrin*. Can you tell me if it is a composition of merit?"

I assured her that it was a composition of the highest merit.

"It is many years since I have heard an opera," she pursued. "In my day the works of the Italians were much applauded. But I doubt if Mozart will be surpassed. I hope you admire the *Nozze?*"

You will not need me to tell you that I came out of Mrs. Gregory St. Michael's house little wiser than I went in. My experience did not lead me to abandon all hope. I paid other visits to other ladies; but these answered my inquiries in much the same sort of way as had the lady who admired Mozart. They spoke delightfully of travel, books, people, and of the colonial renown of Kings Port and its leading families; but it is scarce an exaggeration to say that Mozart was as near the cake, the wedding, or the steel wasp as I came with any of them. By patience, however, and mostly at our boarding-house table, I gathered a certain knowledge, though small in amount. If the health of John Mayrant's mother, I learned, had allowed that lady to bring him up herself, many follies might have been saved the youth. His aunt, Miss Eliza St. Michael, though a pattern of good intentions, was not always a pattern of wisdom.   Moreover, how should a spinster bring up a boy fitly?

Of the Rieppes, father and daughter, I also learned a little more.   They did not (most people believed) come from Georgia.   Natchez and Mobile seemed to divide the responsibility of giving them to the world.   It was quite certain the General had run away from Chattanooga.   Nobody disputed this, or offered any other battle as the authentic one.   Of late the Rieppes were seldom to be seen in Kings Port.   Their house (if it had ever been their own property, which I heard hotly argued both ways) had been sold more than two years ago, and their recent brief sojourns in the town were generally beneath the roof of hospitable friends — people by the name of Cornerly, "whom we do not know," as I was carefully informed by more than one member of the St. Michael family.   The girl had disturbed a number of mothers whose sons were prone to slip out of the strict hereditary fold in directions where beauty or champagne was to be found; and the Cornerlys dined late, and had champagne.   Miss Hortense had "splurged it" a good deal here, and the measure of her success with the male youth was the measure of her condemnation by their female elders.

Such were the facts which I gathered from women and from the few men whom I saw in Kings Port.   This town seemed to me almost as

empty of men as if the Pied Piper had passed
through here and lured them magically away to
some distant country. It was on the happy day
that saw Miss Eliza La Heu again providing me
with sandwiches and chocolate that my knowledge of the wedding and the bride and groom
began really to take some steps forward.

It was not I who, at my sequestered lunch at
the Woman's Exchange, began the conversation
the next time. That confection, "Lady Baltimore," about which I was not to worry myself,
had, as they say, "broken the ice" between the
girl behind the counter and myself.

"He has put it off!" This, without any
preliminaries, was her direct and stimulating
news.

I never was more grateful for the solitude of
the Exchange, where I had, before this, noted and
blessed an absence of lunch customers as prevail-
ing as the trade winds; the people I saw there
came to talk, not to purchase. Well, I was certainly henceforth coming for both!

I eagerly plunged in with the obvious question : —

"Indefinitely?"

"Oh, no! Only Wednesday week."

"But will it keep?"

My ignorance diverted her. "Lady Baltimore?
Why, the *i*dea!" And she laughed at me from
the immense distance that the South is from the
North.

"Then he'll have to pay for two?"

"Oh, no! I wasn't going to make it till Tues-
day."

"I didn't suppose that kind of thing *would* keep," I muttered rather vaguely.

Her young spirits bubbled over. "Which kind of thing? The wedding — or the cake?"

This produced a moment of laughter on the part of us both; we giggled joyously together amid the silence and wares for sale, the painted cups, the embroidered souvenirs, the new food, and the old family "pieces."

So this delightful girl was a verbal skirmisher! Now nothing is more to my liking than the verbal skirmish, and therefore I began one immediately. "I see you quite know," was the first light shot that I hazarded.

Her retort to this was merely a very bland and inquiring stare.

I now aimed a trifle nearer the mark. "About him — her — it! Since you practically live in the Exchange, how can you exactly help yourself?"

Her laughter came back. "It's all, you know, so much later than 1812."

"Later! Why, a lot of it is to happen yet!"

She leaned over the counter. "Tell me what you know about it," she said with caressing insinuation.

"Oh, well — but probably they mean to have your education progress chronologically."

"I think I can pick it up anywhere. We had to at the plantation."

It was from my table in the distant dim back of the room, where things stood lumpily under mosquito netting, that I told her my history. She made me go there to my lunch. She seemed to desire that our talk over the counter should not longer continue. And so, back there, over my chocolate and sandwiches, I brought out my gleaned and arranged knowledge which rang out across the distance, comically, like a lecture. She, at her counter, now and then busy with her ledger, received it with the attentive solemnity of a lecture. The ledger might have been notes that she was dutifully and improvingly taking. After I had finished she wrote on for a little while in silence. The curly white dog rose into sight, looked amiably and vaguely about, stretched himself, and sank to sleep again out of sight.

"That's all?" she asked abruptly.

"So far," I answered.

"And what do you think of such a young man?" she inquired.

"I know what I think of such a young woman."

She was still pensive. "Yes, yes, but then that is so simple."

I had a short laugh. "Oh, if you come to the simplicity!"

She nodded, seeming to be doing sums with her pencil.

"Men are always simple — when they're in love."

I assented. "And women — you'll agree? — are always simple when they're not!"

She finished her sums. "Well, *I* think he's foolish!" she frankly stated. "Didn't Aunt Josephine think so, too?"

"Aunt Josephine?"

"Miss Josephine St. Michael — my great-aunt — the lady who embroidered. She brought me here from the plantation."

" No, she wouldn't talk about it.   But don't you think it is your turn now? "

" I've taken my turn! "

" Oh, not much.   To say you think he's foolish isn't much.   You've seen him since? "

" Seen him?   Since when? "

" Here.   Since the postponement.   I take it he came himself about it."

" Yes, he came.   You don't suppose we discussed the reasons, do you? "

" My dear young lady, I suppose nothing, except that you certainly must have seen how he looked (he can blush, you know, handsomely), and that you may have some knowledge or some guess — "

" Some guess why it's not to be until Wednesday week?   Of course he said why.   Her poor, dear father, the General, isn't very well."

" That, indeed, must be an anxiety for Johnny," I remarked.

This led her to indulge in some more merriment.   " But he does," she then said, " seem anxious about something."

" Ah," I exclaimed.   " Then you admit it, too! "

She resorted again to the bland, inquiring stare.

" What *he* won't admit," I explained, "even to his intimate Aunt, because he's so honorable."

" He certainly is simple," she commented, in soft and pensive tones.

"Isn't there some one," I asked, " who could — not too directly, of course — suggest that to him? "

"I think I prefer men to be simple," she returned somewhat quickly.

"Especially when they're in love," I reminded her somewhat slowly.

"Do you want some Lady Baltimore to-day?" she inquired in the official Exchange tone.

I rose obediently. "You're quite right, I should have gone back to the battle of Cowpens long ago, and I'll just say this — since you asked me what I thought of him — that if he's descended from that John Mayrant who fought the *Serapis* under Paul Jones — "

"He is!" she broke in eagerly.

"Then there's not a name in South Carolina that I'd rather have for my own."

I intended that thrust to strike home, but she turned it off most competently. "Oh, you mustn't accept us because of our ancestors. That's how we've been accepting ourselves, and only look where we are in the race!"

"Ah!" I said, as a parting attempt, "don't pretend you're not perfectly satisfied — all of you — as to where you are in the race!"

"We don't pretend anything!" she flashed back.

V

THE BOY OF THE CAKE

ONE is unthankful, I suppose, to call a day dreary when one has lunched under the circumstances that I have attempted to indicate; the bright spot ought to shine over the whole. But you haven't an idea what a nightmare in the daytime Cowpens was beginning to be.

I had thumbed and scanned hundreds of ancient pages, some of them manuscript; I had sat by ancient shelves upon hard chairs, I had sneezed with the ancient dust, and I had not put my finger upon a trace of the right Fanning. I should have given it up, left unexplored the territory that remained staring at me through the backs of unread volumes, had it not been for my Aunt Carola. To her I owed constancy and diligence, and so I kept at it; and the hermit hours I spent at Court and Chancel streets grew worse as I knew better what rarely good company was ready to receive me. This Kings Port, this little city of oblivion, held, shut in with its lavender and pressed-rose memories, a handful of people who were like that great society of the world, the high society of distinguished men and women who exist no more, but who touched history with a light hand, and left their mark upon it in a host of memoirs and letters that we read to-day with a starved and homesick longing in the midst of our sullen welter of

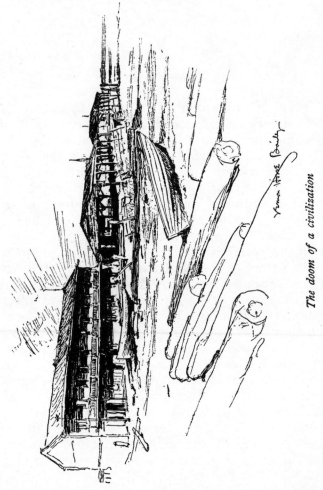

The doom of a civilization

democracy.   With its silent houses and gardens,
its silent streets, its silent vistas of the blue water

in the sunshine, this beautiful, sad place was winning my heart and making it ache.   Nowhere
else in America such charm, such character,
such true elegance as here — and nowhere else
such an overwhelming sense of finality! — the
doom of a civilization founded upon a crime. And
yet, how much has the ballot done for that race?
Or, at least, how much has the ballot done for the
majority of that race?   And what way was it to
meet this problem with the sudden sweeping folly
of the Fifteenth Amendment?   To fling the "door
of hope" wide open before those within had learned
the first steps of how to walk sagely through it!
Ah, if it comes to blame, who goes scatheless in
this heritage of error?   I could have shaped (we
all could, you know) a better scheme for the universe, a plan where we should not flourish at each
other's expense, where the lion should be lying
down with the lamb *now*, where good and evil
should not be husband and wife, indissolubly
married by a law of creation.

With such highly novel thoughts as these I
descended the steps from my researches at the
corner of Court and Chancel streets an hour
earlier than my custom, because — well, I couldn't,
that day, stand Cowpens for another minute.   Up
at the corner of Court and Worship the people
were going decently into church ; it was a sweet,
gentle late Friday in Lent.   I had intended keeping out-of-doors, to smell the roses in the gardens,
to bask in the soft remnant of sunshine, to loiter
and peep in through the Kings Port garden gates,
up the silent walks to the silent verandas.   But
the slow stream of people took me, instead, into

church with the deeply veiled ladies of Kings Port, hushed in their perpetual mourning for not only,

Up the silent walks to the silent verandas

I think, those husbands and brothers and sons whom the war had turned to dust forty years ago, but also for the Cause, the lost Cause, that died with them. I sat there among these Christians suckled in a creed outworn, envying them their well-regulated faith; it, too, was part of the town's repose and sweetness, together with the old-fashioned roses and the old-fashioned ladies. Men, also, were in the congregation — not many, to be sure, but all unanimously wearing that expression of remarkable virtue which seems always to visit, when he goes to church, the average good fellow who is no better than he should be. I became, myself, filled with this same decorous inconsistency, and was singing the hymn, when I caught sight of John Mayrant. What lady was he with? It was just this that most annoyingly I couldn't make out, because the unlucky disposition of things hid it. I caught myself craning my neck and singing the hymn simultaneously and with no difficulty, because all my childhood was in that hymn; I couldn't tell when I hadn't known words and music by heart. Who was she? I tried for a clear view when we sat down, and also, let me confess, when we knelt down; I saw even less of her so; and my hope at the end of the service was dashed by her slow but entire disappearance amid the engulfing exits of the other ladies. I followed where I imagined she had gone, out by a side door, into the beautiful graveyard; but among the flowers and monuments she was not, nor was he; and next I saw, through the iron gate, John Mayrant in the street, walking with his intimate aunt and her more severe sister, and Miss La Heu. I somewhat superfluously hastened to the gate and greeted them, to which they responded with polite, masterly discouragement. He, however, after taking off his hat to them, turned back, and I watched them pursuing their leisurely, reticent course toward the South Place. Why should the old ladies strike me as looking like a tremendously proper pair of conspirators? I was wondering this as I turned back among the tombs, when I perceived John Mayrant coming along one of the churchyard paths. His approach was made at right angles with that of another personage, the respectful negro custodian of the place. This dignitary was evidently hoping to lead me among the monuments, recite to me their old histories, and benefit by my consequent gratitude; he had even got so far as smiling and removing his hat when John Mayrant stopped him. The young man hailed the negro by his first name with that particular and affectionate superiority which few Northerners can understand and none can acquire, and which resembles nothing so much as the way in which you speak to your old dog who has loved you and followed you, because you have cared for him.

"Not this time," John Mayrant said. "I wish to show our relics to this gentleman myself — if he will permit me?" This last was a question put to me with a courteous formality, a formality which a few minutes more were to see smashed to smithereens.

I told him that I should consider myself undeservedly privileged.

"Some of these people are my people," he said, beginning to move.

The old custodian stood smiling, familiar,

respectful, disappointed. " Some of 'em *my* people, too, Mas' John," he cannily observed.

I put a little silver in his hand. " Didn't I see a box somewhere," I said, " with something on it about the restoration of the church ? "

"Something on it, but nothing in it!" exclaimed Mayrant; at which moderate pleasantry the custodian broke into extreme African merriment and ambled away. " You needn't have done it," protested the Southerner, and I naturally claimed my stranger's right to pay my respects in this manner. Such was our introduction, agreeable and unusual.

A silence then unexpectedly ensued and the formality fell colder than ever upon us. The custodian's departure had left us alone, looking at each other across all the unexpressed knowledge that each knew the other had. Mayrant had come impulsively back to me from his aunts, without stopping to think that we had never yet exchanged a word; both of us were now brought up short, and it was the cake that was speaking volubly in our self-conscious dumbness. It was only after this brief, deep gap of things unsaid that John Mayrant came to the surface again, and began a conversation of which, on both our parts, the first few steps were taken on the tiptoes of an archaic politeness; we trod convention like a polished French floor; you might have expected us, after such deliberate and graceful preliminaries, to dance a verbal minuet. We, however, danced something quite different, and that conversation lasted during many days, and led us, like a road, up hill and down dale to a perfect acquaintance. No, not perfect, but de-

lightful; to the end he never spoke to me of the
matter most near him, and I but honor him the
more for his reticence.

Of course his first remark had to be about Kings
Port and me; had he understood rightly that this
was my first visit?

My answer was equally traditional.

It was, next, correct that he should allude to
the weather; and his reference was one of the
two or three that it seems a stranger's destiny always to hear in a place new to him: he apologized
for the weather — so cold a season had not, in his
memory, been experienced in Kings Port; it was
to the highest point exceptional.

I exclaimed that it had been, to my Northern
notions, delightfully mild for March. "Indeed,"
I continued, "I have always said that if March
could be cut out of our Northern climate, as the
core is cut out of an apple, I should be quite satisfied with eleven months, instead of twelve. I
think it might prolong one's youth."

The fire of that season lighted in his eyes, but
he still stepped upon polished convention. He
assured me that the Southern September hurricane
was more deplorable than any Northern March
could be. "Our zone should be called the *In*tem-
perate zone," said he.

"But never in Kings Port," I protested; "with
your roses out-of-doors — and your ladies indoors!"

He bowed. "You pay us a high compliment."

I smiled urbanely. "If the truth is a compliment!"

"Our young ladies *are* roses," he now admitted
with a delicate touch of pride.

"Don't forget your old ones! I never shall."

There was pleasure in his face at this tribute, which, he could see, came from the heart. But, thus pictured to him, the old ladies brought a further idea quite plainly into his expression; and he announced it. "Some of them are not without thorns."

"What would you give," I quickly replied, "for anybody — man or woman — who could not, on an occasion, make themselves sharply felt?"

To this he returned a full but somewhat absent-minded assent. He seemed to be reflecting that he himself didn't care to be the "occasion" upon which an old lady rose should try her thorns; and I was inclined to suspect that his intimate aunt had been giving him a wigging.

Anyhow, I stood ready to keep it up, this interchange of lofty civilities. I, too, could wear the courtly red-heels of eighteenth-century procedure, and for just as long as his Southern upbringing inclined him to wear them; I hadn't known Aunt Carola for nothing! But we, as I have said, were not destined to dance any minuet.

We had been moving, very gradually, and without any attention to our surroundings, to and fro in the beautiful sweet churchyard. Flowers were everywhere, growing, budding, blooming; color and perfume were parts of the very air, and beneath these pretty and ancient tombs, graven with old dates and honorable names, slept the men and women who had given Kings Port her high place in our history. I have never, in this country, seen any churchyard comparable to this one; happy, serene dead, to sleep amid such blossoms and consecration! Good taste prevailed here; distinguished men lay beneath memorial stones that came no higher than your waist or shoulder; there was a total absence of obscure grocers reposing under gigantic obelisks;

A total absence of obscure grocers reposing under gigantic obelisks

to earn a monument here you must win a battle, or do, at any rate, something more than adulterate sugar and oil. The particular monument by which young John Mayrant and I found ourselves standing, when we reached the point about the ladies and the thorns, had a look of importance and it caught his eye, bringing him back to where we were. Upon his pointing to it, and before we had spoken or I had seen the name, I inquired eagerly: "Not the lieutenant of the *Bon Homme Richard?*" and then saw that Mayrant was not the name upon it.

My knowledge of his gallant sea-fighting namesake visibly gratified him. "I wish it were," he said; "but I am descended from this man, too. He was a statesman, and some of his brilliant powers were inherited by his children — but they have not come so far down as me. In 1840, his daughter, Miss Beaufain — "

I laid my hand right on his shoulder. "Don't you do it, John Mayrant!" I cried. "Don't you tell me that. Last night I caught myself saying that instead of my prayers."

Well, it killed the minuet dead; he sat flat down on the low stone coping that bordered the path to which we had wandered back — and I sat flat down opposite him. The venerable custodian, passing along a neighboring path, turned his head and stared at our noise.

"Lawd, see those chillun goin' on!" he muttered. "Mas' John, don't you get too scandalous, tellin' strangers 'bout the old famblies."

Mayrant pointed to me. "He's responsible, Daddy Ben. I'm being just as good as gold. Honest injun!"

The custodian marched slowly on his way, shak-

ing his head. "Mas' John he do go on," he repeated. His office was not alone the care and
the showing off of the graveyard, but another duty,
too, as native and peculiar to the soil as the very
cotton and the rice: this loyal servitor cherished
the honor of the "old famblies," and chid their
young descendants whenever he considered that
they needed it.

Mayrant now sat revived after his collapse of
mirth, and he addressed me from his gravestone.
"Yes, I ought to have foreseen it."

"Foreseen —?" I didn't at once catch the
inference.

"All my aunts and cousins have been talking
to you."

"Oh, Miss Beaufain and the Earl of Mainridge!
Well, but it's quite worth — "

"Knowing by heart!" he broke in with new
merriment.

I kept on. "Why not? They tell those things
everywhere — where they're so .lucky as to possess them! It's a flawless specimen."

"Of 1840 repartee?" He spoke with increasing pauses. "Yes. We do at least possess that.
And some wine of about the same date — and
even considerably older."

"All the better for age," I exclaimed.

But the blue eyes of Mayrant were far away
and full of shadow. "Poor Kings Port," he said
very slowly and quietly. Then he looked at me
with the steady look and the smile that one sometimes has when giving voice to a sorrowful conviction against which one has tried to struggle.
"Poor Kings Port," he affectionately repeated.

" ' Be honest and say that you think so, too ' "

His hand tapped lightly two or three times upon
the gravestone upon which he was seated. "Be
honest and say that you think so, too," he demanded, always with his smile.

But how was I to agree aloud with what his
silent hand had expressed? Those inaudible taps
on the stone spoke clearly enough; they said:
"Here lies Kings Port, here lives Kings Port.
Outside of this is our true death, on the vacant
wharves, in the empty streets. All that we have
left is the immortality which these historic names
have won." How could I tell him that I thought
so, too? Nor was I as sure of it then as he was.
And besides, this was a young man whose spirit
was almost surely, in suffering; ill fortune, both
material and of the heart, I seemed to suspect, had
made him wounded and bitter in these immediate
days; and the very suppression he was exercising
hurt him the more deeply. So I replied, honestly,
as he had asked: "I hope you are mistaken."

"That's because you haven't been here long
enough," he declared.

Over us, gently, from somewhere across the
gardens and the walls, came a noiseless water
breeze, to which the roses moved and nodded
among the tombs. They gave him a fanciful
thought. "Look at them! They belong to us,
and they know it. They're saying, 'Yes; yes;
yes,' all day long. I don't know why on earth
I'm talking in this way to you!" he broke off
with vivacity. "But you made me laugh so."

VI

IN THE CHURCHYARD

"THEN it was a good laugh, indeed!" I
cried heartily.

"Oh, don't let's go back to our fine manners!"
he begged comically. "We've satisfied each
other that we have them! I feel so lonely; and
my aunt just now — well, never mind about that.
But you really must excuse us about Miss Beaufain, and all that sort of thing. I see it, because
I'm of the new generation, since the war, and —
well, I've been to other places, too. But Aunt
Eliza, and all of them, you know, can't see it.
And I wouldn't have them, either! So I don't
ever attempt to explain to them that the world has
to go on. They'd say, 'We don't see the necessity!' When slavery stopped, they stopped, you
see, just like a clock. Their hand points to 1865
— it has never moved a minute since. And some
day" — his voice grew suddenly tender — "they'll
go, one by one, to join the still older ones. And
I shall miss them very much."

For a moment I did not speak, but watched
the roses nodding and moving. Then I said:
"May I say that I shall miss them, too?"

He looked at me. "Miss our old Kings Port
people?" He didn't invite outsiders to do that!

"Don't you see how it is?" I murmured. "It
was the same thing once with us."

"The same thing — in the North?" His tone still held me off.

"The same sort of dear old people — I mean charming, peppery, refined, courageous people; in Salem, in Boston, in New York, in every place that has been colonial, and has taken a hand in the game." And, as certain beloved memories of men and women rose in my mind, I continued: "If you knew some of the Boston elder people as I have known them, you would warm with the same admiration that is filling me as I see your people of Kings Port."

"But politics?" the young Southerner slowly suggested.

"Oh, hang slavery! Hang the war!" I exclaimed. "Of course, we had a family quarrel. But we *were* a family once, and a fine one, too! We knew each other, we visited each other, we wrote letters, sent presents, kept up relations; we, in short, coherently joined hands from one generation to another; the fibres of the sons tingled with the current from their fathers, back and back to the old beginnings, to Plymouth and Roanoke and Rip Van Winkle! It's all gone, all done, all over. You have to be a small, well-knit country for that sort of exquisite personal unitedness. There's nothing united about these States any more, except Standard Oil and discontent. We're no longer a small people living and dying for a great idea; we're a big people living and dying for money. And these ladies of yours — well, they have made me homesick for a national and a social past which I never saw, but which my old people knew. They're like legends, still living,

still warm and with us. In their quiet clean-cut
faces I seem to see a reflection of the old serene
candlelight we all once talked and danced in —
sconces, tall mirrors, candles burning inside glass
globes to keep them from the moths and the draft
that, of a· warm evening, blew in through handsome mahogany doors; the good bright silver;
the portraits by Copley and Gilbert Stuart; a
young girl at a square piano, singing Moore's melodies — and Mr. Pinckney or Commodore Perry,
perhaps, dropping in for a hot supper!'"

John Mayrant was smiling and looking at the
graves. "Yes, that's it; that's all it," he mused.
"You do understand."

But I had to finish my flight. "Such quiet
faces are gone now in the breathless, competing
North: ground into oblivion between the clashing
trades of the competing men and the clashing
jewels and chandeliers of their competing wives
— while yours have lingered on, spared by your
very adversity. And that's why I shall miss your
old people when they follow mine — because
they're the last of their kind, the end of the chain,
the bold original stock, the great race that made
our glory grow and saw that it did grow through
thick and thin: the good old native blood of independence."

I spoke as a man can always speak when he
means it; and my listener's face showed that my
words had gone where meant words always go —
home to the heart. But he merely nodded at me.
His nod, however, telling as it did of a quickly
established accord between us, caused me to bring
out to this new acquaintance still more of those

thoughts which I condescend to expose to very few old ones.

"Haven't you noticed," I said, "or don't you feel it, away down here in your untainted isolation, the change, the great change, that has come over the American people?"

He wasn't sure.

"They've lost their grip on patriotism."

He smiled. "We did that here in 1861."

"Oh, no! You left the Union, but you loved what you considered was your country, and you love it still. That's just my point, just my strange discovery in Kings Port. You retain the thing we've lost. Our big men fifty years ago thought of the country, and what they could make it; our big men to-day think of the country and what they can make *out* of it. Rather different, don't you see? When I walk about in the North, I merely meet members of trusts or unions — according to the length of the individual's purse; when I walk about in Kings Port, I meet *Americans*. — Of course," I added, taking myself up, "that's too sweeping a statement. The right sort of American isn't extinct in the North by any means. But there's such a commercial deluge of the wrong sort, that the others sometimes seem to me sadly like a drop in the bucket."

"You certainly understand it all," John Mayrant repeated. "It's amazing to find you saying things that I have thought were my own private notions."

I laughed. "Oh, I fancy there are more than two of us in the country."

"Even the square piano and Mr. Pinckney," he

went on. " I didn't suppose anybody had thought things like that, except myself."

"Oh," I again said lightly, "any American — any, that is, of the world — who has a colonial background for his family, has thought, probably, very much the same sort of things. Of course it would be all Greek or gibberish to the new people."

He took me up with animation. " The new people! My goodness, sir, yes! Have you seen them? Have you seen Newport, for instance?" His diction now (and I was to learn it was always in him a sign of heightening intensity) grew more and more like the formal speech of his ancestors. " You have seen Newport?" he said.

"Yes; now and then."

" But lately, sir? I knew we were behind the times down here, sir, but I had not imagined how much. Not by any means! Kings Port has a long road to go before she will consider marriage provincial and chastity obsolete."

"Dear me, Mr. Mayrant! Well, I must tell you that it's not all quite so — so advanced — as that, you know. That's not the whole of Newport."

He hastened to explain. " Certainly not, sir! I would not insult the honorable families whom I had the pleasure to meet there, and to whom my name was known because they had retained their good position since the days when my great-uncle had a house and drove four horses there himself. I noticed three kinds of Newport, sir."

" Three?"

" Yes. Because I took letters; and some of the

letters were to people who — who once *had* been,
you know; it was sad to see the thing, sir, so plain
against the glaring proximity of the other thing.
And so you can divide Newport into those who
have to sell their old family pictures, those who
have to buy their old family pictures, and the lucky
few who need neither buy nor sell, who are neither
going down nor bobbing up, but who have kept
their heads above the American tidal wave from
the beginning and continue to do so. And I
don't believe that there are any nicer people in the
world than those."

"Nowhere!" I exclaimed. "When New York
does her best, what's better? — If only those best
set the pace!"

"If only!" he assented. "But it's the others
who get into the papers, who dine the drunken
dukes, and make poor chambermaids envious a
thousand miles inland!"

"There should be a high tariff on drunken
dukes," I said.

"You'll never get it!" he declared. "It's the
Republican party whose daughters marry them."

I rocked with enjoyment where I sat; he was
so refreshing. And I agreed with him so well.
"You're every bit as good as Miss Beaufain," I
cried.

"Oh, no; oh, no! But I often think if we could
only deport the negroes and Newport together to
one of our distant islands, how happily our two
chief problems would be solved!"

I still rocked. "Newport would, indeed, enjoy
your plan for it. Do go on!" I entreated him.
But he had, for the moment, ceased; and I rose

to stretch my legs and saunter among the old headstones and the wafted fragrance.

His aunt (or his cousin, or whichever of them it had been) was certainly right as to his inheriting a pleasant and pointed gift of speech; and a responsive audience helps us all. Such an audience I certainly was for young John Mayrant, yet beneath the animation that our talk had filled his eyes with lay (I seemed to see or feel) that other mood all the time, the mood which had caused the girl behind the counter to say to me that he was "anxious about something." The unhappy youth, I was gradually to learn, was much more than that — he was in a tangle of anxieties. He talked to me as a sick man turns in bed from pain; the pain goes on, but the pillow for a while is cool.

Here there broke upon us a little interruption, so diverting, so utterly like the whole quaint tininess of Kings Port, that I should tell it to you, even if it did not bear directly upon the matter which was beginning so actively to concern me — the love difficulties of John Mayrant.

It was the letter-carrier.

We had come, from our secluded seats, round a corner, and so by the vestry door and down the walk beside the church, and as I read to myself the initials upon the stones wherewith the walk was paved, I drew near the half-open gateway upon Worship Street. The postman was descending the steps of the post-office opposite. He saw me through the gate and paused. He knew me, too! My face, easily marked out amid the resident faces he was familiar with, had at once caught his attention; very likely he, too, had by now learned that I was interested in the battle of Cowpens; but I did not ask him this. He crossed over and handed me a letter.

"No use," he said most politely, "takin' it away down to Mistress Trevise's when you're right here, sir. Northern mail eight hours late today," he added, and bowing, was gone upon his route.

My home letter, from a man, an intimate running mate of mine, soon had my full attention, for on the second page it said: —

"I have just got back from accompanying her to Baltimore. One of us went as far as Washington with her on the train. We gave her a dinner yesterday at the March Hare by way of farewell. She tried our new toboggan fire-escape on a bet. Clean from the attic, my boy. I imagine our native girls will rejoice at her departure. However, nobody's engaged to her, at least nobody here. How many may fancy themselves so elsewhere I can't say. Her name is Hortense Rieppe."

I suppose I must have been silent after finishing this letter.

"No bad news, I trust?" John Mayrant inquired.

I told him no; and presently we had resumed our seats in the quiet charm of the flowers.

I now spoke with an intention. "What a lot you seem to have seen and suffered of the advanced Newport!"

The intention wrought its due and immediate effect. "Yes. There was no choice. I had gone to Newport upon—upon an urgent matter, which took me among those people."

He dwelt upon the pictures that came up in his mind. But he took me away again from the "urgent matter." "I saw," he resumed more briskly, "fifteen or twenty—most amazing, sir! —young men, some of them not any older than I am, who had so many millions that they could easily—" he paused, casting about for some expression adequate—"could buy Kings Port and put it under a glass case in a museum—my aunts and all—and never know it!" He livened with disrespectful mirth over his own picture of his aunts, purchased by millionaire steel or coal for the purposes of public edification.

"And a very good thing if they could be," I declared.

He wondered a moment. "My aunts? Under a glass case?"

"Yes, indeed—and with all deference be it said! They'd be more invaluable, more instructive, than the classics of a thousand libraries."

He was prepared not to be pleased. "May I ask to whom and for what?"

"Why, you ought to see! You've just been saying it yourself. They would teach our bulging automobilists, our unlicked boy cubs, our alcoholic girls who shout to waiters for 'high-balls' on country club porches—they would teach these wallowing creatures, whose money has merely gilded their bristles, what American refinement once was. The manners we've lost, the decencies we've banished, the standards we've lowered, their light is still flickering in this passing generation of yours. It's the last torch. That's why I wish it could, somehow, pass on the sacred fire."

He shook his head. "They don't want the sacred fire. They want the high-balls —and they have money enough to be drunk straight through the next world!" He was thoughtful. "They are the classics," he added.

I didn't see that he had gone back to my word. "Roman Empire, you mean?"

"No, the others; the old people we're bidding good-by to. Roman Republic! Simple lives, gallant deeds, and one great uniting inspiration. Liberty winning her spurs. They were moulded under that, and they are our true American classics. Nothing like them will happen again."

"Perhaps," I suggested, "our generation is uneasily living in a 'bad quarter-of-an-hour' — good old childhood gone, good new manhood not yet come, and a state of chicken-pox between whiles." And on this I made to him a much-used and consoling quotation about the old order changing.

"Who says that?" he inquired; and upon my telling him, "I hope so," he said, "I hope so. But just now Uncle Sam 'aspires to descend.'"

I laughed at his counter-quotation. "You know *your* classics, if you don't know Tennyson."

He, too, laughed. "Don't tell Aunt Eliza!"

"Tell her what?"

"That I didn't recognize Tennyson. My Aunt Eliza educated me — and she thinks Tennyson about the only poet worth reading since — well, since Byron and Sir Walter at the very latest! Neither she nor Sir Walter come down to modern

poetry — or to alcoholic girls." His tone, on these
last words, changed.

Again, as when he had said "an urgent matter,"
I seemed to feel hovering above us what must be
his ceaseless preoccupation ; and I wondered if he
had found, upon visiting Newport, Miss Hortense
sitting and calling for "high-balls."

I gave him a lead. "The worst of it is that a girl
who would like to behave herself decently finds
that propriety puts her out of the running. The
men flock off to the other kind."

He was following me with watching eyes.

"And you know," I continued, "what an anxious Newport parent does on finding her girl on
the brink of being a failure."

"I can imagine," he answered, "that she scolds
her like the dickens."

"Oh, nothing so ineffectual! She makes her
keep up with the others, you know. Makes her do
things she'd rather not do."

"High-balls, you mean?"

"Anything, my friend ; anything to keep up."

He had a comic suggestion. "Driven to drink
by her mother! Well, it's, at any rate, a new
cause for old effects." He paused. It seemed
strangely to bring to him some sort of relief.
"That would explain a great deal," he said.

Was he thus explaining to himself his lady-love,
or rather certain Newport aspects of her which
had, so to speak, jarred upon his Kings Port
notions of what a lady might properly do? I sat
on my gravestone with my wonder, and my now-
dawning desire to help him (if improbably I could),
to get him out of it, if he were really in it ; and

he sat on his gravestone opposite, with the path between us, and the little noiseless breeze rustling the white irises, and bearing hither and thither the soft perfume of the roses. His boy face, lean, high-strung, brooding, was full of suppressed contentions. I made myself, during our silence, state his possible problem: " He doesn't love her any more, he won't admit this to himself; he intends to go through with it, and he's catching at any justification of what he has seen in her that has chilled him, so that he may, poor wretch! coax back his lost illusion." Well, if that was it, what in the world could I, or anybody, do about it?

His next remark was transparent enough. " Do you approve of young ladies smoking? "

I met his question with another: " What reasons can be urged against it? "

He was quick. " Then you don't mind it? " There was actual hope in the way he rushed at this.

I laughed. " I didn't say I didn't mind it." (As a matter of fact I do mind it; but it seemed best not to say so to him.)

He fell off again. " I certainly saw very nice people doing it up there."

I filled this out. "You'll see very nice people doing it everywhere."

" Not in Kings Port! At least, not *my* sort of people!" He stiffly proclaimed this.

I tried to draw him out. " But is there, after all, any valid objection to it? "

But he was off on a preceding speculation. " A mother or any parent," he said, " might encourage the daughter to smoke, too. And the girl might take it up so as not to be thought peculiar where she was, and then she might drop it very gladly."

I became specific. " Drop it, you mean, when she came to a place where doing it would be thought — well, in bad style?"

" Or for the better reason," he answered, "that she didn't really like it herself."

" How much *you* don't ' really like it' *your*self!" I remarked.

This time he was slow. "Well — well — why need they? Are not their lips more innocent than ours? Is not the association somewhat — ? "

" My dear fellow," I interrupted, " the association is, I think you'll have to agree, scarcely of *their* making!"

" That's true enough," he laughed. " And, as you say, very nice people do it everywhere. But not here. Have you ever noticed," he now inquired with continued transparency, " how much harder they are on each other than we are on them?"

" Oh, yes! I've noticed that." I surmised it was this sort of thing he had earlier choked himself off from telling me in his unfinished complaint about his aunt; but I was to learn later that on this occasion it was upon the poor boy himself and not on the smoking habits of Miss Rieppe, that his aunt had heavily descended. I also reflected that if cigarettes were the only thing he deprecated in the lady of his choice, the lost illusion might be coaxed back. The trouble was that *I* deprecated something fairly distant from cigarettes. The cake was my quite sufficient trouble; it stuck in my throat worse than the probably magnified gossip I had heard; this, for the present, I could manage to swallow.

He came out now with a personal note. " I suppose you think I'm a ninny."

" Never in the wildest dream! "

" Well, but too innocent for a man, anyhow."

" That would be an insult," I declared laughingly.

" For I'm not innocent in the least. You'll find we're all men here, just as much as any men in the North you could pick out. South Carolina has never lacked sporting blood, sir. But in Newport — well, sir, we gentlemen down here, when we wish a certain atmosphere and all that, have always been accustomed to seek the *demi-monde*."

" So it was with us until the women changed it."

" The women, sir? " He *was* innocent!

" The 'ladies,' as you Southerners so chivalrously continue to style them. The rich new fashionable ladies became so desperate in their competition for men's allegiance that they — well, some of them would, in the point of conversation, greatly scandalize the smart *demi-monde*."

He nodded. " Yes. I heard men say things in drawing-rooms to ladies that a gentleman here would have been taken out and shot for. And don't you agree with me, sir, that good taste itself should be a sort of religion? I don't mean to say anything sacrilegious, but it seems to me that even if one has ceased to believe some parts of

the Bible, even if one does not always obey the
Ten Commandments, one is bound, not as a
believer but as a *gentleman*, to remember the difference between grossness and refinement, between
excess and restraint — that one can have and keep,
just as the pagan Greeks did, a moral elegance."

He astonished me, this ardent, ideal, troubled
boy; so innocent regarding the glaring facts of
our new prosperity, so finely penetrating as to
some of the mysteries of the soul. But he was
of old Huguenot blood, and of careful and gentle
upbringing; and it was delightful to find such a
young man left upon our American soil untainted
by the present fashionable idolatries.

"I bow to your creed of 'moral elegance,'" I
cried. "It never dies. It has outlasted all the
mobs and all the religions."

"They seemed to think," he continued, pursuing his Newport train of thought, "that to prove
you were a dead game sport you must behave like
— behave like —"

"Like a herd of swine," I suggested.

He was merry. "Ah, if they only would —
completely!"

"Completely what?"

"Behave so. Rush over a steep place into the
sea."

We sat in the quiet relish of his Scriptural
idea, and the western crimson and the twilight
began to come and mingle with the perfumes.
John Mayrant's face changed from its vivacity to
a sort of pensive wistfulness, which, for all the
dash and spirit in his delicate features, was somehow the final thing one got from the boy's expres-

sion. It was as though the noble memories of
his race looked out of his eyes, seeking new
chances for distinction, and found instead a soil
laid waste, an empty fatherland, a people benumbed
past rousing. Had he not said, "Poor Kings
Port!" as he tapped the gravestone? Moral elegance could scarcely permit a sigh more direct.

"I am glad that you believe it never dies," he
resumed. "And I am glad to find somebody to
— talk to, you know. My friends here are everything friends and gentlemen should be, but they
don't — I suppose it's because they have not had
my special experiences."

I sat waiting for the boy to go on with it. How
plainly he was telling me of his "special experiences"! He and his creed were not merely in
revolt against the herd of swine; there would be
nothing special in that; I had met people before
who were that; but he was tied by honor, and
soon to be tied by the formidable nuptial knot, to
a specimen devotee of the cult. He shouldn't
marry her if he really did not want to, and I could
stop it! But how was I to begin spinning the
first faint web of plan how I might stop it, unless
he came right out with the whole thing? I didn't
believe he was the man to do that ever, even under
the loosening inspiration of drink. In wine lies
truth, no doubt; but within him, was not moral
elegance the bottom truth that would, even in his
cups, keep him a gentleman, and control all such
revelations? He might smash the glasses, but he
would not speak of his misgivings as to Hortense
Rieppe.

He began again, "Nor do I believe that a

really nice girl would continue to think as those
few do, if she once got safe away from them.
Why, my dear sir," he stretched out his hand in
emphasis, "you do not have to do anything
untimely and extreme if you are in good earnest
a dead game sport. The time comes, and you
meet the occasion as the duck swims. There was
one of them — the right kind."

"Where?" I asked.

"Why — you're leaning against her headstone!"

The little incongruity made us both laugh, but
it was only for the instant. The tender mood of
the evening, and all that we had said, sustained
the quiet and almost grave undertone of our conference. My own quite unconscious act of rising
from the grave and standing before him on the
path to listen brought back to us our harmonious
pensiveness.

"She was born in Kings Port, but educated in
Europe. I don't suppose until the time came
that she ever did anything harder than speak
French, or play the piano, or ride a horse. She
had wealth and so had her husband. He was
killed in the war, and so were two of her sons.
The third was too young to go. Their fortune
was swept away, but the plantation was there, and
the negroes were proud to remain faithful to the
family. She took hold of the plantation, she
walked the rice-banks in high boots. She had an
overseer, who, it was told her, would possibly take
her life by poison or by violence. She nevertheless lived in that lonely spot with no protector
except her pistol and some directions about anti-
dotes. She dismissed him when she had proved

he was cheating her; she made the planting pay
as well as any man did after the war; she educated her last son, got him into the navy, and
then, one evening, walking the river-banks too
late, she caught the fever and died. You will
understand she went with one step from cherished
ease to single-handed battle with life, a delicately
nurtured lady, with no preparation for her trials."

"Except moral elegance," I murmured.

"Ah, that was the point, sir! To see her you
would never have guessed it! She kept her bur-
dens from the sight of all. She wore tribulation
as if it were a flower in her bosom. We children
always looked forward to her coming, because she
was so gay and delightful to us, telling us stories
of the old times — old rides when the country was
wild, old journeys with the family and servants to
the Hot Springs before the steam cars were invented, old adventures, with the battle of New
Orleans or a famous duel in them — the sort of
stories that begin with (for you seem to know
something of it yourself, sir) 'Your grandfather,
my dear John, the year that he was twenty, got
himself into serious embarrassments through paying his attentions to two reigning beauties at
once.' She was full of stories which began in
that sort of pleasant way."

I said: "When a person like that dies, an
impoverishment falls upon us; the texture of life
seems thinner."

"Oh, yes, indeed! I know what you mean — to
lose the people one has always seen from the
cradle. Well, she has gone away, she has taken
her memories out of the world, the old times, the

old stories. Nobody, except a little nutshell of people here, knows or cares anything about her any more; and soon even the nutshell will be empty." He paused, and then, as if brushing aside his churchyard mood, he translated into his changed thought another classic quotation: " But we can't dawdle over the ' tears of things'; it's Nature's law. Only, when I think of the rice-banks and the boots and the pistol, I wonder if the Newport ladies, for all their high-balls, could do any better!"

The crimson had faded, the twilight was altogether come, but the little noiseless breeze was blowing still; and as we left the quiet tombs behind us, and gained Worship Street, I could not help looking back where slept that older Kings Port about which I had heard and had said so much. Over the graves I saw the roses, nodding and moving, as if in acquiescent revery.

VII

THE GIRL BEHIND THE COUNTER — II

"WHICH of them is idealizing?" This was
the question that I asked myself, next morning, in my boarding-house, as I dressed for breakfast; the next morning is — at least I have always
found it so — an excellent time for searching questions; and to-day I had waked up no longer beneath the strong, gentle spell of the churchyard.
A bright sun was shining over the eastern waters
of the town, I could see from my upper veranda
the thousand flashes of the waves; the steam yacht
rode placidly and competently among them, while
a coastwise steamer was sailing by her, out to sea,
to Savannah, or New York; the general world
was going on, and — which of them was idealizing? It mightn't be so bad, after all. Hadn't I,
perhaps, over-sentimentalized to myself the case
of John Mayrant? Hadn't I imagined for him
ever so much more anxiety than the boy actually
felt? For people can idealize *down* just as readily
as they can idealize *up*. Of Miss Hortense Rieppe
I had now two partial portraits — one by the displeased aunts, the other by their chivalric nephew;
in both she held between her experienced lips,
a cigarette; there the similarity ceased. And
then, there was the toboggan fire-escape. Well, I
must meet the living original before I could de-

cide whether (for me, at any rate) she was the
" brute " as seen by the eyes of Mrs. Gregory St.
Michael, or the " really nice girl " who was going
to marry John Mayrant on Wednesday week.
Just at this point my thoughts brought up hard
again at the cake. No; I couldn't swallow that
any better this morning than yesterday afternoon!
Allow the gentleman to pay for the feast! Better
to have omitted all feast; nothing simpler, and it
would have been at least dignified, even if arid.
But then, there was the lady (a cousin or an aunt
— I couldn't remember which this morning) who
had told me she wasn't solicitous. What did she
mean by that? And she had looked quite queer
when she spoke about the phosphates. Oh, yes,
to be sure, she was his intimate aunt! Where,
by the way, was Miss Rieppe?

By the time I had eaten my breakfast and
walked up Worship Street to the post-office I
was full of it all again; my searching thoughts
hadn't simplified a single point. I always called
for my mail at the post-office, because I got it
sooner; it didn't come to the boarding-house before I had departed on my quest for royal blood,
whereas, this way, I simply got my letters at the
corner of Court and Worship streets and walked
diagonally across and down Court a few steps to
my researches, which I could vary and alleviate
by reading and answering news from home.

It was from Aunt Carola that I heard to-day.
Only a little of what she said will interest you.
There had been a delightful meeting of the Selected
Salic Scions. The Baltimore Chapter had paid her
Chapter a visit. Three ladies and one very highly

connected young gentleman had come—an encouragingly full and enthusiastic meeting. They had
lunched upon cocoa, sherry, and croquettes; after
which all had been more than glad to listen to a
paper read by a descendant of Edward the Third;
and the young gentleman, a descendant of Cather-
ine of Aragon, had recited a beautiful original
poem, entitled " My Queen Grandmother." Aunt
Carola regretted that I could not have had the
pleasure and the benefit of this meeting; the
young gentleman had turned out to be, also, a
refined and tasteful musician, playing upon the
piano a favorite gavotte of Louis the Thirteenth.
" And while you are in Kings Port," my aunt said,
" I expect you to profit by associating with the
survivors of our good American society — people
such as one could once meet everywhere when I
was young, but who have been destroyed by the
invasion of the proletariat. You are in the last
citadel of good-breeding. By the way, find out,
if you can, if any of the Bombo connection are
extant; as through them I should like, if possible,
to establish a chapter of the Scions in South Carolina. Have you met a Miss Rieppe, a decidedly
striking young woman, who says she is from Kings
Port, and who recently passed through here with
a very common man dancing attendance on her?
He owns the *Hermana*, and she is said to be
engaged to him."

This wasn't as good as meeting Miss Rieppe myself; but the new angle at which I got her from
my Aunt was distinctly a contribution toward
the young woman's likeness; I felt that I should
know her at sight, if ever she came within seeing

Between the silent walls of commerce desolated

distance. And it would be entertaining to find
that she was a Bombo; but that could wait; what

couldn't wait was the *Hermana*. I postponed the
Fannings, hurried by the door where they waited for
me, and, coming to the end of Court Street, turned
to the right and sought among the wharves the nearest vista that could give me a view of the harbor.
Between the silent walls of commerce desolated,
and by the empty windows from which Prosperity
once looked out, I threaded my way to a point
upon the town's eastern edge.   Yes, that was the
steam yacht's name: the *Hermana*.   I didn't make
it out myself, she lay a trifle too far from shore;
but I could read from a little fluttering pennant
that her owner was not on board; and from the
second loafer whom I questioned I learned, besides
her name, that she had come from New York here
to meet her owner, whose name he did not know
and whose arrival was still indefinite.   This was
not very much to find out; but it was so much
more than I had found out about the Fannings
that, although I now faithfully returned to my researches, and sat over open books until noon, I
couldn't tell you a word of what I read.   Where
was Miss Rieppe, and where was the owner of
the *Hermana?*   Also, precisely how ill was the
hero of Chattanooga, her poor dear father?

At the Exchange I opened the door upon a
conversation which, in consequence, broke off
abruptly; but this much I came in for:—

" Nothing but the slightest bruise above his eye.
The other one is in bed."

It was the severe lady who said this; I mean
that lady who, among all the severe ones I had
met, seemed capable of the highest exercise of this
quality, although she had not exercised it in my

presence. She looked, in her veil and her black
street dress, as aloof, and as coldly scornful of the
present day, as she had seemed when sitting over
her embroidery; but it was not of 1812, or even
1840, that she had been talking just now: it was
this morning that somebody was bruised, somebody was in bed.

The handsome lady acknowledged my saluta-
tion completely, but not encouragingly, and then,
on the threshold, exchanged these parting sentences with the girl behind the counter:—

"They will have to shake hands. He was not
very willing, but he listened to me. Of course,
the chastisement was right — but it does not
affect my opinion of his keeping on with the
position."

"No, indeed, Aunt Josephine!" the girl agreed.
"I wish he wouldn't. Did you say it was his right
eye?"

"His left." Miss Josephine St. Michael inclined
her head once more to me and went out of the
Exchange. I retired to my usual table, and the
girl read in my manner, quite correctly, the feelings which I had not supposed I had allowed to
be evident. She said:—

"Aunt Josephine always makes strangers think
she's displeased with them."

I replied like the young ass which I constantly
tell myself I have ceased to be: "Oh, displeasure
is as much notice as one is entitled to from Miss
St. Michael."

The girl laughed with her delightful sweet
mockery.

"I declare, you're huffed! Now don't tell me

you're not. But you mustn't be. When you
know her, you'll know that that awful manner
means Aunt Josephine is just being shy. Why,
even *I'm* not afraid of her George Washington
glances any more!"

"Very well," I laughed, "I'll try to have your
courage." Over my chocolate and sandwiches I
sat in curiosity discreditable, but natural. Who
was in bed — who would have to shake hands?
And why had they stopped talking when I came
in? Of course, I found myself hoping that John
Mayrant had put the owner of the *Hermana* in
bed at the slight cost of a bruise above his left
eye. I wondered if the cake was again counter-
manded, and I started upon that line. "I think
I'll have to-day, if you please, another slice of that
Lady Baltimore." And I made ready for another
verbal skirmish.

"I'm so sorry! It's a little stale to-day. You
can have the last slice, if you wish."

"Thank you, I will." She brought it. "It's
not so very stale," I said. "How long since it
has been made?"

"Oh, it's the same you've been having. You're
its only patron just now."

"Well, no. There's Mr. Mayrant."

"Not for a week yet, you remember."

So the wedding was on yet. Still, John might
have smashed the owner of the *Hermana*.

"Have you seen him lately?" I asked.

There was something special in the way she
looked. "Not to-day. Have you?"

"Never in the forenoon. He has his duties
and I have mine."

She made a little pause, and then, " What do
you think of the President? "

" The President? "   I was at a loss.

" But I'm afraid you would take his view — the
Northern view," she mused.

It gave me, suddenly, her meaning. " Oh, the
President of the United States! How you do
change the subject! "

Her eyes were upon me, burning with sectional
indignation, but she seemed to be thinking too
much to speak.   Now, here was a topic that I had
avoided, and she had plumped it at me.   Very
well; she should have my view.

" If you mean that a gentleman cannot invite
any respectable member of any race he pleases to
dine privately in his house — "

" *His* house! "   She was glowing now with it.
" I think he is — I think he is — to have one of
them — and even if *he* likes it, not to remember —
I cannot speak about him! " she wound up; " I
should say unbecoming things."   She had walked
out, during these words, from behind the counter,
and as she stood there in the middle of the long
room you might have thought she was about to
lead a cavalry charge.   Then, admirably, she put
it all under, and spoke on with perfect self-control.
" Why can't somebody explain it to him?   If I
knew him, I would go to him myself, and I would
say, ' Mr. President, we need not discuss our different tastes as to dinner company.   Nor need we
discuss how much you benefit the colored race by
an act which makes every member of it immediately think that he is fit to dine with any king in
the world.   But you are staying in a house which

is partly our house, ours, the South's, for we, too,
pay taxes, you know.   And since you also know
our deep feeling — you may even call it a prejudice, if it so pleases you — do you not think that, so
long as you are residing in that house, you should
not gratuitously shock our deep feeling?'" She
swept a magnificent low curtsy at the air.

"By Jove, Miss La Heu!" I exclaimed, "you
put it so that it's rather hard to answer."

"I'm glad it strikes you so."

"But did it make them all think they were
going to dine?"

"Hundreds of thousands.   It was proof to them
that they were as good as anybody — just as good,
without reading or writing or anything.   The
very next day some of the laziest and dirtiest
where we live had a new strut, like the monkey
when you put a red flannel cap on him — only the
monkey doesn't push ladies off the sidewalk.
And that state of mind, you know," said Miss La
Heu, softening down from wrath to her roguish
laugh, "isn't the right state of mind for racial
progress!   But I wasn't thinking of this.   You
know he has appointed one of them to office
here."

A light entered my brain: John Mayrant had a
position at the Custom House!   John Mayrant
was subordinate to the President's appointee!   She
hadn't changed the subject so violently, after all.

I came squarely at it.   "And so you wish him
to resign his position?"

But I was ahead of her this time.

"The Chief of Customs?" she wonderingly
murmured.

I brought her up with me now. "Did Miss Josephine St. Michael say it was over his left eye?"

The girl instantly looked everything she thought. "I believe you were present!" This was her highly comprehensive exclamation, accompanied also by a blush as splendidly young as John Mayrant's had been while he so stammeringly brought out his wishes concerning the cake. I at once decided to deceive her utterly, and therefore I spoke the exact truth: "No, I wasn't present."

They did their work, my true words; the false impression flowed out of them as smoothly as California claret from a French bottle.

"I wonder who told you?" my victim remarked. "But it doesn't really matter. Everybody is bound to know it. You surely were the last person with him in the churchyard?"

"Gracious!" I admitted again with splendidly mendacious veracity. "How we do find each other out in Kings Port!"

It was not by any means the least of the delights which I took in the company of this charming girl that sometimes she was too much for me, and sometimes I was too much for her. It was, of course, just the accident of our ages; in a very few years she would catch up, would pass, would always be too much for me. Well, to-day it was happily my turn; I wasn't going to finish lunch without knowing all she, at any rate, could tell me about the left eye and the man in bed.

"Forty years ago," I now, with ingenuity, remarked, "I suppose it would have been pistols."

She assented. " And I like that better — don't
you — for gentlemen ? "
" Well, you mean that fists are — "
" Yes," she finished for me.

" All the same," I maintained, "don't you think
that there ought to be some correspondence, some
proportion, between the gravity of the cause and
the gravity of — "
" Let the coal-heavers take to their fists ! " she
scornfully cried. " People of our class can't descend — "
" Well, but," I interrupted, "then you give the
coal-heavers the palm for discrimination."
" How's that ? "
" Why, perfectly ! Your coal-heaver kills for
some offences, while for lighter ones he — gets a
bruise over the left eye."
" You don't meet it, you don't meet it ! What
is an insult ever but an insult ? "
" Oh, we in the North notice certain degrees —
insolence, impudence, impertinence, liberties, rudeness — all different."
She took up my phrase with a sudden odd
quietness. " You in the North."
" Why, yes. We have, alas ! to expect and
allow for rudeness sometimes, even in our chosen
few, and for liberties in *their* chosen few ; it's only
the hotel clerk and the head waiter from whom we
usually get impudence ; while insolence is the
chronic condition of the Wall Street rich."
" You in the North ! " she repeated. " And so
your Northern eyes can't see it, after all ! " At
these words my intelligence sailed into a great
blank, while she continued : " Frankly — and for-

give me for saying it — I was hoping that you were one Northerner who would see it."

"But see *what?*" I barked in my despair.

She did not help me. "If I had been a man, nothing could have insulted me more than that. And that's what you don't see," she regretfully finished. "It seems so strange."

I sat in the midst of my great blank, while her handsome eyes rested upon me. In them was that look of a certain inquiry and a certain remoteness with which one pauses, in a museum, before some specimen of the cave-dwelling man.

"You comprehend so much," she meditated slowly, aloud; "you've been such an agreeable disappointment, because your point of view is so often the same as ours." She was still surveying me with the specimen expression, when it suddenly left her. "Do you mean to sit there and tell me," she broke out, "that you wouldn't have resented it yourself?"

"O dear!" my mind lamentably said to itself, inside. Of what may have been the exterior that I presented to her, sitting over my slice of Lady Baltimore, I can form no impression.

"Put yourself in his place," the girl continued.

"Ah," I gasped, "that is always so easy to say and so hard to do."

My remark proved not a happy one. She made a brief, cold pause over it, and then, as she wheeled round from me, back to the counter: "No Southerner would let pass such an affront."

It was final. She regained her usual place, she resumed her ledger; the curly dog, who had come out to hear our conversation, went in again; I was

" She was still surveying me with the specimen expression "

disgraced. Not only with the profile of her short, belligerent nose, but with the chilly way in which she made her pencil move over the ledger, she told me plainly that my self-respect had failed to meet her tests. This was what my remarkable ingenuity had achieved for me. I swallowed the last crumbs of Lady Baltimore, and went forward to settle the account.

"I suppose I'm scarcely entitled to ask for a fresh one to-morrow," I ventured. "I am so fond of this cake."

Her officialness met me adequately. "Certainly. The public is entitled to whatever we print upon our bill-of-fare."

Now this was going to be too bad! Henceforth I was to rank merely as "the public," no matter how much Lady Baltimore I should lunch upon! A happy thought seized me, and I spoke out instantly on the strength of it.

"Miss La Heu, I've a confession to make."

But upon this beginning of mine the inauspicious door opened and young John Mayrant came in. It was all right about his left eye; anybody could see *that* bruise!

"Oh!" he exclaimed, hearty, but somewhat disconcerted. "To think of finding you here! You're going? But I'll see you later?"

"I hope so," I said. "You know where I work."

"Yes—yes. I'll come. We've all sorts of things more to say, haven't we? We—good-by!"

Did I hear, as I gained the street, something being said about the General, and the state of his health?

VIII

"MIDSUMMER-NIGHT'S DREAM"

YOU may imagine in what state of wondering I went out of that place, and how little I could now do away with my curiosity. By the droll looks and head-turnings which followed me from strangers that passed me by in the street, I was made aware that I must be talking aloud to myself, and the words which I had evidently uttered were these: "But who in the world can he have smashed up?"

Of course, beneath the public stare and smile I kept the rest of my thoughts to myself; yet they so possessed and took me from my surroundings, that presently, while crossing Royal Street, I was nearly run down by an electric car. Nor did even this serve to disperse my preoccupation; my walk back to Court and Chancel streets is as if it had not been; I can remember nothing about it, and the first account that I took of external objects was to find myself sitting in my accustomed chair in the Library, with the accustomed row of books about the battle of Cowpens waiting on the table in front of me. How long we had thus been facing each other, the books and I, I've not a notion. And with such mysterious machinery are we human beings filled — machinery that is in motion all the while, whether we are aware of

it or not — that now, with some part of my
mind, and with my pencil assisting, I composed
several stanzas to my kingly ancestor, the goal of
my fruitless search; and yet during the whole
process of my metrical exercise I was really
thinking and wondering about John Mayrant,
his battles and his loves.

ODE ON INTIMATIONS OF ROYALTY

I sing to thee, thou Great Unknown,
Who dost connect me with a throne
Through uncle, cousin, aunt, or sister,
But not, I trust, through bar sinister.

Chorus:

Gules ! Gules ! and a cuckoo peccant !

Such was the frivolous opening of my poem,
which, as it progressed, grew even less edifying;
I have quoted this fragment merely to show you
how little reverence for the Selected Salic Scions
was by this time left in my spirit, and not because
the verses themselves are in the least meritorious;
they should serve as a model for no serious-minded
singer, and they afford a striking instance of that
volatile mood, not to say that inclination to rib-
aldry, which will at seasons crop out in me, do
what I will. It is my hope that age may help me
to subdue this, although I have observed it in
some very old men.

I did not send my poem to Aunt Carola, but
I wrote her a letter, even there and then, couched
in terms which I believe were altogether respectful. I deplored my lack of success in discovering
the link that was missing between me and king's

blood; I intimated my conviction that further
effort on my part would still be met with failure;
and I renounced with fitting expressions of disappointment my candidateship for the Scions,
thanking Aunt Carola for her generosity, by which
I must now no longer profit. I added that I
should remain in Kings Port for the present, as I
was finding the climate of decided benefit to my
health, and the courtesy of the people an education in itself.

Whatever pain at missing the glory of becoming a Scion may have lingered with me after this
was much assuaged in a few days by my reading
an article in a New York paper, which gave an
account of a meeting of my Aunt's Society, held
in that city. My attention was attracted to this
article by the prominent heading given to it:
THEY WORE THEIR CROWNS. This,
in very conspicuous Roman capitals, caused me
to sit up. There must have been truth in some
of it, because the food eaten by the Scions was
mentioned as consisting of sandwiches, sherry,
and croquettes; yet I think that the statement
that the members present addressed each other
according to the royal families from which they
severally traced descent, as, for example, Brother
Guelph and Sister Plantagenet, can scarce have
been aught but an exaggeration; nevertheless,
the article brought me undeniable consolation for
my disappointment.

After finishing my letter to Aunt Carola I
should have hastened out to post it and escape
from Cowpens, had I not remembered that John
Mayrant had more or less promised to meet me

here. Now, there was but a slender chance that
the boy would speak to me on the subject of his
late encounter; this I must learn from other
sources; but he might speak to me about something that would open a way for my hostile prepa-
rations against Miss Rieppe. So far he had not
touched upon his impending marriage in any
way, but this reserve concerning a fact generally
known among the people whom I was seeing
could hardly go on long without becoming ridiculous. If he should shun mention of it to-day, I
would take this as a plain sign that he did not
look forward to it with the enthusiasm which a
lover ought to feel for his approaching bliss; and
on such silence from him I would begin, if I
could, to undermine his intention of keeping
an engagement of the heart when the heart no
longer entered into it.

While my thoughts continued to be busied
over this lover and his concerns, I noticed the
works of William Shakespeare close beside me
upon a shelf; and although it was with no special
purpose in mind that I took out one of the volumes and sat down with it to wait for John
Mayrant, in a little while an inspiration came to
me from its pages, so that I was more anxious
than ever the boy should not fail to meet me here
in the Library.

Was it the bruise on his forehead that had per-
turbed his manner just now when he entered the
Exchange? No, this was not likely to be the
reason, since he had been full as much embarrassed
that first day of my seeing him there, when he
had given his order for Lady Baltimore so lamely

that the girl behind the counter had come to his
aid. And what could it have been that he had
begun to tell her to-day as I was leaving the
place? Was the making of that cake again to be
postponed on account of the General's precarious
health? And what had been the nature of the
insult which young John Mayrant had punished
and was now commanded to shake hands over?
Could it in truth be the owner of the *Hermana*
whom he had thrashed so well as to lay him up in
bed? That incident had damaged two people at
least, the unknown vanquished combatant in his
bodily welfare, and me in my character as an up-
standing man in the fierce feminine estimation of
Miss La Heu; but this injury it was my intention to set right; my confession to the girl behind
the counter was merely delayed. As I sat with
Shakespeare open in my lap, I added to my store
of reasoning one little new straw of argument in
favor of my opinion that John Mayrant was no
longer at ease or happy about his love affair. I
had never before met any young man in whose
manner nature was so finely tempered with good
bringing-up; forwardness and shyness were alike
absent from him, and his bearing had a sort of
polished unconsciousness as far removed from raw
diffidence as it was from raw conceit; it was altogether a rare and charming address in a youth of
such true youthfulness, but it had failed him upon
two occasions which I have already mentioned.
Both times that he had come to the Exchange he
had stumbled in his usually prompt speech, lost
his habitual ease, and betrayed, in short, all the
signs of being disconcerted. The matter seemed

suddenly quite plain to me: it was the nature of
his errands to the Exchange. The first time he
had been ordering the cake for his own wedding,
and to-day it was something about the wedding
again. Evidently the high mettle of his delicacy
and breeding made him painfully conscious of the
view which others must take of the part that Miss
Rieppe was playing in all this — a view from
which it was out of his power to shield her; and
it was this consciousness that destroyed his composure. From what I was soon to learn of his
fine and unmoved disregard for unfavorable
opinion when he felt his course to be the right
one, I know that it was no thought at all of his
own scarcely heroic rôle during these days, but
only the perception that outsiders must detect in
his affianced lady some of those very same
qualities which had chilled his too precipitate
passion for her, and left him alone, without romance, without family sympathy, without social
acclamations, with nothing indeed save his high-
strung notion of honor to help him bravely face
the wedding march. How appalling must the
wedding march sound to a waiting bridegroom
who sees the bride, that he no longer looks at
except with distaste and estrangement, coming
nearer and nearer to him up the aisle! A funeral
march would be gayer than that music, I should
think! The thought came to me to break out
bluntly and say to him: "Countermand the cake!
She's only playing with you while that yachtsman
is making up his mind." But there could be but
one outcome of such advice to John Mayrant:
two people, instead of one, would be in bed suffer-

ing from contusions. As I mused on the boy and
his attractive and appealing character, I became
more rejoiced than ever that he had thrashed
somebody, I cared not very much who nor yet
very much why, so long as such thrashing had
been thorough, which seemed quite evidently and
happily the case. He stood now in my eyes, in
some way that is too obscure for me to be
able to explain to you, saved from some reproach
whose subtlety likewise eludes my powers of an-
alysis.

It was already five minutes after three o'clock,
my dinner hour, when he at length appeared in
the Library; and possibly I put some reproach
into my greeting: "Won't you walk along with
me to Mrs. Trevise's?" (That was my boarding-
house.)

"I could not get away from the Custom House
sooner," he explained; and into his eyes there
came for a moment that look of unrest and preoccupation which I had observed at times while
we had discussed Newport and alcoholic girls.
The two subjects seemed certainly far enough
apart! But he immediately began upon a conversation briskly enough — so briskly that I suspected at once he had got his subject ready in
advance; he didn't want me to speak first, lest I
turn the talk into channels embarrassing, such as
bruised foreheads or wedding cake. Well, this
should not prevent me from dropping in his cup the
wholesome bitters which I had prepared.

"Well, sir! Well, sir!" such was his hearty
preface. "I wonder if you're feeling ashamed of
yourself?"

"Never when I read Shakespeare," I answered, restoring the volume to its place.

He looked at the title. "Which one?"

"One of the unsuitable love affairs that was prevented in time."

"Romeo and Juliet?"

"No; Bottom and Titania — and Romeo and Juliet were not prevented in time. They had their bliss once and to the full, and died before they caused each other anything but ecstasy. No weariness of routine, no tears of disenchantment; complete love, completely realized — and finis! It's the happiest ending of all the plays."

He looked at me hard. "Sometimes I believe you're ironic!"

I smiled at him. "A sign of the highest civilization, then. But please to think of Juliet after ten years of Romeo and his pin-headed intelligence and his preordained infidelities. Do you imagine that her predecessor, Rosamond, would have had no successors? Juliet would have been compelled to divorce Romeo, if only for the children's sake."

"The children!" cried John Mayrant. "Why, it's for their sake deserted women abstain from divorce!"

"Juliet would see deeper than such mothers. She could not have her little sons and daughters grow up and *comprehend* their father's absences, and see their mother's submission to his returns; for such discovery would scorch the marrow of any hearts they had."

At this, as we came out of the Library, he made an astonishing rejoinder, and one which I cannot in the least account for: "South Carolina does not allow divorce."

"Then I should think," I said to him, "that all you people here would be doubly careful as to what manner of husbands and wives you chose for yourselves."

Such a remark was sailing, you may say, almost within three points of the wind; and his own accidental allusion to Romeo had brought it about with an aptness and a celerity which were better for my purpose than anything I had privately developed from the text of Bottom and Titania; none the less, however, did I intend to press into my service that fond couple also as basis for a moral, in spite of the sharp turn which those last words of mine now caused him at once to give to our conversation. His quick reversion to the beginning of the talk seemed like a dodging of remarks that hit too near home for him to relish hearing pursued.

"Well, sir," he resumed with the same initial briskness, "I was ashamed if you were not."

"I still don't make out what impropriety we have jointly committed."

"What do you think of the views you expressed about our country?"

"Oh! When we sat on the gravestones."

"What do you think about it to-day?"

I turned to him as we slowly walked toward Worship Street. "Did you say anything then that you would take back now?"

He pondered, wrinkling his forehead. "Well, but all the same, didn't we give the present hour a pretty black eye?"

"The present hour deserves a black eye, and two of them!"

He surveyed me squarely. "I believe you're a pessimist!"

"That is the first trashy thing I've heard you say."

"Thank you! At least admit you're scarcely an optimist."

"Optimist! Pessimist! Why, you're talking just like a newspaper!"

He laughed. "Oh, don't compare a gentleman to a newspaper."

"Then keep your vocabulary clean of bargain-counter words. A while ago the journalists had a furious run upon the adjective 'un-American.' Anybody or anything that displeased them was 'un-American.' They ran it into the ground, and in its place they have lately set up 'pessimist,' which certainly has a threatening appearance. They don't know its meaning, and in their mouths it merely signifies that what a man says makes them feel personally uncomfortable. The word has become a dusty rag of slang. The arrested burglar very likely calls the policeman a pessimist; and, speaking reverently and with no intention to shock you, the scribes and Pharisees would undoubtedly have called Christ a pessimist when He called them hypocrites, had they been acquainted with the word."

Once more my remarks drew from the boy an unexpected rejoinder. We had turned into Worship Street, and, as we passed the churchyard, he stopped and laid his hand upon the railing of the gate.

"You don't shock me," he said; and then: "But you would shock my aunts." He paused, gazing into the churchyard, before he continued more slowly: "And so should I — if they knew it — shock them."

"If they knew what?" I asked.

His hand indicated a sculptured crucifix near by.

"Do you believe everything still?" he answered. "Can you?"

As he looked at me, I suppose that he read negation in my eyes.

"No more can I," he murmured. Again he looked in among the tombstones and flowers, where the old custodian saw us and took off his hat. "Howdy, Daddy Ben!" John Mayrant returned pleasantly, and then resuming to me: "No more can I believe everything." Then he gave a brief, comical laugh. "And I hope my aunts won't find that out! They would think me gone to perdition indeed. But I always go to church here" (he pointed to the quiet building, which, for all its modest size and simplicity, had a stately and inexpressible charm), "because I like to kneel where my mother said her prayers, you know." He flushed a little over this confidence into which he had fallen, but he continued: "I like the words of the service, too, and I don't ask myself over-curiously what I do believe; but there's a permanent something within us — a Greater Self — don't you think?"

"A permanent something," I assented, "which has created all the religions all over the earth from the beginning, and of which Christianity itself is merely one of the present temples."

He made an exclamation at my word "present."
"Do you think anything in this world is final?" I asked him.

"But—" he began, somewhat at a loss.

"Haven't you found out yet that human nature is the one indestructible reality that we know?"

"But—" he began again.

"Don't we have the 'latest thing' all the time, and never the ultimate thing, never, never? The latest thing in women's hats is that huge-brimmed affair with the veil as voluminous as a double-bed mosquito netting. That hat will look improbable next spring. The latest thing in science is radium. Radium has exploded the conservation of energy theory — turned it into a last year's hat. Answer me, if Christianity is the same as when it wore among its savage ornaments a devil with horns and a flaming Hell! Forever and forever the human race reaches out its hand and shapes some system, some creed, some government, and declares: 'This is at length the final thing, the cure-all,' and lo and behold, something flowing and eternal in the race itself presently splits the creed and the government to pieces! Truth is a very marvellous thing. We feel it; it can fill our eyes with tears, our hearts with joy, it can make us die for it; but once our human lips attempt to formulate and thus imprison it, it becomes a lie. You cannot shut truth up in any words."

"But it shall prevail!" the boy exclaimed with a sort of passion.

"Everything prevails," I answered him.

"I don't like that," he said.

"Neither do I," I returned. "But Jacob got Esau's inheritance by a mean trick."

"Jacob was punished for it."

"Did that help Esau much?"

"You are a pessimist!"

"Just because I see Jacob and Esau to-day, alive and kicking in Wall Street, Washington, Newport, everywhere?"

"You're no optimist, anyhow!"

"I hope I'm blind in neither eye."

"You don't give us credit —"

"For what?"

"For what we've accomplished since Jacob."

"Printing, steam, and electricity, for instance? They spread the Bible and the yellow journal with equal velocity."

"I don't mean science. Take our institutions."

"Well, we've accomplished hospitals and the stock market — a pretty even set-off between God and the devil."

He laughed. "You don't take a high view of us!"

"Nor a low one. I don't play ostrich with any of the staring permanences of human nature. We're just as noble to-day as David was sometimes, and just as bestial to-day as David was sometimes, and we've every possibility inside us all the time, whether we paint our naked skins, or wear steel armor or starched shirts."

"Well, I believe good is the guiding power in the world."

"Oh, John Mayrant! Good and evil draw us on like a span of horses, sometimes like a tandem, taking turns in the lead. Order has melted into disorder, and disorder into new order — how many times ? "

" But better each time."

" How can you know, who never lived in any age but your own ? "

" I know we have a higher ideal."

" Have we ? The Greek was taught to love his neighbor as himself. He gave his great teacher a cup of poison. We gave ours the cross."

Again he looked away from me into the sweet old churchyard. " I can't answer you, but I don't believe it."

This brought me to gayety. " That's unanswerable, anyhow ! "

He still stared at the graves. . " Those people in there didn't think all these uncomfortable things."

" Ah, no ! They belonged in the first volume of the history of our national soul, before the bloom was off us."

" That's an odd notion ! And pray what volume are we in now ? "

" Only the second."

" Since when ? "

" Since that momentous picnic, the Spanish War ! "

" I don't see how that took the bloom off us."

" It didn't. It merely waked Europe up to the facts."

" Our battleships, you mean ? "

" Our steel rails, our gold coffers, our roaring affluence."

" And our very accurate shooting ! " he insisted ; for he was a Southerner, and man's gallantry appealed to him more than man's industry.

I laughed. "Yes, indeed! We may say that the Spanish War closed our first volume with a bang. And now in the second we bid good-by to the virgin wilderness, for it's explored; to the Indian, for he's conquered; to the pioneer, for he's dead; we've finished our wild, romantic adolescence and we find ourselves a recognized world-power of eighty million people, and of general commercial endlessness, and playtime over."

"I think," John Mayrant now asserted, "that it is going too far to say the bloom is off us."

"Oh, you'll find snow in the woods away into April and May. The freedom-loving American, the embattled farmer, is not yet extinct in the far recesses. But the great cities grow like a creeping paralysis over freedom, and the man from the country is walking into them all the time because the poor, restless fellow believes wealth awaits him on their pavements. And when he doesn't go to them, they come to him. The Wall Street bucket-shop goes fishing in the woods with wires a thousand miles long; and so we exchange the solid trail-blazing enterprise of Volume One for Volume Two's electric unrest. In Volume One our wagon was hitched to the star of liberty. Capital and labor have cut the traces. The labor union forbids the workingman to labor as his own virile energy and skill prompt him. If he disobeys, he is expelled and called a 'scab.' Don't let us call ourselves the land of the free while such things go on. We're all thinking a deal too much about our pockets nowadays. Eternal vigilance cannot watch liberty and the ticker at the same time."

"Well," said John Mayrant, "we're not thinking about our pockets in Kings Port, because "(and
here there came into his voice and face that
sudden humor which made him so delightful)—
"because we haven't got any pockets to think of!"
This brought me down to cheerfulness from
my flight among the cold clouds.

He continued: "Any more lamentations, Mr.
Jeremiah?"

"Those who begin to call names, John Mayrant—but never mind! I could lament you sick
if I chose to go on about our corporations and
corruption that I see with my pessimistic eye;
but the other eye sees the American man himself
—the type that our eighty millions on the whole
melt into and to which my heart warms each time
I land again from more polished and colder shores
—my optimistic eye sees that American dealing
adequately with these political diseases. For
stronger even than his kindness, his ability, and
his dishonesty is his self-preservation. He's
going to stand up for the 'open shop' and sit down
on the 'trust'; and I assure you that I don't in
the least resemble the *Evening Post*."

A look of inquiry was in John Mayrant's
features.

"The New York *Evening Post*," I repeated
with surprise. Still the inquiry of his face remained.

"Oh, fortunate youth!" I cried. "To have
escaped the New York *Evening Post!*"

"Is it so heinous?"

"Well! . . . well! . . . how exactly describe it?
. . . make you see it? . . . It's partially tongue-

tied, a sad victim of its own excesses. Habitual over-indulgence in blaming has given it a painful stutter when attempting praise; it's the sprucely written sheet of the supercilious; it's the after-dinner pill of the American who prefers Europe; it's our Republic's common scold, the Xantippe of journalism, the paper without a country."

"The paper without a country! That's very good!"

"Oh, no! I'll tell you something much better. but it is not mine. A clever New Yorker said that what with *The Sun* —"

"I know that paper."

"— what with *The Sun* making vice so attractive in the morning and the *Post* making virtue so odious in the evening, it was very hard for a man to be good in New York."

"I fear I should subscribe to *The Sun*," said John Mayrant. He took his hand from the church-gate railing, and we had turned to stroll down Worship Street when he was unexpectedly addressed.

For some minutes, while John Mayrant and I had been talking, I had grown aware, without taking any definite note of it, that the old custodian of the churchyard, Daddy Ben, had come slowly near us from the distant corner of his demesne, where he had been (to all appearances) engaged in some trifling activity among the flowers — perhaps picking off the faded blossoms. It now came home to me that the venerable negro had really been, in a surreptitious way, watching John Mayrant, and waiting for something —

In Worship Street

either for the right moment to utter
what he now uttered, or his own delayed decision to utter it at all.

" Mas' John ! " he called quite softly. His tone was fairly padded with caution, and I saw that in the pause which followed, his eye shot a swift look at the bruise on Mayrant's forehead, and another look, equally swift, at me.

" Well, Daddy Ben, what is it ? "

The custodian shuffled close to the gate which separated him from us. " Mas' John, I speck de Presi*dent* he dun' know de cullud people like we knows 'um, else he nebber bin 'pint dat ar boss in de Cussum House, no, sah."

After this effort he wiped his forehead and breathed hard.

To my astonishment, the effort brought immediately a stern change over John Mayrant's face; then he answered in the kindest tones, " Thank you, Daddy Ben."

This answer interpreted for me the whole thing, which otherwise would have been obscure enough: the old man held it to be an indignity that his young " Mas' John " should, by the President's act, find himself the subordinate of a member of the black race, and he had just now, in his perspiring effort, expressed his sympathy ! Why he had chosen this particular moment (after quite obvious debate with himself) I did not see until somewhat later.

He now left us standing at the gate; and it was not for some moments that John Mayrant spoke again, evidently closing, for our two selves, this delicate subject.

" I wish we had not got into that second volume of yours."

" That's not progressive."

"I hate progress."

"What's the use? Better grow old gracefully!

> "'Qui n'a pas l'esprit de son âge
> De son âge a tout le malheur.'"

"Well, I'm personally not growing old, just yet."

"Neither is the United States."

"Well, I don't know. It's too easy for sick or worthless people to survive nowadays. They are clotting up our square miles very fast. Philanthropists don't seem to remember that you can beget children a great deal faster than you can educate them; and at this rate I believe universal suffrage will kill us off before our time."

"Do not believe it! We are going to find out that universal suffrage is like the appendix — useful at an early stage of the race's evolution but to-day merely a threat to life."

He thought this over. "But a surgical operation is pretty serious, you know."

"It'll be done by absorption. Why, you've begun it yourselves, and so has Massachusetts. The appendix will be removed, black and white — and I shouldn't much fear surgery. We're not nearly civilized enough yet to have lost the power of recuperation, and in spite of our express-train speed, I doubt if we shall travel from crudity to rottenness without a pause at maturity."

"That is the old, old story," he said.

"Yes; is there anything new under the sun?"

He was gloomy. "Nothing, I suppose." Then the gloom lightened. "Nothing new under the sun — except the fashionable families of Newport!"

This again brought us from the clouds of speculation down to Worship Street, where we were
walking toward South Place. It also unexpectedly furnished me with the means to lead
back our talk so gently, without a jolt or a jerk,
to my moral and the delicate topic of matrimony
from which he had dodged away, that he never
awoke to what was coming until it had come.
He began pointing out, as we passed them, certain houses which were now, or had at some period
been, the dwellings of his many relatives: " My
cousin Julia So-and-so lives there," he would say;
or, " My great-uncle, known as Regent Tom,
owned that before the War "; and once, " The
Rev. Joseph Priedieu, my great-grandfather, built
that house to marry his fifth wife in, but the grave
claimed him first."

So I asked him a riddle.   " What is the difference between Kings Port and Newport? "

This he, of course, gave up.

" Here you are all connected by marriage, and
there they are all connected by divorce."

" That's true! " he cried.   " That's very true.
I met the most embarrassingly cater-cornered
families."

" Oh, they weren't embarrassed! " I interjected.

" No, but *I* was," said John.

" And you told me you weren't innocent! " I
exclaimed.   " They are going to institute a divorce
march," I continued.   " ' Lohengrin ' or ' Midsummer-Night's Dream ' played backward.   They
have not settled which.   It is to be taught in the
nursery with the other kindergarten melodies."

He was still unsuspectingly diverted; and we

walked along until we turned in the direction of my boarding-house.

"Did you ever notice," I now said, "what a perpetual allegory 'Midsummer-Night's Dream' contains?"

"I thought it was just a fairy sort of thing."

"Yes, but when a great poet sets his hand to a fairy sort of thing, you get — well, you get poor Titania."

"She fell in love with a jackass," he remarked. "Puck bewitched her."

"Precisely. A lovely woman with her arms around a jackass. Does that never happen in Kings Port?"

He began smiling to himself. "I'm afraid Puck isn't all dead yet."

I was now in a position to begin dropping my bitters. "Shakespeare was probably too gallant to put it the other way, and make Oberon fall in love with a female jackass. But what an allegory!"

"Yes," he muttered. "Yes."

I followed with another drop. "Titania got out of it. It is not always solved so easily."

"No," he muttered. "No." It was quite evident that the flavor of my bitters reached him.

He was walking slowly, with his head down, and frowning hard. We had now come to the steps of my boarding-house, and I dropped my last drop. "But a disenchanted woman has the best of it — before marriage, at least."

He looked up quickly. "How?"

I evinced surprise. "Why, she can always break off honorably, and we never can, I suppose."

We had now come to the steps of my boarding-house

For the third time this day he made me an astonishing rejoinder: "Would you like to take orders from a negro?"

It reduced me to stammering. " I have never —such a juncture has never — "

" Of course you wouldn't. Even a Northerner ! "
His face, as he said this, was a single glittering piece of fierceness. I was still so much taken aback that I said rather flatly : " But who has to ? "

" I have to." With this he abruptly turned on his heel and left me standing on the steps. For a moment I stared after him ; and then, as I rang the bell, he was back again ; and with that formality which at times overtook him he began : " I will ask you to excuse my hasty — "

" Oh, John Mayrant ! What a notion ! "
But he was by no means to be put off, and he proceeded with stiffer formality : " I feel that I have not acted politely just now, and I beg to assure you that I intended no slight."

My first impulse was to lay a hand upon his shoulder and say to him : " My dear fellow, stuff and nonsense ! " Thus I should have treated any Northern friend ; but here was no Northerner. I am glad that I had the sense to feel that any careless, good-natured putting away of his deliberate and definitely tendered apology would seem to him a " slight " on my part. His punctilious value for certain observances between man and man reached me suddenly and deeply, and took me far from the familiarity which breeds contempt.

" Why, John Mayrant," I said, " you could never offend me unless I thought that you wished to, and how should I possibly think that ? "

" Thank you," he replied very simply.

I rang the bell a second time. "If we can get into the house," I suggested, "won't you stop and dine with me?"

He was going to accept. "I shall be —" he had begun, in tones of gratification, when in one instant his face was stricken with complete dismay. "I had forgotten," he said; and this time he was gone indeed, and in a hurry most apparent. It resembled a flight.

What was the matter now? You will naturally think that it was an appointment with his lady-love which he had forgotten; this was certainly my supposition as I turned again to the front door. There stood one of the waitresses, glaring with her white eyes half out of her black face at the already distant back of John Mayrant.

"Oh!" I thought; but, before I could think any more, the tall, dreadful boarder — the lady whom I secretly called Juno — swept up the steps, and by me into the house, with a dignity that one might term deafening.

The waitress now muttered, or rather sang, a series of pious apostrophes. "Oh, Lawd, de rampages and de ructions! Oh, Lawd, sinner is in my way, Daniel!" She was strongly, but I think pleasurably, excited; and she next turned to me with a most natural grin, and saying, "Chick'n's mos' gone, sah," she went back to the dining room.

This admonition sent me upstairs to make as hasty a toilet as I could.

IX

JUNO

EACH recent remarkable occurrence had obliterated its predecessor, and it was with difficulty that I made a straight parting in my hair. Had it been Miss Rieppe that John so suddenly ran away to? It seemed now more as if the boy had been running away *from* somebody. The waitress had stared at him with extraordinary interest; she had seen his bruise; perhaps she knew how he had got it. Her excitement — had he smashed up his official superior at the custom house? That would be an impossible thing, I told myself instantly; as well might a nobleman cross swords with a peasant. Perhaps the stare of the waitress had reminded him of his bruise, and he might have felt disinclined to show himself with it in a company of gossiping strangers. Still, that would scarcely account for the dismay with which he had so suddenly left me. Was Juno the cause — she had come up behind me; he must have seen her and her portentous manner approaching — had the boy fled from her? And then, his fierce outbreak about taking orders from a negro when I was moralizing over the misfortune of marrying a jackass! I got a sort of parting in my hair, and went down to the dining room.

Juno was there before me, with her bonnet, or rather her headdress, still on, and I heard her making apologies to Mrs. Trevise for being so late. Mrs. Trevise, of course, sat at the head of her table, and Juno sat at her right hand. I was very glad not to have a seat near Juno, because this lady was, as I have already hinted, an intolerable person to me. Either her Southern social position or her rent (she took the whole second floor, except Mrs. Trevise's own rooms) was of importance to Mrs. Trevise; but I assure you that her ways kept our landlady's cold, impervious tact watchful from the beginning to the end of almost every meal. Juno was one of those persons who possess so many and such strong feelings themselves that they think they have all the feelings there are; at least, they certainly consider no one's feelings but their own. She possessed an inexhaustible store of anecdote, but it was exclusively about our Civil War; you would have supposed that nothing else had ever happened in the world. When conversation among the rest of us became general, she preserved a cold and acrid inattention; when the fancy took her to open her own mouth, it was always to begin some reminiscence, and the reminiscence always began: " In September, 1862, when the Northern vandals," etc., etc., or " When the Northern vandals were repulsed by my husband's cousin, General Braxton Bragg," etc., etc. Now it was not that I was personally wounded by the term, because at the time of the vandals I was not even born, and also because I know that vandals cannot be kept out of any army. Deeply as I believed the March to

the Sea to have been imperative, of " Sherman's
bummers " and their excesses I had a fair historic
knowledge and a very poor opinion ; and this I
should have been glad to tell Juno, had she ever
given me the chance ; but her immodest sympathy for herself froze all sympathy for her. Why
could she not preserve a well bred silence upon
her sufferings, as did the other old ladies I had
met in Kings Port? Why did she drag them in,
thrust them, poke them, shove them at you?
Thus it was that for her insulting disregard of
those whom her words might wound I detested
Juno ; and as she was a woman, and nearly old
enough to be my grandmother, it was, of course,
out of the question that I should retaliate. When
she got very bad indeed, it was calm Mrs. Trevise's
last, but effective, resort to tinkle a little handbell and scold one of the waitresses whom its
sound would then summon from the kitchen.
This bell was tinkled not always by any means
for my sake ; other travellers from the North there
were who came and went, pausing at Kings Port
between Florida and their habitual abodes.

At present our company consisted of Juno; a
middle-class Englishman employed in some business capacity in town ; a pair of very young
honeymooners from the " up-country"; a Louisi-
ana poetess, who wore the long, cylindrical ring-
lets of 1830, and who was attending a convention
of the Daughters of Dixie; two or three males and
females, best described as et ceteras ; and myself.

" I shall only take a mouthful for the sake of
nourishment," Juno was announcing, "and then I
shall return to his bedside."

" Is he very suffering ?" inquired the poetess, in melodious accent.

" It was an infamous onslaught," Juno replied. The poetess threw up her eyes and crooned, " Noble, doughty champion ! "

" You may say so indeed, madam," said Juno.

" Raw beefsteak's jolly good for your eye," observed the Briton.

This suggestion did not appear to be heard by Juno.

" I had a row with a chap," the Briton continued. " He's my best friend now. He made me put raw beefsteak — "

" I thank you," interrupted Juno. " He requires no beefsteak, raw or cooked."

The face of the Briton reddened. " Too groggy to eat, is he ? "

Mrs. Trevise tinkled her bell. " Daphne ! I have said to you twice to hand those yams."

" I done handed 'em twice, ma'am."

" Hand them right away, Daphne, and don't be so forgetful." It was not easy to disturb the composure of Mrs. Trevise.

The poetess now took up the broken thread. " Had I a son," she declared, " I would sooner witness him starve than hear him take orders from a menial race."

" But mightn't starving be harder for him to experience than for you to witness, y' know?" asked the Briton.

At this one of the et ceteras made a sort of snuffling noise, and ate his dinner hard.

It was the male honeymooner who next spoke. " Must have been quite a tussle, ma'am."

" It was an infamous onslaught!" repeated Juno.

" Wish I'd seen it!" sighed the honeymooner.

His bride smiled at him beamingly. " You'd have felt right lonesome to be out of it, David."

" No apology has yet been offered," continued Juno.

" But must your nephew apologize besides taking a licking?" inquired the Briton.

Juno turned an awful face upon him. " It is from his brutal assailant that apologies are due. Mr. Mayrant's family " (she paused here for blighting emphasis) "are well-bred people, and he will be coerced into behaving like a gentleman for once."

I checked an impulse here to speak out and express my doubts as to the family coercion being founded upon any dissatisfaction with John's conduct.

" I wonder if reading or recitation might not soothe your nephew?" said the poetess, now.

" I should doubt it," answered Juno. " I have just come from his bedside."

" I should so like to soothe him, if I could," the poetess murmured. " If he were well enough to hear my convention ode — "

" He is not nearly well enough," said Juno.

The et cetera here coughed and blew his nose so remarkably that we all started.

A short silence followed, which Juno relieved. " I will give the young ruffian's family the credit they deserve," she stated. " The whole connection despises his keeping the position."

Another et cetera now came into it. " Is it known what exactly precipitated the occurrence?"

Juno turned to him. "My nephew is a gentleman from whose lips no unworthy word could ever fall."

"Oh!" said the et cetera, mildly. "He said something, then?"

"He conveyed a well-merited rebuke in fitting terms."

"What were the terms?" inquired the Briton.

Juno again did not hear him. "It was after a friendly game of cards. My nephew protested against any gentleman remaining at the custom house since the recent insulting appointment."

I was now almost the only member of the party who had preserved strict silence throughout this very interesting conversation, because, having no wish to converse with Juno at any time, I especially did not desire it now, just after her seeing me (I thought she must have seen me) in amicable conference with the object of her formidable displeasure.

"Every Mayrant is ferocious that I ever heard of," she continued. "You cannot trust that seemingly delicate and human exterior. His father had it, too — deceiving exterior and raging interior, though I will say for that one that he would never have stooped to humiliate the family name as his son is doing. His regiment was near by when the Northern vandals burned our courthouse, and he made them run, I can tell you! It's a mercy for that poor girl that the scales have dropped from her eyes and she has broken her engagement with him."

"With the father?" asked a third et cetera.

Juno stared at the intruder.

Mrs. Trevise drawled a calm contribution. "The father died before this boy was born." "Oh, I see!" murmured the et cetera, gratefully.

Juno proceeded. "No woman's life would be safe with him."

"But mightn't he be safer for a person's niece than for their nephew?" said the Briton.

Mrs. Trevise's hand moved toward the bell. But Juno answered the question mournfully: "With such hereditary bloodthirstiness, who can tell?" And so Mrs. Trevise moved her hand away again.

"Excuse me, but do you know if the other gentleman is laid up, too?" inquired the male honeymooner, hopefully.

"I am happy to understand that he is," replied Juno.

In sheer amazement I burst out, "Oh!" and abruptly stopped.

But it was too late. I had instantly become the centre of interest. The et ceteras and honeymooners craned their necks; the Briton leaned toward me from opposite; the poetess, who had worn an absent expression since being told that the injured champion was not nearly well enough to listen to her ode, now put on her glasses and gazed at me kindly; while Juno reared her headdress and spoke, not to me, but to the air in my general neighborhood.

"Has any one later intelligence than what I bring from my nephew's bedside?"

So she hadn't perceived who my companion at the step had been! Well, she should be enlightened, they all should be enlightened, and vengeance was mine. I spoke with gentleness : —

"Your nephew's impressions, I fear, are still confused by his deplorable misadventure."

"May I ask what you know about his impressions?"

Out of the corner of my eye I saw the hand of Mrs. Trevise move toward her bell; but she wished to hear all about it more than she wished concord at her harmonious table; and the hand stopped.

Juno spoke again. "Who, pray, has later news than what I bring?"

My enemy was in my hand; and an enemy in the hand is worth I don't know how many in the bush.

I answered most gently: "I do not come from Mr. Mayrant's bedside, because I have just left him at the front door in sound health — saving a bruise over his left eye."

During a second we all sat in a high-strung silence, and then Juno became truly superb. "Who sees the scars he brazenly conceals?"

It took away my breath; my battle would have been lost, when the Briton suggested: "But mayn't he have shown those to his Aunt?"

We sat in no silence now; the first et cetera made extraordinary sounds on his plate, Mrs. Trevise tinkled her handbell with more unction than I had ever yet seen in her; and while she and Daphne interchanged streams of severe words which I was too disconcerted to follow, the other et ceteras and the honeymooners hectically effervesced into small talk. I presently found myself eating our last course amid a reëstablished calm, when, with a rustle, Juno swept out from among us, to return (I suppose) to the bedside. As she passed behind the Briton's chair, that invaluable person kicked me under the table, and on my raising my eyes to him he gave me a large, robust wink.

X

HIGH WALK AND THE LADIES

I NOW burned to put many questions to the rest of the company. If, through my foolish and outreaching slyness with the girl behind the counter, the door of my comprehension had been shut, Juno had now opened it sufficiently wide for a number of facts to come crowding in, so to speak, abreast. Indeed, their simultaneous arrival was not a little confusing, as if several visitors had burst in upon me and at once begun speaking loudly, each shouting a separate and important matter which demanded my intelligent consideration. John Mayrant worked in the custom house, and Kings Port frowned upon this; not merely Kings Port in general — which counted little with the boy, if indeed he noticed general opinion at all — but the boy's particular Kings Port, his severe old aunts, and his cousins, and the pretty girl at the Exchange, and the men he played cards with, all these frowned upon it, too; yet even this condemnation one could disregard if some lofty personal principle, some pledge to one's own sacred honor, were at stake — but here was no such thing: John Mayrant hated the position himself. The salary? No, the salary would count for nothing in the face of such a prejudice as I had seen glitter from his eye! A strong, clever youth of twenty-three, with the

world before him, and no one to support — stop!
Hortense Rieppe! *There* was the lofty personal
principle, the sacred pledge to honor; he was
engaged presently to endow .her with all his
worldly goods; and to perform this faithfully a
bridegroom must not, no matter how little he
liked "taking orders from a negro," fling away
his worldly goods some few days before he was
to pronounce his bridegroom's vow. So here,
at Mrs. Trevise's dinner-table, I caught for one
moment, to the full, a vision of the unhappy
boy's plight; he was sticking to a task which
he loathed that he might support a wife whom
he no longer desired. Such, as he saw it, was
his duty; and nobody, not even a soul of his
kin or his kind, gave him a word or a thought
of understanding, gave him anything except the
cold shoulder. Yes; from one soul he had got
a sign — from aged Daddy Ben, at the churchyard gate; and amid my jostling surmises and
conclusions, that quaint speech of the old negro,
that little act of fidelity and affection from the
heart of a black man, took on a strange pathos
in its isolation amid the general harshness of his
white superiors. Over this it was that I was
pausing when, all in a second, perplexity again
ruled my meditations. Juno had said that the
engagement was broken. Well, if that were the
case — But was it likely to be the case?
Juno's agreeable habit, a habit grown familiar to
all of us in the house, was to sprinkle about,
along with her vitriol, liberal quantities of the
by-product of inaccuracy. Mingled with her
latest lustrations, she had poured out for us one

good dose of falsehood, the antidote for which it had been my happy office to administer on the spot. If John Mayrant wasn't in bed from the wounds of combat, as she had given us to suppose, perhaps Hortense Rieppe hadn't released him from his plighted troth, as Juno had also announced; and distinct relief filled me when I reasoned this out. I leave others to reason out why it was relief, and why a dull disappointment had come over me at the news that the match was off. This, for me, should have been good news, when you consider that I had been so lately telling myself such a marriage must not be, that I must myself, somehow (since no one else would), step in and arrest the calamity; and it seems odd that I should have felt this blankness and regret upon learning that the parties had happily settled it for themselves, and hence my difficult and delicate assistance was never to be needed by them.

Did any one else now sitting at our table know of Miss Rieppe's reported act? What particulars concerning John's fight had been given by Juno before my entrance? It didn't surprise me that her nephew was in bed from Master Mayrant's lusty blows. One could readily guess the manner in which young John, with his pent-up fury over the custom house, would "land" his chastisement all over the person of any rash critic! And what a talking about it must be going on everywhere to-day! If Kings Port tongues had been set in motion over me and my small notebook in a library, the whole town must be buzzing over every bruise given and taken in this evidently emphatic battle. I had hoped to glean some

more precise information from my fellow-boarders
after Juno had disembarrassed us of her sonorous
presence; but even if they were possessed of all
the facts which I lacked, Mrs. Trevise in some
masterly fashion of her own banished the subject
from further discussion. She held us off from it
chiefly, I think, by adopting a certain upright
posture in her chair, and a certain tone when she
inquired if we wished a second help of the pud-
ding. After thirty-five years of boarders and
butchers, life held no secrets or surprises for her;
she was a mature, lone, disenchanted, able lady,
and even her silence was like an arm of the law.

An all too brief conversation, nipped by Mrs.
Trevise at a stage even earlier than the bud,
revealed to me that perhaps my fellow-boarders
would have been glad to ask me questions, too.

It was the male honeymooner who addressed
me. " Did I understand you to say, sir, that Mr.
Mayrant had received a bruise over his left eye?"

"Daphne!" called out Mrs. Trevise, " Mr.
Henderson will take an orange."

And so we finished our meal without further
reference to eyes, or noses, or anything of the
sort. It was just as well, I reflected, when I
reached my room, that I on my side had been
asked no questions, since I most likely knew less
than the others who had heard all that Juno had
to say; and it would have been humiliating, after
my superb appearance of knowing more, to explain
that John Mayrant had walked with me all the
way from the Library, and never told me a word
about the affair.

This reflection increased my esteem for the

boy's admirable reticence. What private matter
of his own had I ever learned from him? It was
other people, invariably, who told me of his
troubles. There had been that single, quickly
controlled outbreak about his position in the
Custom House, and also he had let fall that touching word concerning his faith and his liking to
say his prayers in the place where his mother had
said them; beyond this, there had never yet been
anything of all that must at the present moment
be intimately stirring in his heart.

Should I "like to take orders from a negro"?
Put personally, it came to me now as a new idea,
came as something which had never entered my
mind before, not even as an abstract hypothesis.
I didn't have to think before reaching the answer,
though; something within me, which you may
call what you please — convention, prejudice,
instinct — something answered most promptly
and emphatically in the negative. I revolved it
in my mind as I tried to pack into a box a number of objects that I had bought in one or two
"antique" shops. They wouldn't go in, the
objects; they were of defeating and recalcitrant
shapes, and of hostile materials — glass and brass
— and I must have a larger box made, and in
that case I would buy this afternoon the other
kettle-supporter (I forget its right name) and have
the whole lot decently packed. Take orders from
a colored man? Have him give you directions,
dictate you letters, discipline you if you were
unpunctual? No, indeed! And if such were
my feeling, how must this young Southerner feel?
With this in my mind, I made sure that the part

in my back hair was right, and after that precaution soon found myself on my way, in a way somewhat roundabout, to the kettle-supporter, sauntering northward along High Walk, and stopping often; the town, and the water, and the

The town, and the water, and the distant shores . . . melted
into one gentle impression of wistfulness and tenderness

distant shores all were so lovely, so belonged to one another, so melted into one gentle impression of wistfulness and tenderness! I leaned upon the stone parapet and enjoyed the quiet which every surrounding detail brought to my senses. How could John Mayrant endure such a situation?

I continued to wonder; and I also continued to
assure myself it was absurd to suppose that the
engagement was broken.

The shutting of a front door across the street
almost directly behind me attracted my attention
because of its being the first sound that had happened in noiseless, empty High Walk since I had
been strolling there; and I turned from the parapet to see that I was no longer the solitary person
in the street.   Two ladies, one tall and one diminutive, both in black and with long black veils
which they had put back from their faces, were
evidently coming from a visit.   As the tall one
bowed to me I recognized Mrs. Gregory St.
Michael, and took off my hat.   It was not until
they had crossed the street and come up the stone
steps near where I stood on High Walk that
the little lady also bowed to me; she was Mrs.
Weguelin St. Michael, and from something in her
prim yet charming manner I gathered that she
held it to be not perfectly well-bred in a lady to
greet a gentleman across the width of a public
highway, and that she could have wished that
her tall companion had not thus greeted me,
a stranger likely to comment upon Kings Port
manners.   In her eyes, such free deportment evidently went with her tall companion's method of
speech: hadn't the little lady informed me during
our first brief meeting that Kings Port at times
thought Mrs. Gregory St. Michael's tongue " too
downright "?

The two ladies having graciously granted me
permission to join them while they took the air,
Mrs. Gregory must surely have shocked Mrs.

Weguelin by saying to me, " I haven't a penny
for your thoughts, but I'll exchange."

" Would you thus bargain in the dark, madam ? "

" Oh, I'll risk that; and, to say truth, even your
back, as we came out of that house, was a back of
thought."

" Well, I confess to some thinking. Shall I
begin ? "

It was Mrs. Weguelin who quickly replied, smiling: " Ladies first, you know. At least we still
keep it so in Kings Port."

" Would we did everywhere ! " I exclaimed de-
voutly; and I was quite aware that beneath the
little lady's gentle smile a setting down had lurked,
a setting down of the most delicate nature, administered to me not in the least because I had
deserved one, but because she did not like Mrs.
Gregory's " downright " tongue, and could not
stop her.

Mrs. Gregory now took the prerogative of ladies,
and began. " I was thinking of what we had all
just been saying during our visit across the way
— and with which you are not going to agree —
that our young people would do much better to
let us old people arrange their marriages for them,
as it is done in Europe."

" O dear ! "

" I said that you would not agree; but that is
because you are so young."

" I don't know that twenty-eight is so young."

" You will know it when you are seventy-three."
This observation again came from Mrs. Weguelin
St. Michael, and again with a gentle and attractive
smile. It was only the second time that she had

spoken; and throughout the talk into which we
now fell as we slowly walked up and down High
Walk, she never took the lead; she left that to
the "downright" tongue — but I noticed, however, that she chose her moments to follow the
lead very aptly. I also perceived plainly that
what we were really going to discuss was not at
all the European principle of marriage-making,
but just simply young John and his Hortense;
they were the true kernel of the nut with whose
concealing shell Mrs. Gregory was presenting me,
and in proposing an exchange of thoughts she
would get back only more thoughts upon the same
subject. It was pretty evident how much Kings
Port was buzzing over all this! They fondly
believed they did not like it; but what would they
have done without it? What, indeed, were they
going to do when it was all over and done with,
one way or another? As a matter of fact, they
ought to be grateful to Hortense for contributing
illustriously to the excitement of their lives.

"Of course, I am well aware," Mrs. Gregory
pursued, "that the young people of to-day believe
they can all 'teach their grandmothers to suck
eggs,' as we say in Kings Port."

"We say it elsewhere, too," I mildly put in.

"Indeed? I didn't know that the North, with
its pest of Hebrew and other low immigrants, had
retained any of the good old homely saws which
we brought from England. But do you imagine
that if the control of marriage rested in the hands
of parents and grandparents (where it properly
belongs), you would be witnessing in the North
this disgusting spectacle of divorce?"

" But, Mrs. St. Michael — "

" We didn't invite you to argue when we invited you to walk ! " cried the lady, laughing.

" We should like you to answer the question," said Mrs. Weguelin St. Michael.

" And tell us," Mrs. Gregory continued, " if it's your opinion that a boy who has never been married is a better judge of matrimony's pitfalls than his father."

" Or than any older person who has bravely and worthily gone through with the experience," Mrs. Weguelin added.

" Ladies, I've no mind to argue.   But we're ahead of Europe; we don't need their clumsy old plan."

Mrs. Gregory gave a gallant, incredulous snort. " I shall be interested to learn of anything that is done better here than in Europe."

" Oh, many things, surely !   But especially the mating of the fashionable young.   They don't need any parents to arrange for them; it's much better managed through precocity."

" Through precocity?   I scarcely follow you."

And Mrs. Weguelin softly added, " You must excuse us if we do not follow you."   But her softness nevertheless indicated that if there were any one present needing leniency, it was myself.

" Why, yes," I told them, " it's through pre-cocity.   The new-rich American no longer com-mits the blunder of keeping his children innocent. You'll see it beginning in the dancing-class, where I heard an exquisite little girl of six say to a little boy, ' Go away; I can't dance with you, because my mamma says your mamma only keeps a maid

to answer the doorbell.' When they get home
from the dancing-class, tutors in poker and bridge
are waiting to teach them how to gamble for each
other's little dimes. I saw a little boy in knicker-
bockers and a wide collar throw down the evening paper — "

" At that age? They read the *papers?*" interrupted Mrs. Gregory.

" They read nothing else at any age. He threw
it down and said, ' Well, I guess there's not much
behind this raid on Steel Preferred.' What need
has such a boy for parents or grandparents?
Presently he is travelling to a fashionable board-
ing-school in his father's private car. At college
all his adolescent curiosities are lavishly gratified.
His sister at home reads the French romances,
and by eighteen she, too, knows (in her head at
least) the whole of life, so that she can be perfectly trusted; she would no more marry a mere
half-millionnaire just because she loved him than
she would appear twice in the same ball-dress.
She and her ball-dresses are described in the
papers precisely as if she were an animal at a
show — which indeed is what she has become;
and she's eager to be thus described, because she
and her mother — even if her mother was once a
lady and knew better — are haunted by one perpetual, sickening fear, the fear of being *left out !*
And if you desire to pay correct ballroom compliments, you no longer go to her mother and tell
her she's looking every bit as young as her
daughter; you go to the daughter and tell her
she's looking every bit as old as her mother, for
that's what she wishes to do, that's what she tries

for, what she talks, dresses, eats, drinks, goes to
indecent plays and laughs for.   Yes, we manage
it through precocity, and the new-rich American
parent has achieved at least one new thing
under the sun, namely, the corruption of the
child."

My ladies silently consulted each other's expressions, after which, in equal silence, their gaze
returned to me ; but their equally intent scrutiny
was expressive of quite different things.   It was
with expectancy that Mrs. Gregory looked at me
—she wanted more.   Not so Mrs. Weguelin ;
she gave me disapproval ; it was shadowed in
her beautiful, lustrous eyes that burned dark in
her white face with as much fire as that of youth,
yet it was not of youth, being deeply charged
with retrospection.

In what, then, had I sinned ?   For the little
lady's next words, coldly murmured, increased in
me an uneasiness, as of sin : —

" You have told us much that we are not accustomed to hear in Kings Port."

" Oh, I haven't begun to tell you ! "   I exclaimed cheerily.

" You certainly have not told us," said Mrs.
Gregory, " how your 'precocity' escapes this
divorce degradation."

" *Escape* it ?   Those people think it is — well,
provincial — not to have been divorced at least
once ! "

Mrs. Gregory opened her eyes, but Mrs. Weguelin shut her lips.

I continued : " Even the children, for their
own little reasons, like it.   Only last summer, in

Newport, a young boy was asked how he enjoyed having a father and an ex-father."

" *Ex*-father ! " said Mrs. Gregory. " *Vice*-father is what I should call him."

" Maria ! " murmured Mrs. Weguelin, " how can you jest upon such topics ? "

" I am far from jesting, Julia. Well, young gentleman, and what answer did this precious Newport child make ? "

" He said (if you will pardon my giving you his little sentiment in his own quite expressive idiom), ' Me for two fathers ! Double money birthdays and Christmases. See ? ' That was how *he* saw divorce."

Once again my ladies consulted each other's expressions ; we moved along High Walk in such silence that I heard the stiff little rustle which the palmettos were making across the street ; even these trees, you might have supposed, were whispering together over the horrors that I had recited in their decorous presence.

It was Mrs. Gregory who next spoke. " I can translate that last boy's language, but what did the other boy mean about a ' raid on Steel Preferred ' — if I've got the jargon right ? "

While I translated this for her, I felt again the disapproval in Mrs. Weguelin's dark eyes ; and my sins — for they were twofold — were presently made clear to me by this lady.

" Are such subjects as — as *stocks* " (she softly cloaked this word in scorn immeasurable) — " are such subjects mentioned in your good society at the North ? "

I laughed heartily. " Everything's mentioned ! "

The lady paused over my reply. " I am afraid
you must feel us to be very old-fashioned in
Kings Port," she then said.

" But I rejoice in it ! "

She ignored my not wholly dexterous compliment. " And some subjects," she pursued, " seem
to us so grave that if we permit ourselves to
speak of them at all we cannot speak of them
lightly."

No, they couldn't speak of them lightly ! Here,
then, stood my two sins revealed ; everything I
had imparted, and also my tone of imparting it,
had displeased Mrs. Weguelin St. Michael, not
with the thing, but with *me*. I had transgressed
her sound old American code of good manners, a
code slightly pompous no doubt, but one in which
no familiarity was allowed to breed contempt. To
her good taste, there were things in the world
which had, apparently, to exist, but which one
banished from drawing-room discussion as one
conceals from sight the kitchen and outhouses ;
one dealt with them only when necessity compelled, and never in small-talk ; and here had I
been, so to speak, small-talking them in that glib,
modern, irresponsible cadence with which our
brazen age rings and clatters like the beating of
triangles and gongs. Not triangles and gongs,
but rather strings and flutes, had been the music
to which Kings Port society had attuned its
measured voice.

I saw it all, and even saw that my own dramatic
sense of Mrs. Weguelin's dignity had perversely
moved me to be more flippant than I actually felt ;
and I promised myself that a more chastened tone

should forthwith redeem me from the false position I had got into.

"My dear," said Mrs. Gregory to Mrs. Weguelin, "we must ask him to excuse our provin-
cialism."

For the second time I was not wholly dexterous.
"But I like it so much!" I exclaimed; and both
ladies laughed frankly.

Mrs. Gregory brought in a fable. "You'll find
us all 'country mice' here."

This time I was happy. "At least, then, there'll
be no cat!" And this caused us all to make little
bows.

But the word "cat" fell into our talk as does a
drop of some acid into a chemical solution, instantly changing the whole to an unexpected new
color. The unexpected new color was, in this
instance, merely what had been latently lurking
in the fluid of our consciousness all through;
and now it suddenly came out.

Mrs. Gregory stared over the parapet at the
harbor. "I wonder if anybody has visited that
steam yacht?"

"The *Hermana?*" I said. "She's waiting, I
believe, for her owner, who is enjoying himself
very much on land." It was a strong temptation
to add, "enjoying himself with the cat," but I
resisted it.

"Oh!" said Mrs. Gregory. "Possibly a friend
of yours?"

"Even his name is unknown to me. But I
gather that he may be coming to Kings Port —
to attend Mr. John Mayrant's wedding next
Wednesday week."

I hadn't gathered this; but one is at times
driven to improvising.   I wished so much to
know if Juno was right about the engagement
being broken, and I looked hard at the ladies as
my words fairly grazed the "cat." This time I
expected them to consult each other's expressions,
and such, indeed, was their immediate proceeding.

"The Wednesday following, you mean," Mrs.
Weguelin corrected.

"Postponed again?   Dear me!"

Mrs. Gregory spoke this time.   "General
Rieppe.   Less well again, it seems."

It would be like Juno to magnify a delay into a
rupture.   Then I had a hilarious thought, which
I instantly put to the ladies.   "If the poor General were to die completely, would the wedding
be postponed completely?"

"There would not be the slightest chance of
that," Mrs. Gregory declared.   And then she
pronounced a sentence that was truly oracular:
"She's coming at once to see for herself."

To which Mrs. Weguelin added with deeper
condemnation than she had so far employed at
all: "There is a rumor that she is actually coming in an automobile."

My silence upon these two remarks was the
silence of great and sudden interest; but it led
Mrs. Weguelin St. Michael to do my perceptions
a slight injustice, and she had no intention that I
should miss the quality of her opinion regarding
the vehicle in which Hortense was reported to
be travelling.

"Miss Rieppe has the extraordinary taste to

come here in an automobile," said Mrs. Weguelin St. Michael, with deepened severity.

Though I understood quite well, without this emphasizing, that the little lady would, with her unbending traditions, probably think it more respectable to approach Kings Port in a wheelbarrow, I was absorbed by the vague but copious import of Mrs. Gregory's announcement. The oracles, moreover, continued.

" But she is undoubtedly very clever to come and see for herself," was Mrs. Weguelin's next comment.

Mrs. Gregory's face, as she replied to her companion, took on a censorious and superior expression. " You'll remember, Julia, that I told Josephine St. Michael it was what they had to expect."

" But it was not Josephine, my dear, who at any time approved of taking such a course. It was Eliza's whole doing."

It was fairly raining oracles round me, and they quite resembled, for all the help and light they contained, their Delphic predecessors.

" And yet Eliza," said Mrs. Gregory, " in the face of it, this very morning, repeated her eternal assertion that we shall all see the marriage will not take place."

" Eliza," murmured Mrs. Weguelin, " rates few things more highly than her own judgment."

Mrs. Gregory mused. " Yet she is often right when she has no right to be right."

I could not bear it any longer, and I said, " I heard to-day that Miss Rieppe had broken her engagement."

"And where did you hear *that* nonsense?"
asked Mrs. Gregory.

My heart leaped, and I told her where.

"Oh, well! you will hear anything in a boarding-house. Indeed, that would be a great deal too
good to be true."

"May I ask where Miss Rieppe is all this
while?"

"The last news was from Palm Beach, where
the air was said to be necessary for the General."

"But," Mrs. Weguelin repeated, "we have
every reason to believe that she is coming here
in an automobile."

"We shall have to call, of course," added Mrs.
Gregory to her, not to me; they were leaving me
out of it. Yes, these ladies were forgetting about
me in their rising preoccupation over whatever
crisis it was that now hung over John Mayrant's
love affairs — a preoccupation which was evidently
part of Kings Port's universal buzz to-day, and
which my joining them in the street had merely
mitigated for a moment. I did not wish to be
left out of it; I cannot tell you why — perhaps it
was contagious in the local air — but a veritable
madness of craving to know about it seized upon
me. Of course, I saw that Miss Rieppe was,
almost too grossly and obviously, "playing for
time"; the health of people's fathers did not
cause weekly extensions of this sort. But what
was it that the young lady expected time to effect
for her? Her release, formally, by her young
man, on the ground of his worldly ill fortune?
Or was it for an offer from the owner of the
Hermana that she was waiting, before she should

take the step of formally releasing John Mayrant?
No, neither of these conjectures seemed to furnish
a key to the tactics of Miss Rieppe; and the
theory that each of these affianced parties was
strategizing to cause the other to assume the
odium of breaking their engagement, with no
result save that of repeatedly countermanding a
wedding-cake, struck me as belonging admirably
to a stage-comedy in three acts, but scarcely to
life as we find it. Besides, poor John Mayrant
was, all too plainly, not strategizing; he was playing as straight a game as the honest heart of a
gentleman could inspire. And so, baffled at all
points, I said (for I simply had to try something
which might lead to my sharing in Kings Port's
vibrating secret):—

"I can't make out whether she wants to marry
him or not."

Mrs. Gregory answered. "That is just what
she is coming to see for herself."

"But since her love was for his phosphates
only —!" was my natural exclamation.

It caused (and this time I did not expect it) my
inveterate ladies to consult each other's expressions. They prolonged their silence so much
that I spoke again:—

"And backing out of this sort of thing can be
done, I should think, quite as cleverly, and much
more simply, from a distance."

It was Mrs. Weguelin who answered now, or,
rather, who headed me off. "Have you been
able to make out whether he wants to marry her
or not?"

"Oh, he never comes near any of that with
me!"

"Certainly not. But we all understand that he has taken a fancy to you, and that you have talked much with him."

So they all understood this, did they? This, too, had played its little special part in the buzz? Very well, then, nothing of my private impressions should drop from my lips here, to be quoted and misquoted and battledored and shuttlecocked, until it reached the boy himself (as it would inevitably) in fantastic disarrangement. I laughed. "Oh, yes! I have talked much with him. Shakespeare, I think, was our latest subject."

Mrs. Weguelin was plainly watching for something to drop. "Shakespeare!" Her tone was of surprise.

I then indulged myself in that most delightful sort of impertinence, which consists in the other person's not seeing it. "You wouldn't be likely to have heard of that yet. It occurred only before dinner to-day. But we have also talked optimism, pessimism, sociology, evolution — Mr. Mayrant would soon become quite —" I stopped myself on the edge of something very clumsy.

But sharp Mrs. Gregory finished for me. "Yes, you mean that if he didn't live in Kings Port (where we still have reverence, at any rate), he would imbibe all the shallow quackeries of the hour and resemble all the clever young donkeys of the minute."

"Maria!" Mrs. Weguelin murmurously expostulated.

Mrs. Gregory immediately made me a handsome but equivocal apology. "I wasn't thinking of you at all!" she declared gayly; and it set me

doubting if perhaps she hadn't, after all, compre-
hended my impertinence. " And, thank Heaven! "
she continued, " John is one of us, in spite of his
present stubborn course."

But Mrs. Weguelin's beautiful eyes were rest-
ing upon me with that disapproval I had come
to know. To her, sociology and evolution and
all the " isms " were new-fangled inventions and
murky with offence; to touch them was defile-
ment, and in disclosing them to John Mayrant I
was a corrupter of youth. She gathered it all up
into a word that was radiant with a kind of lovely
maternal gentleness: —

"We should not wish John to become radical."

In her voice, the whole of old Kings Port was
enshrined: hereditary faith and hereditary standards, mellow with the adherence of generations
past, and solicitous for the boy of the young generation. I saw her eyes soften at the thought of
him; and throughout the rest of our talk to its
end her gaze would now and then return to me,
shadowed with disapproval.

I addressed Mrs. Gregory. " By his ' present
stubborn course' I suppose you mean the Custom
House."

" All of us deplore his obstinacy. His Aunt
Eliza has strongly but vainly expostulated with
him. And after that, Miss Josephine felt obliged
to tell him that he need not come to see her again
until he resigned a position which reflects
ignominy upon us all."

I suppressed a whistle. I thought (as I have
said earlier) that I had caught a full vision of
John Mayrant's present plight. But my imagi-

nation had not soared to the height of Miss
Josephine St. Michael's act of discipline. This,
it must have been, that the boy had checked himself from telling me in the churchyard. What a
character of sterner times was Miss Josephine!
I thought of Aunt Carola, but even she was not
quite of this iron, and I said so to Mrs. Gregory.
"I doubt if there be any old lady left in the
North," I said, "capable of such antique severity."

But Mrs. Gregory opened my eyes still further.
"Oh, you'd have them if you had the negro to
deal with as we have him. Miss Josephine," she
added, "has to-day removed her sentence of
banishment."

I felt on the verge of new discoveries. "What!"
I exclaimed, "and did she relent?"

"New circumstances intervened," Mrs. Gregory
loftily explained. "There was an occurrence —
an encounter, in fact — in which John Mayrant
fittingly punished one who had presumed. Upon
hearing of it, this morning, Miss Josephine sent
a message to John that he might resume visiting
her."

"But that is perfectly grand!" I cried in my
delight over Miss Josephine as a character.

"It is perfectly natural," returned Mrs. Gregory,
quietly. "John has behaved with credit throughout. He was at length made to see that circumstances forbade any breach between his family
and that of the other young man. John held back
— who would not, after such an insult? — but
Miss Josephine was firm, and he has promised to
call and shake hands. My cousin, Doctor Beau-
garcon, assures me that the young man's injuries

are trifling — a week will see him restored and presentable again."

"A week? A mere nothing!" I answered. "Do you know," I now suggested, "that you have forgotten to ask me what I was thinking about when we met?"

"Bless me, young gentleman! and was it so remarkable?"

"Not at all, but it partly answers what Mrs. Weguelin St. Michael asked me. If a young man does not really wish to marry a young woman, there are ways well known by which she can be brought to break the engagement."

"Ah," said Mrs. Gregory, "of course; gayeties and irregularities — "

"That is, if he's not above them," I hastily subjoined.

"Not always, by any means," Mrs. Gregory returned. ".Kings Port has been treated to some episodes — "

Mrs. Weguelin put in a word of defence. "It is to be said, Maria, that John's irregularities have invariably been conducted with perfect propriety."

"Oh," said Mrs. Gregory, "no Mayrant was ever known to be gross!"

"But this particular young lady," said Mrs. Weguelin, "would not be estranged by any masculine irregularities and gayeties. Not by any."

"How about infidelities?" I suggested. "If he should flagrantly lose his heart to another?"

Mrs. Weguelin replied quickly. "That answers very well where hearts are in question."

"But," said I, "since phosphates are no longer — ? "

There was a pause. "It would be a new dilemma," Mrs. Gregory then said slowly, "if she turned out to care for him, after all."

Throughout all this I was getting more and more the sense of how a total circle of people, a well-filled, wide circle of interested people, surrounded and cherished John Mayrant, made itself the setting of which he was the jewel; I felt in it, even stronger than the manifestation of personal affection (which certainly was strong enough), a collective sense of possession in him, a clan value, a pride and a guardianship concentrated and jealous, as of an heir to some princely estate, who must be worthy for the sake of a community even before he was worthy for his own sake. Thus he might amuse himself — it was in the code that princely heirs so should do, *pour se déniaiser*, as they neatly put it in Paris — thus might he and must he fight when his dignity was assailed; but thus might he not marry outside certain lines prescribed, or depart from his circle's established creeds, divine and social, especially to hold any position which (to borrow Mrs. Gregory's phrase) "reflected ignominy" upon them all. When he transgressed, their very value for him turned them bitter against him. I know that all of us are more or less chained to our community, which is pleased to expect us to walk its way, and mightily displeased when we please ourselves instead by breaking the chain and walking our own way; and I know that we are forgiven very slowly; but I had not dreamed what a prisoner to communal criticism a young American could be until I beheld Kings Port over John Mayrant.

And to what estate was this prince heir? Alas, his inheritance was all of it the Past and none of it the Future; was the full churchyard and the empty wharves! He was paying dear for his princedom! And then, there was yet another sense of this beautiful town that I got here completely, suddenly crystallized, though slowly gathering ever since my arrival: all these old people were clustered about one young one. That was it; that was the town's ultimate tragic note: the old timber of the forest dying and the too sparse new growth appearing scantily amid the tall, fine, venerable, decaying trunks. It had been by no razing to the ground and sowing with salt that the city had perished; a process less violent but more sad had done away with it. Youth, in the wake of commerce, had ebbed from Kings Port, had flowed out from the silent, mourning houses, and sought life North and West, and wherever else life was to be found. Into my revery floated a phrase from a melodious and once favorite song: *O tempo passato perchè non ritorni?*

And John Mayrant? Why, then, had he tarried here himself? That is a hard saying about crabbed age and youth, but are not most of the sayings hard that are true? What was this young man doing in Kings Port with his brains, and his pride, and his energetic adolescence? If the Custom House galled him, the whole country was open to him; why not have tried his fortune out and away, over the hills, where the new cities

lie, all full of future and empty of past? Was it
much to the credit of such a young man to find
himself at the age of twenty-three or twenty-four,
sound and lithe of limb, yet tied to the apron
strings of Miss Josephine, and Miss Eliza, and
some thirty or forty other elderly female relatives?

With these thoughts I looked at the ladies and
wondered how I might lead them to answer me
about John Mayrant, without asking questions
which might imply something derogatory to him or
painful to them. I could not ever say to them a
word which might mean, however indirectly, that
I thought their beautiful, cherished town no
place for a young man to go to seed in; this cut
so close to the quick of truth that discourse must
keep wide away from it. What, then, could I ask
them? As I pondered, Mrs. Weguelin solved it
for me by what she was saying to Mrs. Gregory,
of which, in my preoccupation, I had evidently
missed a part: —

" — if he should share the family bad taste
in wives."

" Eliza says she has no fear of that."

" Were I Eliza, Hugh's performance would
make me very uneasy."

" Julia, John does not resemble Hugh."

" Very decidedly, in coloring, Maria."

" And Hugh found that girl in Minneapolis,
Julia, where there was doubtless no pick for the
poor fellow. And remember that George chose
a lady, at any rate."

Mrs. Weguelin gave to this a short assent.
" Yes." It portended something more behind,
which her next words duly revealed. " A lady;

but do — any — ladies ever seem quite like our
own ? "

" Certainly not, Julia."

You see, they were forgetting me again; but
they had furnished me with a clue.

" Mr. John Mayrant has married brothers ? "

" Two," Mrs. Gregory responded. " John is
the youngest of three children."

" I hadn't heard of the brothers before."

" They seldom come here. They saw fit to
leave their home and their delicate mother."

" Oh ! "

" But John," said Mrs. Gregory, " met his
responsibility like a Mayrant."

" Whatever temptations he has yielded to,"
said Mrs. Weguelin, " his filial piety has stood
proof."

" He refused," added Mrs. Gregory, " when
George (and I have never understood how George
could be so forgetful of their mother) wrote twice,
offering him a lucrative and rising position in the
railroad company at Roanoke."

" That was hard ! " I exclaimed.

She totally misapplied my sympathy. " Oh,
Anna Mayrant," she corrected herself, " John's
mother, Mrs. Hector Mayrant, had harder things
than forgetful sons to bear ! I've not laid eyes on
those boys since the funeral."

" Nearly two years," murmured Mrs. Weguelin.
And then, to me, with something that was almost
like a strange severity beneath her gentle tone :
" Therefore we are proud of John, because the
better traits in his nature remind us of his forefathers, whom we knew."

"In Kings Port," said Mrs. Gregory, "we prize those who ring true to the blood."

By way of response to this sentiment, I quoted some French to her. "*Bon chien chasse de race.*" It pleased Mrs. Weguelin. Her guarded attitude toward me relented. "John mentioned your cultivation to us," she said. "In these tumble-down days it is rare to meet with one who still lives, mentally, on the gentlefolks' plane — the *piano nobile* of intelligence!"

I realized how high a compliment she was paying me, and I repaid it with a joke. "Take care! Those who don't live there would call it the *piano snobile.*"

"Ah!" cried the delighted lady, "they'd never have the wit!"

"Did you ever hear," I continued, "the Bostonian's remark — 'The mission of America is to vulgarize the world'?"

"I never expected to agree so totally with a Bostonian!" declared Mrs. Gregory.

"Nothing so hopeful," I pursued, "has ever been said of us. For refinement and thoroughness and tradition delay progress, and we are sweeping them out of the road as fast as we can."

"Come away, Julia," said Mrs. Gregory. "The young gentleman is getting flippant again, and we leave him."

The ladies, after gracious expressions concerning the pleasure of their stroll, descended the steps at the north end of High Walk, where the parapet stops, and turned inland from the water through a little street. I watched them until they went out of my sight round a corner; but the two silent, leisurely figures, moving in their black and their veils along an empty highway, come back to me often in the pictures of my thoughts; come back most often, indeed, as the human part

Leafy enclosures dipping below sight among quaint and huddled quadrangles

of what my memory sees when it turns to look at Kings Port. For, first, it sees the blue frame of quiet sunny water, and the white town within its frame beneath the clear, untainted air; and then

it sees the high-slanted roofs, red with their old
corrugated tiles, and the tops of leafy enclosures
dipping below sight among quaint and huddled
quadrangles ; and, next, the quiet houses standing
in their separate grounds, their narrow ends to the
street and their long, two-storied galleries open to
the south, but their hushed windows closed as if
against the prying, restless Present that must not
look in and disturb the motionless memories which
sit brooding behind these shutters ; and between
all these silent mansions lie the narrow streets,
the quiet, empty streets, along which, as my
memory watches them, pass the two ladies silently,
in their black and their veils, moving between
high, mellow-colored garden walls over whose
tops look the oleanders, the climbing roses, and
all the taller flowers of the gardens.

And if Mrs. Gregory and Mrs. Weguelin
seemed to me at moments as narrow as those
streets, they also seemed to me as lovely as those
serene gardens ; and if I had smiled at their prejudices, I had loved their innocence, their deep
innocence, of the poisoned age which has succeeded their own ; and if I had wondered this day
at their powers for cruelty, I wondered the next
day at the glimpse I had of their kindness.   For
during a pelting cold rainstorm, as I sat and
shivered in a Royal Street car, waiting for it to
start upon its north-bound course, the house-door
opposite which we stood at the end of the track
opened, and Mrs. Weguelin's head appeared,
nodding to the conductor as she sent her black
servant out with hot coffee for him!   He took
off his hat, and smiled, and thanked her ; and

when we had started and I, the sole passenger in
the chilly car, asked him about this, he said with
native pride: "The ladies always watches out for
us conductors in stormy weather, sir.   That's
Mistress Weguelin St. Michael, one of our finest."
And then he gave me careful directions how to
find a shop that I was seeking.

Think of this happening in New York!   Think
of the aristocracy of that metropolis warming up
with coffee the — but why think of it, or of a
New York conductor answering your questions
with careful directions!   It is not New York's
fault, it is merely New York's misfortune: New
York is in a hurry; and a world of haste cannot
be a world either of courtesy or of kindness.   But
we have progress, progress, instead; and that is
a tremendous consolation.

XI

DADDY BEN AND HIS SEED

BUT what was Hortense Rieppe coming to see for herself?

Many dark things had been made plain to me by my talk with the two ladies; yet while disclosing so much, they had still left this important matter in shadow. I was very glad, however, for what they had revealed. They had showed me more of John Mayrant's character, and more also of the destiny which had shaped his ends, so that my esteem for him had increased; for some of the words that they had exchanged shone like bright lanterns down into his nature upon strength and beauty lying quietly there, — young strength and beauty, yet already tempered by manly sacrifice. I saw how it came to pass through this, through renunciation of his own desires, through performance of duties which had fallen upon him not quite fairly, that the eye of his spirit had been turned away from self; thus had it grown strong-sighted and able to look far and deep, as his speech sometimes revealed, while still his flesh was of his youthful age, and no saint's flesh either. This had the ladies taught me during the fluttered interchange of their reminders and opinions, and by their eager agreements and disagreements, I was also grateful to them in that I could once

more correct Juno.   The pleasure should be mine
to tell them in the public hearing of our table
that Miss Rieppe was still engaged to John Mayrant.

But what was this interesting girl coming to see
for herself?

This little hole in my knowledge gave me discomfort as I walked along toward the antiquity
shop where I was to buy the other kettle-supporter.   The ladies, with all their freedom of
comment and censure, had kept something from
me.   I reviewed, I pieced together, their various
remarks, those oracles, especially, which they had
let fall, but it all came back to the same thing :
I did not know, and they did, what Hortense
Rieppe was coming to see for herself.   At all
events, the engagement was not broken, the
chance to be instrumental in having it broken
was still mine ; I might still save John Mayrant
from his deplorable quixotism ; and as this reflection grew with me I took increasing comfort in
it, and I stepped onward toward my kettle-supporter, filled with that sense of moral well-being
which will steal over even the humblest of us
when we feel that we are beneficently minding
somebody else's business.

Whenever the arrangement did not take me
too widely from my course, I so mapped out my
walks and errands in Kings Port that I might
pass by the churchyard and church at the corner
of Court and Worship streets.   Even if I did not
indulge myself by turning in to stroll and loiter
among the flowers, it was enough pleasure to
walk by that brick-wall.   If you are willing to

wander curiously in our old towns, you may still
find in many of them good brick walls standing
undisturbed, and equal in their color and simple
excellence to those of Kings Port; but fashion
has pushed these others out of its sight, among
back streets and all sorts of forgotten purlieus
and abandoned dignity, and takes its walks to-day
amid cold, expensive ugliness; while the old brick
walls of Kings Port continually frame your steps
with charm. No one workman famous for his
skill built them so well proportioned, so true to
comeliness; it was the general hand of their age
that could shape nothing wrong, as the hand of
to-day can shape nothing right, save by a rigid
following of the old.

I gave myself the pleasure this afternoon of
walking by the churchyard wall; and when I
reached the iron gate, there was Daddy Ben. So
full was I of my thoughts concerning John Mayrant, and the vicissitudes of his heart, and the
Custom House, that I was moved to have words
with the old man upon the general topic.

" Well," I said, " and so Mr. John is going to
be married."

No attempt to start a chat ever failed more
signally. He assented with a manner of mingled
civility and reserve that was perfection, and after
the two syllables of which his answer consisted,
he remained as impenetrably respectful as before.
I felt rather high and dry, but I tried it again : —

" And I'm sure, Daddy Ben, that you feel as
sorry as any of the family that the phosphates
failed."

Again he replied with his two syllables of

assent, and again he stood mute, respectful, a
little bent with his great age ; but now his good
manners — and better manners were never seen —
impelled him to break silence upon some subject,
since he would not permit himself to speak concerning the one which I had introduced. It was
the phosphates which inspired him.

" Dey is mighty fine prostrate wukks heah, sah."

" Yes, I've been told so, Daddy Ben."

" On dis side up de ribber an' tudder side
down de ribber 'cross de new bridge. Wuth
visitin' fo' strangers, sah."

I now felt entirely high and dry. I had attempted to enter into conversation with him
about the intimate affairs of a family to which
he felt that he belonged ; and with perfect tact he
had not only declined to discuss them with me,
but had delicately informed me that I was a
stranger and as such had better visit the phosphate works among the other sights of Kings
Port. No diplomat could have done it better ;
and as I walked away from him I knew that he
regarded me as an outsider, a Northerner, belonging to a race hostile to his people ; he had seen
Mas' John friendly with me, but that was Mas'
John's affair. And so it was that if the ladies
had kept something from me, this cunning, old,
polite, coal-black African had kept everything
from me.

If all the negroes in Kings Port were like
Daddy Ben, Mrs. Gregory St. Michael would not
have spoken of having them " to deal with," and
the girl behind the counter would not have been
thrown into such indignation when she alluded to

their conceit and ignorance.   Daddy Ben had, so
far from being puffed up by the appointment in
the Custom House, disapproved of this.   I had
heard enough about the difference between the
old and new generations of the negro of Kings
Port to believe it to be true, and I had come to
discern how evidently it lay at the bottom of
many things here : John Mayrant and his kind
were a band united by a number of strong ties,
but by nothing so much as by their hatred of the
modern negro in their town.   Yes, I was obliged
to believe that the young Kings Port African,
left to freedom and the ballot, was a worse African than his slave parents ; but this afternoon
brought me a taste of it more pungent than all
the assurances in the world.

I bought my kettle-supporter, and learned from
the robber who sold it to me (Kings Port prices
for " old things " are the most exorbitant that I
know anywhere) that a carpenter lived not far
from Mrs. Trevise's boarding-house, and that he
would make for me the box in which I could pack
my various purchases.

" That is, if he's working this week," added the
robber.

" What else would he be doing ? "

" It may be his week for getting drunk on what
he earned the week before."   And upon this he
announced with as much bitterness as if he had
been John Mayrant or any of his aunts, " That's
what Boston philanthropy has done for him."

I flared up at this.   " I suppose that's a Southern argument for reëstablishing slavery."

" I am not Southern ; Breslau is my native

town, and I came from New York here to live five
years ago.   I've seen what your emancipation has
done for the black, and I say to you, my friend,
honest I don't know a fool from a philanthropist
any longer."

He had much right upon his side ; and it can
be seen daily that philanthropy does not always
walk hand-in-hand with wisdom.   Does anything
or anybody always walk so?   Moreover, I am a
friend to not many superlatives, and have perceived no saying to be more true than the one
that extremes meet : they meet indeed, and folly
is their meeting-place.   Nor could I say in the
case of the negro which folly were the more ridiculous ; — that which expects a race which has
lived no one knows how many thousand years in
mental nakedness while Confucius, Moses, and
Napoleon were flowering upon adjacent human
stems, should put on suddenly the white man's
intelligence, or that other folly which declares we
can do nothing for the African, as if Hampton
had not already wrought excellent things for him.
I had no mind to enter into all the inextricable
error with this Teuton, and it was he who continued : —

" Oh, these Boston philanthropists; oh, these
know-it-alls !   Why don't they stay home ?   Why
do they come down here to worry us with their
ignorance?   See here, my friend, let me show
you ! "

He rushed about his shop in a search of dis-
traught eagerness, and with a multitude of small
exclamations, until, screeching jubilantly once,
he pounced upon a shabby and learned-looking

volume. This he brought me, thrusting it with
his trembling fingers between my own, and shuf-
fling the open pages. But when the apparently
right one was found, he exclaimed, " No, I have
better ! " and dashed away to a pile of pamphlets
on the floor, where he began to plough and harrow.
Wondering if I was closeted with a maniac, I
looked at the book in my passive hand, and saw
diagrams of various bones to me unknown, and
men's names of which I was equally ignorant —
Mivart, Topinard, and more, — but at last that of
Huxley. But this agreeable sight was spoiled at
once by the quite horrible words *Nycticebidæ*,
platyrrhine, catarrhine, from which I raised my
eyes to see him coming at me with two pamphlets,
and scolding as he came.

" Are you educated, yes ? Have been to college,
yes ? Then perhaps you will understand."

Certainly I understood immediately that he and
his pamphlets were as bad as the book, or worse,
in their use of a vocabulary designed to cause
almost any listener the gravest inconvenience.
Common Eocene ancestors occurred at the beginning of his lecture; and I believed that if it got
no stronger than this, I could at least preserve the
appearance of comprehending him; but it got
stronger, and at *sacro-iliac notch* I may say, without using any grossly exaggerated expression, that
I became unconscious. At least, all intelligence
left me. When it returned, he was saying : —

"But this is only the beginning. Come in here
to my crania and jaws."

Evidently he held me hypnotized, for he now
hurried me unresisting through a back door into

a dark little room, where he turned up the gas, and I saw shelves as in a museum, to one of which he led me. I suppose that it was curiosity that rendered me thus sheep-like. Upon the shelf were a number of skulls and jaws in admirable condition and graded arrangement, beginning to the left with that flat kind of skull which one associates with gorillas. He resumed his scolding harangue, and for a few brief moments I understood him. Here, told by themselves, was as much of the story of the skulls as we know, from man-like apes through glacial man to the modern senator or railroad president. But my intelligence was destined soon to die away again.

"That is the Caucasian skull: your skull," he said, touching a specimen at the right.

"Interesting," I murmured. "I'm afraid I know nothing about skulls."

"But you shall know someding before you leave," he retorted, wagging his head at me; and this time it was not the book, but a specimen, that he pushed into my grasp. He gave it a name, not as bad as *platyrrhine*, but I feared worse was coming; then he took it away from me, gave me another skull, and while I obediently held it, pronounced something quite beyond me.

"And what is the translation of that?" he demanded excitedly.

"Tell me," I feebly answered.

He shouted with overweening triumph: "The translation of that is *South Carolina nigger!* Notice well this so egcellent specimen. Prognathous, megadont, plàtyrrhine."

"Ha! Platyrrhine!" I saluted the one word I recognized as I drowned.

"You have said it yourself!" was his extraordinary answer; — for what had I said? Almost as if he were going to break into a dance for joy, he took the Caucasian skull and the other two, and set the three together by themselves, away from the rest of the collection. The picture which they thus made spoke more than all the measurements and statistics which he now chattered out upon me, reading from his book as I contemplated the skulls. There was a similarity of shape, a kinship there between the three, which stared you in the face; but in the contours of vaulted skull, the projecting jaws, and the great molar teeth — what was to be seen? Why, in every respect that the African departed from the Caucasian, he departed in the direction of the ape! Here was zoölogy mutely but eloquently telling us why there had blossomed no Confucius, no Moses, no Napoleon, upon that black stem; why no Iliad, no Parthenon, no Sistine Madonna, had ever risen from that tropic mud.

The collector touched my sleeve. "Have you now learned someding about skulls, my friend? Will you invite those Boston philanthropists to stay home? They will get better results in civilization by giving votes to monkeys than teaching Henry Wadsworth Longfellow to niggers."

Retaliation rose in me. "Haven't you learned to call them negroes?" I remarked. But this was lost upon the Teuton. I was tempted to tell him that I was no philanthropist, and no Bostonian, and that he need not shout so loud, but my more dignified instincts restrained me. I withdrew my sleeve from his touch (it was this act of his, I think,

that had most to do with my displeasure), and
merely bidding him observe that the enormous
price of the kettle-supporter had been reduced
for me by his exhibition to a bagatelle, I left the
shop of the screaming anatomist — or Afropath,
or whatever it may seem most fitting that he should
be called.

I bore the kettle-supporter with me, tied up
objectionably in newspaper, and knotted with un-
gainly string; and it was this bundle which prevented my joining the girl behind the counter, and
ending by a walk with a young lady the afternoon
that had begun by a walk with two old ones. I
should have liked to make my confession to her.
She was evidently out for the sake of taking the
air, and had with her no companion save the big
curly white dog; confession would have been very
agreeable; but I looked again at my ugly newspaper bundle, and turned in a direction that she
was not herself pursuing.

Twice, as I went, I broke into laughter over my
interview in the shop, which I fear has lost its
comical quality in the relating. To enter a door
and come serenely in among dingy mahogany and
glass objects, to bargain haughtily for a brass
bauble with the shopkeeper, and to have a few exchanged remarks suddenly turn the whole place
into a sort of bedlam with a gibbering scientist
dashing skulls at me to prove his fixed idea, and
myself quite furious — I laughed more than twice;
but, by the time I had approached the neighborhood of the carpenter's shop, another side of it
had brought reflection to my mind. Here was a
foreigner to whom slavery and the Lost Cause

"No companion save the big curly white dog"

were nothing, whose whole association with the
South had begun but five years ago; and the race
question had brought his feelings to this pitch!
He had seen the Kings Port negro with the eyes
of the flesh, and not with the eyes of theory, and
as a result the reddest rag for him was pale beside
a Boston philanthropist!

Nevertheless, I have said already that I am no
lover of superlatives, and in doctrine especially is
this true. We need not expect a Confucius from
the negro, nor yet a Chesterfield; but I am an
enemy also of that blind and base hate against him,
which conducts nowhere save to the de-civilizing
of white and black alike. Who brought him here?
Did he invite himself? Then let us make the
best of it and teach him, lead him, compel him to
live self-respecting, not as statesman, poet, or finan-
cier, but by the honorable toil of his hand and sweat
of his brow. Because "the door of hope" was
once opened too suddenly for him is no reason for
slamming it now forever in his face.

Thus mentally I lectured back at the Teuton as
I went through the streets of Kings Port; and
after a while I turned a corner which took me
abruptly, as with one magic step, out of the white
man's world into the blackest Congo. Even the
well-inhabited quarter of Kings Port (and I had
now come within this limited domain) holds narrow lanes and recesses which teem and swarm with
negroes. As cracks will run through fine porcelain, so do these black rifts of Africa lurk almost
invisible among the gardens and the houses. The
picture that these places offered, tropic, squalid,
and fecund, often caused me to walk through them

As cracks will run through fine porcelain, so do these black rifts of Africa lurk almost invisible among the gardens

and watch the basking population ; the intricate, broken wooden galleries, the rickety outside stair-

cases, the red and yellow splashes of color on the
clothes lines, the agglomerate rags that stuffed
holes in decaying roofs or hung nakedly on human
frames, the small, choked dwellings, bursting open
at doors and windows with black, round-eyed babies
as an overripe melon bursts with seeds, the children
playing marbles in the court, the parents playing cards in the room, the grandparents smoking
pipes on the porch, and the great-grandparents upstairs gazing out at you like creatures from the
Old Testament or the jungle.   From the jungle
we had stolen them, North and South had stolen
them together, long ago, to be slaves, not to be
citizens, and now here they were, the fruits of our
theft; and for some reason (possibly the Teuton
was the reason) that passage from the Book of
Exodus came into my head: "For I the Lord thy
God am a jealous God, visiting the iniquity of the
fathers upon the children."

These thoughts were interrupted by sounds as
of altercation. I had nearly reached the end of
the lane, where I should again emerge into the
white man's world, and where I was now walking
the lane spread into a broader space with ells and
angles and rotting steps, and habitations mostly
too ruinous to be inhabited.   It was from a sash-
less window in one of these that the angry
voices came. The first words which were distinct aroused my interest quite beyond the scale
of an ordinary altercation: —

"Calls you'self a reconstuckted niggah?"

This was said sharply and with prodigious
scorn. The answer which it brought was lengthy
and of such a general sullen incoherence that I

could make out only a frequent repetition of
"custom house," and that somebody was going to
take care of somebody hereafter.

Into this the first voice broke with tones of highest contempt and rapidity : —

"Presi*dent* gwine to gib brekfus' an' dinnah an
suppah to de likes ob *you* fo' de whole remaindah
ob youh wuthless nat'ral life? Get out ob my
sight, you reconstuckted niggah. I come out ob
de St. Michael."

There came through the window immediately
upon this sounds of scuffling and of a fall, and
then cries for help which took me running into
the dilapidated building. Daddy Ben lay on the
floor, and a thick, young savage was kicking him.
In some remarkable way I thought of the solidity
of their heads, and before the assailant even knew
that he had a witness, I sped forward, aiming my
kettle-supporter, and with its sharp brass edge I
dealt him a crack over his shin with astonishing accuracy. It was a dismal howl that he
gave, and as he turned he got from me another
crack upon the other shin. I had no time to
be alarmed at my deed, or I think that I should
have been very much so; I am a man above all
of peace, and physical encounters are peculiarly
abhorrent to me; but, so far from assailing me,
the thick, young savage, with the single muttered
remark, "He hit me fust," got himself out of the
house with the most agreeable rapidity.

Daddy Ben sat up, and his first inquiry greatly
reassured me as to his state. He stared at my
paper bundle. "You done make him hollah wid
dat, sah!"

I showed him the kettle-supporter through a rent in its wrapping, and I assisted him to stand upright.   His injuries proved fortunately to be slight (although I may say here that the shock to his ancient body kept him away for a few days from the churchyard), and when I began to talk to him about the incident, he seemed unwilling to say much in answer to my questions.   And when I offered to accompany him to where he lived, he declined altogether, assuring me that it was close, and that he could walk there as well as if nothing had happened to him; but upon my asking him if I was on the right way to the carpenter's shop, he looked at me curiously.

" No use you gwine dah, sah.   Dat shop close up.   He not wukkin, dis week, and dat why fo' I jaw him jus' now when you come in an' stop him. He de cahpentah, my gran'son, Cha's Coteswuth."

XII

FROM THE BEDSIDE

NEXT morning when I saw the weltering sky I resigned myself to a day of dulness; yet before its end I had caught a bright new glimpse of John Mayrant's abilities, and also had come, through tribulation, to a further understanding of the South; so that I do not, to-day, regret the tribulation. As the rain disappointed me of two outdoor expeditions, to which I had been for some little while looking forward, I dedicated most of my long morning to a sadly neglected correspondence, and trusted that the expeditions, as soon as the next fine weather visited Kings Port, would still be in store for me. Not only everybody in town here, but Aunt Carola, up in the North also, had assured me that to miss the sight of Live Oaks when the azaleas in the gardens of that country seat were in flower would be to lose one of the rarest and most beautiful things which could be seen anywhere; and so I looked out of my window at the furious storm, hoping that it might not strip the bushes at Live Oaks of their bloom, which recent tourists at Mrs. Trevise's had described as drawing near the zenith of its luxuriance. The other excursion to Udolpho with John Mayrant was not so likely to fall through. Udolpho was a sort of hunting lodge

or country club near Tern Creek and an old
colonial church, so old that it bore the royal
arms upon a shield still preserved as a sign of its
colonial origin. A note from Mayrant, received
at breakfast, informed me that the rain would
take all pleasure from such an excursion, and that
he should seize the earliest opportunity the
weather might afford to hold me to my promise.
The wet gale, even as I sat writing, was beating
down some of the full-blown flowers in the garden
next Mrs. Trevise's house, and as the morning
wore on I watched the paths grow more strewn
with broken twigs and leaves.

I filled my correspondence with accounts of
Daddy Ben and his grandson, the carpenter,
doubtless from some pride in my part in that, but
also because it had become, through thinking it
over, even more interesting to-day than it had been
at the moment of its occurrence; and in reply-
ing to a sort of postscript of Aunt Carola's in
which she hurriedly wrote that she had forgotten
to say she had heard the La Heu family in South
Carolina was related to the Bombos, and should
be obliged to me if I would make inquiries about
this, I told her that it would be easy, and then
described to her the Teuton, plying his "antiquity" trade externally while internally cherishing
his collected skulls and nursing his scientific rage.
All my letters were the more abundant concerning these adventures of mine from my having kept
entirely silent upon them at Mrs. Trevise's tea-
table. I dreaded Juno when let loose upon the
negro question; and the fact that I was beginning to understand her feelings did not at all make

me wish to be deafened by them.   Neither Juno,
therefore, nor any of them learned a word from
me about the kettle-supporter incident.   What I
did take pains to inform the assembled company
was my gratification that the report of Mr. Mayrant's engagement being broken was unfounded;
and this caused Juno to observe that in that case
Miss Rieppe must have the most imperative
reasons for uniting herself to such a young man.

Unintimidated by the rain, this formidable creature had taken herself off to her nephew's bedside
almost immediately after breakfast; and later in
the day I, too, risked a drenching for the sake of
ordering the packing-box that I needed.   When I
returned, it was close on tea-time; I had seen Mrs.
Weguelin St. Michael send out the hot coffee to
the conductor, and I had found a negro carpenter
whose week it happily was to stay sober; and
now I learned that, when tea should be finished,
the poetess had in store for us, as a treat, her
ode.

Our evening meal was not plain sailing, even
for the veteran navigation of Mrs. Trevise; Juno
had returned from the bedside very plainly displeased (she was always candid even when silent)
by something which had happened there; and
before the joyful moment came when we all
learned what this was, a very gouty Boston lady
who had arrived with her husband from Florida
on her way North — and whose nature you will
readily grasp when I tell you that we found ourselves speaking of the man as Mrs. Braintree's
husband and never as Mr. Braintree — this
crippled lady, who was of a candor equal to Juno's,

embarked upon a conversation with Juno that compelled Mrs. Trevise to tinkle her bell for Daphne after only two remarks had been exchanged.

I had been sorry at first that here in this Southern boarding-house Boston should be represented only by a lady who appeared to unite in herself all the stony products of that city, and none of the others; for she was as convivial as a statue and as well-informed as a spelling-book; she stood no more for the whole of Boston than did Juno for the whole of Kings Port. But my sorrow grew less when I found that in Mrs. Braintree we had indeed a capable match for her Southern counterpart. Juno, according to her custom, had remembered something objectionable that had been perpetrated in 1865 by the Northern vandals.

" Edward," said Mrs. Braintree to her husband, in a frightfully clear voice, " it was at Chambersburg, was it not, that the Southern vandals burned the house in which were your father's title-deeds ? "

Edward, who, it appeared, had fought through the whole Civil War, and was in consequence perfectly good-humored and peaceable in his feelings upon that subject, replied hastily and amiably : " Oh, yes, yes ! Why, I believe it was ! "

But this availed nothing; Juno bent her great height forward, and addressed Mrs. Braintree. " This is the first time I have been told Southerners were vandals."

" You will never be able to say that again ! " replied Mrs. Braintree.

After the bell and Daphne had stopped, the

invaluable Briton addressed a genial generalization to us all: " I often think how truly awful your war would have been if the women had fought it, y'know, instead of the men."

" Quite so ! " said the easy-going Edward. " Squaws ! Mutilation ! Yes ! " and he laughed at his little joke, but he laughed alone.

I turned to Juno. " Speaking of mutilation, I trust your nephew is better this evening."

I was rejoiced by receiving a glare in response. But still more joy was to come.

" An apology ought to help cure him a lot," observed the Briton.

Juno employed her policy of not hearing him.

" Indeed, I trust that your nephew is in less pain," said the poetess.

Juno was willing to answer this. "The injuries, thank you, are the merest trifles — all that such a light-weight could inflict." And she shrugged her shoulders to indicate the futility of young John's pugilism.

" But," the surprised Briton interposed, " I thought you said your nephew was too feeble to eat steak or hear poetry."

Juno could always stem the eddy of her own contradictions — but she did raise her voice a little. " I fancy, sir, that Doctor Beaugarçon knows what he is talking about."

" Have they apologized yet ? " inquired the male honeymooner from the up-country.

" My nephew, sir, nobly consented to shake hands this afternoon. He did it entirely out of respect for Mr. Mayrant's family, who coerced him into this tardy reparation, and who feel un-

able to recognize him since his treasonable attitude in the Custom House."

"Must be fairly hard to coerce a chap you can't
recognize," said the Briton.

An et cetera now spoke to the honeymoon
bride from the up-country: "I heard Doctor
Beaugarçon say he was coming to visit you this
evening."

"Yais,"assented the bride. "Doctor Beaugarçon
is my mother's fourth cousin."

Juno now took — most unwisely, as it proved
— a vindictive turn at me. "I knew that your
friend, Mr. Mayrant, was intemperate," she began.

I don't think that Mrs. Trevise had any intention to ring for Daphne at this point — her curiosity was too lively; but Juno was going to risk
no such intervention, and I saw her lay a pre-
cautionary hand heavily down over the bell.
"But," she continued, "I did not know that Mr.
Mayrant was a gambler."

"Have you ever seen him intemperate?" I
asked.

"That would be quite needless," Juno returned.
"And of the gambling I have ocular proof, since
I found him, cards, counters, and money, with my
sick nephew. He had actually brought cards in
his pocket."

"I suppose," said the Briton, "your nephew
was too sick to resist him."

The male honeymooner, with two of the et
ceteras, made such unsteady demonstrations at
this that Mrs. Trevise protracted our sitting no
longer. She rose, and this meant rising for us
all.

A sense of regret and incompleteness filled me, and finding the Briton at my elbow as our company proceeded toward the sitting room, I said: " Too bad!"

His whisper was confident. "We'll get the rest of it out of her yet."

But the rest of it came without our connivance.

In the sitting room Doctor Beaugarçon sat waiting, and at sight of Juno entering the door (she headed our irregular procession) he sprang up and lifted admiring hands. "Oh, why didn't I have an aunt like you!" he exclaimed, and to Mrs. Trevise as she followed: "She pays her nephew's poker debts."

"How much, cousin Tom?" asked the up-country bride.

And the gay old doctor chuckled, as he kissed her: "Thirty dollars this afternoon, my darling."

At this the Briton dragged me behind a door in the hall, and there we danced together.

"That Mayrant chap will do," he declared; and we composed ourselves for a proper entrance into the sitting room, where the introductions had been made, and where Doctor Beaugarçon and Mrs. Braintree's husband had already fallen into war reminiscences, and were discovering with mutual amiability that they had fought against each other in a number of battles.

"And you generally licked us," smiled the Union soldier.

"Ah! don't I know myself how it feels to run!" laughed the Confederate. "Are you down at the club?"

But upon learning from the poetess that her

"Too sick to resist him"

ode was now to be read aloud, Doctor Beaugarçon
paid his fourth cousin's daughter a brief, though
affectionate, visit, lamenting that a very ill patient
should compel him to take himself away so immediately, but promising her presently in his stead
two visitors much more interesting.

"Miss Josephine St. Michael desires to call
upon you," he said, "and I fancy that her nephew
will escort her."

"In all this rain?" said the bride.

"Oh, it's letting up, letting up! Good night,
Mistress Trevise. Good night, sir; I am glad to
have met you." He shook hands with Mrs.
Braintree's husband. "We fellows," he whispered,
"who fought in the war have had war enough."
And bidding the general company good night, and
kissing the bride again, he left us even as the
poetess returned from her room with the manuscript.

I soon wished that I had escaped with him, because I feared what Mrs. Braintree might say
when the verses should be finished; and so, I
think, did her husband. We should have taken
the hint which tactful Doctor Beaugarçon had
meant, I began to believe, to give us in that whispered remark of his. But it had been given too
lightly, and so we sat and heard the ode out. I
am sure that the poetess, wrapped in the thoughts
of her own composition, had lost sight of all but
the phrasing of her poem and the strong feelings
which it not unmusically voiced; there is no other
way to account for her being willing to read it in
Mrs. Braintree's presence.

Whatever gayety had filled me when the Boston

lady had clashed with Juno was now changed to
deprecation and concern.¹ Indeed, I myself felt
almost as if I were being physically struck by the
words, until mere bewilderment took possession
of me; and after bewilderment, a little, a very
little, light, which, however, rapidly increased.
We were the victors, we the North, and we had
gone upon our way with songs and rejoicing —
able to forget, because we were the victors. We
had our victory; let the vanquished have their
memory. But here was the cry of the vanquished,
coming after forty years. It was the time which
at first bewildered me; Juno had seen the war,
Juno's bitterness I could comprehend, even if I
could not comprehend her freedom in expressing
it; but the poetess could not be more than a year
or two older than I was; she had come after it
was all over. Why should she prolong such
memories and feelings? But my light increased
as I remembered she had not written this for us,
and that if she had not seen the flames of war, she
had seen the ashes; for the ashes I had seen myself here in Kings Port, and had been overwhelmed by the sight, forty years later, more
overwhelmed than I could possibly say to Mrs.
Gregory St. Michael, or Mrs. Weguelin, or anybody. The strain of sitting and waiting for the
end made my hands cold and my head hot, but
nevertheless the light which had come enabled me
to bend instantly to Mrs. Braintree and murmur a
great and abused quotation to her: —

"*Tout comprendre c'est tout pardonner.*"

But my petition could not move her. She was
too old; she had seen the flames of war; and so
she said to her husband: —

" Edward, will you please help me upstairs ? "

And thus the lame, irreconcilable lady left the
room with the assistance of her unhappy warrior,
who must have suffered far more keenly than I
did.

This departure left us all in a constraint which
was becoming unbearable when the blessed doorbell rang and delivered us, and Miss Josephine St.
Michael entered with John Mayrant. He wore a
most curious expression ; his eyes went searching
about the room, and at length settled 'upon Juno
with a light in them as impish as that which had
flickered in my own mood before the ode.

To my surprise, Miss Josephine advanced and
gave me a special and marked greeting. Before
this she had always merely bowed to me ; to-night
she held out her hand. " Of course my visit is
not to you ; but I am very glad to find you here
and express the appreciation of several of us for
your timely aid to Daddy Ben. He feels much
shame in having said nothing to you himself."

And while I muttered those inevitable modest
nothings which fit such occasions, Miss St. Michael
recounted to the bride, whom she was ostensibly
calling upon, and to the rest of our now once more
harmonious circle, my adventures in the alleys
of Africa. These loomed, even with Miss St.
Michael's perfectly quiet and simple rendering of
them, almost of heroic size, thanks doubtless to
Daddy Ben's tropical imagery when he first told
the tale ; and before they were over Miss St.
Michael's marked recognition of me actually
brought from Juno some reflected recognition —
only this resembled in its graciousness the origi-

nal about as correctly as a hollow spoon reflects the human countenance divine. Still, it was at Juno's own request that I brought down from my chamber and displayed to them the kettle-supporter.

I have said that Miss St. Michael's visit was *ostensibly* to the bride: and that is because for some magnetic reason or other I felt diplomacy like an undercurrent passing among our chairs. Young John's expression deepened, whenever he watched Juno, to a devilishness which his polite manners veiled no better than a mosquito netting; and I believe that his aunt, on account of the battle between their respective nephews, had for family reasons deemed it advisable to pay, indirectly, under cover of the bride, a state visit to Juno; and I think that I saw Juno accepting it as a state visit, and that the two together, without using a word of spoken language, gave each other to understand that the recent deplorable circumstances were a closed incident. I think that his Aunt Josephine had desired young John to pay a visit likewise, and, to make sure of his speedy compliance, had brought him along with her — coerced him, as Juno would have said. He wore somewhat the look of having been "coerced," and he contributed remarkably few observations to the talk.

It was all harmonious, and decorous, and properly conducted, this state visit; yet even so, Juno and John exchanged at parting some verbal sweetmeats which rather stuck out from the smooth meringue of diplomacy.

She contemplated his bruise. "You are feeling

" Miss St. Michael's visit was *ostensibly* to the bride "

stronger, I hope, than you have been lately? A
bridegroom's health should be good."

He thanked her. "I am feeling better to-night
than for many weeks."

The rascal had the thirty dollars visibly bulging
that moment in his pocket. I doubt if he had acquainted his aunt with this episode, but she was
certain to hear it soon; and when she did hear it,
I rather fancy that she wished to smile—as I completely smiled alone in my bed that night thinking
young John over.

But I did not go to sleep smiling; listening to
the "Ode for the Daughters of Dixie" had been an
ordeal too truly painful, because it disclosed live
feelings which I had thought were dead, or rather,
it disclosed that those feelings smouldered in the
young as well as in the old. Doctor Beaugarçon
didn't have them — he had fought them out, just
as Mr. Braintree had fought them out; and Mrs.
Braintree, like Juno, retained them, because she
hadn't fought them out; and John Mayrant didn't
have them, because he had been to other places;
and I didn't have them — never had had them in
my life, because I came into the world when it
was all over. Why then — Stop, I told myself,
growing very wakeful, and seeing in the darkness
the light which had come to me, you have beheld
the ashes, and even the sight has overwhelmed
you; these others were born in the ashes, and
have had ashes to sleep in and ashes to eat. This
I said to myself; and I remembered that *War*
hadn't been all; that *Reconstruction* came in due
season; and I thought of the "reconstructed"
negro, as Daddy Ben had so ingeniously styled

him.   These white people, my race, had been
set beneath the reconstructed negro.   Still, still,
this did not justify the whole of it to me ; my perfectly innocent generation seemed to be included
in the unforgiving, unforgetting ode.   " I must
have it out with somebody," I said.   And in time
I fell asleep.

XIII

THE GIRL BEHIND THE COUNTER — III

I WAS still thinking the ode over as I dressed for breakfast, for which I was late, owing to my hair, which the changes in the weather had rendered somewhat recalcitrant. Yes; decidedly I must have it out with somebody. The weather was once more superb; and in the garden beneath my window men were already sweeping away the broken twigs and débris of the storm. I say "already," because it had not seemed to me to be the Kings Port custom to remove débris, or anything, with speed. I also had it in my mind to perform at lunch Aunt Carola's commission, and learn if the family of La Heu were indeed of royal descent through the Bombos. I intended to find this out from the girl behind the counter, but the course which our conversation took led me completely to forget about it.

As soon as I entered the Exchange I planted myself in front of the counter, in spite of the discouragement which I too plainly perceived in her countenance; the unfavorable impression which I had made upon her at our last interview was still in force.

I plunged into it at once. " I have a confession to make."

"You do me surprising honor."

"Oh, now, don't begin like that! I suppose you never told a lie."

"I'm telling the truth now when I say that I do not see why an entire stranger should confess anything to me."

"Oh, my goodness! Well, I told you a lie, anyhow; a great, successful, deplorable lie."

She opened her mouth under the shock of it, and I recited to her unsparingly my deception; during this recital her mouth gradually closed.

"Well, I declare, declare, declare!" she slowly and deliciously breathed over the sum total; and she considered me at length, silently, before her words came again, like a soft soliloquy. "I could never have believed it in one who"— here gayety flashed in her eyes suddenly — "parts his back hair so rigidly. Oh, I beg your pardon for being personal!" And her gayety broke in ripples. Some habitual instinct moved me to turn to the looking-glass. "Useless!" she cried, "you can't see it in that. But it's perfectly splendid to-day."

Nature has been kind to me in many ways — nay, prodigal; it is not every man who can perceive the humor in a jest of which he is himself the subject. I laughed with her. "I trust that I am forgiven," I said.

"Oh, yes, you are forgiven! Come out, General, and give the gentleman your right paw, and tell him that he is forgiven — if only for the sake of Daddy Ben." With these latter words she gave me a gracious nod of understanding. They were all thanking me for the kettle-supporter! She probably knew also the tale of John Mayrant, the cards, and the bedside.

The curly dog came out, and went through his part very graciously.

"I can guess his last name," I remarked.

"General's? How? Oh, you've heard it! I don't believe in you any more."

"That's not a bit handsome, after my confession. No, I'm getting to understand South Carolina a little. You came from the 'up-country,' you call your dog General; his name is General Hampton!"

Her laughter assented. "Tell me some more about South Carolina," she added with her caressing insinuation.

"Well, to begin with — "

"Go sit down at your lunch-table first. Aunt Josephine would never tolerate my encouraging gentlemen to talk to me over the counter."

I went back obediently, and then resumed: "Well, what sort of people are those who own the handsome garden behind Mrs. Trevise's!"

"I don't know them."

"Thank you; that's all I wanted."

"What do you mean?"

"They're new people. I could tell it from the way you stuck your nose in the air."

"Sir!"

"Oh, if you talk about my hair, I can talk about your nose, I think. I suspected that they were 'new people' because they cleaned up their garden immediately after the storm this morning. Now, I'll tell you something else: the whole South looks down on the whole North."

She made her voice kind. "Do you mind it *very* much?"

I joined in her latent mirth. " It makes life not
worth living! But more than this, South Carolina looks down on the whole South."

" Not Virginia."

" Not? An ' entire stranger,' you know, sometimes notices things which escape the family eye
— family likenesses in the children, for instance."

" Never Virginia," she persisted.

" Very well, very well! Somehow you've admitted the rest, however."

She began to smile.

" And next, Kings Port looks down on all the
rest of South Carolina."

·She now laughed outright. " An up-country
girl will not deny that, anyhow! "

" And finally, your aunts — "

" My aunts *are* Kings Port."

" The whole of it ? "

" If you mean the thirty thousand negroes — "

" No, there are other white people here — there
goes your nose again! "

" I will *not* have you so impudent, sir! "

" A thousand pardons, I'm on my knees. But
your aunts — "

There was such a flash of war in her eye that
I stopped.

" May I not even mention them ? " I asked her.

And suddenly upon this she became serious and
gentle. " I thought that you understood ·them.
Would you take them from their seclusion, too ?
It is all they have left — since you burned the
rest in 1865."

. I had made her say what I wanted! That " you "
was what I wanted. Now I should presently have

it out with her. But, for the moment, I did not
disclaim the "you." I said: —

"The burning in 1865 was horrible, but it was
war."

"It was outrage."

"Yes, the same kind as England's, who burned
Washington in 1812, and whom you all so deeply
admire."

She had, it seemed, no answer to this. But we
trembled on the verge of a real quarrel. It was
in her voice when she said: —

"I think I interrupted you."

I pushed the risk one step nearer the verge,
because of the words I wished finally to reach.
"In 1812, when England burned our White
House down, we did not sit in the ashes; we set
about rebuilding."

And now she burst out. "That's not fair, that's
perfectly inexcusable! Did England then set
loose on us a pack of black savages and politicians
to *help* us rebuild? Why, this very day I cannot
walk on the other side of the river, I dare not
venture off the New Bridge; and you who
first beat us and then unleashed the blacks to
riot in a new 'equality' that they were no more
fit for than so many apes, you sat back at ease in
your victory and your progress, having handed
the vote to the negro as you might have handed a
kerosene lamp to a child of three, and let us
crushed, breathless people cope with the chaos
and destruction that never came near you. Why,
how can you dare — " Once again, admirably,
she pulled herself up as she had done when she
spoke of the President. "I mustn't!" she de-

clared, half whispering, and then more clearly and
calmly, " I mustn't." And she shook her head as
if shaking something off. " Nor must you," she
finished, charmingly and quietly, with a smile.

" I will not," I assured her. She was truly
noble.

" But I did think that you understood us," she
said pensively.

" Miss La Heu, when you talked to me about
the President and the White House, I said that
you were hard to answer. Do you remember?"

" Perfectly. I said I was glad you found me so."

" You helped me to understand you then, and
now I want to be helped to further understanding. Last night I heard the 'Ode for the
Daughters of Dixie.' I had a bad time listening
to that."

" Do you presume to criticise it? Do we
criticise your Grand Army reunions, and your
'Marching through Georgia,' and your 'John
Brown's Body,' and your Arlington Museum?
Can we not be allowed to celebrate our heroes
and our glories and sing our songs?"

She had helped me already! Still, still, the
something I was groping for, the something which
had given me such pain during the ode, remained
undissolved, remained unanalyzed between us; I
still had to have it out with her, and the point
was that it had to be with her, and not simply
with myself alone. We must thrash out *together*
the way to an understanding; an agreement was
not in the least necessary — we could agree to
differ, for that matter, with perfect cordiality —
but an understanding we must reach. And as I

was thinking this my light increased, and I saw clearly the ultimate thing which lay at the bottom of my own feeling, and which had been strangely confusing me all along. This discovery was the key to the whole remainder of my talk; I never let go of it. The first thing it opened for me was that Eliza La Heu didn't understand *me*, which was quite natural, since I had only just this moment become clear to myself.

" Many of us," I began, " who have watched the soiling touch of politics make dirty one clean thing after another, would not be wholly desolated to learn that the Grand Army of the Republic had gone to another world to sing its songs and draw its pensions."

She looked astonished, and then she laughed. Down in the South here she was too far away to feel the vile uses to which present politics had turned past heroism.

" But," I continued, " we haven't any Daughters of the Union banded together and handing it down."

" It?" she echoed. " Well, if the deeds of your heroes are not a sacred trust to you, don't invite us, please, to resemble you."

I waited for more, and a little more came.

" We consider Northerners foreigners, you know."

Again I felt that hurt which hearing the ode had given me, but I now knew how I was going to take it, and where we were presently coming out; and I knew she didn't mean quite all that — didn't mean it every day, at least — and that my speech had driven her to saying it.

" No, Miss La Heu ; you don't consider Northerners, who understand you, to be foreigners."

" We have never met any of that sort."

(" Yes," I thought, " but you really want to.
Didn't you say you hoped I was one ?   Away
down deep there's a cry of kinship in you ; and
that you don't hear it, and that we don't hear it,
has been as much our fault as yours.   I see that
very well now, but I'm afraid to tell you so, yet.")

What I said was: " We're handing the ' sacred
trust ' down, I hope."

" I understood you to say you weren't."

" I said we were not handing ' it ' down."

I didn't wonder that irritation again moulded her
reply.   " You must excuse a daughter of Dixie if
she finds the words of a son of the Union beyond
her.   We haven't had so many advantages."

There she touched what I had thought over
during my wakeful hours : the tale of the ashes,
the desolate ashes!   The war had not prevented
my parents from sending me to school and college,
but here the old had seen the young grow up
starved of what their fathers had given them, and
the young had looked to the old and known their
stripped heritage.

" Miss La Heu," I said, " I could not tell you,
you would not wish me to tell you, what the sight
of Kings Port has made me feel.   But you will
let me say this : I have understood for a long
while about your old people, your old ladies, whose
faces are so fine and sad."

I paused, but she merely looked at me, and her
eyes were hard.

" And I may say this, too.   I thank you very

sincerely for bringing completely home to me
what I had begun to make out for myself. I hope
the Daughters of Dixie will go on singing of their
heroes."

I paused again, and now she looked away, out
of the window into Royal Street.

"Perhaps," I still continued, "you will hardly
believe me when I say that I have looked at your
monuments here with an emotion more poignant
even than that which Northern monuments raise
in me."

"Why?"

"Oh!" I exclaimed. "Need you have asked
that? The North won."

"You are quite dispassionate!" Her eyes were
always toward the window.

"That's *my* 'sacred trust.'"

It made her look at me. "Yours?"

"Not yours — yet! It would be yours if you
had won." I thought a slight change came in her
steady scrutiny. "And, Miss La Heu, it was
awful about the negro. It *is* awful. The young
North thinks so just as much as you do. Oh, we
shock our old people! We don't expect *them* to
change, but they mustn't expect us *not* to. And
even some of them have begun to whisper a little
doubtfully. But never mind them — here's the
negro. We can't kick him out. That plan is
childish. So, it's like two men having to live in
one house. The white man would keep the house
in repair, the black would let it rot. Well, the
black must take orders from the white. And it
will end so."

She was eager. "Slavery again, you think?"

"Oh, never! It was too injurious to ourselves. But something between slavery and equality." And I ended with a quotation: "'Patience, cousin, and shuffle the cards.'"

"You may call me cousin — this once — because you have been, really, quite nice — for a Northerner."

Now we had come to the place where she must understand me.

"Not a Northerner, Miss La Heu."

She became mocking. "Scarcely a Southerner, I presume?"

But I kept my smile and my directness. "No more a Southerner than a Northerner."

"Pray what, then?"

"An American."

She was silent.

"It's the 'sacred trust' — for me."

She was still silent.

"If my state seceded from the Union to-morrow, I should side with the Union against her."

She was frankly astonished now. "Would you really?" And I think some light about me began to reach her. A Northerner willing to side against a Northern state! I was very glad that I had found that phrase to make clear to her my American creed.

I proceeded. "I shall help to hand down all the glories and all the sadnesses; Lee's, Lincoln's, everybody's. But I shall not hand 'it' down."

This checked her.

"It's easy for *me*, you know," I hastily explained. "Nothing noble about it at all. But from noble people "— and I looked hard at her —" one expects, sooner or later, noble things."

She repressed something she had been going to reply.

" If ever I have children," I finished, "they shall know 'Dixie' and 'Yankee Doodle' by heart, and never know the difference. By that time I should think they might have a chance of hearing 'Yankee Doodle' in Kings Port."

Again she checked a rapid retort. " Well," she, after a pause, repeated, "you have been really quite nice."

" May I tell you what you have been? "

" Certainly not. Have you seen Mr. Mayrant to-day? "

" We have an engagement to walk this afternoon. May I go walking with you sometime? "

" May he, General? " A wagging tail knocked on the floor behind the counter. " General says that he will think about it. What makes you like Mr. Mayrant so much? "

This question struck me as an odd one; nor could I make out the import of the peculiar tone in which she put it. " Why, I should think everybody would like him — except, perhaps, his double victim."

" Double? "

" Yes, first of his fist and then of — of his hand! "

But she didn't respond.

" Of his hand — his poker hand," I explained.

" Poker hand? " She remained honestly vague.

It rejoiced me to be the first to tell her. " You haven't heard of Master John's last performance?

Well, finding himself forced by that immeasurable
old Aunt Josephine of yours to shake hands, he
shook 'em all right, but he took thirty dollars
away as a little set-off for his pious docility."

" Oh ! " she murmured, overwhelmed with astonishment. Then she broke into one of her delicious peals of laughter.

" Anybody," I said, " likes a boy who plays a
hand — and a fist — to that tune." I continued
to say a number of commendatory words about
young John, while her sparkling eyes rested upon
me. But even as I talked I grew aware that
these eyes were not sparkling, were starry rather,
and distant, and that she was not hearing what
I said ; so I stopped abruptly, and at the stopping she spoke, like a person waking up.

" Oh, yes ! Certainly he can take care of himself. Why not ? "

" Rather creditable, don't you think ? "

" Creditable ? "

" Considering his aunts and everything."

She became haughty on the instant. " Upon
my word ! And do you suppose the women of
South Carolina don't wish their men to be men ?
Why " — she returned to mirth and that arch
mockery which was her special charm — " we
South Carolina women consider virtue *our* business, and we don't expect the men to meddle
with it ! "

" Primal, perpetual, necessary ! " I cried. " When
that division gets blurred, society is doomed. Are
you sure John can take care of himself *every* way?"

" I have other things than Mr. Mayrant to think
about." She said this quite sharply.

It surprised me. "To be sure," I assented.
" But didn't you once tell me that you thought he
was simple?"

She opened her ledger.   "It's a great honor to
have one's words so well remembered."

I was still at a loss. "Anyhow, the wedding is
postponed," I continued; "and the cake. Of
course one can't help wondering how it's all coming out."

She was now working at her ledger, bending
her head over it.   "Have you ever met Miss
Rieppe?"   She inquired this with a sort of wonderful softness — which I was to hear again upon
a still more memorable occasion.

"Never," I answered, "but there's nobody at
present living whom I long to see so much."

She wrote on for a little while before saying,
with her pencil steadily busy, "Why?"

"Why? Don't you? After all this fuss?"

" Oh, certainly," she drawled. "She is so much
admired — by Northerners."

" I do hope John is able to take care of himself!"
I purposely repeated.

" Take care of *your*self!" she laughed angrily
over her ledger.

"Me? Why? I understand you less and
less!"

"Very likely."

"Why, I want to help him!" I protested. " I
don't want him to marry her. Oh, by the way,
do you happen to know what it is that she is
coming here to see for herself?"

In a moment her ledger was left, and she was
looking at me straight. Coming? When?

"Soon. In an automobile. To see something for herself."

She pondered for quite a long moment; then her eyes returned, searchingly, to me. "You didn't make that up?"

I laughed, and explained. "Some of them, at any rate," I finished, "know what she's coming for. They were rather queer about it, I thought."

She pondered again. I noticed that she had deeply flushed, and that the flush was leaving her. Then she fixed her eyes on me once more. "They wouldn't tell you?"

"I think that they came inadvertently near it, once or twice, and remembered just in time that I didn't know about it."

"But since you *do* know pretty much about it!" she laughed.

I shook my head. "There's something else, something that's turned up; the sort of thing that upsets calculations. And I merely hoped that you'd know."

On those last words of mine she gave me quite an extraordinary look, and then, as if satisfied with what she saw in my face: —

"They don't talk to me."

It was an assurance, it was true, it had the ring of truth, that evident genuineness which a piece of real confidence always possesses; she meant me to know that we were in the same boat of ignorance to-day. And yet, as I rose from my lunch and came forward to settle for it, I was aware of some sense of defeat, of having been held off just as the ladies on High Walk had held me off.

"Well," I sighed, "I pin my faith to the aunt who says he'll never marry her."

Miss La Heu had no more to say upon the subject. "Haven't you forgotten something?" she inquired gayly; and, as I turned to see what I had left behind — "I mean, you had no Lady Baltimore to-day."

"I clean forgot it!"

"No loss. It is very stale; and to-morrow I shall have a fresh supply ready."

As I departed through the door I was conscious of her eyes following me, and that she had spoken of Lady Baltimore precisely because she was thinking of something else.

XIV

THE REPLACERS

SHE had been strange, perceptibly strange, had Eliza La Heu; that was the most which I could make out of it. I had angered her in some manner wholly beyond my intention or understanding and not all at one fixed point in our talk; her irritation had come out and gone in again in spots all along the colloquy, and it had been a displeasure wholly apart from that indignation which had flashed up in her over the negro question. This, indeed, I understood well enough, and admired her for, and admired still more her gallant control of it; as for the other, I gave it up.

A sense of guilt — a very slight one, to be sure — dispersed my speculations when I was preparing for dinner, and Aunt Carola's postscript, open upon my writing-table, reminded me that I had never asked Miss La Heu about the Bombos. Well, the Bombos could keep! And I descended to dinner a little late (as too often) to feel instantly in the air that they had been talking about me. I doubt if any company in the world, from the Greeks down through Machiavelli to the present moment, has ever been of a subtlety adequate to conceal from an observant person entering a room the fact that he has been the subject of their conversation. This company, at any rate, did not conceal it from me. Not even when the up-country bride astutely greeted me with: —

"Why, we were just speaking of you! We were just saying it would be a perfect shame if you missed those flowers at Live Oaks." And, at this, various of the guests assured me that another storm would finish them; upon which I assured every one that to-morrow should see me embark upon the Live Oaks excursion boat, knowing quite well in my heart that some decidedly different question concerning me had been hastily dropped upon my appearance at the door. It poked up its little concealed head, did this question, when the bride said later to me, with immense archness: —

"How any gentleman can help falling just daid in love with that lovely young girl at the Exchange, I don't see!"

"But I haven't helped it!" I immediately exclaimed.

"Oh!" declared the bride with unerring perception, "that just shows he hasn't been smitten at all! Well, I'd be ashamed, if I was a single gentleman." And while I brought forth additional phrases concerning the distracted state of my heart, she looked at me with large, limpid eyes. "Anybody could tell you're not afraid of a rival," was her resulting comment; upon which several of the et ceteras laughed more than seemed to me appropriate.

I left them all free again to say what they pleased; for John Mayrant called for me to go upon our walk while we were still seated at table,

and at table they remained after I had excused
myself.

The bruise over John's left eye was fading out,
but traces of his spiritual battle were deepening.
During the visit which he had paid (under com-
pulsion, I am sure) to Juno at our boarding-house
in company with Miss Josephine St. Michael, his
recent financial triumph at the bedside had filled
his face with diabolic elation as he confronted his
victim's enraged but checkmated aunt; when to
the thinly veiled venom of her inquiry as to a
bridegroom's health he had retorted with venom
as thinly veiled that he was feeling better that
night than for many weeks, he had looked better,
too; the ladies had exclaimed after his departure
what a handsome young man he was, and Juno
had remarked how fervently she trusted that marriage might cure him of his deplorable tendencies.
But to-day his vitality had sagged off beneath the
weight of his preoccupation: it looked to me as
if, by a day or two more, the boy's face might be
grown haggard.

Whether by intention, or, as is more likely, by
the perfectly natural and spontaneous working of
his nature, he speedily made it plain to me that
our relation, our acquaintance, had progressed to
a stage more friendly and confidential. He did
not reveal this by imparting any confidence to me;
far from it; it was his silence that indicated the
ease he had come to feel in my company. Upon
our last memorable interview he had embarked at
once upon a hasty yet evidently predetermined
course of talk, because he feared that I might
touch upon subjects which he wished excluded

from all discussion between us; to-day he embarked upon nothing, made no conventional effort of any sort, but walked beside me, content with my mere society; if it should happen that either of us found a thought worth expressing aloud, good! and if this should not happen, why, good also! And so we walked mutely and agreeably together for a long while. The thought which was growing clear in my mind, and which was decidedly worthy of expression, was also unluckily one which his new reliance upon my discretion completely forbade my uttering in even the most shadowy manner; but it was a conviction which Miss Josephine St. Michael should have been quick to force upon him for his good. Quite apart from selfish reasons, he had no right to marry a girl whom he had ceased to care for. The code which held a "gentleman" to his plighted troth in such a case did more injury to the "lady" than any "jilting" could possibly do. Never until now had I thought this out so lucidly, and I was determined that time and my own tact should assuredly help me find a way to say it to him, if he continued in his present course.

"Daddy Ben says you can't be a real Northerner."

This was his first observation, and I think that we must have walked a mile before he made it.

"Because I pounded a negro? Of course, he retains your Southern *ante-bellum* mythical notion of Northerners — all of us willing to have them marry our sisters. Well, there's a lady at our boarding-house who says you are a real gambler."

The impish look came curling round his lips, but for a moment only, and it was gone.

" That shook Daddy Ben up a good deal."

" Having his grandson do it, do you mean ? "

" Oh, he's used to his grandson ! Grandsons in that race might just as well be dogs for all they know or care about their progenitors. Yet Daddy Ben spent his savings on educating Charles Cotesworth and two more — but not one of them will give the old man a house to-day. If ever I have a home — " John stopped himself, and our silence was no longer easy ; our unspoken thoughts looked out of our eyes so that they could not meet. Yet no one, unless directly invited by him, had the right to say to him what I was thinking, except some near relative. Therefore, to relieve this silence which had ceased to be agreeable, I talked about Daddy Ben and his grandsons, and negro voting, and the huge lie of " equality " which our lips vociferate and our lives daily disprove. This took us comfortably away from weddings and cakes into the subject of lynching, my violent condemnation of which surprised him ; for our discussion had led us over a wide field, and one fertile in well-known disputes of the evergreen sort, conducted by the North mostly with more theory than experience, and by the South mostly with more heat than light ; whereas, between John and me, I may say that our amiability was surpassed only by our intelligence ! Each allowed for the other's standpoint, and both met in many views : he would have voted against the last national Democratic ticket but for the Republican upholding of negro equality, while I assured him that such stupid and criminal upholding was on the wane. He informed me that he did not believe the pure-

blooded African would ever be capable of taking
the intellectual side of the white man's civilization,
and I informed him that we must patiently face
this probability, and teach the African whatever
he could profitably learn and no more; and each
of us agreed with the other. I think that we were
at one, save for the fact that I was, after all, a
Northerner — and that is a blemish which nobody
in Kings Port can quite get over. John, therefore, was unprepared for my wholesale denuncia-
tion of lynching.

"With your clear view of the negro," he
explained.

"My dear man, it's my clear view of the white!
It's the white, the American citizen, the 'hope of
humanity,' as he enjoys being called, who, after
our English-speaking race has abolished public
executions, degenerates back to the Stone Age.
It's upon him that lynching works the true injury."

"They're nothing but animals," he muttered.

"Would you treat an animal in that way?" I
inquired.

He persisted. "You'd do it yourself if you had
to suffer from them."

"Very probably. Is that an answer? What
I'd never do would be to make a show, an entertainment, a circus, out of it, run excursion trains
to see it — come, should you like your sister to
buy tickets for a lynching?"

This brought him up rather short. "I should
never take part myself," he presently stated, "unless it were immediate personal vengeance."

"Few brothers or husbands would blame you!"
I returned. "It would be hard to wait for the

law. But let no community which treats it as a public spectacle presume to call itself civilized."

He gave a perplexed smile, shaking his head over it. "Sometimes I think civilization costs —"

"Civilization costs all you've got!" I cried.

"More than *I've* got!" he declared. "I'm mortal tired of civilization."

"Ah, yes! What male creature is not? And neither of us will live quite long enough to see the smash-up of our own."

"Aren't you sometimes inconsistent?" he inquired, laughing.

"I hope so," I returned. "Consistency is a form of death. The dead are the only perfectly consistent people."

"And sometimes you sound like a Socialist," he pursued, still laughing.

"Never!" I shouted. "Don't class me with those untrained puppies of thought. And you'll generally observe," I added, "that the more nobly a Socialist vaporizes about the rights of humanity, the more wives and children he has abandoned penniless along the trail of his life."

He was livelier than ever at this. "What date have you fixed for the smash-up of our present civilization?"

"Why fix dates? Is it not diversion enough to watch, and step handsomely through one's own part, with always a good sleeve to laugh in?"

Pensiveness returned upon him. "I shall be able to step through my own part, I think." He paused, and I was wondering secretly, "Does that include the wedding?" when he continued: "What's there to laugh at?"

"Why, our imperishable selves! For instance :
we swear by universal suffrage. Well, sows' ears
are an invaluable thing in their place, on the head
of the animal; but send them to make your laws,
and what happens? Bribery, naturally. The silk
purse buys the sow's ear. We swear by Christianity, but dishonesty is our present religion.
That little phrase 'In God We Trust' is about
as true as the silver dollar it's stamped on — worth
some thirty-nine cents. We get awfully serious
about whether or no good can come of evil, when
every sky-scraping thief of finance is helping hospitals with one hand while the other's in my
pocket; and good and evil attend each other, lead
to each other, are such Siamese twins that if
separated they would both die. We make phrases
about peace, pity, and brotherhood, while every
nation stands prepared for shipwreck and for the
sinking plank to which two are clinging and the
stronger pushes the weaker into the flood and
thus floats safe. Why, the old apple of wisdom,
which Adam and Eve swallowed and thus lost
their innocence, was a gentle nursery drug compared with the new apple of competition, which,
as soon as chewed, instantly transforms the heart
into a second brain. But why worry, when nothing is final? Haven't you and I, for instance,
lamented the present rottenness of· smart society?
Why, when kings by the name of George sat on
the throne of England, society was just as drunken,
just as dissolute! Then a decent queen came,
and society behaved itself; and now, here we come
round again to the Georges, only with the name
changed! There's nothing final. So, when things

are as you don't like them, remember that and
bear them; and when they're as you do like them,
remember it and make the most of them — and
keep a good sleeve handy!"

"Have you got any creed at all?" he demanded.

"Certainly; but I don't live up to it."

"That's not expected. May I ask what it is?"

"It's in Latin."

"Well, I can probably bear it. Aunt Eliza had
a classical tutor for me."

I always relish a chance to recite my favorite
poet, and I began accordingly: —

> "Lætus in præsens animus quod ultra est
> Oderit curare et — "

"I know that one!" he exclaimed, interrupting
me. "The tutor made me put it into English
verse. I had the severest sort of a time. I ran
away from it twice to a deer-hunt." And he, in
his turn, recited: —

> "Who hails each present hour with zest
> Hates fretting what may be the rest,
> Makes bitter sweet with lazy jest;
> Naught is in every portion blest."

I complimented him, in spite of my slight
annoyance at being deprived by him of the chance
to declaim Latin poetry, which is an exercise that
I approve and enjoy; but of course, to go on with
it, after he had intervened with his translation,
would have been flat.

"You have written good English, and very
close to the Latin, too," I told him, "particularly
in the last line." And I picked up from the bridge

Where glimpses of cabin and plantation serve to increase the silence and the soft, mysterious loneliness

which we were crossing, an oyster-shell, and sent it skimming over the smooth water that stretched between the low shores, wide, blue, and vacant.

" I suppose you wonder why we call this the New Bridge,' " he remarked.

" I did wonder when I first came," I replied.

He smiled. " You're getting used to us ! "

This long structure wore, in truth, no appearance of yesterday. It was newer than the " New Bridge " which it had replaced some fifteen years ago, and which for forty years had borne the same title. Spanning the broad river upon a legion of piles, this wooden causeway lies low against the face of the water, joining the town with a serene and pensive country of pines and live oaks and level opens, where glimpses of cabin and plantation serve to increase the silence and the soft, mysterious loneliness. Into this the road from the bridge goes straight and among the purple vagueness gently dissolves away.

We watched a slow, deep-laden boat sliding down toward the draw, across which we made our way, and drew near the further end of the bridge. The straight avenue of the road in front of us took my eyes down its quiet vista, until they were fixed suddenly by an alien object, a growing dot, accompanied by dust, whence came the small, distorted honks of an automobile. These fat, importunate sounds redoubled as the machine rushed toward the bridge, growing up to its full staring, brazen dimensions. Six or seven figures sat in it, all of the same dusty, shrouded likeness, their big glass eyes and their masked mouths suggesting some fabled, unearthly race, a family of replete and bilious ogres ; so that as they flew honking by us I called out to John : —

" Behold the yellow rich ! " and then remembered that his Hortense probably sat among them.

The honks redoubled, and we turned to see that the drawbridge had no thought of waiting for them. We also saw a bewildered curly white dog and a young girl, who called despairingly to him as he disappeared beneath the automobile. The engine of murder could not, as is usual, proceed upon its way, honking, for the drawbridge was visibly swinging open to admit the passage of the boat. When John and I had run back near enough to become ourselves a part of the incident, the white dog lay still behind the stationary automobile, whose passengers were craning their muffled necks and glass eyes to see what they had done, while one of their number had got out, and was stooping to examine if the machine had sustained any injuries. The young girl, with a face of anguish, was calling the dog's name as she hastened toward him, and her voice aroused him: he lifted his head, got on his legs, and walked over to her, which action on his part brought from the automobile a penetrating female voice : —

"Well, he's in better luck than that Savannah dog!"

But General was not in luck. He lay quietly down at the feet of his mistress and we soon knew that life had passed from his faithful body. The first stroke of grief, dealt her in such cruel and sudden form, overbore the poor girl's pride and reserve; she made no attempt to remember or heed surroundings, but kneeling and placing her arms about the neck of her dead servant, she spoke piteously aloud: —

"And I raised him, I raised him from a puppy!"

The female voice, at this, addressed the traveller who was examining the automobile: "Charley, a five or a ten spot is what her feelings need."

The obedient and munificent Charley straightened up from his stooping among the mechanical entrails, dexterously produced money, and advanced with the selected bill held out politely in his hand, while the glass eyes and the masks peered down at the performance. Eliza La Heu had perceived none of this, for she was intent upon General; nor had John Mayrant, who had approached her with the purpose of coming to her aid. But when Charley, quite at hand, began to speak words which were instantly obliterated from my memory by what happened, the young girl realized his intention and straightened stiffly, while John, with the rapidity of light, snatched the extended bill from Charley's hand, and tearing it in four pieces, threw it in his face.

A foreign voice cackled from the automobile: "Oh la la! il a du panache!"

But Charley now disclosed himself to be a true man of the world — the financial world — by picking the pieces out of the mud; and, while he wiped them and enclosed them in his handkerchief and with perfect dignity returned them to his pocket, he remarked simply, with a shrug: "As you please." His accent also was ever so little foreign — that New York downtown foreign, of the second generation, which stamps so many of our bankers.

The female now leaned from her seat, and

with the tone of setting the whole thing right, explained: "We had no idea it was a lady."

"Doubtless you're not accustomed to their appearance," said John to Charley.

I don't know what Charley would have done about this; for while the completely foreign voice was delightedly whispering, "Toujours le panache!" a new, deep, and altogether different female voice exclaimed:—

"Why, John, it's you!"

So that was Hortense, then! That rich and quiet utterance was hers, a schooled and studied management of speech. I found myself surprised, and I knew directly why; that word of one of the old ladies, "I consider that she looks like a steel wasp," had implanted in me some definite anticipations to which the voice certainly did not correspond. How fervently I desired that she would lift her thick veil, while John, with hat in hand, was greeting her, and being presented to her companions! Why she had not spoken to John sooner was of course a recondite question, and beyond my power to determine with merely the given situation to guide me. Hadn't she recognized him before? Had her thick veil, and his position, and the general slight flurry of the misadventure, intercepted recognition until she heard his voice when he addressed Charley? Or had she known her lover at once, and rapidly decided that the moment was an unpropitious one for a first meeting after absence, and that she would pass on to Kings Port unrevealed, but then had found this plan become impossible through the collision between Charley and John? It was

not until certain incidents of the days following
brought Miss Rieppe's nature a good deal further
home to me, that a third interpretation of her
delay in speaking to John dawned upon my mind;
that I was also måde aware how a woman's understanding of the words "Steel wasp," when applied
by her to one of her own sex, may differ widely
from a man's understanding of them; and that
Miss Rieppe, through her thick veil, saw from her
seat in the automobile something which my own
unencumbered vision had by no means detected.

But now, here on the bridge, even her outward
appearance was as shrouded as her inward qualities — save such as might be audible in that voice,
as her skilful, well-placed speeches to one and
the other of the company tided over and carried
off into ease this uneasy moment. All men, at
such a voice, have pricked up their ears since the
beginning; there was much woman in it; each
slow, schooled syllable called its challenge to
questing man. But I got no chance to look in
the eye that went with that voice; she took all
the advantages which her veil gave her; and how
well she used them I was to learn later.

In the general smoothing-out process which she
was so capably effecting, her attention was about to
reach me, when my name was suddenly called out
from behind her. It was Beverly Rodgers, that
accomplished and inveterate bachelor of fashion.
Ten years before, when I had seen much of him,
he had been more particular in his company, frequently declaring in his genial, irresponsible way
that New York society was going to the devil.
But many tempting dances on the land, and cruises

on the water, had taken him deep among our
lower classes that have boiled up from the bottom
with their millions — and besides, there would be
nothing to marvel at in Beverly's presence in any
company that should include Hortense Rieppe, if
she carried out the promise of her voice.

Beverly was his customary, charming, effusive
self, coming out of the automobile to me with his
" By Jove, old man," and his " Who'd have thought
it, old fellow? " and sprinkling urbane little drops
of jocosity over us collectively, as the garden
water-turning apparatus sprinkles a lawn. His
knowing me, and the way he brought it out, and
even the tumbling into the road of a few wraps
and chattels of travel as he descended from the
automobile, and the necessity of picking these up
and handing them back with delightful little
jocular apologies, such as, " By Jove, what a lout I
am," all this helped the meeting on prodigiously,
and got us gratefully away from the disconcert-
ing incident of the torn money. Charley was
helpful, too; you would never have supposed from
the polite small-talk which he was now offering to
John Mayrant that he had within some three
minutes received the equivalent of a slap across
the eyes from that youth, and carried the soiled
consequences in his pocket. And such a thing is
it to be a true man of the world of finance, that
upon the arrival now of a second automobile, also
his property, and containing a set of maids and
valets, and also some live dogs sitting up, covered
with glass eyes and wrappings like their owners,
munificent Charley at once offered the dead dog
and his mistress a place in it, and begged she

would let it take her wherever she wished to go.
Everybody exclaimed copiously and condolingly
over the unfortunate occurrence. What a fine
animal he was, to be sure! What breed was he?
Of course, he wasn't used to automobiles! Was
it quite certain that he was dead? Quel dom-
mage! And Charley would be so happy to replace him.

And how was Eliza La Heu bearing herself
amid these murmurously chattered infelicities?
She was listening with composure to the murmurs
of Hortense Rieppe, more felicitous, no doubt.
Miss Rieppe, through her veil, was particularly
devoting herself to Miss La Heu. I could not
hear what she said; the little chorus of condolence
and suggestion intercepted all save her tone, and
that, indeed, coherently sustained its measured
cadence through the texture of fragments uttered
by Charley and the others. Eliza La Heu had
now got herself altogether in hand, and, saving
her pale cheeks, no sign betrayed that the young
girl's feelings had been so recently too strong for
her. To these strangers, ignorant of her usual
manner, her present strange quietness may very
well have been accepted as her habit.

" Thank you," she replied to munificent Charley's
offer that she would use his second automobile.
She managed to make her polite words cut like a
scythe. " I should crowd it."

" But they shall get out and walk; it will be
good for them," said Charley, indicating the valets
and maids, and possibly the dogs, too.

Beverly Rodgers did much better than Charley.
With a charming gesture and bow, he offered his

own seat in the first automobile. "I am going
to walk in any case," he assured her.

"One gentleman among them," I heard John
Mayrant mutter behind me.

Miss La Heu declined, the chorus urged, but
Beverly (who was indeed a gentleman, every inch
of him) shook his head imperceptibly at Charley;
and while the little exclamations — "Do come!
So much more comfortable! So nice to see more
of you!" — dropped away, Miss La Heu had settled her problem quite simply for herself. A little
procession of vehicles, townward bound, had gathered on the bridge, waiting until the closing of the
draw should allow them to continue upon their
way. From these most of the occupants had descended, and were staring with avidity at us all;
the great glass eyes and the great refulgent cars
held them in timidity and fascination, and the
poor lifeless white body of General, stretched
beside the way, heightened the hypnotic mystery;
one or two of the boldest had touched him, and
found no outward injury upon him; and this had
sent their eyes back to the automobile with increased awe. Eliza La Heu summoned one of
the onlookers, an old negro; at some word she
said to him he hurried back and returned, leading
his horse and empty cart, and General was lifted
into this. The girl took her seat beside the old
driver.

"No," she said to John Mayrant, "certainly
not."

I wondered at the needless severity with which
she declined his offer to accompany her and help
her.

He stood by the wheel of the cart, looking up at her and protesting, and I joined him.

"Thank you," she returned, "I need no one. You will both oblige me by saying no more about it."

"John!" It was the slow, well-calculated utterance of Hortense Rieppe. Did I hear in it the caressing note of love?

John turned.

The draw had swung to, the mast and sail of the vessel were separating away from the bridge with a stealthy motion, men with iron bars were at work fastening the draw secure, and horses' hoofs knocked nervously upon the wooden flooring as the internal churning of the automobiles burst upon their innocent ears.

"John, if Mr. Rodgers is really not going with us —"

Thus Hortense; and at that Miss La Heu:—

"Why do you keep them waiting?" There was no caress in *that* note! It was polished granite.

He looked up at her on her high seat by the extremely dilapidated negro, and then he walked forward and took his place beside his veiled fiancée, among the glass eyes. A hiss of sharp noise spurted from the automobiles, horses danced, and then, smoothly, the two huge engines were gone with their cargo of large, distorted shapes, leaving behind them — quite as our present epoch will leave behind it — a trail of power, of ingenuity, of ruthlessness, and a bad smell.

"Hold hard, old boy!" chuckled Beverly, to whom I communicated this sentiment. "How do

you know the stink of one generation does not
become the perfume of the next?" Beverly, when
he troubled to put a thing at all (which was seldom
— for he kept his quite good brains well-nigh per-
petually turned out to grass — or rather to grass-
widows) always put it well, and with a bracing
vocabulary. "Hullo!" he now exclaimed, and
walked out into the middle of the roadway, where
he picked up a parasol. "Kitty will be in a jolly
old stew. None of its expensive bones broken,
however." And then he hailed me by a name of
our youth. "What are you doing down here, you
old sourbelly?"

"Watching you sun yourself on the fat cushions
of the yellow rich."

"Oh, shucks, old man, they're not so yellow!"

"Charley strikes me as yellower than his own
gold."

"Charley's not a bad little sort. Of course, he
needs coaching a bit here and there — just now,
for instance, when he didn't see that that girl
wouldn't think of riding in the machine that had
just killed her dog. By Jove, give that girl a year
in civilization and she'd do! Who was the young
fire-eater?"

"Fire-eater! He's a lot more decent than you
or I."

"But that's saying so little, dear boy!"

"Seriously, Beverly."

"Oh, hang it with your 'seriously'! Well, then,
seriously, melodrama was the correct ticket and
all that in 1840, but we've outgrown it; it's
devilish *démodé* to chuck things in people's
faces."

" I'm not sorry John Mayrant did it! " I brought
out his name with due emphasis.

" All the same," Beverly was beginning, when
the automobile returned rapidly upon us, and,
guessing the cause of this, he waved the parasol.
Charley descended to get it — an unnecessary act,
prompted, I suppose, by the sudden relief of finding that it was not lost.

He made his thanks marked.   " It is my sister's,"
he concluded, to me, by way of explanation, in his
slightly foreign accent.   " It is not much, but it
has got some stones and things in the handle."

We were favored with a bow from the veiled
Hortense, shrill thanks from Kitty, and the car,
turning, again left us in a moment.

" You've got a Frenchman along," I said.

" Little Gazza," Beverly returned.   " Italian;
though from his morals you'd never guess he
wasn't Parisian.   Great people in Rome.   Hereditary right to do something in the presence of the
Pope — or not to do it, I forget which.   Not a bit
of a bad little sort, Gazza.   He has just sold a lot
of old furniture — Renaissance — Lorenzo du Bor-
gia — that sort of jolly old truck — to Bohm, you
know."

I didn't know.

" Oh, yes, you do, old boy.   Harry Bohm, of
Bohm & Cohn.   Everybody knows Bohm, and
we'll all be knowing Cohn by next year.   Gazza
has sold *him* a lot of furniture, too.   Bohm's from
Pittsfield, or South Lee, or East Canaan, or West
Stockbridge, or some of those other back-country
cider presses that squirt some of the hardest propo-
sitions into Wall Street.   He's just back from buy-

ing a railroad, and four or five mines in Mexico. Bohm represents Christianity in the firm. At Newport they call him the military attaché to Jerusalem. He's the big chap that sat behind me in the car. He'll marry Kitty as soon as she can get her divorce. Bohm's a jolly old sort — and I tell you, you old sourbelly, you're letting this Southern moss grow over you a bit. Hey? What? 'Yellow rich' isn't half bad, and I'll say it myself, and pretend it's mine ; but hang it, old man, their children won't be worse than lemon-colored, and the grandchildren will be white!"

"Just in time," I exclaimed, "to take a back seat with their evaporated fortunes!"

Beverly chuckled. "Well, if they do evaporate, there will be new ones. Now don't walk along making Mayflower eyes at me. I'm no Puritan, and my people have had a front seat since pretty early in the game, which I'm holding on to, you know. And by Jove, old man, I tell you, if you wish to hold on nowadays, you can't be drawing lines! If you don't want to see yourself jolly well replaced, you must fall in with the replacers. Our blooming old republic is merely the quickest process of endless replacing yet discovered, and you take my tip, and back the replacers! That's where Miss Rieppe, for all her Kings Port traditions, shows sense."

I turned square on him. "Then she has broken it?"

"Broken what?"

"Her engagement to John Mayrant. You mean to say that you didn't —?"

"See here, old man. Seriously. The fire-eater?"

I was so very much bewildered that I merely
stared at Beverly Rodgers. Of course, I might
have known that Miss Rieppe would not feel the
need of announcing to her rich Northern friends
an engagement which she had fallen into the
habit of postponing.

But Beverly had a better right to be taken
aback. " I suppose you must have some reason
for your remark," he said.

" You don't mean that *you're* engaged to her? "
I shot out.

" Me? With my poor little fifteen thousand a
year? Consider, dear boy! Oh, no, we're merely
playing at it, she and I. She's a good player.
But Charley —"

" *He* is? " I shouted.

" I don't know, old man, and I don't think he
knows — yet."

" Beverly," said I, " let me tell you." And I
told him.

After he had got himself adjusted to the
novelty of it he began to take it with a series of
thoughtful chuckles.

Into these I dropped with : " Where's her
father, anyhow? " I began to feel, fantastically,
that she mightn't have a father.

" He stopped in Savannah," Beverly answered.
" He's coming over by the train. Kitty — Charley's sister, Mrs. Bleecker — did the chaperoning
for us."

" Very expertly, I should guess," I said.

" Perfectly; invisibly," said Beverly. And he
returned to his thoughts and his chuckles.

" After all, it's simple," he presently remarked.

" Doesn't that depend on what she's here for ? "

" Oh, to break it."

" Why come for that ? "

He took another turn among his cogitations. I took a number of turns among my own, but it was merely walking round and round in a circle.

" When will she announce it, then ? " he demanded.

" Ah ! " I murmured. " You said she was a good player."

" But a fire-eater ! " he resumed. " For her. Oh, hang it ! She'll let him go ! "

" Then why hasn't she ? "

He hesitated. " Well, of course her game could be spoiled by — "

His speech died away into more cogitation, and I had to ask him what he meant.

" By love getting into it somewhere."

We walked on through Worship Street, which we had reached some while since, and the chief features of which I mechanically pointed out to him.

" Jolly old church, that," said Beverly, as we reached my favorite corner and brick wall. " Well, I'll not announce it ! " he murmured gallantly.

" My dear man," I said, " Kings Port will do all the announcing for you to-morrow."

XV

WHAT SHE CAME TO SEE

BUT in this matter my prognostication was thoroughly at fault; yet surely, knowing Kings Port's sovereign habit, as I had had good cause to know it, I was scarce beyond reasonable bounds in supposing that the arrival of Miss Rieppe would heat up some very general and very audible talk about this approaching marriage, against which the prejudices of the town were set in such compact array. I have several times mentioned that Kings Port, to my sense, was buzzing over John Mayrant's affairs; buzzing in the open, where one could hear it, and buzzing behind closed doors, where one could somehow feel it; I can only say that henceforth this buzzing ceased, dropped wholly away, as if Gossip were watching so hard that she forgot to talk, giving place to a great stillness in her kingdom. Such occasional words as were uttered sounded oddly and egregiously clear in the new-established void.

The first of these words sounded, indeed, quite enormous, issuing as it did from Juno's lips at our breakfast-table, when yesterday's meeting on the New Bridge was investing my mind with many thoughts. She addressed me in one of her favorite tones (I have met it, thank God! but in two or

three other cases during my whole experience),
which always somehow conveyed to you that you
were personally to blame for what she was going
to tell you.

"I suppose you know that your friend, Mr.
Mayrant, has resigned from the Custom House?"

I was, of course, careful not to give Juno the
pleasure of seeing that she had surprised me. I
bowed, and continued in silence to sip a little
coffee; then, setting my coffee down, I observed
that it would be some few days yet before the
resignation could take effect; and, noticing that
Juno was getting ready some new remark, I
branched off and spoke to her of my excursion up
the river this morning to see the azaleas in the
gardens at Live Oaks.

"How lucky the weather is so magnificent!" I
exclaimed.

"I shall be interested to hear," said Juno,
"what explanation he finds to give Miss Josephine
for his disrespectful holding out against her, and
his immediate yielding to Miss Rieppe."

Here I deemed it safe to ask her, was she quite
sure it had been at the instance of Miss Rieppe
that John had resigned?

"It follows suspiciously close upon her arrival,"
stated Juno. She might have been speaking of a
murder. "And how he expects to support a wife
now — well, that is no affair of mine," Juno concluded, with a washing-her-hands-of-it air, as if up
to this point she had always done her best for the
wilful boy. She had blamed him savagely for
not resigning, and now she was blaming him
because he had resigned; and I ate my breakfast

in much entertainment over this female acrobat
in censure.

No more was said; I think that my manner of
taking Juno's news had been perfectly successful
in disappointing her. John's resignation, if it had
really occurred, did certainly follow very close
upon the arrival of Hortense; but I had spoken
one true thought in intimating that I doubted if
it was due to the influence of Miss Rieppe. It
seemed to me to the highest degree unlikely that
the boy in his present state of feeling would do
anything he did not wish to do because his lady-
love happened to wish it — except marry her!
There was apparently no doubt that he would do
that. Did she want him, poverty and all? Was
she, even now, with eyes open, deliberately taking
her last farewell days of automobiles and of steam
yachts? That voice of hers, that rich summons,
with its quiet certainty of power, sounded in my
memory. "John," she had called to him from the
automobile; and thus John had gone away in it,
wedged in among Charley and the fat cushions
and all the money and glass eyes. And now he
had resigned from the Custom House! Yes, that
was, whatever it signified, truly amazing — if true.

So I continued to ponder quite uselessly, until
the up-country bride aroused me. She, it appeared,
had been greatly carried away by the beauty of
Live Oaks, and was making her David take her
there again this morning; and she was asking me
didn't I hope we shouldn't get stuck? The people had got stuck yesterday, three whole hours,
right on a bank in the river; and wasn't it a sin
and a shame to run a boat with ever so many

passengers aground? By the doctrine of chances, I informed her, we had every right to hope for better luck to-day; and, with the assurance of how much my felicity was increased by the prospect of having her and David as company during the expedition, I betook myself meanwhile to my own affairs, which meant chiefly a call at the Exchange to inquire for Eliza La Heu, and a visit to the post-office before starting upon a several hours' absence.

A few steps from our front door I came upon John Mayrant, and saw at once too plainly that no ease had come to his spirit during the hours since the bridge. He was just emerging from an adjacent house.

"And have you resigned?" I asked him.

"Yes. That's done. You haven't seen Miss Rieppe this morning?"

"Why, she's surely not boarding with Mrs. Trevise?"

"No; stopping here with her old friend, Mrs. Cornerly." He indicated the door he had come from. "Of course, you wouldn't be likely to see her pass!" And with that he was gone.

That he was greatly stirred up by something there could be no doubt; never before had I seen him so abrupt; it seemed clear that anger had taken the place of despondency, or whatever had been his previous mood; and by the time I reached the post-office I had already imagined and dismissed the absurd theory that John was jealous of Charley, had resigned from the Custom House as a first step toward breaking his engagement, and had rung Mrs. Cornerly's

bell at this early hour with the purpose of informing his lady-love that all was over between them.
Jealousy would not be likely to produce this
set of manifestations in young, foolish John; and
I may say here at once, what I somewhat later
learned, that the boy had come with precisely the
opposite purpose, namely, to repeat and reënforce
his steadfast constancy, and that it was something
far removed from jealousy which had spurred him
to this.

I found the girl behind the counter at her post,
grateful to me for coming to ask how she was after
the shock of yesterday, but unwilling to speak of
it at all; all which she expressed by her charming
manner, and by the other subjects she chose for
conversation, and especially by the way in which
she held out her hand when I took my leave.

Near the post-office I was hailed by Beverly
Rodgers, who proclaimed to me at once a comic
but genuine distress. He had already walked, he
said (and it was but half-past nine o'clock, as he
bitterly bade me observe on the church dial), more
miles in search of a drink than his unarithmetical
brain had the skill to compute. And he con-
founded such a town heartily; he should return
as soon as possible to Charley's yacht, where there
was civilization, and where he had spent the night.
During his search he had at length come to a door
of promising appearance, and gone in there, and
they had explained to him that it was a dispensary. A beastly arrangement. What was the
name of the razor-back hog they said had invented
it? And what did you do for a drink in this con-
founded water-hole?

He would find it no water-hole, I told him; but
there were methods which a stranger upon his first
morning could scarce be expected to grasp. " I
could direct you to a Dutchman," I said, "but
you're too well dressed to win his confidence at
once."

" Well, old man," began Beverly, " I don't speak
Dutch, but give me a crack at the confidence."

However, he renounced the project upon learning what a Dutchman was. Since my hours were
no longer dedicated to establishing the presence
of royal blood in my veins I had spent them upon
various local investigations of a character far more
entertaining and akin to my taste. It was in
truth quite likely that Beverly could in a very few
moments, with his smile and his manner, find his
way to any Dutchman's heart; he had that divine
gift of winning over to him quickly all sorts and
conditions of men; and my account of the ingenious and law-baffling contrivances, which you
found at these little grocery shops, at once roused
his curiosity to make a trial; but he decided that
the club was better, if less picturesque. And he
told me that all the men of the automobile party
had received from John Mayrant cards of invitation to the club.

" Your fire-eater is a civil chap," said Beverly.
" And by the way, do you happen to know," here
he pulled from his pocket a letter and consulted
its address, " Mrs. Weguelin St. Michael?"

I was delighted that he brought an introduction
to this lady; Hortense Rieppe could not open for
him any of those haughty doors; and I wished
not only that Beverly (since he was just the man

to appreciate it and understand it) should see the
fine flower of Kings Port, but also that the fine
flower of Kings Port should see him; the best
blood of the South could not possibly turn out
anything better than Beverly Rodgers, and it was
horrible and humiliating to think of the other
Northern specimens of men whom Hortense had
imported with her. I was here suddenly reminded
that the young woman was a guest of the Cornerlys, the people who swept their garden, the
people whom Eliza La Heu at the Exchange did
not "know"; and at this the remark of Mrs.
Gregory St. Michael, when I had walked with her
and Mrs. Weguelin, took on an added lustre of
significance: —

"We shall have to call."

Call on the Cornerlys! Would they do that?
Were they ready to stand by their John to
that tune? A hotel would be nothing; you
could call on anybody at a hotel, if you had to;
but here would be a *démarche* indeed! Yet,
nevertheless, I felt quite certain that, if Hortense,
though the Cornerlys' guest, was also the guaran-
teed fiancée of John Mayrant, the old ladies would
come up to the scratch, hate and loathe it as they
might, and undoubtedly would: they could be
trusted to do the right thing.

I told Beverly how glad I was that he would
meet Mrs. Weguelin St. Michael. "The rest of
your party, my friend," I said, "are not very likely
to." And I generalized to him briefly upon the
town of Kings Port. "Supposing I take you to
call upon Mrs. St. Michael when I come back this
afternoon?" I suggested.

Beverly thought it over, and then shook his head. " Wouldn't do, old man. If these people are particular and *know*, as you say they do, hadn't I better leave the letter with my card, and then wait till she sends some word ? "

He was right, as he always was, unerringly. Consorting with all the Charleys, and the Bohms, and the Cohns, and the Kitties hadn't taken the fine edge from Beverly's good inheritance and good bringing up; his instinct had survived his scruples, making of him an agile and charming cynic, whom you could trust to see the right thing always, and never do it unless it was absolutely necessary; he would marry any amount of Kitties for their money, and always know that beside his mother and sisters they were as dirt; and he would see to it that his children took after their father, went to school in England for a good accent and enunciation, as he had done, went to college in America for the sake of belonging in their own country, as he had done, and married as many fortunes, and had as few divorces, as possible.

" Who was that girl on the bridge ? " he now inquired as we reached the steps of the post-office; and when I had told him again, because he had asked me about Eliza La Heu at the time, " She's the real thing," he commented. " Quite extraordinary, you know, her dignity, when poor old awful Charley was messing everything — he's so used to mere money, you know, that half the time he forgets people are not dollars, and you have to kick him to remind him — yes, quite perfect dignity. Gad, it took a lady to climb up and sit by that ragged old darky and take her dead dog away in the cart! The cart and the darky only made her look what she was all the more. Poor Kitty couldn't do that — she'd look like a chambermaid! Well, old man, see you again."

I stood on the post-office steps looking after Beverly Rodgers as he crossed Court Street. His admirably good clothes, the easy finish of his whole appearance, even his walk, and his back, and the slope of his shoulders, were unmistakable. The Southern men, going to their business in Court Street, looked at him. Alas, in his outward man he was as a rose among weeds! And certainly, no well-born American could unite with an art more hedonistic than Beverly's the old school and the *nouveau jeu !*

Over at the other corner he turned and stood, admiring the church and gazing at the other buildings, and so perceived me still on the steps. With a gesture of remembering something he crossed back again.

" You've not seen Miss Rieppe ? "

" Why, of course I haven't ! " I exclaimed. Was everybody going to ask me that?

" Well, something's up, old boy. Charley has got the launch away with him — and I'll bet he's got her away with him, too. Charley lied this morning."

" Is lying, then, so rare with him ? "

" Why, it rather is, you know. But I've come to be able to spot him when he does it. Those little bulgy eyes of his look at you particularly straight and childlike. He said he had to hunt up a man on business — V-C Chemical Company, he called it — "

" There is such a thing here," I said.

" Oh, Charley'd never make up a thing, and get found out in that way ! But he was lying all the same, old man."

" Do you mean they've run off and got married ? "

" What do you take them for ? Much more like them to run off and not get married. But they haven't done that either. And, speaking of that, I believe I've gone a bit adrift. Your fire-eater, you know—she is an extraordinary woman ! " And Beverly gave his mellow, little humorous chuckle. " Hanged if I don't begin to think she does fancy him."

" Well ! " I cried, " that would explain — no, it wouldn't. Whence comes your theory ? "

" Saw her look at him at dinner once last night. We dined with some people — Cornerly. She looked at him just once. Well, if she intends — by gad, it upsets one's whole notion of her ! "

" Isn't just one look rather slight basis for — "

" Now, old man, you know better than that ! " Beverly paused to chuckle. " My grandmother Livingston," he resumed, " knew Aaron Burr, and she used to say that he had an eye which no honest woman could meet without a blush. I don't know whether your fire-eater is a Launce-lot, or a Galahad, but that girl's eye at dinner — "

" Did *he* blush ? " I laughed.

" Not that I saw. But really, old man, confound it, you know ! He's no sort of husband for her. How can he make her happy and how can she make him happy, and how can either of them hit it off with the other the least little bit? She's expensive, he's not; she's up-to-date, he's not; she's of the great world, he's provincial. She's all derision, he's all faith. Why, hang it, old boy, what does she want him for?"

Beverly's handsome brow was actually furrowed with his problem; and, as I certainly could furnish him no solution for it, we stood in silence on the post-office steps. "What *can* she want him for?" he repeated. Then he threw it off lightly with one of his chuckles. "So glad I've no daughters to marry! Well — I must go draw some money."

He took himself off with a certain alacrity, giving an impatient cut with his stick at a sparrow in the middle of Worship Street, nor did I see him again this day, although, after hurriedly getting my letters (for the starting hour of the boat had now drawn near), I followed where he had gone down Court Street, and his cosmopolitan figure would have been easy to descry at any distance along that scantily peopled pavement. He had evidently found the bank and was getting his money.

David of the yellow hair and his limpid-looking bride were on the horrible little excursion boat, watching for me and keeping with some difficulty a chair next themselves that I might not have to stand up all the way; and, as I came aboard, the bride called out to me her relief, she had made sure that I would be late.

"David said you wouldn't," she announced in her clear up-country accent across the parasols and heads of huddled tourists, "but I told him a gentleman that's late to three meals aivry day like as not would forget boats can't be kept hot in the kitchen for you."

I took my place in the chair beside her as hastily as possible, for there is nothing that I so much dislike as being made conspicuous for any reason whatever; and my thanks to her were, I fear, less gracious in their manner than should have been the case. Nor did she find me, I must suppose, as companionable during this excursion — during the first part of it, at any rate — as a limpid-looking bride, who has kept at some pains a seat beside her for a single gentleman, has the right to expect; the brief hours of this morning had fed my preoccupation too richly, and I must often have fallen silent.

The horrible little tug, or ferry, or wherry, or whatever its contemptible inconvenience makes it fitting that this unclean and snail-like craft should be styled, cast off and began to lumber along the edges of the town with its dense cargo of hats and parasols and lunch parcels. We were a most extraordinary litter of man and womankind. There was the severe New England type, improving each shining hour, and doing it in bleak costume and with a thoroughly northeast expression; there were pink sunbonnets from (I should imagine) Spartanburg, or Charlotte, or Greenville; there were masculine boots which yet bore incrusted upon their heels the red mud of Aiken or of Camden; there was one fat, jewelled exhalation who spoke of Palm Beach with the true stockyard twang, and looked as if she swallowed a million

every morning for breakfast, and God knows how
many more for the ensuing repasts; she was the
only detestable specimen among us; sunbonnets,
boots, and even ungenial New England proved on
acquaintance kindly, simple, enterprising Americans; yet who knows if sunbonnets and boots and
all of us wouldn't have become just as detestable
had we but been as she was, swollen and puffy
with the acute indigestion of sudden wealth?

This reflection made me charitable, which I
always like to be, and I imparted it to the bride.

"My!" she said.   And I really don't know
what that meant.

But presently I understood well why people
endured the discomfort of this journey. I forgot
the cinders which now and then showered upon
us, and the heat of the sun, and the crowded
chairs; I forgot the boat and myself, in looking
at the passing shores.   Our course took us round
Kings Port on three sides. The calm, white town
spread out its width and length beneath a blue
sky softer than the tenderest dream; the white
steeples shone through the enveloping brightness, taking to each other, and to the distant roofs
beneath them, successive and changing relations,
while the dwindling mass of streets and edifices
followed more slowly the veering of the steeples,
folded upon itself, and refolded, opened into new
shapes and closed again, dwindling always, and
always white and beautiful; and as the far-off
vision of it held the eye, the few masts along the
wharves grew thin and went out into invisibility,
the spires became as masts, the distant drawbridge
through which we had passed sank down into a

mere stretching line, and shining Kings Port was
dissolved in the blue of water and of air.

The curving and the narrowing of the river
took it at last from view ; and after it disappeared
the spindling chimneys and their smoke, which
were along the bank above the town and bridge,
leaving us to progress through the solitude of
marsh and wood and shore. The green levels of stiff
salt grass closed in upon the breadth of water, and
we wound among them, looking across their silence
to the deeper silence of the woods that bordered
them, the brooding woods, the pines and the live-
oaks, misty with the motionless hanging moss, and
misty also in that Southern air that deepened when
it came among their trunks to a caressing, mysterious, purple veil. Every line of this landscape,
the straight forest top, the feathery breaks in it
of taller trees, the curving marsh, every line and
every hue and every sound inscrutably spoke sadness. I heard a mocking-bird once in some blos-
soming wild fruit tree that we gradually reached
and left gradually behind; and more than once
I saw other blossoms, and the yellow of the trail-
ing jessamine; but the bird could not sing the
silence away, and spring with all her abundance
could not hide this spiritual autumn.

Dreams, a land of dreams, where even the high
noon itself was dreamy; a melting together of
earth and air and water in one eternal gentleness
of revery ! Whence came the melancholy of this?
I had seen woods as solitary and streams as silent,
I had felt nature breathing upon me a greater awe ;
but never before such penetrating and quiet sad-

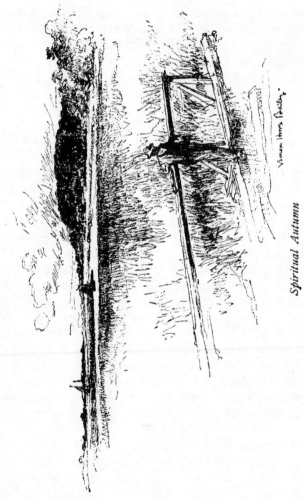

Spiritual Autumn

ness. I only know that this is the perpetual mood
of those Southern shores, those rivers that wind
in from the ocean among their narrowing marshes

and their hushed forests, and that it does not come
from any memory of human hopes and disasters,
but from the elements themselves.

So did we move onward, passing in due time
another bridge and a few dwellings and some
excavations, until the river grew quite narrow, and
there ahead was the landing at Live Oaks, with
negroes idly watching for us, and a launch beside
the bank, and Charley and Hortense Rieppe about
to step into it. Another man stood up in the launch
and talked to them where they were on the landing platform, and pointed down the river as we
approached; but evidently he did not point at us.
I looked hastily to see what he was indicating to
them, but I could see nothing save the solitary
river winding away between the empty woods and
marshes.

So this was Hortense Rieppe! It was not wonderful that she had caused young John to lose his
heart, or, at any rate, his head and his senses; nor
was it wonderful that Charley, with his little bulging eyes, should take her in his launch whenever
she would go; the wonderful thing was that John,
at his age and with his nature, should have got
over it — if he had got over it! I felt it tingling
in me; any man would. Steel wasp indeed!

She was slender, and oh, how well dressed!
She watched the passengers get off the boat, and
I could not tell you from that first sight of her
what her face was like, but only her hair, the sun-
burnt amber of its masses making one think of
Tokay or Chateau-Yquem. She was watching
me, I felt, and then saw; and as soon as I was
near she spoke to me without moving, keeping

one gloved hand lightly posed upon the railing of
the platform, so that her long arm was bent with
perfect ease and grace. I swear that none but a
female eye could have detected any toboggan fire-
escape.

Her words dropped with the same calculated
deliberation, the same composed and rich indifference. " These gardens are so beautiful."

Such was her first remark, chosen with some
purpose, I knew quite well ; and I observed that
I hoped I was not too late for their full perfection,
if too late to visit them in her company.

She turned her head slightly toward Charley.
" We have been enjoying them so much."

It was of absorbing interest to feel simultaneously in these brief speeches he vouchsafed —
speeches consummate in their inexpressive flatness
— the intentional coldness and the latent heat of
the creature. Since Natchez and Mobile (or
whichever of them it had been that had witnessed
her beginnings) she had encountered many men
and women, those who could be of use to her and
those who could not ; and in dealing with them
she had tempered and chiselled her insolence to a
perfect instrument, to strike or to shield.   And of
her greatest gift, also, she was entirely aware —
how could she help being, with her evident experience ? She knew that round her whole form
swam a delicious, invisible sphere, a distillation
that her veriest self sent forth, as gardenias do
their perfume, moving where she moved and staying where she stayed, and compared with which
wine was a feeble vapor for a man to get drunk on.

" Flowers are always so delightful."

" None but a female eye could have detected any toboggan fire-escape "

That was her third speech, pronounced just
like the others, in a low, clear voice — simplicity
arrived at by much well-practised complexity.
And she still looked at Charley.

Charley now responded in his little banker
accent. " It is a magnificent collection." This
he said looking at me, and moving a highly
polished finger-nail along a very slender mustache.

The eyes of Hortense now for a moment
glanced at the mixed company of boat-passen-
gers, who were beginning to be led off in pilgrim
groups by the appointed guides.

" We were warned it would be too crowded,"
she remarked.

Charley was looking at her foot. I can't say
whether or not the two light taps that the foot
now gave upon the floor of the landing brought
out for me a certain impatience which I might
otherwise have missed in those last words of hers.
From Charley it brought out, I feel quite sure, the
speech which (in some form) she had been expect-
ing from him as her confederate in this unwelcome
and inopportune interview with me, and which
his less highly schooled perceptions had not suggested to him until prompted by her.

" I should have been very glad to include you
in our launch party if I had known you were
coming here to-day," lied little Charley.

" Thank you so much!" I murmured; and I
fancy that after this Hortense hated me worse
than ever. Well, why should I play her game ?
If anybody had any claim upon me, was it she ?
I would get as much diversion as I could from this
encounter.

Hortense had looked at Charley when she spoke for my benefit, and it now pleased me very much to look at him when I spoke for hers.

"I could almost give up the gardens for the sake of returning with you," I said to him.

This was most successful in producing a perceptible silence before Hortense said, "Do come."

I wanted to say to her, "You are quite splendid — as splendid as you look, through and through! *You* wouldn't have run away from any battle of Chattanooga!" But what I did say was, "These flowers here will fade, but may I not hope to see you again in Kings Port?"

She was looking at me with eyes half closed; half closed for the sake of insolence — and better observation; when eyes like that take on drowsiness, you will be wise to leave all your secrets behind you, locked up in the bank, or else toss them right down on the open table. Well, I tossed mine down, thereto precipitated by a warning from the stranger in the launch: —

"We shall need all the tide we can get."

"I'm sure you'd be glad to know," I then said immediately (to Charley, of course), "that Miss La Heu, whose dog you killed, is back at her work as usual this morning."

"Thank you," returned Charley. "If there could be any chance for me to replace — "

"Miss La Heu is her name?" inquired Hortense. "I did not catch it yesterday. She works, you say?"

"At the Woman's Exchange. She bakes cakes for weddings — among her other activities."

"So interesting!" said Hortense; and bowing

to me, she allowed the spellbound Charley to help
her down into the launch.

Each step of the few that she had to take was
upon unsteady footing, and each was taken with
slow security and grace, and with a mastery of
her skirts so complete that they seemed to do it
of themselves, falling and folding in the soft, delicate curves of discretion.

For the sake of not seeming too curious about
this party, I turned from watching it before the
launch had begun to move, and it was immediately hidden from me by the bank, so that I did
not see it get away.   As I crossed an open space
toward the gardens I found myself far behind the
other pilgrims, whose wandering bands I could
half discern among winding walks and bordering
bushes.   I was soon taken into somewhat repri-
manding charge by an admirable, if important,
negro, who sighted me from a door beneath the
porch of the house, and advanced upon me speedily.   From him I learned at once the rule of the
place, that strangers were not allowed to "go
loose," as he expressed it; and recognizing the
perfect propriety of this restriction, I was humble,
and even went so far as to put myself right with
him by quite ample purchases of the beautiful
flowers that he had for sale; some of these would
be excellent for the up-country bride, who certainly
ought to have repentance from me in some form
for my silence as we had come up the river: the
scenery had caused me most ungallantly to forget
her.

My rule-breaking turned out all to my advantage.   The admirable and important negro was

so pacified by my liberal amends that he not only placed the flowers which I had bought in a bucket of water to wait in freshness until my tour of the gardens should be finished and the moment for me to return upon the boat should arrive, but he also honored me with his own special company; and instead of depositing me in one of the groups of other travellers, he took me to see the sights alone, as if I were somebody too distinguished to receive my impressions with the common herd. Thus I was able to linger here and there, and even to return to certain points for another look.

I shall not attempt to describe the azaleas at Live Oaks. You will understand me quite well, I am sure, when I say that I had heard the people at Mrs. Trevise's house talk so much about them, and praise them so superlatively, that I was not prepared for much: my experience of life had already included quite a number of azaleas. Moreover, my meeting with Hortense and Charley had taken me far away from flowers. But when that marvellous place burst upon me, I forgot Hortense. I have seen gardens, many gardens, in England, in France, in Italy; I have seen what can be done in great hothouses, and on great terraces; what can be done under a roof, and what can be done in the open air with the aid of architecture and sculpture and ornamental land and water; but no horticulture that I have seen devised by mortal man approaches the unearthly enchantment of the azaleas at Live Oaks. It was not like seeing flowers at all; it was as if there, in the heart of the wild and mystic wood, in the gray gloom of those trees veiled and muffled

in their long webs and skeins of hanging moss,
a great, magic flame of rose and red and white
burned steadily. You looked to see it vanish;
you could not imagine such a thing would stay.
All idea of individual petals or species was swept
away in this glowing maze of splendor, this transparent labyrinth of rose and red and white, through
which you looked beyond, into the gray gloom of
the hanging moss and the depths of the wild forest
trees.

I turned back as often as I could, and to the
last I caught glimpses of it, burning, glowing, and
shining like some miracle, some rainbow exorcism,
with its flooding fumes of orange-rose and red
and white, merging magically. It was not until I
reached the landing, and made my way on board
again, that Hortense returned to my thoughts.
She hadn't come to see the miracle; not she! I
knew that better than ever. And who was the
other man in the launch?

"Wasn't it perfectly elegant!" exclaimed the
up-country bride. And upon my assenting, she
made a further declaration to David: "It's just
aivry bit as good as the Isle of Champagne."

This I discovered to be a comic opera, mounted
with spendthrift brilliance, which David had taken
her to see at the town of Gonzales, just before they
were married.

As we made our way down the bending river
she continued to make many observations to me
in that up-country accent of hers, which is a
fashion of speech that may be said to differ as
widely from the speech of the low-country as
cotton differs from rice. I began to fear that,

in spite of my truly good intentions, I was again
failing to be as "attentive" as the occasion demanded; and so I presented her with my floral
tribute.

She was immediately ·arch. "I'd surely be
depriving *some*body!" and on this I got to the
full her limpid look.

I assured her that this would not be so, and
pointed to the other flowers I had.

Accordingly, after a little more archness, she
took them, as she had, of course, fully meant to
do from the first; she also took a woman's re-
venge. "I'll not be any more lonesome going
down than I was coming up," she said. "David's
enough." And this led me definitely to conclude
that David had secured a helpmate who could
take care of herself, in spite of the limpidity of
her eyes.

A steel wasp? Again that misleading description
of Mrs. Weguelin St. Michael's, to which, since my
early days in Kings Port, my imagination may be
sai.: to have been harnessed, came back into my
mind. I turned its injustice over and over beneath
the light which the total Hortense now shed upon it
— or rather, not the total Hortense, but my whole
impression of her, as far as I had got; I got a
good deal further before we had finished. To the
slow, soft accompaniment of these gliding river
shores, where all the shadows had changed since
morning, so that new loveliness stood revealed at
every turn, my thoughts dwelt upon this perfected
specimen of the latest American moment — so
late that she contained nothing of the past, and a
great deal of to-morrow. I basked myself in the

memory of her achieved beauty, her achieved dress,
her achieved insolence, her luxurious complexity.
She was even later than those quite late athletic
girls, the Amazons of the links, whose big, hard,
football faces stare at one from public windows and
from public prints, whose giant, manly strides take
them over leagues of country and square miles of
dance-floor, and whose bursting, blatant, immodest
health glares upon sea-beaches and round supper tables. Hortense knew that even now the
hour of such is striking, and that the American
boy will presently turn with relief to a creature
who will more clearly remind him that he is a man
and that she is a woman.

But why was the insolence of Hortense offen-
sive, when the insolence of Eliza La Heu was not?
Both these extremely feminine beings could exercise that quality in profusion, whenever they so
wished; wherein did the difference lie?   Perhaps,
I thought, in the spirit of its exercise; Eliza was
merely insolent when she happened to feel like
it; and man has always been able to forgive
woman for that — whether the angels do or not;
but Hortense, the world-wise, was insolent to all
people who could not be of use to her; and all I
have to say is, that if the angels can forgive *that*,
they're welcome; I can't!

Had I made sure of anything at the landing?
Yes; Hortense didn't care for Charley in the least,
and never would. A woman can stamp her foot
at a man and love him simultaneously; but those
two light taps, and the measure that her eyes took
of Charley, meant that she must love his posses-
sions very much to be able to bear him at all.

Then, what was her feeling about John Mayrant?
As Beverly had said, what could she want him
for? He hadn't a thing that she valued or needed.
His old-time notions of decency, the clean simplicity of his make, his good Southern position, and
his collection of nice old relatives — what did these
assets look like from an automobile, or on board
the launch of a modern steam yacht? And
wouldn't it be amusing if John should grow need-
lessly jealous, and have a " difficulty" with Charley? — not a mere flinging of torn paper money
in the banker's face, but some more decided
punishment for the banker's presuming to rest
his predatory eyes upon John's affianced lady.

I stared at the now broadening river, where the
reappearance of the bridge, and of Kings Port,
and the nearer chimneys pouring out their smoke
a few miles above the town, betokened that our
excursion was drawing to its end. And then
from the chimney's neighborhood, from the water-
side where their factories stood, there shot out into
the smoothness of the stream a launch. It crossed
into our course ahead of us, preceded us quickly,
growing soon into a dot, went through the bridge,
and so was seen no longer; and its occupants
must have reached town a good half hour before
we did. And now, suddenly, I was stunned with
a great discovery. The bride's voice sounded in
my ear. " Well, I'll always say you're a prophet,
anyhow!"

I looked at her, dull and dazed by the internal
commotion the discovery had raised in me.

"You said we wouldn't get stuck in the mud,
and we didn't," said the bride.

I pointed to the chimneys.   "Are those the phosphate works?"

"Yais.   Didn't you know?"

"The V-C phosphate works?"

"Why, yais.   Haven't you been to see them yet?   He ought to, oughtn't he, David? 'Specially now they've found those deposits up the river were just as rich as they hoped, after all."

"Whose?   Mr. Mayrant's?" I asked with such sharpness that the bride was surprised.

David hadn't attended to the name.   It was some trust estate, he thought; Regent Tom, or some such thing.

"And they thought it was no good," said the bride.   "And it's aivry bit as good as the Coosaw used to be.   Better than Florida or Tennessee."

My eyes instinctively turned to where they had last seen the launch ; of course it wasn't there any more.   Then I spoke to David.

"Do you know what a phosphate bed looks like?   Can one see it?"

"This kind you can," he answered.   "But it's not worth your trouble.   Just a kind of a square hole you dig along the river till you strike the stuff.   What you want to see is the works."

No, I didn't want to see even the works; they smelt atrociously, and I do not care for vats, and acids, and processes : and besides, had I not seen enough?   My eyes went down the river again where that launch had gone ; and I wondered if the wedding-cake would be postponed any more.

Regent Tom?   Oh, yes, to be sure! John Mayrant had pointed out to me the house where

he had lived; he had been John's uncle. So the
old gentleman had left his estate in trust! And
now —! But certainly Hortense would have won
the battle of Chattanooga!

"Don't be too sure about all this," I told myself
cautiously. But there are times when cautioning
one's self is quite as useiess as if somebody else
had cautioned one; my reason leaped with the
rapidity of intuition; I merely sat and looked on
at what it was doing. All sorts of odds and ends,
words I hadn't understood, looks and silences I
hadn't interpreted, little signs that I had thought
nothing of at first, but which I had gradually,
through their multiplicity, come to know meant
something, all these broken pieces fitted into each
other now, fell together and made a clear pattern
of the truth, without a crack in it — Hortense had
never believed in that story about the phosphates
having failed — "pinched out," as they say of ore
deposits. There she had stood between her two
suitors, between her affianced John and the besieg-
ing Charley, and before she would be off with the
old love and on with the new, she must personally
look into those phosphates. Therefore she had
been obliged to have a sick father and postpone
the wedding two or three times, because her affairs
— very likely the necessity of making certain of
Charley — had prevented her from coming sooner
to Kings Port. And having now come hither,
and having beheld her Northern and her Southern
lovers side by side — had the comparison done
something to her highly controlled heart? Was
love taking some hitherto unknown liberties with
that well-balanced organ? But what an outrage

had been perpetrated upon John! At that my
deductions staggered in their rapid course. How
could his aunts — but then it had only been one
of them; Miss Josephine had never approved of
Miss Eliza's course; it was of that that Mrs.
Weguelin St. Michael had so emphatically reminded Mrs. Gregory in my presence when we
had strolled together upon High Walk, and those
two ladies had talked oracles in my presence.
Well, they were oracles no longer!

When the boat brought us back to the wharf,
there were the rest of my flowers unbestowed, and
upon whom should I bestow them? I thought
first of Eliza La Heu, but she wouldn't be at the
Exchange so late as this. Then it seemed well
to carry them to Mrs. Weguelin. Something,
however, prompted me to pass her door, and continue vaguely walking on until I came to the
house where Miss Josephine and Miss Eliza
lived; and here I rang the bell and was admitted.

They were sitting as I had seen them first, the
one with her embroidery, and the other on the
further side of a table, whereon lay an open letter,
which in a few moments I knew must have been
the subject of the discussion which they finished
even as I came forward.

"It was only prolonging an honest mistake."
That was Miss Eliza.

"And it has merely resulted in clinching what
you meant it to finish." That was Miss Josephine.

I laid my flowers upon the table, and saw that
the letter was in John Mayrant's hand. Of course

I avoided looking at it again; but what had he written, and why had he written? His daily steps turned to this house — unless Miss Josephine had banished him again.

The ladies accepted my offering with gracious expressions, and while I told them of my visit to Live Oaks, and poured out my enthusiasm, the servant was sent for and brought water and two beautiful old china bowls, in which Miss Eliza proceeded to arrange the flowers with her delicate white hands. She made them look exquisite with an old lady's art, and this little occupation went on as we talked of indifferent subjects.

But the atmosphere of that room was charged with the subject of which we did not speak. The letter lay on the table; and even as I struggled to sustain polite conversation, I began to know what was in it, though I never looked at it again; it spoke out as clearly to me as the launch had done. I had thought, when I first entered, to tell the ladies something of my meeting with Hortense Rieppe; I can only say that I found this impossible. Neither of them referred to her, or to John, or to anything that approached what we were all thinking of; for me to do so would have assumed the dimensions of a liberty; and in consequence of this state of things, constraint sat upon us all, growing worse, and so pervading our small-talk with discomfort that I made my visit a very short one. Of course they were civil about this when I rose, and begged me not to go so soon; but I knew better. And even as I was getting my hat and gloves in the hall I could tell by their tones that they had returned to the subject of that letter. But in truth they had never left it; as the front door shut behind me I felt as if they had read it aloud to me.

XVI

THE STEEL WASP

CERTAINLY Hortense Rieppe would have won the battle of Chattanooga! I know not from which parent that young woman inherited her gift of strategy, but she was a master. To use the resources of one lover in order to ascertain if another lover had any; to lay tribute on everything that Charley possessed; on his influence in the business world, which enabled him to walk into the V-C Chemical Company's office and borrow an expert in the phosphate line; on his launch in which to pop the expert and take him up the river, and see in his company and learn from his lips just what resources of worldly wealth were likely to be in store for John Mayrant; and finally (which was the key to all the rest) on his inveterate passion for her, on his bankerlike determination through all the thick and thin of discouragement, and worse than discouragement, of contemptuous coquetry, to possess her at any cost he could afford ;—to use all this that Charley had, in order that she might judiciously arrive at the decision whether she would take him or his rival, left one lost in admiration. And then, not to waste a moment! To reach town one evening, and next morning by ten o'clock to have that expert safe in the launch

on his way up the river to the phosphate dig-
gings! The very audacity of such unscrupulous-
ness commanded my respect: successful dishonor
generally wins louder applause than successful
virtue. But to be married to her! Oh! not for
worlds! Charley might meet such emergency,
but poor John, never!

I nearly walked into Mrs. Weguelin and Mrs.
Gregory taking their customary air slowly in
South Place.

"But why a steel wasp?" I said at once to Mrs.
Weguelin. It was a more familiar way of beginning with the little, dignified lady than would
have been at all possible, or suitable, if we had
not had that little joke about the *piano snobile*
between us. As it was, she was not wholly displeased. These Kings Port old ladies grew, I
suspect, very slowly and guardedly accustomed
to any outsider; they allowed themselves very
seldom to suffer any form of abruptness from him,
or from any one, for that matter. But, once they
were reassured as to him, then they might sometimes allow the privileged person certain de-
partures from their own rule of deportment,
because his conventions were recognized to be
different from theirs. Moreover, in reminding
Mrs. Weguelin of the steel wasp, I had put my
abruptness in "quotations," so to speak, by the
tone I gave it, just as people who are particular
in speech can often interpolate a word of current
slang elegantly by means of the shade of emphasis
which they lay upon it.

So Mrs. Weguelin smiled and her dark eyes
danced a little. "You remember I said that, then?"

" I remember everything that you said."

" How much have you seen of the creature?" demanded Mrs. Gregory, with her head pretty high.

" Well, I'm seeing more, and more, and more every minute. She's rather endless."

Mrs. Weguelin looked reproachful. "You surely cannot admire her, too?"

Mrs. Gregory hadn't understood me. " Oh, if you really can keep her away, you're welcome!"

" I only meant," I explained to the ladies, "that you don't really begin to see her till you *have* seen her : it's afterward, when you're out of reach of the spell." And I told them of the interview which I had not been able to tell to Miss Josephine and Miss Eliza. " I doubt if it lasted more than four minutes," I assured them.

" Up the river?" repeated Mrs. Gregory.

" At the landing," I repeated. And the ladies consulted each other's expressions. But that didn't bother me any more.

" And you can admire her?" Mrs. Weguelin persisted.

" May I tell you exactly, precisely?"

" Oh, do!" they both exclaimed.

" Well, I think many wise men would find her immensely desirable — as somebody else's wife!"

At this remark Mrs. Weguelin dropped her eyes, but I knew they were dancing beneath their lids. "I should not have permitted myself to say that, but I am glad that it has been said."

Mrs. Gregory turned to her companion. " Shall we call to-morrow?"

" Don't you feel it must be done?" returned

Mrs. Weguelin, and then she addressed me. "Do you know a Mr. Beverly Rodgers?"

I gave him a golden recommendation and took my leave of the ladies.

So they were going to do the handsome thing; they would ring the Cornerlys' bell; they would cross the interloping threshold, they would recognize the interloping girl; and this meant that they had given it up. It meant that Miss Eliza had given it up, too, had at last abandoned her position that the marriage would never take place. And her own act had probably drawn this down upon her. When the trustee of that estate had told her of the apparent failure of the phosphates, she had hailed it as an escape for her beloved John, and for all of them, because she made sure that Hortense would never marry a virtually penniless man. And when the work went on, and the rich fortune was unearthed after all, her influence had caused that revelation to be delayed because she was so confident that the engagement would be broken. But she had reckoned without Hortense; worse than that, she had reckoned without John Mayrant; in her meddling attempt to guide his affairs in the way that she believed would be best for him, she forgot that the boy whom she had brought up was no longer a child, and thus she unpardonably ignored his rights as a man. And now Miss Josephine's disapproval was vindicated, and her own casuistry was doubly punished. Miss Rieppe's astute journey of investigation — for her purpose had evidently become suspected by some of them beforehand — had forced Miss Eliza to disclose the truth about the phosphates to her nephew before it should be told him by the girl herself; and the intolerable position of apparent duplicity precipitated two wholly inevitable actions on his part; he had bound himself more than ever to marry Hortense, and he had made a furious breach with his Aunt Eliza. That was what his letter had contained; this time he had banished himself from that house. What was his Aunt Eliza going to do about it? I wondered. She was a stiff, if indiscreet, old lady, and it certainly did not fall within her view of the proprieties that young people should take their elders to task in furious letters. But she had been totally in the wrong, and her fault was irreparable, because important things had happened in consequence of it; she might repent the fault in sackcloth and ashes, but she couldn't stop the things. Would she, then, honorably wear the sackcloth, or would she dishonestly shirk it under the false issue of her nephew's improper tone to her? Women can justify themselves with more appalling skill than men.

One drop there was in all this bitter bucket, which must have tasted sweet to John. He had resigned from the Custom House: Juno had got it right this time, though she hadn't a notion of the real reason for John's act. This act had been, since morning, lost for me, so to speak, in the shuffle of more absorbing events; and it now rose to view again in my mind as a telling stroke in the full-length portrait that all his acts had been painting of the boy during the last twenty-four hours. Notwithstanding a meddlesome aunt, and an arriving sweetheart, and imminent wedlock, he

hadn't forgotten to stop " taking orders from a
negro " at the very first opportunity which came
to him ; his phosphates had done this for him, at
least, and I should have the pleasure of correcting
Juno at tea.

But I did not have this pleasure. They were
all in an excitement over something else, and my
own different excitement hadn't a chance against
this greater one; for people seldom wish to hear
what you have to say, even under the most favorable circumstances, and never when they have
anything to say themselves. With an audience
so hotly preoccupied I couldn't have sat on Juno
effectively at all, and therefore I kept it to myself,
and attended very slightly to what they were telling me about the Daughters of Dixie.

I bowed absently to the poetess. " And your
poem ? " I said. " A great success, I am sure ? "

" Why, didn't you hear me say so ? " said the up-
country bride ; and then, after a smile at the
others, " I'm sure your flowers were graciously
accepted."

" Ask Miss Josephine St. Michael," I replied.

" Oh, oh, oh ! " went the bride. " How would
she know ? "

I gave myself no pains to improve or arrest
this tiresome joke, and they went back to their
Daughters of Dixie ; but it is rather singular how
sometimes an utterly absurd notion will be the
cause of our taking a step which we had not contemplated. I did carry some flowers to Miss La
Heu the next day. I was at some trouble to find
any ; for in Kings Port shops of this kind are by
no means plentiful, and it was not until I had

paid a visit to a quite distant garden at the extreme northwestern edge of the town that I lighted upon anything worthy of the girl behind the counter. The Exchange itself was apt to have flowers for sale, but I hardly saw my way to buying them there, and then immediately offering them to the fair person who had sold them to me. As it was, I did much better; for what I brought her were decidedly superior to any that were at the Exchange when I entered it at lunch time.

They were, as the up-country bride would have put it, "graciously accepted." Miss La Heu stood them in water on the counter beside her ledger. She was looking lovely.

"I expected you yesterday," she said. "The new Lady Baltimore was ready."

"Well, if it is not all eaten yet — "

"Oh, no! Not a slice gone."

"Ah, nobody does your art justice here!"

"Go and sit down at your table, please."

It was really quite difficult to say to her from that distance the sort of things that I wished to say; but there seemed to be no help for it, and I did my best.

"I shall miss my lunches here very much when I'm gone."

"Did you say coffee to-day?"

"Chocolate. I shall miss — "

"And the lettuce sandwiches?"

"Yes. You don't realize how much these lunches — "

"Have cost you?" She seemed determined to keep laughing.

"You have said it. They have cost me my — "

" I can give you the receipt, you know."

" The receipt ? "

" For Lady Baltimore, to take with you."

" You'll have to give me a receipt for a lost heart."

" Oh, his heart! General, listen to — " From habit she had turned to where her dog used to lie ; and sudden pain swept over her face and was mastered. " Never mind ! " she quickly resumed. " Please don't speak about it. And you have a heart somewhere ; for it was very nice in you to come in yesterday morning after — after the bridge."

" I hope I have a heart," I began, rising ; for, really, I could not go on in this way, sitting down away back at the lunch table.

But the door opened, and Hortense Rieppe came into the Woman's Exchange.-

It was at me that she first looked, and she gave me the slightest bow possible, the least sign of conventional recognition that a movement of the head could make and be visible at all ; she didn't bend her head down, she tilted it ever so little up. It wasn't new to me, this form of greeting, and I knew that she had acquired it at Newport, and that it denoted, all too accurately, the size of my importance in her eyes ; she did it, as she did everything, with perfection. Then she turned to Eliza La Heu, whose face had become miraculously sweet.

" Good morning," said Hortense.

It sounded from a quiet well of reserve music ; just a cupful of melodious tone dipped lightly out of the surface. Her face hadn't become anything ;

but it was equally miraculous in its total void of
all expression relating to this moment, or to any
moment; just her beauty, her permanent stationary beauty, was there glowing in it and through
it, not skin deep, but going back and back into
her lazy eyes, and shining from within the modu-
lated bloom of her color and the depths of her
amber hair. She was choosing, for this occasion,
to be as impersonal as some radiant hour in nature, some mellow, motionless day when the
leaves have turned, but have not fallen, and it is
drowsily warm; but it wasn't so much of nature
that she, in her harmonious lustre, reminded me,
as of some beautiful silken-shaded lamp, from
which color rather than light came with subdued
ampleness.

I saw her eyes settle upon the flowers that I
had brought Eliza La Heu.

" How beautiful those are! " she remarked.

" Is there something that you wish? " inquired
Miss La Heu, always miraculously sweet.

"Some of your good things for lunch; a very
little, if you will be so kind."

I had gone back to my table while the " very
little " was being selected, and I felt, in spite of
how slightly she counted me, that it would be in-
adequate in me to remain completely dumb.

" Mr. Mayrant is still at the Custom House? " I
observed.

"For a few days, yes. Happily we shall soon
break that connection." And she smelt my
flowers.

" 'We,' " I thought to myself, "is rather tremendous."

It grew more tremendous in the silence as Eliza La Heu brought me my orders. Miss Rieppe did not seat herself to take the light refreshment which she found enough for lunch. Her plate and cup were set for her, but she walked about, now with one, and now with the other, taking her time over it, and pausing here and there at some article of the Exchange stock.

Of course, she hadn't come there for any lunch; the Cornerlys had midday lunch and dined late; these innovated hours were a part of Kings Port's deep suspicion of the Cornerlys; but what now became interesting was her evident indifference to our perceiving that lunch was merely a pretext with her; in fact, I think she wished it to be perceived, and I also think that those turns which she took about the Exchange — her apparent inspection of an old mahogany table, her examination of a pewter set — were a symbol (and meant to be a symbol) of how she had all the time there was, and the possession of everything she wished including the situation, and that she enjoyed having this sink in while she was rearranging whatever she had arranged to say, in consequence of finding that I should also hear it. And how well she was worth looking at, no matter whether she stood, or moved, or what she did! Her age lay beyond the reach of the human eye; if she was twenty-five, she was marvellous in her mastery of her appearance; if she was thirty-four, she was marvellous in her mastery of perpetuating it, and by no other means than perfect dress personal to herself (for she had taken the fashion and welded it into her own plasticity) and perfect health;

for without a trace of the athletic, her graceful shape teemed with elasticity. There was a touch of "sport" in the parasol she had laid down; and with all her blended serenity there was a touch of "sport" in *her*. Experience could teach her beauty nothing more; it wore the look of having been made love to by many married men.

Quite suddenly the true light flashed upon me. I had been slow-sighted indeed! So *that* was what she had come here for to-day! Miss Hortense was going to pay her compliments to Miss La Heu. I believe that my sight might still have been slow but for that miraculous sweetness upon the face of Eliza. She was ready for the compliments! Well, I sat expectant — and disappointment was by no means my lot.

Hortense finished her lunch. "And so this interesting place is where you work?"

Eliza, thus addressed, assented.

"And you furnish wedding cakes also?"

Eliza was continuously and miraculously sweet. "The Exchange includes that."

"I shall hope you will be present to taste some of yours on the day it is mine."

"I shall accept the invitation if my friends send me one."

No blood flowed from Hortense at this, and she continued with the same smooth deliberation.

"The list is of necessity very small; but I shall see that it includes you."

"You are not going to postpone it any more, then?"

No blood flowed at this, either. "I doubt if John — if Mr. Mayrant — would brook further

"With all her blended serenity, there was a touch of 'sport' in her"

delay, and my father seems stronger, at last. How much do I owe you for your very good food ? "

It is a pity that a larger audience could not have been there to enjoy this skilful duet, for it held me hanging on every musical word of it. There, at the far back end of the long room, I sat alone at my table, pretending to be engaged over a sandwich that was no more in existence — external, I mean — and a totally empty cup of chocolate. I lifted the cup, and bowed over the plate, and used the paper Japanese napkin, and generally went through the various discreet paces of eating, quite breathless, all the while, to know which of them was coming out ahead. There was no fairness in their positions; Hortense had Eliza in a cage, penned in by every fact; but it doesn't do to go too near some birds, even when they're caged, and, while these two birds had been giving their sweet manifestations of song, Eliza had driven a peck or two home through the bars, which, though they did not draw visible blood, as I have said, probably taught Hortense that a Newport education is not the only instruction which fits you for drawing-room war to the knife.

Her small reckoning was paid, and she had drawn on one long, tawny glove. Even this act was a luxury to watch, so full it was of the feminine, of the stretching, indolent ease that the flesh and the spirit of this creature invariably seemed to move with. But why didn't she go? This became my wonder now, while she slowly drew on the second glove. She was taking more time than it needed.

"Your flowers are for sale, too?"

This, after her silence, struck me as being something planned out after her original plan. The original plan had finished with that second assertion of her ownership of John (or, I had better say, of his ownership in her), that doubt she had expressed as to his being willing to consent to any further postponement of their marriage. Of course she had expected, and got herself ready for, some thrust on the postponement subject.

Eliza crossed from behind her counter to where the Exchange flowers stood on the opposite side of the room and took some of them up.

"But those are inferior," said Hortense. "These." And she touched lightly the bowl in which my roses stood close beside Eliza's ledger.

Eliza paused for one second. "Those are not for sale."

Hortense paused, too. Then she hung to it. "They are so much the best." She was holding her purse.

"I think so, too," said Eliza. "But I cannot let any one have them."

Hortense put her purse away. "You know best. Shall you furnish us flowers as well as cake?"

Eliza's sweetness rose an octave, softer and softer. "Why, they have flowers there! Didn't you know?"

And to this last and frightful peck through the bars Hortense found no retaliation. With a bow to Eliza, and a total oblivion of me, she went out of the Exchange. She had flaunted "her" John in Eliza's face, she had, as they say, rubbed it in

that he was "her" John; — but was it such a neat,
tidy victory, after all? She had given away the
last word to Eliza, presented her with that poison-
ous speech which when translated meant: —

"Yes, he's 'your' John; and you're climbing
up him into houses where you'd otherwise be
arrested for trespass." For it was in one of the
various St. Michael houses that the marriage
would be held, owing to the nomadic state of the
Rieppes.

Yes, Hortense had gone altogether too close to
the cage at the end, and, in that repetition of her
taunt about "furnishing" supplies for the wedding, she had at length betrayed something which
her skill and the intricate enamel of her experience
had hitherto, and with entire success, concealed —
namely, the latent vulgarity of the woman. She
was wearing, for the sake of Kings Port, her best
behavior, her most knowing form, and, indeed,
it was a well-done imitation of the real thing; it
would last through most occasions, and it would
deceive most people. But here was the trouble:
she was *wearing* it; while, through the whole encounter, Eliza La Heu had worn nothing but her
natural and perfect dignity; yet with that disadvantage (for good breeding, alas! is at times a sort
of disadvantage, and can be battered down and
covered with mud so that its own fine grain is invisible) Eliza had, after a somewhat undecisive
battle, got in that last frightful peck! But what
had led Hortense, after she had come through
pretty well, to lose her temper and thus, at the
finish, expose to Eliza her weakest position? That
her clothes were paid for by a Newport lady who

had taken her to Worth, that her wedding feast was to be paid for by the bridegroom, these were not facts which Eliza would deign to use as weapons; but she was marrying inside the doors of Eliza's Kings Port, that had never opened to admit her before, and she had slipped into putting this chance into Eliza's hand — and how had she come to do this?

To be sure, my vision had been slow! Hortense had seen, through her thick veil, Eliza's interest in John in the first minute of her arrival on the bridge, that minute when John had run up to Eliza after the automobile had passed over poor General. And Hortense had not revealed herself at once, because she wanted a longer look at them. Well, she had got it, and she had got also a look at her affianced John when he was in the fire-eating mood, and had displayed the conduct appropriate to 1840, while Charley's display had been so much more modern. And so first she had prudently settled that awkward phosphate difficulty, and next she had paid this little visit to Eliza in order to have the pleasure of telling her in four or five different ways, and driving it in deep, and turning it round: "*Don't you wish you may get him?*"

"That's all clear as day," I said to myself. "But what does her loss of temper mean?"

Eliza was writing at her ledger. The sweetness hadn't entirely gone; it was too soon for that, and besides, she knew I must be looking at her.

"Couldn't you have told her they were my flowers?" I asked her at the counter, as I prepared to depart.

Eliza did not look up from her ledger. " Do
you think she would have believed me ? "

" And why shouldn't — "

" Go out! " she interrupted imperiously and with
a stamp of her foot. " You've been here long
enough! "

You may imagine my amazement at this. It
was not until I had reached Mrs. Trevise's, and
was sitting down to answer a note which had been
left for me, that light again came. Hortense
Rieppe had thought those flowers were from John
Mayrant, and Eliza had let her think so.

Yes, that was light, a good bright light shed on
the matter; but a still more brilliant beam was
cast by the up-country bride when I came into the
dining-room. I told her myself, at once, that I had
taken flowers to Miss La Heu; I preferred she
should hear this from me before she learned it
from the smiling lips of gossip. It surprised me
that she should immediately inquire what kind of
flowers?

" Why, roses," I answered; and she went into
peals of laughter.

" Pray share the jest," I begged her with some
dignity.

" Didn't you know," she replied, " the language
that roses from a single gentleman to a young
lady speak in Kings Port ? "

I stood staring and stiff, taking it in, taking
myself, and Eliza, and Hortense, and the impli-
cated John, all in.

" Why, *aivry*body in Kings Port knows that! "
said the bride; and now my mirth rose even
above hers.

XVII

DOING THE HANDSOME THING

IT by no means lessened my pleasure to discern that Hortense must feel herself to be in a predicament; and as I sat writing my answer to the note, which was from Mrs. Weguelin St. Michael and contained an invitation to me for the next afternoon, I thought of those pilots whose dangers have come down to us from distant times through the songs of ancient poets. The narrow and tempestuous channel between Scylla and Chàrybdis bristled unquestionably with violent problems, but with none, I should suppose, that called for a nicer hand upon the wheel, or an eye more alert, than this steering of your little trireme to a successful marriage, between one man who believed himself to be your destined bridegroom and another who expected to be so, meanwhile keeping each in ignorance of how close you were sailing to the other. In Hortense's place I should have wished to hasten the wedding now, have it safely performed this afternoon, say, or to-morrow morning; thus precipitated by some invaluable turn in the health of her poor dear father. But she had worn it out, his health, by playing it for decidedly as much as it could bear; it couldn't be used again without risk; the date must stand fixed; and, uneasy as she might have begun to be

about John, Hortense must, with no shortening
of the course, get her boat in safe without smash-
ing it against either John or Charley.   I wondered
a little that she should feel any uncertainty about
her affianced lover.   She must know how much
his word was to him, and she had had his word
twice, given her the second time to put his own
honor right with her on the score of the phosphates.   But perhaps Hortense's rich experiences
of life had taught her that a man's word to a
woman should not be subjected to the test of
another woman's advent.   On the whole, I suppose it was quite natural those flowers should
annoy her, and equally natural that Eliza, the
minx, should allow them to do so!   There's a
joy to the marrow in watching your enemy har-
ried and discomfited by his own gratuitous contrivances; you look on serenely at a show which
hasn't cost you a groat.   However, poor Eliza
had not been so serene at the very end, when she
stormed out at me.   For this I did not have to
forgive her, of course, little as I had merited such
treatment.   Had she not accepted my flowers?
But it was a gratification to reflect that in my
sentimental passages with her I had not gone to
any great length; nothing, do I ever find, is so
irksome as the sense of having unwittingly been
in a false position.   Was John, on his side, in love
with her?   Was it possible he would fail in his
word?   So with these thoughts, while answering
and accepting Mrs. Weguelin St. Michael's invitation to make one of a party of strangers to
whom she was going to show another old Kings
Port church, " where many of my ancestors lie,"

as her note informed me, I added one sentence
which had nothing to do with the subject. " She
is a steel wasp," I ventured to say. And when
on the next afternoon I met the party at the
church, I received from the little lady a look of
highly spiced comprehension as she gently remarked, " I was glad to get your acceptance."

When I went down to the dinner-table, Juno
sat in her best clothes, still discussing the Daughters of Dixie.

I can't say that I took much more heed of this
at dinner than I had done at tea; but I was
interested to hear Juno mention that she, too,
intended to call upon Hortense Rieppe. Kings
Port, she said, must take a consistent position;
and for her part, so far as behavior went, she
didn't see much to' choose between the couple.
" As to whether Mr. Mayrant had really concealed the discovery of his fortune," she continued, " I asked Miss Josephine — in a perfectly
nice way, of course. But old Mr. St. Michael
Beaugarçon, who has always had the estate in
charge, did that. It is only a life estate, unless
Mr. Mayrant has lawful issue. Well, he will
have that now, and all that money will be his to
squander."

Aunt Carola had written me again this morning, but I had been in no haste to open her letter;
my neglect of the Bombos did not weigh too
heavily upon me, I fear, but I certainly did put off
reading what I expected to be a reprimand. And
concerning this I was right; her first words
betokened reprimand at once. " My dear nephew
Augustus," she began, in her fine, elegant hand-

writing. That was always her mode of address to me when something was coming, while at other times it would be, less portentously, " My dear Augustus," or " My dear nephew "; but whenever my name and my relationship to her occurred conjointly, I took the communication away with me to some corner, and opened it in solitude.

It wasn't about the Bombos, though; and for what she took me to task I was able to defend myself, I think, quite adequately. She found fault with me for liking the South too much, and this she based upon the enthusiastic accounts of Kings Port and its people that I had written to her; nor had she at all approved of my remarks on the subject of the negro, called forth by Daddy Ben and his grandson Charles Cotesworth.

"When I sent you (wrote Aunt Carola) to admire Kings Port good-breeding, I did not send you to forget your country. Remember that those people were its mortal enemies; that besides their treatment of our prisoners in Libby and Andersonville (which killed my brother Alexander) they displayed in their dealings, both social and political, an arrogance in success and a childish petulance at opposition, which we who saw and suffered can never forget, any more than we can forget our loved ones who laid down their lives for this cause."

These were not the only words with which Aunt Carola reproved what she termed my "disloyalty," but they will serve to indicate her feeling about the Civil War. It was — on her side — precisely the feeling of all the Kings Port old ladies on *their* side. But why should it be mine?

And so, after much thinking how I might best reply respectfully yet say to Aunt Carola what my feeling was, I sat down upstairs at my window, and, after some preliminary sentences, wrote : —

" There are dead brothers here also, who, like your brother, laid down their lives for what they believed was their country, and whom their sisters never can forget as you can never forget him. I read their names upon sad church tablets, and their boy faces look out at me from cherished miniatures and dim daguerreotypes. Upon their graves the women who mourn them leave flowers as you leave flowers upon the grave of your young soldier. You will tell me, perhaps, that since the bereavement is equal, I have not justified my sympathy for these people. But the bereavement was not equal. More homes here were robbed by death of their light and promise than with us; and to this you must add the material desolation of the homes themselves. Our roofs were not laid in ashes, and to-day we sit in affluence while they sit in privation. You will say to this, perhaps, that they brought it upon themselves. But even granting that they did so, surely to suffer and to lose is more bitter than to suffer and to win. My dear aunt, you could not see what I have seen here, and write to me as you do ; and if those years have left upon your heart a scar which will not vanish, do not ask me, who came afterward, to wear the scar also. I should then resemble certain of the younger ones here, with less excuse than is theirs. As for the negro, forgive me if I assure you that you retain an Abolitionist exaltation for a creature who does not exist, or whose existence is an ineffectual drop in the bucket, a creature on grateful knees raising faithful eyes to one who has struck off his chains of slavery, whereas the creature who does exist is — "

I paused here in my letter to Aunt Carola, and sought for some fitting expression that should characterize for her with sufficient severity the new type of deliberately worthless negro; and as I sought, my eyes wandered to the garden next door, the garden of the Cornerlys. On a bench near a shady arrangement of vines over bars sat Hortense Rieppe. She was alone, and, from her attitude, seemed to be thinking deeply. The high walls of the garden shut her into a privacy that her position near the shady vines still more increased. It was evident that she had come here for the sake of being alone, and I regretted that she was so turned from me that I could not see her face. But her solitude did not long continue; there came into view a gentleman of would-be venerable appearance, who approached her with a walk carefully constructed for public admiration, and who, upon reaching her, bent over with the same sort of footlight elaboration and gave her a paternal kiss. I did not need to hear her call him father; he was so obviously General Rieppe, the prudent hero of Chattanooga, that words would have been perfectly superfluous in his identification.

I was destined upon another day to hear the tones of his voice, and thereupon may as well state now that they belonged altogether with the rest of him. There is a familiar type of Northern fraud, and a Southern type, equally familiar, but

totally different in appearance. The Northern
type has the straight, flat, earnest hair, the shaven
upper lip, the chin-beard, and the benevolent religious expression. He will be the president of
several charities, and the head of one great business. He plays no cards, drinks no wine, and
warns young men to beware of temptation. He
is as genial as a hair-sofa; and he is seldom found
out by the public unless some financial crash in
general affairs uncovers his cheating, which lies
most often beyond the law's reach; and because
he cannot be put in jail, he quite honestly believes
heaven is his destination. We see less of him
since we have ceased to be a religious country,
religion no longer being an essential disguise for
him. The Southern type, with his unction and
his juleps, is better company, unless he is the hero
of too many of his own anecdotes. He is com-
monly the possessor of a poetic gaze, a mane of
silvery hair, and a noble neck. As war days and
cotton-factor days recede into a past more and
more filmed over with romance, he too grows rare
among us, and I regret it, for he was in truth a
picturesque figure. General Rieppe was perfect.

At first I was sorry that the distance they were
from me rendered hearing what they were saying
impossible; very soon, however, the frame of my
open window provided me with a living picture
which would have been actually spoiled had the
human voice disturbed its eloquent pantomime.

General Rieppe's daughter responded to her
father's caress but languidly, turning to him her
face, with its luminous, stationary beauty. He
pointed to the house, and then waved his hand

toward the bench where she sat; and she, in
response to this, nodded slightly.   Upon which
the General, after another kiss of histrionic pater-
nity administered to her forehead, left her sitting
and proceeded along the garden walk at a stately
pace, until I could no longer see him.   Hortense,
left alone upon the bench, looked down at the
folds of her dress, extended a hand and slowly
rearranged one of them, and then, with the same
hand, felt her hair from front to back.   This had
scarce been accomplished when the General re-
appeared, ushering Juno along the walk, and
bearing a chair with him.   When they turned
the corner at the arbor, Hortense rose, and greetings ensued.   Few objects could be straighter
than was Juno's back; her card-case was in her
hand, but her pocket was not quite large enough
for the whole of her pride, which stuck out so
that it could have been seen from a greater distance than my window.   The General would have
departed, placing his chair for the visitor, when
Hortense waved for him an inviting hand toward
the bench beside her; he waved a similarly inviting hand, looking at Juno, who thereupon sat
firmly down upon the chair.   At this the General
hovered heavily, looking at his daughter, who gave
him no look in return, as she engaged in conversation with Juno; and presently the General left
them.   Juno's back and Hortense's front, both
entirely motionless as they interviewed each other,
presented a stiff appearance, with Juno half turned
in her seat and Hortense's glance following her
slight movement; the two then rose, as the General came down the walk with two chairs and

Mrs. Gregory and Mrs. Weguelin St. Michael.
Juno, with a bow to them, approached Hortense
by a step or two, a brief touch of their fingers was
to be seen, and Juno's departure took place, attended by the heavy hovering of General Rieppe.

"That's why!" I said to myself aloud, suddenly,
at my open window. Immediately, however, I
added, "but can it be?" And in my mind a
whole little edifice of reasons for Hortense's
apparent determination to marry John instantly
fabricated itself — and then fell down.

Through John she was triumphantly bringing
stiff Kings Port to her, was forcing them to accept her. But this was scarce enough temptation
for Hortense to marry; she could do very well
without Kings Port — indeed, she was not very
likely to show herself in it, save to remind them,
now and then, that she was there, and that they
could not keep her out any more; this might
amuse her a little, but the society itself would not
amuse her in the least. What place had it for
her to smoke her cigarettes in?

Eliza La Heu, then? Spite? The pleasure
of taking something that somebody else wanted?
The pleasure of spoiling somebody else's pleasure?
Or, more accurately, the pleasure of power? Well,
yes; that might be it, if Hortense Rieppe were
younger in years, and younger, especially, in soul;
but her museum was too richly furnished with
specimens of the chase, she had collected too
many bits and bibelots from life's Hotel Druot
and the great bazaar of female competition, to pay
so great a price as marriage for merely John;
particularly when a lady, even in Newport, can

have but one husband at a time in her collection.
If she did actually love John, as Beverly Rodgers
had reluctantly come to believe, it was most inappropriate in her !   Had I followed out the
train of reasoning which lay coiled up inside
the word *inappropriate*, I might have reached
the solution which eventually Hortense herself
gave me, and the jewelled recesses of her nature
would have blazed still more brilliantly to my
eyes to-day; but in truth, my soul wasn't old
enough yet to work Hortense out by itself, un-
aided !

While Mrs. Gregory and Mrs. Weguelin sat on
their chairs, and Hortense sat on her bench, tea
was brought and a table laid, behind whose white-
ness and silver Hortense began slight offices with
cups and sugar tongs.   She looked inquiry at her
visitors, in answer to which Mrs. Gregory indicated acceptance, and Mrs. Weguelin refusal.
The beauty of Hortense's face had strangely increased since the arrival of these two visitors.   It
shone resplendent behind the silver and the white
cloth, and her movement, as she gave the cup to
Mrs. Gregory St. Michael, was one of complete
grace and admirable propriety.   But once she looked
away from them in the direction of the path.
Her two visitors rose and left her, Mrs. Gregory
setting her tea-cup down with a gesture that said
she would take no more, and, after their bows of
farewell, Hortense sat alone again pulling about
the tea things.

I saw that by the table lay a card-case on the
ground, evidently dropped by Mrs. Gregory; but
Hortense could not see it where she sat.   Her

quick look along the path heralded more company and the General with more chairs. Young people now began to appear, the various motions of whom were more animated than the approaches and greetings and farewells of their elders; chairs were moved and exchanged, the General was useful in handling cups, and a number of faces unknown to me came and went, some of them elderly ones whom I had seen in church, or passed while walking; the black dresses of age mingled with the brighter colors of youth; and on her bench behind the cups sat Hortense, or rose up at right moments, radiant, restrained and adequate, receiving with deferential attention the remarks of some dark-clothed elder, or, with sufficiently interested countenance, inquiring something from a brighter one of her own generation; but twice I saw her look up the garden path. None of them stayed long, although when they were all gone the shadow of the garden wall had come as far as the arbor; and once again Hortense sat alone behind the table, leaning back with arms folded, and looking straight in front of her. At last she stirred, and rose slowly, and then, with a movement which was the perfection of timidity, began to advance, as John, with his Aunt Eliza, came along the path. To John, Hortense with familiar yet discreet brightness gave a left hand, as she waited for the old lady; and then the old lady went through with it. What that embrace of acknowledgment cost her cannot be measured, and during its process John stood like a sentinel. Possibly this was the price of his forgiveness to his Aunt Eliza.

The visitors accepted tea, and the beauty in

Hortense's face was now supreme. The old lady sat, forgetting to drink her tea, but very still in outward attitude, as she talked with Hortense; and the sight of one hand in its glove lying motionless upon her best dress, suddenly almost drew unexpected tears to my eyes. John was nearly as quiet as she, but the glove that he held was twisted between his fingers. I expected that he would stay with his Hortense when his aunt took her leave; he, however, was evidently expected by the old lady to accompany her out and back, I suppose, to her house, as was proper.

But John's departure from Hortense differed from his meeting her. She gave no left hand to him now; she gazed at him, and then, as the old lady began to go toward the house, she moved a step toward him, and then she cast herself into his arms! It was no acting, this, no skilful simulation; her head sank upon his shoulder, and true passion spoke in every line of that beautiful surrendered form, as it leaned against her lover's.

"So *that's* why!" I exclaimed, once more aloud.

It was but a moment; and John, released, followed Miss Eliza. The old lady walked slowly, with that half-failing step that betokens the body's weariness after great mental or moral strain. Indeed, as John regained her side, she put her arm in his as if her feebleness needed his support. Thus they went away together, the aunt and her beloved boy, who had so sorely grieved and disappointed her.

But if this sight touched me, this glimpse of the vanquished leaving the field after supreme

acknowledgment of defeat, upon Hortense it
wrought another effect altogether. She stood
looking after them, and as she looked, the whole
woman from head to foot, motionless as she was,
seemed to harden. Yet still she looked, until at
length, slowly turning, her eyes chanced to fall
upon Mrs. Gregory St. Michael's card-case.
There it lay, the symbol of Kings Port's capitulation. She swooped down and up with a flying
curve of grace, holding her prey caught; and
then, catching also her handsome skirts on either
side, she danced like a whirling fan among the
empty chairs.

XVIII

BUT a little while, and all that I had just witnessed in such vivid dumb-show might have
seemed to me in truth some masque; so smooth
had it been, and voiceless, coming and going like
a devised fancy. And after the last of the players
was gone from the stage, leaving the white cloth,
and the silver, and the cups, and the groups of
chairs near the pleasant arbor, I watched the
deserted garden whence the sunlight was slowly
departing, and it seemed to me more than ever
like some empty and charming scene in a play-
house, to which the comedians would in due time
return to repeat their delicate pantomime. But
these were mental indulgences, with which I sat
playing until the sight of my interrupted letter to
Aunt Carola on the table before me brought the
reality of everything back into my thoughts; and
I shook my head over Miss Eliza. I remembered
that hand of hers, lying in despondent acqui-
escence upon her lap, as the old lady sat in her
best dress, formally and faithfully accepting the
woman whom her nephew John had brought upon
them as his bride-elect — formally and faithfully
accepting this distasteful person, and thus aton-
ing as best she could to her beloved nephew for
the wrong that her affection had led her to do

him in that ill-starred and inexcusable tampering
with his affairs.

But there was my letter waiting. I took my
pen, and finished what I had to say about the
negro and the injustice we had done to *him*, as
well as to our own race, by the Fifteenth Amendment. I wrote : —

"I think Northerners must often seem to these
people strangely obtuse in their attitude. And
they deserve such opinion, since all they need to
do is come here and see for themselves what the
War did to the South.

"You may have a perfectly just fight with a
man and beat him rightly; but if you are able to
go on with your work next day, while his health
is so damaged that for a long while he limps about
as a cripple, you must not look up from your busy
thriving and reproach him with his helplessness,
and remind him of its cause; nor must you be surprised that he remembers the fight longer than
you have time for. I know that the North meant
to be magnanimous, that the North *was* magnanimous, that the spirit of Grant at Appomattox filled
many breasts; and I know that the magnanimity
was not met by those who led the South after
Lee's retirement, and before reconstruction set in,
and that the Fifteenth Amendment was brought
on by their own doings : when have two wrongs
made a right? And to place the negro above
these people was an atrocity. You cannot expect
them to inquire very industriously how magnanimous this North *meant* to be, when they have
suffered at her hands worse, far worse, than France
suffered from Germany's after 1870.

" I do think there should be a different spirit
among some of the later-born, but I have come
to understand even the slights and suspicions
from which I here and there suffer, since to their
minds, shut in by circumstance, I'm always a
' Yankee.'

" We are prosperous ; and prosperity does not
bind, it merely *assembles* people — at dinners and
dances. It is adversity that *binds* — beside the
gravestone, beneath the desolated roof. Could
you come here and see what I have seen, the
retrospect of suffering, the long, lingering con-
valescence, the small outlook of vigor to come,
and the steadfast sodality of affliction and affection and fortitude, your kind but unenlightened
heart would be wrung, as mine has been, and is
being, at every turn."

After I had posted this reply to Aunt Carola,
I had some fears that my pen had run away with
me, and that she might now descend upon me
with that reproof which she knew so well how to
exercise in cases of disrespect. But there was
actually a certain pathos in her mildness when it
came. She felt it her duty to go over a good deal
of history first, but : —

" I do not understand the present generation,"
she finished, " and I suppose that I was not
meant to."

The little sigh in these words did great credit
to Aunt Carola.

This vindication off my mind, and relieved by
it of the more general thoughts about Kings Port
and the South, which the pantomime of Kings
Port's forced capitulation to Hortense had raised

in me, I returned to the personal matters between
that young woman and John, and Charley.   How
much did Charley know ?   How much would
Charley stand ?   How much would John stand,
if he came to know ?

Well, the scene in the garden now helped me
to answer these questions much better than I
could have answered them before its occurrence.
With one fact — the great fact of love — established, it was not difficult to account for at least
one or two of the several things that puzzled me.
There could be no doubt that Hortense loved
John Mayrant, loved him beyond her own control.
When this love had begun, made no matter.   Perhaps it began on the bridge, when the money was
torn, and Eliza La Heu had appeared.   The Kings
Port version of Hortense's indifference to John
before the event of the phosphates might well
enough be true.   It might even well enough be
true that she had taken him and his phosphates
at Newport for lack of anything better at hand,
and because she was sick of disappointed hopes.
In this case, Charley's subsequent appearance as
something very much better (if the phosphates
were to fail) would perfectly explain the various
postponements of the wedding.

So I was able to answer my questions to myself thus : How much did Charley know ? — Just
what he could see for himself, and what he had
most likely heard from Newport gossip.   He
could have heard of an old engagement, made
purely for money's sake, and of recent delays
created by the lady ; and he could see the gentleman — an impossible husband from a Wall Street

standpoint! — to whom Hortense was evidently
tempering her final refusal by indulgently taking
an interest in helping along his phosphate fortune. Charley would not refuse to lend her his
aid in this estimable benevolence; nor would it
occur to Charley's sensibilities how such benevolence would be taken by John if John were not
"taken" himself. Yes, Charley was plainly fooled,
and fooled the more readily because he had the
old version of the truth. How should he suspect
there was a revised version? How should he discover that passion had now changed sides, that it
was now John who allowed himself to be loved?
The signs of this did not occur before his eyes.
Of course, Charley would not stay fooled forever;
the hours of that were numbered, — but their
number was quite beyond my guessing!

How much would Charley stand? He would
stand a good deal, because the measure of
his toleration was the measure of his desire for
Hortense; and it was plain that he wanted her
very much indeed. But how much would John
stand? How soon would his "fire-eating" traditions produce a "difficulty"? Why had they
not done this already? Well, the garden had in
some way helped me to frame a fairly reasonable
answer for this also. Poor Hortense had become
as powerless to woo John to warmth as poor
Venus had been with Adonis; and passion, in
changing sides, had advanced the boy's knowledge. He knew now the difference between the
embraces of his lady when she had merely wanted
his phosphates, and these other caresses now that
she wanted *him*. In his ceaseless search for some

possible loophole of escape, his eye could not have overlooked the chance that lay in Charley, and he was far too canny to blast his forlorn hope. He had probably wondered what had changed the nature of Hortense's caresses, and the adventure of the torn money could scarce have failed to suggest itself to the mind of a youth who, little as he had trodden the ways of the world, evidently possessed some lively instincts regarding the nature of women. To batter Charley as he had battered Juno's nephew, might result in winding the arms of Hortense around his own neck more tightly than ever.

Why Hortense should keep Charley " on " any longer, was what I could least fathom, but I trusted her to have excellent reasons for anything that she did. " It's sure to be quite simple, once you know it," I told myself; and the near future proved me to be right.

Thus I laid most of my enigmas to rest; there was but one which now and then awakened still. Were Hortense a raw girl of eighteen, I could easily grant that the " fire-eater " in John would be sure to move her. But Hortense had travelled many miles away from the green forests of romance; her present fields were carpeted, not with grass and flowers, but with Oriental mats and rugs, and it was electric lights, not the moon and stars, that shone upon her highly seasoned nights. No, torn money and all, it was not *appropriate* in a woman of her experience; and so I still found myself inquiring in the words of Beverly Rodgers, " But what can she want him for ? "

The next time that I met Mrs. Gregory St. Michael it was on my way to join the party at the old church, which Mrs. Weguelin was going to show them. The card-case was in her hand, and the sight of it prompted me to allude to Hortense Rieppe.

"I find her beauty growing upon me," I declared.

Mrs. Gregory did not deny the beauty, although she spoke with reserve at first. "It is to be said that she knows how to write a suitable note," the lady also admitted.

She didn't tell me what the note was about, naturally; but I could imagine with what joy in the exercise of her art Hortense had constructed that communication which must have accompanied the prompt return of the card-case.

Then Mrs. Gregory's tongue became downright. "Since you're able to see so much of her, why don't you tell her to marry that little steam-yacht gambler? I'm sure he's dying to, and he's just the thing for her?"

"Ah," I returned, "Love so seldom knows what's just the thing for marriage."

"Then your precocity theory falls," declared Mrs. St. Michael. And as she went away from me along the street, I watched her beautiful stately walk; for who could help watching a sight so good?

Charley, then, was no secret to John's people. Was John still a secret to Charley? Could Hortense possibly have managed this? I hoped for a chance to observe the two men with her during the visit of Mrs. Weguelin St. Michael and her party to the church.

This party was already assembled when I arrived upon the spot appointed. In the street, a few paces from the church, stood Bohm and Charley and Kitty and Gazza, with Beverly Rodgers, who, as I came near, left them and joined me.

"Oh, she's somewhere off with her fire-eater," responded Beverly to my immediate inquiry for Hortense. "Do you think she was asked, old man?"

Probably not, I thought. "But she goes so well with the rest," I suggested.

Beverly gave his chuckle. "She goes where she likes. She'll meet us here when we're finished, I'm pretty sure."

"Why such certainty?"

"Well, she has to attend to Charley, you know!"

Mrs. Weguelin, it appeared, had met the party here by the church, but had now gone somewhere in the immediate neighborhood to find out why the gate was not opened to admit us, and to hasten the unpunctual custodian of the keys. I had not looked for precisely such a party as Mrs. Weguelin's invitation had gathered, nor could I imagine that she had fully understood herself what she was gathering; and this I intimated to Beverly Rodgers, saying: —

"Do you suppose, my friend, that she suspected the feather of the birds you flock with?"

Beverly took it lightly. "Hang it, old boy, of course everybody can't be as nice as I am!" But he took it less lightly before it was over.

We stood chatting apart, he and I, while Bohm and Charley and Kitty and Gazza walked across

the street to the window of a shop, where old furniture was for sale at a high price; and it grew
clearer to me what Beverly had innocently brought
upon Mrs. Weguelin, and how he had brought it.
The little quiet, particular lady had been pleased
with his visit, and pleased with him. His good
manners, his good appearance, his good English-
trained voice, all these things must have been extremely to her taste; and then — more important
than they — did she not know about his people?
She had inquired, he told me, with interest about
two of his uncles, whom she had last seen in
1858. "She's awfully the right sort," said Beverly.
Yes, I saw well how that visit must have gone:
the gentle old lady reviving in Beverly's presence,
and for the sake of being civil to him, some memories of her girlhood, some meetings with those
uncles, some dances with them; and generally
shedding from her talk and manner the charm of
some sweet old melody — and Beverly, the facile,
the appreciative, sitting there with her at a correct, deferential angle on his chair, admirably
sympathetic and in good form, and playing the
old school. (He had no thought to deceive her;
the old school was his by right, and genuinely in
his blood, he took to it like a duck to the water.)
How should Mrs. Weguelin divine that he also
took to the *nouveau jeu* to the tune of Bohm and
Charley and Kitty and Gazza? And so, to show
him some attention, and because she couldn't ask
him to a meal, why, she would take him over the
old church, her colonial forefathers'; she would
tell him the little legends about them; he was
precisely the young man to appreciate such things

— and she would be pleased if he would also bring the friends with whom he was travelling.

I looked across the street at Bohm and Charley and Kitty and Gazza. They were now staring about them in all their perfection of stare: small Charley in a sleek slate-colored suit, as neat as any little barber; Bohm, massive, portentous, his strong shoes and gloves the chief note in his dress, and about his whole firm frame a heavy mechanical strength, a look as of something that did something rapidly and accurately when set going — cut or cracked or ground or smashed something better and faster than it had ever been cut or cracked or ground or smashed before, and would take your arms and legs off if you didn't stand well back from it; it was only in Bohm's eye and lips that you saw he wasn't made entirely of brass and iron, that champagne and shoulders décolletés received a punctual share of his valuable time. And there was Kitty, too, just the wife for Bohm, so soon as she could divorce her husband, to whom she had united herself before discovering that all she married him for, his old Knickerbocker name, was no longer in the slightest degree necessary for social acceptance; while she could feed people, her trough would be well thronged. Kitty was neat, Kitty was trig, Kitty was what Beverly would call " swagger "; her skilful tailor-made clothes sheathed her closely and gave her the excellent appearance of a well-folded English umbrella; it was in her hat that she had gone wrong — a beautiful hat in itself, one which would have wholly become Hortense; but for poor Kitty it didn't do at all. Yes, she was a well-folded English umbrella, only the umbrella had for its handle the head of a bulldog or the leg of a ballet-dancer. And these were the Replacers, whom Beverly's clear-sighted eyes saw swarming round the temple of his civilization, pushing down the aisles, climbing over the backs of the benches, walking over each other's bodies, and seizing those front seats which his family had sat in since New York had been New York; and so the wise fellow very prudently took every step that would insure the Replacers' inviting him to occupy one of his own chairs. I had almost forgotten little Gazza, the Italian nobleman, who sold old furniture to new Americans. Gazza was not looking at the old furniture of Kings Port, which must have filled his Vatican soul with contempt; he was strolling back and forth in the street, with his head in the air, humming, now loudly, now softly, "*La-la, la-la, E quando a la predica in chiesa siederai, la-la-la-la;*" and I thought to myself that, were I the Pope, I should kick him into the Tiber.

When Mrs. Weguelin St. Michael came back with the keys and their custodian, Bohm was listening to the slow, clear words of Charley, in which he evidently found something that at length interested him — a little. Bohm, it seemed, did not often speak himself: possibly once a week. His way was to let other people speak to him; when there were signs in his face that he was hearing anything which they said, it was a high compliment to them, and of course Charley could command Bohm's ear; for Charley, although he was as neat as any barber, and let Hortense walk

on him because he looked beyond that, and pur-
posed to get her, was just as potent in the financial world as Bohm, could bring a borrowing
empire to his own terms just as skilfully as could
Bohm; was, in short, a man after Bohm's own —
I had almost said heart: the expression is so ob-
stinately embedded in our language! Bohm, listening, and Charley, talking, had neither of them
noticed Mrs. Weguelin's arrival; they stood ignor-
ing her, while she waited, casting a timid eye upon
them. But Beverly, suddenly perceiving this, and
begging her pardon for them, brought the party
together, and we moved in among the old graves.

"Ah!" said Gazza, bending to read the quaint
words cut upon one of them, as we stopped while
the door at the rear of the church was being
opened, "French!"

"It was the mother-tongue of these colonists,"
Mrs. Weguelin explained to him.

"Ah! like Canada!" cried Gazza. "But what
a pretty bit is that!" And he stood back to
admire a little glimpse, across a street, between
tiled roofs and rusty balconies, of another church
steeple. "Almost, one would say, the Old
World," Gazza declared.

"Our world is not new," said Mrs. Weguelin;
and she passed into the church.

Kings Port holds many sacred nooks, many corners, many vistas, that should deeply stir the
spirit and the heart of all Americans who know
and love their country. The passing traveller
may gaze up at certain windows there, and see
History herself looking out at him, even as she
looks out of the windows of Independence Hall in

"Almost, one would say, the Old World"

Philadelphia.   There are also other ancient buildings in Kings Port, where History is shut up, as in

a strong-box, — such as that stubborn old octagon, the powder-magazine of Revolutionary times, which is a chest holding proud memories of blood and war. And then there are the three churches. Not strong-boxes, these, but shrines, where burn the venerable lamps of faith. And of these three houses of God, that one holds the most precious flame, the purest light, which treasures the holy fire that came from France. The English colonists, who sat in the other two congregations, came to Carolina's soil to better their estate; but it was for liberty of soul, to lift their ardent and exalted prayer to God as their own conscience bade them, and not as any man dictated, that those French colonists sought the New World. No Puritan splendor of independence and indomitable courage outshines theirs. They preached a word as burning as any that Plymouth or Salem ever heard. They were but a handful, yet so fecund was their marvellous zeal that they became the spiritual leaven of their whole community. They are less known than Plymouth and Salem, because men of action, rather than men of letters, have sprung from the loins of the South; but there they stand, a beautiful beacon, shining upon the coasts of our early history. Into their church, then, into the shrine where their small lamp still burns, their devout descendant, Mrs. Weguelin St. Michael led our party, because in her eyes Kings Port could show nothing more precious and significant. There had been nothing to warn her that Bohm and Charley were Americans who neither knew nor loved their country, but merely Americans who knew their country's wealth and loved to acquire every penny of it that they could.

And so, following the steps of our delicate and
courteous guide, we entered into the dimness of
the little building; and Mrs. Weguelin's voice,
lowered to suit the sanctity which the place had for
her, began to tell us very quietly and clearly the
story of its early days.

I knew it, or something of it, from books; but
from this little lady's lips it took on a charm
and graciousness which made it fresh to me. I
listened attentively, until I felt, without at first
seeing the cause, that dulling of enjoyment, that
interference with the receptive attention, which
comes at times to one during the performance of
music when untimely people come in or go out.
Next, I knew that our group of listeners was less
compact; and then, as we moved from the first
point in the church to a new one, I saw that
Bohm and Charley were dropping behind, and I
lingered, with the intention of bringing them
closer.

"But there was nothing in it," I heard Charley's
slow monologue continuing behind me to the
silent Bohm. "We could have bought the
Parsons road at that time. 'Gentlemen,' I said to
them, 'what is there for us in tide-water at Kings
Port?'"

It was not to be done, and I rejoined Mrs.
Weguelin and those of the party who were making
some show of attention to her quiet little histories
and explanations; and Kitty's was the next voice
which I heard ring out: —

"Oh, you must never let it fall to pieces! It's
the cunningest little fossil I've seen in the South."

"So," said Charley behind me, "we let the

other crowd buy their strategic point ; and I guess
they know they got a gold brick."

I moved away from the financiers, I endeavored
not to hear their words ; and in this much I was
successful ; but their inappropriate presence had
got, I suppose upon my nerves ; at any rate, go
where I would in the little church, or attend as I
might and did to what Mrs. Weguelin St. Michael
said about the tablets, and whatever traditions
their inscriptions suggested to her, that quiet, low,
persistent banker's voice of Charley's pervaded the
building like a draft of cold air.   Once, indeed, he
addressed Mrs. Weguelin a question.   She was
telling Beverly (who followed her throughout,
protectingly and charmingly, with his most
devoted attention and his best manner) the honorable deeds of certain older generations of a
family belonging to this congregation, some of
whose tombs outside had borne French inscriptions.

" My mother's family," said Mrs. Weguelin.

" And nowadays," inquired Beverly, " what do
they find instead of military careers ? "

" There are no more of us nowadays ; they —
they were killed in the war."   And immediately
she smiled, and with her hand she made a light
gesture, as if to dismiss this subject from mutual
embarrassment and pain.

" I might have known better," murmured the
understanding Beverly.

But Charley now had his question.   " How
many, did you say ? "

"How many ? " Mrs. Weguelin did not quite
understand him.

" Were killed ? " explained Charley.

Again there was a little pause before Mrs. Weguelin answered, " My four brothers met their deaths."

Charley was interested. " And what was the percentage of fatality in their regiments ? "

" Oh," said Mrs. Weguelin, " we did not think of it in that way." And she turned aside.

" Charley," said Kitty, with some precipitancy, " do make Mr. Bohm look at the church ! " and she turned after Mrs. Weguelin. " It *is* such a *gem* ! "

But I saw the little lady try to speak and fail, and then I noticed that she was leaning against a window-sill.

Beverly Rodgers also noticed this, and he hastened to her.

" Thank you," she returned to his hasty question, " I am quite well. If you are not tired of it, shall we go on ? "

" It is such a *gem* ! " repeated Kitty, throwing an angry glance at Charley and Bohm. And so we went on.

Yes, Kitty did her best to cover it up; Kitty, as she would undoubtedly have said herself, could see a few things. But nobody could cover it up, though Beverly was now vigilant in his efforts to do so. Indeed, Replacers cannot be covered up by human agency; they bulge, they loom, they stare, they dominate the road of life, even as their automobiles drive horses and pedestrians to the wall. Bohm, roused from his financial torpor by Kitty's sharp command, did actually turn his eyes upon the church, which he had now been inside for some twenty minutes without noticing. Instinct and long training had given his eye, when it really looked at anything, a particular glance— the glance of the Replacer — which plainly calculated: " Can this be made worth money to me?" and which died instantly to a glaze of indifference on seeing that no money could be made. Bohm's eye, accordingly, waked and then glazed. Manners, courtesy, he did not need, not yet; he had looked at them with his Replacer glance, and, seeing no money in them, had gone on looking at railroads, and mines, and mills, — and bare shoulders, and bottles. Should manners and courtesy come, some day, to mean money to him, then he could have them, in his fashion, so that his admirers and his apologists should alike declare of him, " A rough diamond, but consider what he has made of himself ! "

" After what, did you say? " This was the voice of Gazza, addressing Mrs. Weguelin St. Michael. It must be said of Gazza that he, too, made a certain pretence of interest in the traditions of Kings Port.

" After the revocation of the Edict of Nantes," replied Mrs. Weguelin.

" Built it in Savannah," Charley was saying to Bohm, "or Norfolk. This is a good place to bury people in, but not money. Now the phosphate proposition — "

Again I dragged my attention by force away from that quiet, relentless monologue, and listened as well as I could to Mrs. Weguelin. There had come to be among us all, I think — Beverly, Kitty, Gazza, and myself — a joint impulse to shield her,

to cluster about her, to follow her steps from each
little lecture that she finished to the new point
where the next lecture began ; and we did it, performed our pilgrimage to the end; but there was
less and less nature in our performance.   I knew
(and it was like a dream which I could not stop)
that we pressed a little too close, that our questions were a little too eager, that we overpainted
our faces with attention ; knowing this did not
help, nothing helped, and we went on to the end,
seeing ourselves doing it ; and it must have been
that Mrs. Weguelin saw us likewise.   But she was
truly admirable in giving no sign, she came out
well ahead ; the lectures were not hurried, one
had no sense of points being skipped to accom-
modate our unworthiness, it required a previous
familiarity with the church to know (as I did) that
there was, indeed, more and more skipping ; yet
the little lady played her part so evenly and with
never a falter of voice nor a change in the gentle
courtesy of her manner, that I do not think —
save for that moment at the window-sill— I could
have been sure what she thought, or how much
she noticed.   Her face was always so pale, it may
well have been all imagination with me that she
seemed, when we emerged at last into the light of
the street, paler than usual ; but I am almost certain that her hand was trembling as she stood
receiving the thanks of the party.   These thanks
were cut a little short by the arrival of one of the
automobiles, and, at the same time, the appearance of Hortense strolling toward us with John
Mayrant.

Charley had resumed to Bohm, " A   tax of

twenty-five cents on the ton is nothing with deposits of this richness," when his voice ceased;
and looking at him to see the cause, I perceived
that his eye was on John, and that his polished
finger-nail was running meditatively along his
thin mustache.

Hortense took the matter — whatever the matter was — in hand.

" You haven't much time," she said to Charley,
who consulted his watch.

" Who's coming to see me off? " he inquired.

" Where's he going? " I asked Beverly.

" She's sending him North," Beverly answered,
and then he spoke with his very best simple manner to Mrs. Weguelin St. Michael. " May I not
walk home with you after all your kindness? "

She was going to say no, for she had had
enough of this party; but she looked at Beverly,
and his face and his true solicitude won her; she
said, " Thank you, if you will." And the two departed together down the shabby street, the little
veiled lady in black, and Beverly with his excellent London clothes and his still more excellent
look of respectful, sheltering attention.

And now Bohm pronounced the only utterance
that I heard fall from his lips during his stay in
Kings Port. He looked at the church he had
come from, he looked at the neighboring larger
church whose columns stood out at the angle of
the street; he looked at the graveyard opposite
that, then at the stale, dusty shop of old furniture,
and then up the shabby street, where no life or
movement was to be seen, except the distant forms
of Beverly and Mrs. Weguelin St. Michael. Then

from a gold cigar-case, curved to fit his breast pocket, he took a cigar and lighted it from a gold match-box. Offering none of us a cigar, he placed the case again in his pocket; and holding his lighted cigar a moment with two fingers in his strong glove, he spoke: —

" This town's worse than Sunday."

Then he got into the automobile. They all followed to see Charley off, and he addressed me.

" I shall be glad," he said, " if you will make one of a little party on the yacht next Sunday, when I come back. And you also," he added to John.

Both John and I expressed our acceptance in suitable forms, and the automobile took its way to the train.

" Your Kings Port streets," I said, as we walked back toward Mrs. Trevise's, " are not very favorable for automobiles."

" No," he returned briefly. I don't remember that either of us found more to say until we had reached my front door, when he asked, " Will the day after to-morrow suit you for Udolpho ? "

" Whenever you say," I told him.

" Weather permitting, of course. But I hope that it will; for after that I suppose my time will not be quite so free."

After we had parted it struck me that this was the first reference to his approaching marriage that John had ever made in my hearing since that day long ago (it seemed long ago, at least) when he had come to the Exchange to order the wedding-cake, and Eliza La Heu had fallen in love with him at sight.   That, in my opinion, looking back now with eyes at any rate partially opened, was what Eliza had done.   Had John returned the compliment then, or since?

XIX

UDOLPHO

I T was to me continuously a matter of satisfaction and of interest to see Hortense disturbed
— whether for causes real or imaginary — about
the security of her title to her lover John, nor can
I say that my misinterpreted bunch of roses diminished this satisfaction. I should have been glad
to know if the accomplished young woman had
further probed that question and discovered the
truth, but it seemed scarce likely that she could
do this without the help of one of three persons,
Eliza and myself who knew all, or John who knew
nothing; for the up-country bride, and whatever
other people in Kings Port there were to whom
the bride might gayly recite the tale of my roses,
were none of them likely to encounter Miss
Rieppe; their paths and hers would not meet
until they met in church at the wedding of Hortense and John. No, she could not have found
out the truth; for never in the world would she,
at this eleventh hour, risk a conversation with
John upon a subject so full of well-packed explo-
sives; and so she must be simply keeping on both
him and Eliza an eye as watchful as lay in her
power. As for Charley, what bait, what persua-
sion, what duress she had been able to find that

took him at an hour so critical from her side to New York, I could not in the least conjecture. Had she said to the little banker, Go, because I must think it over alone? It did not seem strong enough. Or had she said, Go, and on your return you shall have my answer? Not adequate either, I thought. Or had it been, If you don't go, it shall be "no," to-day and forever? This last was better; but there was no telling, nor did Beverly Rodgers, to whom I propounded all my theories, have any notion of what was between Hortense and Charley. He only knew that Charley was quite aware of the existence of John, but had always been merely amused at the notion of him.

"So have you been merely amused," I reminded him.

"Not since that look I saw her give him, old chap. I know she wants him, only not why she wants him. And Charley, you know—well, of course, poor Charley's a banker, just a banker and no more; and a banker is merely the ace in the same pack where the drummer is the two-spot. Our American civilization should be called Drummer's Delight — and there's nothing in your fire-eater to delight a drummer: he's a gentleman, he'll be only so-so rich, and he's away back out of the lime-light, while poor old Charley's a bounder, and worth forty millions anyhow, and right in the centre of the glare. How should he see any danger in John?"

"I wonder if he hasn't begun to?"

"Well, perhaps. He and Hortense have been 'talking business'; I know that. Oh — and why do you think she *said* he must go to New York? To make a better deal for the fire-eater's phos-

phates than his fuddling old trustee here was going to close with. Charley said that could be
arranged by telegram. But she made him go
himself! She's extraordinary. He'll arrive in
town to-morrow, he'll leave next day, he'll reach
here by the Southern on Saturday night in time
for our Sunday yacht picnic, and then something
has got to happen, I should think."

Here was another key, unlocking a further
piece of knowledge for me. I had not been able
to guess why Hortense should be keeping Charley
"on"; but how natural was this policy, when
understood clearly! She still needed Charley's
influence in the world of affairs. Charley's final
service was to be the increasing of his successful
rival's fortune. I wondered what Charley would
do, when the full extent of his usefulness dawned
upon him; and with wonder renewed I thought
of General Rieppe, and this daughter he had
managed to beget. Surely the mother of Hortense, whoever she may have been, must have
been a very richly endowed character!

"Something has most certainly got to happen,
and soon," I said to Beverly Rodgers. "Especially
if my busy boarding-house bodies are right in
saying that the invitations for the wedding are to
be out on Monday."

Well, I had Friday, I had Udolpho; and there,
while on that excursion, when I should be alone
with John Mayrant during many hours, and especially the hours of deep, confidential night, I
swore to myself on oath I would say to the boy
the last word, up to the verge of offence, that my
wits could devise. Apart from a certain dra-

matic excitement as of battle — battle between
Hortense and me — I truly wished to help him
out of the miserable mistake his wrong standard,
his chivalry gone perverted, was spurring him on
to make; and I had a comic image of myself,
summoning Miss Josephine, summoning Miss
Eliza, summoning Mrs. Gregory and Mrs. Weguelin, and the whole company of aunts and cousins,
and handing to them the rescued John with the
single but sufficient syllable: " There! "

He was in apparent spirits, was John, at that
hour of our departure for Udolpho; he pretended
so well that I was for a while altogether deceived.
He had wished to call for me with the conveyance
in which he should drive us out into the lonely
country through the sunny afternoon; but instead,
I chose to walk round to where he lived, and where
I found him stuffing beneath the seats of the
vehicle the baskets and the parcels which contained the provisions for our ample supper.

" I have never seen you drink hearty yet, and
now I purpose to," said John.

As the packing was finishing Miss Josephine
St. Michael came by; and the sight of the erect
old lady reminded me that of all Kings Port figures known to me and seen in the garden paying
their visit of ceremony to Hortense, she alone —
she and Eliza La Heu—had been absent. Eliza's
declining to share in that was well-nigh inevitable,
but Miss Josephine was another matter. Perhaps
she had considered her sister's going there to be
enough; at any rate, she had not been party to
the surrender, and this gave me whimsical satisfaction. Moreover, it had evidently occasioned

no ruffle in the affectionate relations between herself and John.

"John," said she, "as you drive by, do get me
a plumber."

"Much better get a burglar, Aunt Josephine.
Cheaper in the end, and neater work."

It was thus, at the outset, that I came to believe John's spirits were high; and this illusion
he successfully kept up until after we had left the
plumber and Kings Port several sordid miles behind us; the approach to Kings Port this way
lies through dirtiest Africa. John was loquacious;
John discoursed upon the Replacers; Mrs. Weguelin St. Michael had quite evidently expressed to
her own circle what she thought of them; and the
town in consequence, although it did not see them
or their automobiles, because it appeared they
were gone some twenty miles inland upon an
excursion to a resort where was a large hotel, and
a little variety in the way of some tourists of the
Replacer stripe, — the town kept them well in its
mind's eye. The automobiles would have sufficed
to bring them into disrepute, but Kings Port had
a better reason in their conduct in the church;
and John found many things to say to me, as we
drove along, about Bohm and Charley and Kitty.
Gazza he forgot, although, as shall appear in its
place, Gazza was likely to live a long while in his
memory. Beverly Rodgers he, of course, recognized as being a gentleman — it was clear that
Beverly met with Kings Port's approval — and,
from his Newport experiences, John was able to
make out quite as well as if he had heard Beverly
explain it himself the whole wise philosophic

system of joining with the Replacers in order that you be not replaced yourself.

"In his shoes mightn't I do the same?" he surmised. "I fear I'm not as Spartan as my aunts —only pray don't mention it to them!"

And then, because I had been answering him with single syllables, or with nods, or not at all, he taxed me with my taciturnity; he even went so far as to ask me what thoughts kept me so silent — which I did not tell him.

"I am wondering," I told him instead, "how much they steal every week."

"Those financiers?"

"Yes. Bohm is president of an insurance company, and Charley's a director, and reorganizes railroads."

"Well, if other people share your pleasant opinion of them, how do they get elected?"

"Other people share their pleasant spoils — senators, vestrymen — you can't be sure who you're sitting next to at dinner any more. Come live North. You'll find the only safe way is never to know anybody worth more than five millions — if you wish to keep the criminal classes off your visiting list."

This made him merry. "Put 'em in jail, then!"

"Ah, the jail!" I returned. "It's the great American joke. It reverses the rule of our smart society. Only those who have no incomes are admitted."

"But what do you have laws and lawyers for?"

"To keep the rich out of jail. It's called 'professional etiquette.'"

" Your picture flatters ! "

" You flatter me; it's only a photograph. Come North and see."

" One might think, from your account, the American had rather be bad than good."

" O dear, no ! The American had much rather be good than bad ! "

" Your admission amazes me ! "

" But also the American had rather be rich than good. And he is having his wish. And money's golden hand is tightening on the throat of liberty while the labor union stabs liberty in the back — for trusts and unions are both trying to kill liberty. And the soul of Uncle Sam has turned into a dollar inside his great, big, strong, triumphant flesh; so that even his new religion, his own special invention, his last offering to the creeds of the world, his gatherer of converted hordes, his Christian Science, is based upon physical benefit."

John touched the horses. " You're particularly cheerful to-day ! "

" No. I merely summarize what I'm seeing."

" Well, a moral awakening will come," he declared.

" Inevitably. To-morrow, perhaps. The flesh has had a good, long, prosperous day, and the hour of the spirit must be near- striking. And the moral awakening will be followed by a moral slumber, since, in the uncomprehended scheme of things, slumber seems necessary ; and you needn't pull so long a face, Mr. Mayrant, because the slumber will be followed by another moral awakening. The alcoholic society girl you don't like

will very probably give birth to a water-drinking
daughter — who in her turn may produce a bibu-
lous progeny: how often must I tell you that
nothing is final?"

John Mayrant gave the horses a somewhat
vicious lash after these last words of mine; and,
as he made no retort to them, we journeyed some
little distance in silence through the mild, enchanting light of the sun. My deliberate allusion to
alcoholic girls had made plain what I had begun
to suspect. I could now discern that his cloak of
gayety had fallen from him, leaving bare the same
harassed spirit, the same restless mood, which had
been his upon the last occasion when we had
talked at length together upon some of the present social and political phases of our republic —
that day of the New Bridge and the advent of
Hortense. Only, upon that day, he had by his
manner in some subtle fashion conveyed to me
a greater security in my discretion than I felt
him now to entertain. His many observations
about the Replacers, with always the significant
and conspicuous omission of Hortense, proved
more and more, as I thought it over, that his state
was unsteady. Even now, he did not long endure
silence between us; yet the eagerness which he
threw into our discussions did not, it seemed to
me, so much proceed from present interest in their
subjects (though interest there was at times) as
from anxiety lest one particular subject, ever present with him, should creep in unawares. So much
I, at any rate, concluded, and bided my time for
the creeping in unawares, content meanwhile to
parry some of the reproaches which he now and

again cast at me with an earnestness real or feigned.

We had made now considerable progress, and were come to a space of sand and cabins and intersecting railroad tracks, where freight cars and locomotives stood, and negroes of all shapes, but of one lowering and ragged appearance, lounged and stared.

" There used to be a murder here about once a day," said John, " before the dispensary system. Now, it is about once a week."

" That law is of benefit, then ? " I inquired.

" To those who drink the whiskey, possibly; certainly to those who sell it! " And he condensed for me the long story of the state dispensary, which in brief appeared to be that South Carolina had gone into the liquor business. The profits were to pay for compulsory education; the liquor was to be pure; society and sobriety were to be advanced: such had been the threefold promise, of which the threefold fulfilment was — defeat of the compulsory education bill, a political monopoly enriching favored distillers, " and lately," said John, " a thoroughly democratic whiskey for the plain people. Pay ten cents for a bottle of X, if you're curious. It may not poison you — but the murders are coming up again."

" What a delightful example of government ownership! " I exclaimed.

But John in Kings Port was not in the way of hearing that cure-all policy discussed, and I therefore explained it to him. He did not seem to grasp my explanation.

"I don't see how it would change anything," he remarked, "beyond switching the stealing from one set of hands to another."

I put on a face of concern. "What? You don't believe in our patent American short-cuts?"

"Short-cuts?"

"Certainly. Short-cuts to universal happiness, universal honesty, universal everything. For instance: Don't make a boy study four years for a college degree; just cut the time in half, and you've got a short-cut to education. Write it down that man is equal. That settles it. You'll notice how equal he is at once. Write it down that the negro shall vote. You'll observe how instantly he is fit for the suffrage. Now they want it written down that government shall take all the wicked corporations, because then corruption will disappear from the face of the earth. You'll find the farmers presently having it written down that all hens must hatch their eggs in a week, and next, a league of earnest women will advocate a Constitutional amendment that men only shall bring forth children. Oh, we Americans are very thorough!" And I laughed.

But John's face was not gay. "Well," he mused, "South Carolina took a short-cut to pure liquor and sober citizens — and reached instead a new den of thieves. Is the whole country sick?"

"Sick to the marrow, my friend; but young and vigorous still. A nation in its long life has many illnesses before the one it dies of. But we shall need some strong medicine if we do not get well soon."

" What kind ? "

" Ah, that's beyond any one! And we have
several things the matter with us — as bad a case,
for example, of complacency as I've met in history.
Complacency's a very dangerous disease, seldom
got rid of without the purge of a great calamity.
And worse, where does our dishonesty begin, and
where end? The boy goes to college, and there
in football it awaits him; he graduates, and in the
down-town office it smirks at him; he rises into
the confidence of his superiors, the town's chief
citizens, and finds their gray hairs crowned with
it, — the very men he has looked up to, believed
in, his ideals, his examples, the merchant prince,
the railroad magnate, the president of insurance
companies — all dirty rascals ! Presently he faces
worldly success or failure, and then, in the new
ocean of mind that has swallowed morals up, he
sinks with his isolated honesty, like a fool, or
swims to respectability with his brother knaves.
And into this mess the immigrant sewage of
Europe is steadily pouring. Such is our conti-
nent to-day, with all its fair winds and tides and
fields favorable to us, and only our shallow, com-
placent, dishonest selves against us! But don't let
these considerations make you gloomy; for (I must
say it again) nothing is final; and even if we rot
before we ripen — which would be a wholly novel
phenomenon — we shall have made our contribution to mankind in demonstrating by our collapse
that the sow's ear belongs with the rest of the
animal, and not in the voting booth or the legislature, and that the doctrine of universal suffrage
should have waited until men were born honest

and equal. That in itself would be a memorable service to have rendered."

We had come into the divine, sad stillness of the woods, where the warm sunlight shone through the gray moss, lighting the curtained solitudes away and away into the depths of the golden afternoon; and somewhere amid the miles of sleeping wilderness sounded the hoarse honk of the automobile. The Replacers were abroad, enjoying what they could in this country where they did not belong, and which did not as yet belong to them. Once again we heard their honk off to our left, from a farther distance, and I am glad to say that we did not see them at all.

" If," said John Mayrant, "what you have said is true, the nation had better get on its knees and pray God to give it grace."

I looked at the boy and saw that his countenance had grown very fine. "The act," I said, "would bring grace, wherever it comes from."

" Yes," he assented. " If in the stars and awfulness of space there's nothing, that does not trouble me; for my greater self is inside me, safe. And our country has a greater self somewhere. Think!"

" I do not have to think," I replied, "when I know the nobleness we have risen to at times."

" And I," he pursued, "happen to believe it is not all only stars and space; and that God, as much as any ship-builder, rejoices to watch every tiniest boat meet and brave the storm."

Out of his troubles he had brought such mood, sweetness instead of bitterness; he was saying as plainly as if his actual words said it, " Misfortune

has come to me, and I am going to make the best
of it." His nobleness, his moral elegance, compelled him to this, and I envied him, not sure if I
myself, thus placed, would acquit myself so well.
And there was in his sweetness a contagion that
strangely reconciled me to the troubled aspects of
our national hour. I thought, "Invisible among
our eighty millions there is a quiet legion living
untainted in the depths, while the yellow rich, the
prismatic scum and bubbles, boil on the surface."
Yes, he had accidentally helped me, and I wished
doubly that I might help him. It was well enough
he should feel he must not shirk his duty, but how
much better if he could be led to see that marrying where he did not love was no duty of his.

I knew what I had to say to him, but lacked the
beginning of it; and of this beginning I was in
search as we drove up among the live-oaks of
Udolpho to the little club-house, or hunting lodge,
where a negro and his wife received us, and took
the baskets and set about preparing supper. My
beginning sat so heavily upon my attention that
I took scant notice of Udolpho as we walked
about its adjacent grounds in the twilight before
supper, and John Mayrant pointed out to me its
fine old trees, its placid stream, and bade me admire the snug character of the hunting lodge,
buried away for bachelors' delights deep in the
heart of the pleasant forest. I heard him indulging in memories and anecdotes of late sittings
after long hunts; but I was myself always on a
hunt for my beginning, and none of his words
clearly reached my intelligence until I was aware
of his reciting an excellently pertinent couplet: —

" If you would hold your father's land,
   You must wash your throat before your hand — "

and found myself standing by the lodge table, upon which he had set two glasses, containing, I soon ascertained, gin, vermouth, orange bitters, and a cherry at the bottom — all which he had very skilfully mingled himself in the happiest proportions.

"The poetry," he remarked, "is hereditary in my family;" and setting down the empty glasses we also washed our hands. A moon half-grown looked in at the window from the filmy darkness, and John, catching sight of it, paused with the wet soap in his hand and stared out at the dimly visible trees. "Oh, the times, the times!" he murmured to himself, gazing long; and then with a sort of start he returned to the present moment, and rinsed and dried his hands. Presently we were sitting at the table, pledging each other in well-cooled champagne ; and it was not long after this that not only the negro who waited on us was plainly revelling in John's remarks, but also the cook, with her bandannaed ebony head poked round the corner of the kitchen door, was doing her utmost to lose no word of this entertainment. For John, taking up the young and the old, the quick and the dead, of masculine Kings Port, proceeded to narrate their private exploits, until by coffee-time he had unrolled for me the richest tapestry of gayeties that I remember, and I sat without breath, tearful and aching, while the two negroes had retired far into the kitchen to muffle their emotions.

"The negro who waited on us"

"Tom, oh Tom! you Tom!" called John May-rant; and after the man had come from the kitchen: "You may put the punch-bowl and things on the table, and clear away and go to bed. My Great-uncle Marston Chartain," he continued to me, "was of eccentric taste, and for the last twenty years of his life never had anybody to dinner but the undertaker." He paused at this point to mix the punch, and then resumed: "But for all that, he appears to have been a lively old gentleman to the end, and left us his version of a saying which is considered by some people an improvement on the original, '*Cherchez la femme.*' Uncle Marston had it, ' Hunt the *other* woman.' Don't go too fast with that punch; it isn't as gentle as it seems."

But John and his Uncle Marston had between them given me my beginning, and, as I sat sipping my punch, I ceased to hear the anecdotes which followed. I sat sipping and smoking, and was presently aware of the deepening silence of the night, and of John no longer at the table, but by the window, looking out into the forest, and muttering once more, "Oh, the times, the times!"

"It's always a triangle," I began.

He turned round from his window. "Triangle?" He looked at my glass of punch, and then at me. "Go easy with the Bombo," he repeated.

"Bombo?" I echoed. "You call this Bombo? You don't know how remarkable that is, but that's because you don't know Aunt Carola, who is very remarkable, too. Well, never mind her now. Point is, it's always a triangle."

" I haven't a doubt of it," he replied.

" There you're right.   And so was your uncle.
He knew.   Triangle."   Here I found myself nodding portentously at John, and beating the table
with my finger very solemnly.

He stood by his window seeming to wait for
me.   And now everything in the universe grew
perfectly clear to me; I rose on mastering tides
of thought, and all problems lay disposed of at my
feet, while delicious strength and calm floated in
my brain and being.   Nothing was difficult for
me.   But I was getting away from the triangle,
and there was John waiting at the window, and I
mustn't say too much, mustn't say too much.   My
will reached out and caught the triangle and
brought it close, and I saw it all perfectly clear
again.

" What are they all," I said, " the old romances?
You take Paris and Helen and Menelaus.   What's
that?   You take Launcelot and Arthur and
Guinevere.   You take Paola and Francesca
and her husband, what's-his-name, or Tristram
and Iseult and Mark.   Two men, one woman.
Triangle and trouble.   Other way around you
get Tannhäuser and Venus and Elizabeth; two
women, one man; more triangle and more trouble.
Yes."   And I nodded at him again.   The tide of
my thought was pulling me hard away from this
to other important world-problems, but my will
held, struggling, and I kept to it.

" You wait," I told him.   " I know what I
mean.   Trouble is, so hard to advise him right."

" Advise who right? " inquired John Mayrant.

It helped me wonderfully.   My will gripped my

floating thoughts and held them to it. "Friend
of mine in trouble; though why he asks me when
I'm not married — I'd be married now, you know,
but afraid of only one wife. Man doesn't love
twice; loves thrice, four, six, lots of times; but
they say only one wife. Ought to be two, anyhow. Much easier for man to marry then."

"Wouldn't it be rather immoral?" John asked.

"Morality is queer thing. Like kaleidoscope.
New patterns all the time. Abraham and wives
— perfectly respectable. You take Pharaohs —
or kings of that sort — married own sisters. All
right then. Perfectly horrible now, of course.
But you ask men about two wives. They'd say
something to be said for that idea. Only there
are the women, you know. They'd never. But
I'm going to tell my friend he's doing wrong.
Going to write him to-night. Where's ink?"

"It won't go to-night," said John. "What are
you going to tell him?"

"Going to tell him, since only one wife, wicked
not to break his engagement."

John looked at me very hard, as he stood by the
window, leaning on the sill. But my will was
getting all the while a stronger hold, and my
thoughts were less and less inclined to stray to
other world-problems; moreover, below the con-
fusion that still a little reigned in them was the
primal cunning of the old Adam, the native man,
quite untroubled and alert — it saw John's look at
me and it prompted my course.

"Yes," I said. "He wants the truth from me.
Where's his letter? No harm reading you without names." And I fumbled in my pocket.

"Letter gone. Never mind. Facts are: friend's asked girl. Girl's said yes. Now he thinks he's bound by that."

"He thinks right," said John.

"Not a bit of it. You take Tannhäuser. Engagement to Venus all a mistake. Perfectly proper to break it. Much more than proper. Only honorable thing he could do. I'm going to write it to him. Where's ink?" And I got up.

John came from his window and sat down at the table. His glass was empty, his cigar gone out, and he looked at me. But I looked round the room for the ink, noting in my search the big fireplace, simple, wooden, unornamented, but generous, and the plain plaster walls of the lodge, whereon hung two or three old prints of game-birds; and all the while I saw John out of the corner of my eye, looking at me.

He spoke first. "Your friend has given his word to a lady; he must stand by it like a gentleman."

"Lot of difference," I returned, still looking round the room, "between spirit and letter. If his heart has broken the word, his lips can't make him a gentleman."

John brought his fist down on the table. "He had no business to get engaged to her! He must take the consequences."

That blow of the fist on the table brought my thoughts wholly clear and fixed on the one subject; my will had no longer to struggle with them, they worked of themselves in just the way that I wanted them to do.

"If he's a gentleman, he must stand to his word," John repeated, "unless she releases him."

I fumbled again for my letter. "That's just about what he says himself," I rejoined, sitting down. "He thinks he ought to take the consequences."

"Of course!" John Mayrant's face was very stern as he sat in judgment on himself.

"But why should *she* take the consequences?" I asked.

"What consequences?"

"Being married to a man who doesn't want her, all her life, until death them do part. How's that? Having the daily humiliation of his indifference, and the world's knowledge of his indifference. How's that? Perhaps having the further humiliation of knowing that his heart belongs to another woman. How's that? That's not what a girl bargains for. His standing to his word is not an act of honor, but a deception. And in talking about 'taking the consequences,' he's patting his personal sacrifice on the back and forgetting all about her and the sacrifice he's putting her to. What's the brief suffering of a broken engagement to that? No: the true consequences that a man should shoulder for making such a mistake is the poor opinion that society holds of him for placing a woman in such a position; and to free her is the most honorable thing he can do. Her dignity suffers less so than if she were a wife chained down to perpetual disregard."

John, after a silence, said: "That is a very curious view."

"That is the view I shall give my friend," I

answered. "I shall tell him that in keeping on he is not at bottom honestly thinking of the girl and her welfare, but of himself and the public opinion he's afraid of, if he breaks his engagement. And I shall tell him that if I'm in church and they come to the place where they ask if any man knows just cause or impediment, I shall probably call out, 'He does! His heart's not in it. This is not marriage that he's committing. You're pronouncing your blessing upon a fraud."

John sat now a long time silent, holding his extinct cigar. The lamp was almost burned dry; we had blown out the expiring candles some while since. "That is a very curious view," he repeated. "I should like to hear what your friend says in answer."

This finished our late sitting. We opened the door and went out for a brief space into the night to get its pure breath into our lungs, and look to the distant place where the moon had sailed. Then we went to bed, or rather, I did; for the last thing that I remembered was John, standing by the window of our bedroom still dressed, looking out into the forest.

XX

WHAT SHE WANTED HIM FOR

HE was neither at the window, nor in his bed, nor anywhere else to be seen, when I opened my eyes upon the world next morning; nor did any answer come when I called his name. I raised myself and saw outside the great branches of the wood, bathed from top to trunk in a sunshine that was no early morning's light; and upon this, the silence of the house spoke plainly to me not of man still sleeping, but of man long risen and gone about his business. I stepped barefoot across the wooden floor to where lay my watch, but it marked an unearthly hour, for I had neglected to wind it at the end of our long and convivial evening — of which my head was now giving me some news. And then I saw a note addressed to me from John Mayrant.

"You are a good sleeper," it began, "but my conscience is clear as to the Bombo, called by some Kill-devil, about which I hope you will remember that I warned you."

He hoped I should remember! Of course I remembered everything; why did he say that? An apology for his leaving me followed; he had been obliged to take the early train because of the Custom House, where he was serving his final days; they would give me breakfast when-

ever I should be ready for it, and I was to make
free of the place; I had better visit the old church
(they had orders about the keys) and drive myself
into Kings Port after lunch; the horses would
know the way, if I did not. It was the boy's closing sentence which fixed my attention wholly,
took it away from Kill-devil Bombo and my Aunt
Carola's commission, for the execution of which I
now held the clue, and sent me puzzling for the
right interpretation of his words:—

" I believe that you will help your friend by that
advice which startled me last night, but which I
now begin to see more in than I did. Only
between alternate injuries, he may find it harder
to choose which is the least he can inflict, than
you, who look on, find it. For in following your
argument, he benefits himself so plainly that the
benefit to the other person is very likely obscured
to him. But, if you wish to, tell him a Southern
gentleman would feel he ought to be shot *either*
way. That's the honorable price for changing
your mind in such a case."

No interpretation of this came to me. I planned
and carried out my day according to his suggestion; a slow dressing with much cold water, a
slow breakfast with much good hot coffee, a slow
wandering beneath the dreamy branches of Udolpho,— this course cleared my head of the Bombo,
and brought back to me our whole evening, and
every word I had said to John, except that I had
lost the solution which, last night, the triangle
had held for me. At that moment, the triangle,
and my whole dealing with the subject of monog-
amy, had seemed to contain the simplicity of

genius; but it had all gone now, and I couldn't

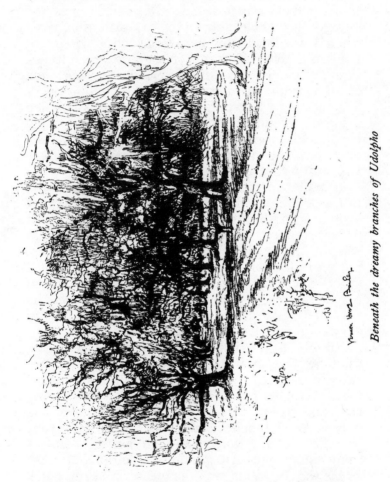

Beneath the dreamy branches of Udolpho

get it back; only, what I had contrived to say to
John about his own predicament had been cer-

tainly well said; I would say that over again
to-day.   It was the boy and the meaning of his
words which escaped me still, baffled me, and
formed the whole subject of my attention, even
when I was inside the Tern Creek church; so that
I retain nothing of that, save a general quaintness,
a general loneliness, a little deserted, forgotten token
of human doings long since done, standing on its
little acre of wilderness amid that solitude which
suggests the departed presence of man, and which
is so much more potent in the flavor of its desolation than the virgin wilderness whose solitude is
still waiting for man to come.

It made no matter whether John had believed
in the friend to whom I intended writing advice,
or had seen through and accepted in good part
my manœuvre ; he had considered my words, that
was the point; and he had not slept in his bed,
but on it, if sleep had come to him at all; this I
found out while dressing.   Several times I read
his note over.   " Between alternate injuries he
may find it harder to choose."   This was not an
answer to me, but an explanation of his own perplexity.   At times it sounded almost like an appeal,
as if he were saying, " Do not blame me for not
being convinced ; " and if it was such appeal, why,
then, taken with his resolve to do right at any
cost, and his night of inward contention, it was
poignant.   " I believe that you will help your
friend."   Those words sounded better.   But —
" tell him a Southern gentleman ought to be shot
either way."   What was the meaning of this ?   A
chill import rose from it into my thoughts, but
that I dismissed.   To die on account of Hortense !

Such a thing was not to be conceived. And yet, given a high-strung nature, not only trapped by its own standards, but also wrought upon during many days by increasing exasperation and unhappiness while helpless in the trap, and with no other outlook but the trap: the chill import returned to me more than once, and was reasoned away, as, with no attention to my surroundings, I took a pair of oars, and got into a boat belonging to the lodge, and rowed myself slowly among the sluggish windings of Tern Creek.

Whence come those thoughts that we ourselves feel shame at? It shamed me now, as I pulled my boat along, that I should have thoughts of John which needed banishing. What tale would this be to remember of a boy's life, that he gave it to buy freedom from a pledge which need never have been binding? What pearl was this to cast before the sophisticated Hortense? Such act would be robbed of its sadness by its absurdity. Yet, surely, the bitterest tragedies are those of which the central anguish is lost amid the dust of surrounding paltriness. If such a thing should happen here, no one but myself would have seen the lonely figure of John Mayrant, standing by the window and looking out into the dark quiet of the wood; his name would be passed down for a little while as the name of a fool, and then he would be forgotten. " I believe that you will help your friend." Yes; he had certainly written that, and it now came to me that I might have said to him one thing more: Had he given Hortense the chance to know what his feelings to her had become? But he would merely have answered that here it was the duty of a gentleman to lie. Or, had he possibly, at Newport, ever become her lover too much for any escaping now? Had his dead passion once put his honor in a pawn which only marriage could redeem? This might fit all that had come, so far; and still, with such a two as they, I should forever hold the boy the woman's victim. But this did not fit what came after. Perhaps it was the late sitting of the night before, and the hushed and strange solitude of my surroundings now, that had laid my mind open to all these thoughts which my reason, in dealing with, answered continually, one by one, yet which returned, requiring to be answered again; for there are times when our uncomfortable eyes see through the appearances we have arranged for daily life, into the actualities which lie forever behind them.

Going about thus in my boat, I rowed sleepiness into myself, and pushed into a nook where shade from some thick growth hid the boat and me from the sun; and there, almost enmeshed in the deep lattice of green, I placed my coat beneath my head, and prone in the boat's bottom I drifted into slumber. Once or twice my oblivion was pierced by the roaming honk of the automobile; but with no more than the half-melted consciousness that the Replacers were somewhere in the wood, oblivion closed over me again; and when it altogether left me, it was because of voices near me on the water, or on the bank. Their calls and laughter pushed themselves into my drowsiness, and soon after I grew aware that the Replacers were come here to see what was to be seen at Udolpho — the club, the old church, a country

" John, after a silence, said . ' That is a very curious view ' "

place with a fine avenue — and that it was the church they now couldn't get into, because my visit had disturbed the usual whereabouts of the key, of which Gazza was now going in search. I could have told him where to find it, but it pleased me not to disturb myself for this, as I listened to him assuring Kitty that it was probably in the cabin beyond the bridge, but not to be alarmed if he did not immediately return with it. Kitty, not without audible mirth, assured him that they should not be alarmed at all, to which the voice of Hortense supplemented, " Not at all."   They were evidently in a boat, which Hortense 'herself was rowing, and which she seemed to bring to the bank, where I gathered that Kitty got out and sat while Hortense remained in the boat. There was the little talk and movement which goes with bor- rowing of a cigarette, a little exclamation about not falling out, accompanied by the rattle of a displaced oar, and then stillness, and the smell of tobacco smoke.

Presently Kitty spoke.   " Charley will be back to-night."

To this I heard no reply.

" What did his telegram say ? " Kitty inquired, after another silence.

" It's all right."   This was Hortense.   Her slow, rich murmur was as deliberate as always.

" Mr. Bohm knew it would be," said Kitty. " He said it wouldn't take five minutes' talk from Charley to get a contract worth double what they were going to accept."

After this, nothing came to me for several minutes, save the odor of the cigarettes.

Of course there was now but one proper course
for me, namely, to utter a discreet cough, and
thus warn them that some one was within ear-
shot. But I didn't! I couldn't! Strength failed,
curiosity won, my baser nature triumphed here,
and I deliberately remained lying quiet and hidden. It was the act of no gentleman, you will
say. Well, it was; and I must simply confess to
it, hoping that I am not the only gentleman in
the world who has, on occasion, fallen beneath
himself.

"Hortense Rieppe," began Kitty, "what do you
intend to say to my brother after what he has
done about those phosphates?"

"He is always so kind," murmured Hortense.

"Well, you know what it means."

"Means?"

"If you persist in this folly, you'll drop out."

Hortense chose another line of speculation.
"I wonder why your brother is so sure of me?"

"Charley is a set man. And I've never seen
him so set on anything as on you, Hortense
Rieppe."

"He is always so kind," murmured Hortense
again.

"He's a man you'll always know just where to
find," declared Kitty. "Charley is safe. He'll
never take you by surprise, never fly out, never do
what other people don't do, never make any one
stare at him by the way he looks, or the way he
acts, or anything he says, or — or — why, how you
can hesitate between those two men after that
ridiculous, childish, conspicuous, unusual scene on
the bridge —"

" Unusual.   Yes," said Hortense.

Kitty's eloquence and voice mounted together.
" I should think it was unusual ! Tearing people's money up, and making a rude, awkward fuss
that everybody had to smooth over as hard as they
could ! Why, even Mr. Rodgers says that sort of
thing isn't done, and you're always saying he
knows."

" No," said Hortense.   " It isn't done."

" Well, I've never seen anything approaching
such behavior in our set.   And he was ready to
go further.   Nobody knows where it might have
gone to, if Charley's perfect coolness hadn't
rebuked him and brought him to his senses.
There's where it is, that's what I mean, Hortense,
by saying you could always feel safe with
Charley."

Hortense put in a languid word.   " I think I
should always feel safe with Mr. Mayrant."

But Kitty was a simple soul.   " Indeed you
couldn't, Hortense ! I assure you that you're
mistaken.   There's where you get so wrong about
men sometimes.   I have been studying that boy
for your sake ever since we got here, and I know
him through and through.   And I tell you, you
cannot count upon him.   He has not been used to
our ways, and I see no promise of his getting used to
them.   He will stay capable of outbreaks like that
horrid one on the bridge.   Wherever you take
him, wherever you put him, no matter how much
you show him of us, and the way we don't allow
conspicuous things like that to occur, believe me,
Hortense, he'll never learn, he'll never smooth
down.   You may brush his hair flat and keep him

appearing like other people for a while, but a time will come, something will happen, and that boy'll be conspicuous. Charley would never be conspicuous."

" No," assented Hortense.

Kitty urged her point. " Why, I never saw or *heard* of anything like that on the bridge — that is, among — among — us ! "

" No," assented Hortense, again, and her voice dropped lower with each statement. " One always sees the same thing. Always hears the same thing. Always the same thing." These last almost inaudible words sank away into the silent pool of Hortense's meditation.

" Have another cigarette," said Kitty. " You've let yours fall into the water."

I heard them moving a little, and then they must have resumed their seats.

" You'll drop out of it," Kitty now pursued.

" Into what shall I drop? "

" Just being asked to the big things everybody goes to and nobody counts. For even with the way Charley has arranged about the phosphates, it will not be enough to keep you in our swim — just by itself. He'll weigh more than his money, because he'll stay different — too different."

" He was not so different last summer."

" Because he was not there long enough, my dear. He learned bridge quickly, and of course he had seen champagne before, and nobody had time to notice him. But he'll be married now, and they will notice him, and they won't want him. To think of your dropping out ! " Kitty became very earnest. " To think of not seeing you among us! You'll be in none of the small things; you'll never be asked to stay at the smart houses — why, not even your name will be in the paper! Not a foreigner you entertain, not a dinner you give, not a thing you wear, will ever be described next morning. And Charley's so set on you, and you're so just exactly made for each other, and it would all be so splendid, and cosey, and jolly! And to throw all this away for that crude boy!" Kitty's disdain was high at the thought of John.

Hortense took a little time over it. "Once," she then stated, "he told me he could drown in my hair as joyfully as the Duke of Clarence did in his butt of Malmsey wine!"

Kitty gave a little scream. "Did you let him?"

"One has to guard one's value at times."

Kitty's disdain for John increased. "How crude!"

Hortense did not make any answer.

"How crude!" Kitty, after some silence, repeated. She seemed to have found the right word.

Steps sounded upon the bridge, and the voice of Gazza cried out that the stupid key was at the imbecile club-house, whither he was now going for it, and not to be alarmed. Their voices answered reassuringly, and Gazza was heard growing distant, singing some little song.

Kitty was apparently unable to get away from John's crudity. "He actually said that?"

"Yes."

"Where was it? Tell me about it, Hortense."

"We were walking in the country on that occasion."

Kitty still lingered with it. " Did he look —
I've never had any man — I wonder if — how did
you feel ? "

" Not disagreeably." And Hortense permitted
herself to laugh musically.

Kitty's voice at once returned to the censorious
tone. " Well, I call such language as that very —
very — "

Hortense helped her. " Operatic ? "

" He could never be taught in those ways
either," declared Kitty. " You would find his
ardor always untrained — provincial."

Once more Hortense abstained from making
any answer.

Kitty grew superior. " Well, if *that's* to your
taste, Hortense Rieppe ! "

" It was none of it like Charley," murmured
Hortense.

" I should think not ! Charley's not crude.
What do you see in that man ? "

" I like the way his hair curls above his ears."

For this Kitty found nothing but an impatient
exclamation.

And now the voice of Hortense sank still deeper
in dreaminess, — down to where the truth lay ;
and from those depths came the truth, flashing
upward through the drowsy words she spoke :
" I think I want him for his innocence."

What light these words may have brought to
Kitty, I had no chance to learn ; for the voice of
Gazza returning with the key put an end to this
conversation. But I doubted if Kitty had it in
her to fathom the nature of Hortense. Kitty was
like a trim little clock that could tick tidily on an

ornate shelf; she could go, she could keep up with time, with the rapid epoch to which she belonged, but she didn't really have many works. I think she would have scoffed at that last languorous speech as a piece of Hortense's nonsense, and that is why Hortense uttered it aloud: she was safe from being understood. But in my ears it sounded the note of revelation, the simple central secret of Hortense's fire, a flame fed overmuch with experience, with sophistication, grown cold under the ministrations of adroitness, and lighted now by the "crudity" of John's love-making. And when, after an interval, I had rowed my boat back, and got into the carriage, and started on my long drive from Udolpho to Kings Port, I found that there was almost nothing about all this which I did not know now. Hortense, like most riddles when you are told the answer, was clear: —

"I think I want him for his innocence."

Yes; she was tired of love-making whose down had been rubbed off; she hungered for love-making with the down still on, even if she must pay for it with marriage. Who shall say if her enlightened and modern eye could not look beyond such marriage (when it should grow monotonous) to divorce?

XXI

HORTENSE'S CIGARETTE GOES OUT

JOHN was the riddle that I could not read. Among my last actions of this day was one that had been almost my earliest, and bedtime found me staring at his letter, as I stood, half undressed, by my table. The calm moon brought back Udolpho and what had been said there, as it now shone down upon the garden where Hortense had danced. I stared at John's letter as if its words were new to me, instead of being words that I could have fluently repeated from beginning to end without an error; it was as if, by virtue of mere gazing at the document, I hoped to wring more meaning from it, to divine what had been in the mind which had composed it; but instead of this, I seemed to get less from it, instead of more. Had the boy's purpose been to mystify me, he could scarce have done better. I think that he had no such intention, for it would have been wholly unlike him; but I saw no sign in it that I had really helped him, had really shaken his old quixotic resolve, nor did I see any of his having found a new way of his own out of the trap. I could not believe that the dark road of escape had taken any lodgement in his thought, but had only passed over it, like a cloud with a heavy shadow. But these are surmises at the

best: if John had formed any plan, I can never
know it, and Juno's remarks at breakfast on Sunday morning sounded strange, like something a
thousand miles away.   For she spoke of the wedding, and of the fact that it would certainly be a
small one.   She went over the names of the people who would have to be invited, and doubted
if she were one of these.   But if she should be,
then she would go — for the sake of Miss Josephine St. Michael, she declared.   In short, it was
perfectly plain that Juno was much afraid of being
left out, and that wild horses could not drag her
away from it, if an invitation came to her.   But,
as I say, this side of the wedding seemed to have
nothing to do with it, when I thought of all that
lay beneath; my one interest to-day was to see
John Mayrant, to get from him, if not by some
word, then by some look or intonation, a knowledge of what he meant to do.   Therefore, disappointment and some anxiety met me when I
stepped from the *Hermana's* gangway upon her
deck, and Charley asked me if he was coming.
But the launch, sent back to wait, finally brought
John, apologizing for his lateness.

Meanwhile, I was pleased to find among the
otherwise complete party General Rieppe.   What
I had seen of him from a distance held promise,
and the hero's nearer self fulfilled it.   We fell to
each other's lot for the most natural of reasons:
nobody else desired the company of either of us.
Charley was making himself the devoted servant
of Hortense, while Kitty drew Beverly, Bohm, and
Gazza in her sprightly wake.   To her, indeed, I
made a few compliments during the first few

minutes after my coming aboard, while every sort of drink and cigar was being circulated among us by the cabin boy. Kitty's costume was the most markedly maritime thing that I have ever beheld in any waters, and her white shoes looked (I must confess) supremely well on her pretty little feet. I am no advocate of sumptuary laws; but there should be one prohibiting big-footed women from wearing white shoes. Did these women know what a spatulated effect their feet so shod produce, no law would be needed. Yes, Kitty was superlatively, stridently maritime; you could have known from a great distance that she belonged to the very latest steam yacht class, and that she was perfectly ignorant of the whole subject. On her left arm, for instance, was worked a red propeller with one blade down, and two chevrons. It was the rating mark for a chief engineer, but this, had she known it, would not have disturbed her.

"I chose it," she told me in reply to my admiration of it, "because it's so pretty. Oh, won't we enjoy ourselves while those stupid old blue-bloods in Kings Port are going to church!" And with this she gave a skip, and ordered the cabin boy to bring her a Remsen cooler. Beverly Rodgers called for dwarf's blood, and I chose a horse's neck, and soon found myself in the society of the General.

He was sipping whiskey and plain water. "I am a rough soldier, sir," he explained to me, "and I keep to the simple beverage of the camp. Had we not 'rather bear those ills we have than fly to others that we know not of'?" And he

waved a stately hand at my horse's neck.   "You
are acquainted with the works of Shakespeare?"

I replied that I had a moderate knowledge of
them, and assured him that a horse's neck was
very simple.

"Doubtless, sir; but a veteran is ever old-
fashioned."

"Papa," said Hortense, "don't let the sun shine
upon your head."

"Thank you, daughter mine."   They said no
more; but I presently felt that for some reason
she watched him.

He moved farther beneath the awning, and I
followed him.   "Are you a father, sir?   No?
Then you cannot appreciate what it is to confide
such a jewel as yon girl to another's keeping."   He
summoned the cabin boy, who brought him some
more of the simple beverage of the camp, and I, feeling myself scarce at liberty to speak on matters so
near to him and so far from me as his daughter's
marriage, called his attention to the beautiful aspect
of Kings Port, spread out before us in a long
white line against the blue water.

The General immediately seized his opportunity.   "'Sweet Auburn, loveliest village of the
plain!'   You are acquainted with the works of
Goldsmith, sir?"

I professed some knowledge of this author
also, and the General's talk flowed ornately onward.   Though I had little to say to him about
his daughter's marriage, he had much to say to
me.   Miss Josephine St. Michael would have
been gratified to hear that her family was considered suitable for Hortense to contract an

alliance with. "My girl is not stepping down, sir," the father assured me; and he commended the St. Michaels and the whole connection. He next alluded tragically but vaguely to misfortunes which had totally deprived him of income. I could not precisely fix what his inheritance had been; sometimes he spoke of cotton, but next it would be rice, and he touched upon sugar more than once; but, whatever it was, it had been vast and was gone. He told me that I could not imagine the feelings of a father who possessed a jewel and no dowry to give her. "A queen's estate should have been hers," he said. "But what! 'Who steals my purse steals trash.'" And he sat up, nobly braced by the philosophic thought. But he soon was shaking his head over his enfeebled health. Was I aware that he had been the cause of postponing the young people's joy twice? Twice had the doctors forbidden him to risk the emotions that would attend his giving his jewel away. He dwelt upon his shattered system to me, and, indeed, it required some dwelling on, for he was the picture of admirable preservation. "But I know what it is myself," he declared, "to be a lover and have bliss delayed. They shall be united now. A soldier must face all arrows. What!"

I had hoped he might quote something here, but was disappointed. His conversation would soon cease to interest me, should I lose the excitement of watching for the next classic; and my eye wandered from the General to the water, where, happily, I saw John Mayrant coming in the launch. I briskly called the General's attention to him, and was delighted with the unexpected result.

"'Oh, young Lochinvar has come out of the West,'" said the General, lifting his glass.

I touched it ceremoniously with mine. "The day will be hot," I said; "'The boy stood on the burning deck.'"

On this I made my escape from him, and, leaving him to his whiskey and his contemplating, I became aware that the eyes of the rest of the party were eager to watch the greeting between Hortense and John. But there was nothing to see. Hortense waited until her lover had made his apologies to Charley for being late, and, from the way they met, she might have been no more to him than Kitty was. Whatever might be thought, whatever might be known, by these onlookers, Hortense set the pace of how the open secret was to be taken. She made it, for all of us, as smooth and smiling as the waters of Kings Port were this fine day. How much did they each know? I asked myself how much they had shared in common. To these Replacers Kings Port had opened no doors; they and their automobile had skirted around the outside of all things. And if Charley knew about the wedding, he also knew that it had been already twice postponed. He, too, could have said, as Miss Eliza had once said to me, "The cake is not baked yet." The General's talk to me (I felt as I took in how his health had been the centred point) was probably the result of previous arrangements with Hortense herself; and she quite as certainly inspired whatever she allowed him to say to Charley.

As for Kitty, she knew that her brother was "set"; she always came back to that.

If Hortense found this Sunday morning a passage of particularly delicate steering, she showed it in no way, unless by that heightened radiance and triumph of beauty which I had seen in her before. No; the splendor of the day, the luxuries of the *Hermana*, the conviviality of the Replacers — all melted the occasion down to an ease and enjoyment in which even John Mayrant, with his grave face, was not perceptible, unless, like myself, one watched him.

It was my full expectation that we should now get under way and proceed among the various historic sights of Kings Port harbor, but of this I saw no signs anywhere on board the *Hermana*. Abeam of the foremast her boat booms remained rigged out on port and starboard, her boats riding to painters, while her crew wore a look as generally lounging as that of her passengers. Beverly Rodgers told me the reason: we had no pilot; the negro waterman engaged for this excursion in the upper waters had failed of appearance, and when Charley was for looking up another, Kitty, Bohm, and Gazza had dissuaded him.

"Kitty," said Beverly, "told me she didn't care about the musty old forts and things, anyhow."

I looked at Kitty, and heard her tongue ticking away, like the little clock she was; she had her Bohm, she had her nautical costume and her Remsen cooler. These, with the lunch that would come in time, were enough for her.

"But it was such a good chance!" I exclaimed in disappointment.

" Chance for what, old man ? "

" To see everything — the forts, the islands — and it's beautiful, you know, all the way to the navy yard."

Beverly followed my glance to where the gay company was sitting among the cracked ice, and bottles, and cigar boxes, chattering volubly, with its back to the scenery.   He gave his *laisser-faire* chuckle, and laid a hand on my shoulder.   " Don't worry 'em with forts and islands, old boy !   They know what they want.   No living breed on earth knows better what it wants."

" Well, they don't get it."

" Ho, don't they ? "

" The cold fear of ennui gnaws at their vitals this minute."

Shrill laughter from Kitty and Gazza served to refute my theory.

" Of course, very few know what's the matter with them," I added.   " You seldom spot an organic disease at the start."

" Hm," said Beverly, lengthily.   " You put a pin through some of 'em.   Hortense hasn't got the disease, though."

" Ah, she spotted it !   She's taking treatment. It's likely to help her — for a time."

He looked at me.   " You know something ? "

I nodded.   He looked at Hortense, who was now seated among the noisy group with quiet John beside her.   She was talking to Bohm, she had no air of any special relation to John, but there was a lustre about her that spoke well for the treatment.

" Then it's coming off ? " said Beverly.

"She has been too much for him," I answered. Beverly misunderstood. "He doesn't look it."

"That's what I mean."

"But the fool can cut loose!"

"Oh, you and I have gone over all that! I've even gone over it with him."

Beverly looked at Hortense again. "And her fire-eater's fortune is about double what it would have been. I don't see how she's going to square herself with Charley."

"She'll wait till that's necessary. It isn't necessary to-day."

We had to drop our subject here, for the owner of the *Hermana* approached us with the amiable purpose, I found, of making himself civil for a while to me.

"I think you would have been interested to see the navy yard," I said to him.

"I have seen it," Charley replied, in his slightly foreign, careful voice. "It is not a navy yard. It is small politics and a big swamp. I was not interested."

"Dear me!" I cried. "But surely it's going to be very fine!"

"Another gold brick sold to Uncle Sam." Charley's words seemed always to drop out like little accurately measured coins from some minting machine. "They should not have changed from the old place if they wanted a harbor that could be used in war-time. Here they must always keep at least one dredge going out at the jetties. So the enemy blows up your dredge and you are bottled in, or bottled out. It is very simple for the enemy. And, for Kings Port, navy

yards do not galvanize dead trade. It was a
gold brick. You have not been on the *Hermana*
before? "

He knew that I had not, but he wished to show
her to me; and I soon noted a difference as radical as it was diverting between this banker-yachts-
man's speech when he talked of affairs on land and
when he attempted to deal with nautical matters.
The clear, dispassionate finality of his tone when
phosphates, or railroads, or navy yards, or imperial
loans were concerned, left him, and changed to
something very like a recitation of trigonometry
well memorized but not at all mastered; he could
do that particular sum, but you mustn't stop him;
and I concluded that I would rather have Charley
for my captain during a panic in Wall Street than
in a hurricane at sea. He, too, wore highly pronounced sea clothes of the ornamental kind; and
though they fitted him physically, they hung bag-
gily upon his unmarine spirit; giving him the air,
as it were, of a broiled quail served on oyster shells.
Beverly Rodgers, the consummate Beverly, was the
only man of us whose clothes seemed to belong to
him; he looked as if he could sail a boat.

While the cabin boy continued to rush among
the guests with siphons, ice, and fresh refresh-
ments, Charley became the *Hermana's* guide-
book for me; and our interview gave me, I may
say, entertainment unalloyed, although there lay
all the while, beneath the entertainment, my sadness and concern about John. Charley was owner
of the *Hermana*, there was no doubt of that; she
had cost him (it was not long before he told me)
fifty thousand dollars, and to run her it cost him

a thousand a month. Yes, he was her owner, but there it stopped, no matter with how solemn a face he inspected each part of her, or spoke of her details; he was as much a passenger on her as myself; and this was as plain on the equally solemn faces of his crew, from the sailing-master down through the two quartermasters to the five deck-hands, as was the color of the *Hermana's* stack, which was, of course, yellow. She was a pole-mast, schooner-rigged steam yacht, Charley accurately told me, with clipper bow and spiked bowsprit.

" About a hundred tons ? " I inquired.

" Yes. A hundred feet long, beam twenty feet, and she draws twelve feet," said Charley; and I thought I detected the mate listening to him.

He now called my attention to the flags, and I am certain that I saw the sailing-master hide his mouth with his hand. Some of the deck-hands seemed to gather delicately nearer to us.

" Sunday, of course," I said; and I pointed to the Jack flying from a staff at the bow.

But Charley did not wish me to tell him about the flags, he wished to tell me about the flags. " I am very strict about all this," he said, his gravity and nauticality increasing with every word. "At the fore truck flies our club burgee."

I went through my part, giving a solemn, silent, intelligent assent.

" That is my private signal at the main truck. It was designed by Miss Rieppe."

As I again intelligently nodded, I saw the boatswain move an elbow into the ribs of one of the quartermasters.

" On the staff at the taffrail I have the United
States yacht ensign," Charley continued.   " That's
all," he said, looking about for more flags, and (to
his disappointment, I think) finding no more.
For he added: " But at twelve o'c — at eight
bells, the crew's meal-flag will be in the port fore
rigging.   While we are at lunch, my meal-flag
will be in the starboard main rigging."

" It should be there all day," I was tempted to
remark to him, as my wandering eye fell on the
cabin boy carrying something more on a plate to
Kitty.   But instead of this I said: " Well, she's a
beautiful boat ! "

Charley shook his head.   " I'm going to get rid
of her."

I was surprised.   " Isn't she all right ? "   It
seemed to me that the crew behind us were very
attentive now.

" There is not enough refrigerator space," said
Charley.   One of the deck-hands whirled round
instantly ; but stolidity sat like adamant upon the
faces of the others as Charley turned in their
direction, and we continued our tour of the *Hermana*.   Thus the little banker let me see his little
soul, deep down ; and there I saw that to pass for
a real yachtsman — which he would never be able
to do — was dearer to his pride than to bring off
successfully some huge and delicate matter in the
world's finance — which he could always do supremely well.   " I'm just like that, too," I thought
to myself ; and we returned to the gay Kitty.

But Kitty, despite her gayety, had serious
thoughts upon her mind.   Charley's attentions to
me had met all that politeness required, and as

we went aft again, his sister caused certain movements and rearrangements to happen with chairs and people. I didn't know this at once, but I knew it when I found myself somehow sitting with her and John, and saw Hortense with Charley. Hortense looked over at Kitty with a something that had in it both raised eyebrows and a shrug, though these visible signs did not occur; and, indeed, so far as anything visible went (except the look) you might have supposed that now Hortense had no thoughts for any man in the world save Charley. And John was plainly more at ease with Kitty! He began to make himself agreeable, so that once or twice she gave him a glance of surprise. There was nothing to mark him out from the others, except his paleness in the midst of their redness. Yachting clothes bring out wonderfully how much you are in the habit of eating and drinking; and an innocent stranger might have supposed that the Replacers were richly sunburned from exposure to the blazing waters of Cuba and the tropics. Kitty deemed it suitable to extol Kings Port to John. "Quaint" was the word that did most of this work for her; she found everything that, even the negroes; and when she had come to the end of it, she supposed the inside must be just as "quaint" as the outside.

"It is," said John Mayrant. He was enjoying Kitty. Then he became impertinent. "You ought to see it."

"Do you stay inside much?" said Kitty.

"We all do," said John. "Some of us never come out."

"But you came out?" Kitty suggested.

"Oh, I've *been* out," John returned. He was getting older. I doubt if the past few years of his life had matured him as much as had the past few days. Then he looked at Kitty in the eyes. "And I'd always come out — if Romance rang the bell."

"Hm!" said Kitty. "Then you know that ring?"

"We begin to hear it early in Kings Port," remarked John. "About the age of fourteen."

Kitty looked at him with an interest that now plainly revealed curiosity also. It occurred to me that he could not have found any great embarrassment in getting on at Newport. "What if I rang the bell myself?" explained Kitty.

"Come in the evening," returned John. "We won't go home till morning."

Kitty kissed her hand to him, and, during the pleased giggle that she gave, I saw her first taking in John and then Hortense. Kitty was thinking, thinking, of John's "crudity." And so I made a little experiment for myself.

"I wonder if men seem as similar in making love as women do in receiving it?"

"They aren't!" shouted both John and Kitty, in the same indignant breath. Their noise brought Bohm to listen to us.

This experiment was so much a success that I promptly made another for the special benefit of Bohm, Kitty's next husband. I find it often delightful to make a little gratuitous mischief, just to watch the victims. I addressed Kitty. "What would you do if a man said he could drown in your hair as joyfully as the Duke of Clarence did in his butt of Malmsey?"

"Why—why—" gasped Kitty, "why—why—"

I suppose it gave John time; but even so he was splendid.

"She has heard it said!" This was his triumphant shout. I should not have supposed that Kitty could have turned any redder, but she did. John buried his nose in his tall glass, and gulped a choking quantity of its contents, and mopped his face profusely; but little good that effected. There sat this altogether innocent pair, deeply suffused with the crimson of apparent guilt, and there stood Kitty's next husband, eying them suspiciously. My little gratuitous mischief was a perfect success, and remains with me as one of the bright spots in this day of pleasure.

Vivacious measures from the piano brought Kitty to her feet.

"There's Gazza!" she cried. "We'll make him sing!" And on the instant she was gone down the companionway. Bohm followed her with a less agitated speed, and soon all were gone below, leaving John and me alone on the deck, sitting together in silence.

John lolled back in his chair, slowly sipping at his tall glass, and neither of us made any remark. I think he wanted to ask me how I came to mention the Duke of Clarence; but I did not see how he very well could, and he certainly made no attempt to do so. Thus did we sit for some time, hearing the piano and the company grow livelier and louder with solos, and choruses, and laughter. By and by the shadow of the awning

shifted, causing me to look up, when I saw the
shores slowly changing; the tide had turned, and
was beginning to run out.   Land and water lay
in immense peace; the long, white, silent picture of
the town with its steeples on the one hand, and on
the other the long, low shore, and the trees behind.
Into this rose the high voice of Gazza, singing
in broken English, "Razzla-dazzla, razzla-dazzla,"
while his hearers beat upon glasses with spoons —
at least so I conjectured.

"Aren't you coming, John?" asked Hortense,
appearing at the companionway.   She looked
very bacchanalian.   Her splendid amber hair was
half riotous, and I was reminded of the toboggan
fire-escape.

He obeyed her; and now I had the deck entirely
to myself, or, rather, but one other and distant
person shared it with me.   The hour had come,
the bells had struck; Charley's crew was eating
its dinner below forward; Charley's guests were
drinking their liquor below aft; Charley's correct
meal-flag was to be seen in the port fore rigging,
as he had said, red and triangular; and away off
from me in the bow was the anchor watch, whom
I dreamily watched trying to light his pipe.   His
matches seemed to be bad; and the brotherly
thought of helping him drifted into my mind —
and comfortably out of it again, without disturbing
my agreeable repose.   It had been really entertaining in John to tell Kitty that she ought to see
the inside of Kings Port; that was like his engaging impishness with Juno.   If by any possible
contrivance (and none was possible) Kitty and her
Replacers could have met the inside of Kings

Port, Kitty would have added one more "quaint" impression to her stock, and gone away in total ignorance of the quality of the impression she had made — and Bohm would probably have again remarked, "Worse than Sunday." No; the St. Michaels and the Replacers would never meet in this world, and I see no reason that they should in the next. John's light and pleasing skirmish with Kitty gave me the glimpse of his capacities which I had lacked hitherto. John evidently "knew his way about," as they say; and I was diverted to think how Miss Josephine St. Michael would have nodded over his adequacy and shaken her head at his squandering it on such a companion. But it was no squandering; the boy's heavy spirit was making a gallant "bluff" at playing up with the lively party he had no choice but to join, and this one saw the moment he was not called upon to play up.

The peaceful loveliness that floated from earth and water around me triumphed over the jangling hilarity of the cabin, and I dozed away, aware that they were now all thumping furiously in chorus, while Gazza sang something that went, " Oh, she's my leetle preety poosee pet." When I roused, it was Kitty's voice at the piano, but no change in the quality of the song or the thumping; and Hortense was stepping on deck. She had a cigarette, her beauty flashed with devilment, and John followed her. " They are going to have an explanation," I thought, as I saw his face. If that were so, then Kitty had blundered in her strategy and hurt Charley's cause; for after the two came Gazza, as obviously "sent" as any emissary ever

looked : Kitty took care of the singing, while
Gazza intercepted any tête-à-tête. I rose and made
a fourth with them, and even as I was drawing
near, the devilment in Hortense's face sank inward
beneath cold displeasure.

I had never been a welcome person to Hortense,
and she made as little effort to conceal this as
usual.   Her indifferent eyes glanced at me with
drowsy insolence, and she made her beautiful,
low voice as remote and inattentive as her skilful
social equipment could render it.

" It is so hot in the cabin."

This was all she had for me.   Then she looked
at Gazza with returning animation.

" Oh, la la ! " said Gazza.   " If it is hot in the
cabin ! "   And he flirted his handkerchief back
and forth.

" I think I had the best of it," I remarked.
" All the melody and none of the temperature."

Hortense saw no need of noticing me further.

" The singer has the worst of it," said Gazza.

" But since you all sang ! " I laughed.

" Miss Rieppe, she is cool," continued Gazza.
" And she danced.   It is not fair."

John contributed nothing.   He was by no
means playing up now.   He was looking away at
the shore.

Gazza hummed a little fragment.   " But after
lunch I will sing you good music."

" So long as it keeps us cool," I suggested.

" Ah, no !   It will not be cool music ! " cried
Gazza — " for those who understand."

" Are those boys bathing ? " Hortense now
inquired.

We watched the distant figures, and presently they flashed into the water.

"Oh, me!" sighed Gazza. "If I were a boy!"

Hortense looked at him. "You would be afraid." The devilment had come out again, suddenly and brilliantly.

"I never have been afraid!" declared Gazza.

"You would not jump in after me," said Hortense, taking his measure more and more provokingly.

Gazza laid his hand on his heart. "Where you go, I will go!"

Hortense looked at him, and laughed very slightly and lightly.

"I swear it! I swear!" protested Gazza.

John's eyes were now fixed upon Hortense.

"Would you go?" she asked him.

"Decidedly not!" he returned. I don't know whether he was angry or anxious.

"Oh, yes, you would!" said Hortense; and she jumped into the water, cigarette and all.

"Get a boat, quick," said John to me; and with his coat flung off he was in the river, whose current Hortense could scarce have reckoned with; for they were both already astern as I ran out on the port boat boom.

Gazza was dancing and shrieking, "Man overboard!" which, indeed, was the correct expression, only it did not apply to himself. Gazza was a very sensible person. I had, as I dropped into the nearest boat, a brisk sight of the sailing-master, springing like a jack-in-the-box on the deserted deck, with a roar of "Where's that haymaker?" His reference was to the anchor watch. The

"'Oh, yes, you would!' said Hortense"

temptation to procure good matches to light his pipe had ended (I learned later) by proving too much for this responsible sailor-man, and he had unfortunately chosen for going below just the unexpected moment when it had entered the daring head of Hortense to perform this extravagance. Of course, before I had pulled many strokes, the deck of the *Hermana* was alive with many manifestations of life-saving and they had most likely been in time.   But I am not perfectly sure of this; the current was strong, and a surprising distance seemed to broaden between me and the *Hermana* before another boat came into sight around her stern.   By then, or just after that (for I cannot clearly remember the details of these few anxious minutes), I had caught up with John, whose face, and total silence, as he gripped the stern of the boat with one hand and held Hortense with the other, plainly betrayed it was high time somebody came.   A man can swim (especially in salt water) with his shoes on, and his clothes add nothing of embarrassment, if his arms are free; but a woman's clothes do not help either his buoyancy or the freedom of his movement.   John now lifted Hortense's two hands, which took a good hold of the boat.   From between her lips the dishevelled cigarette, bitten through and limp, fell into the water.   The boat felt the weight of the two hands to it.

" Take care," I warned John.

Hortense opened her eyes and looked at me; she knew that I meant her.   " I'll not swamp you."   This was her first remark.   Her next was when, after no incautious haste, I had hauled her in over the stern, John working round to the bow for the sake of balance: " I was not dressed for swimming." Very quietly did Hortense speak; very coolly, very evenly; no fainting — and no flippancy; she was too game for either.

After this, whatever emotions she had felt, or was feeling, she showed none of them, unless it was by her complete silence. John's coming into the boat we managed with sufficient dexterity; aided by the horrified Charley, who now arrived personally in the other boat, and was for taking all three of us into that. But this was altogether unnecessary; he was made to understand that such transferences as it would occasion were superfluous, and so one of his men stepped into our boat to help me to row back against the current; and for this I was not unthankful.

Our return took, it appeared to me, a much longer time than everything else which had happened. When I looked over my shoulder at the *Hermana*, she seemed an incredible distance off, and when I looked again, she had grown so very little nearer that I abandoned this fruitless proceeding. Charley's boat had gone ahead to announce the good news to General Rieppe as soon as possible. But if our return was long to me, to Hortense it was not so. She sat beside her lover in the stern, and I knew that he was more to her than ever: it was her spirit also that wanted him now. Poor Kitty's words of prophecy had come perversely true: "Something will happen, and that boy'll be conspicuous." Well, it had happened with a vengeance, and all wrong for Kitty, and all wrong for me! Then I remembered Charley, last of all.   My doubt as to what he would have done, had he been on deck, was settled later by learning from his own lips that he did not know how to swim.

Yes, the sentimental world (and by that I mean the immense and mournful preponderance of fools, and not the few of true sentiment) would soon be exclaiming: " How romantic!   She found her heart!   She had a glimpse of Death's angel, and in that light saw her life's true happiness!"   But I should say nothing like that, nor would Miss Josephine St. Michael, if I read that lady at all right. She didn't know what I did about Hortense, she hadn't overheard Sophistication confessing amorous curiosity about Innocence; but the old Kings Port lady's sound instinct would tell her that a souse in the water wasn't likely to be enough to wash away the seasoning of a lifetime; and she would wait, as I should, for the day when Hortense, having had her taste of John's innocence, and having grown used to the souse in the water, would wax restless for the Replacers, for excitement, for complexity, for the prismatic life.   Then it might interest her to corrupt John; but if she couldn't, where would her occupation be, and how were they going to pull through?

But now, there sat Hortense in the stern, melted into whatever best she was capable of; it had come into her face, her face was to be read — for the first time since I had known it — and, strangely enough, I couldn't read John's at all. It seemed happy, which was impossible.

"Way enough!" he cried suddenly, and, at his command, the sailor and I took in our oars.   Here was the *Hermana's* gangway, and crowding faces above, and ejaculations and tears from Kitty. Yes, Hortense would have liked that return voyage to last longer. I was first on the gangway, and stood to wait and give them a hand out; but she lingered, and, rising slowly, spoke her first word to him, softly: —

"And so I owe you my life."

"And so I restore it to you complete," said John, instantly.

None could have heard it but myself — unless the sailor, beyond whose comprehension it was — and I doubted for a moment if I could have heard right; but it was for a moment only. Hortense stood stiff, and then, turning, came in front of him, and I read her face for an instant longer, before the furious hate in it was mastered to meet her father's embrace, as I helped her up the gangway.

"Daughter mine!" said the General, with a magnificent break in his voice.

But Hortense was game to the end. She took Kitty's hysterics and the men's various grades of congratulation; her word to Gazza would have been supreme, but for his imperishable rejoinder.

"I told you you wouldn't jump," was what she said.

Gazza stretched both arms, pointing to John. "But a native! He was surer to·find you!"

At this they all remembered John, whom they thus far hadn't thought of.

"Where is that lion-hearted boy?" the General called out.

John hadn't got out of the boat; he thought he ought to change his clothes, he said; and when Charley, truly astonished, proffered his entire wardrobe and reminded him of lunch, it was thank you very much, but if he could be put ashore — I looked for Hortense, to see what she would do, but Hortense, had gone below with Kitty to change *her* clothes, and the genuinely hearty protestations from all the rest brought merely pleasantly firm politeness from John, as he put on again the coat he had flung off on jumping. At least he would take a drink, urged Charley. Yes, thank you, he would; and he chose brandy-and-soda, of which he poured himself a remarkably stiff one. Charley and I poured ourselves milder ones, for the sake of company.

" Here's how," said Charley to John.

" Yes, here's how," I added more emphatically.

John looked at Charley with a somewhat extraordinary smile. " Here's unquestionably how!" he exclaimed.

We had a gay lunch; I should have supposed there was plenty of room in the *Hermana's* refrigerator; nor did the absence of Hortense and John, the cause of our jubilation, at all interfere with the jubilation itself; by the time the launch was ready to put me ashore, Gazza had sung several miles of " good music " and double that quantity of " razzla-dazzla," and General Rieppe was crying copiously, and assuring everybody that God was very good to him. But Kitty had told us all that she intended Hortense to remain quiet in her cabin; and she kept her word.

Quite suddenly, as the launch was speeding me toward Kings Port, I exclaimed aloud: " The cake ! "

And, I thought, the cake was now settled forever.

XXII

IT was my lot to attend but one of the weddings which Hortense precipitated (or at least determined) by her plunge into the water; and, truth to say, the honor of my presence at the other was not requested; therefore I am unable to describe the nuptials of Hortense and Charley. But the papers were full of them; what the female guests wore, what the male guests were worth, and what both ate and drank, were set forth in many columns of printed matter; and if you did not happen to see this, just read the account of the next wedding that occurs among the New York yellow rich, and you will know how Charley and Hortense were married; for it's always the same thing. The point of mark in this particular ceremony of union lay in Charley's speech; Charley found a happy thought at the breakfast. The bridal party (so the papers had it) sat on a dais, and was composed exclusively of Oil, Sugar, Beef, Steel, and Union Pacific; merely at this one table five hundred million dollars were sitting (so the papers computed), and it helped the bridegroom to his idea, when, by the importunate vociferations of the company, he was forced to get on his unwilling legs.

"Poets and people of that sort say" (Charley

concluded, after thanking them) " that happiness cannot be bought with money. Well, I guess a poet never does learn how to make a dollar do a dollar's work. But I am no poet ; and I have learned it is as well to have a few dollars around. And I guess that my friends and I, right here at this table, could organize a corner in happiness any day we chose. And if we do, we will let you all in on it."

I am told that the bride looked superb, both in church and at the reception which took place in the house of Kitty; and that General Rieppe, in spite of his shattered health, maintained a noble appearance through the whole ordeal of parting with his daughter. I noticed that Beverly Rodgers and Gazza figured prominently among the invited guests: Bohm did not have to be invited, for some time before the wedding he had become the husband of the successfully divorced Kitty. So much for the nuptials of Hortense and Charley; they were, as one paper pronounced them, " up to date and distingue." The paper omitted the accent in the French word, which makes it, I think, fit this wedding even more happily.

" So Hortense," I said to myself as I read the paper, " has squared herself with Charley after all." And I sat wondering if she would be happy. But she was not constructed for happiness. You cannot be constructed for *all* the different sorts of experiences which this world offers : each of our natures has its specialty. Hortense was constructed for pleasure ; and I have no doubt she got it, if not through Charley, then by other means.

The marriage of Eliza La Heu and John Mayrant was of a different quality; no paper pronounced it " up to date," or bestowed any other
adjectival comments upon it; for, being solemnized in Kings Port, where such purely personal
happenings are still held (by the St. Michael
family, at any rate) to be no business of any one's
save those immediately concerned, the event
escaped the tarnishment of publicity. Yes, this
marriage was *solemnized,* a word that I used above
without forethought, and now repeat with intention; for certainly no respecter of language would
write it of the yellow rich and their blatant
unions. If you're a Bohm or a Charley, you may
trivialize or vulgarize or bestialize your wedding,
but solemnize it you don't, for that is not " up to
date."

And to the marriage of Eliza and John I went;
for not only was the honor of my presence requested, but John wrote me, in both their names,
a personal note, which came to me far away in the
mountains, whither I had gone from Kings Port.
This was the body of the note : —

" To the formal invitation which you will receive, Miss La Heu joins her wish with mine
that you will not be absent on that day. We
should both really miss you. Miss La Heu begs
me to add that if this is not sufficient induce-
ment, you shall have a slice of Lady Baltimore."

Not a long note! But you will imagine how
genuinely I was touched by their joint message.
I was not an old acquaintance, and I had
done little to help them in their troubles,
but I came into the troubles; with their mem-

ory of those days I formed a part, and it was a part which it warmed me to know they did not dislike to recall. I had actually been present at their first meeting, that day when John visited the Exchange to order his wedding-cake, and Eliza had rushed after him, because in his embarrassment he had forgotten to tell her the date for which he wanted it. The cake had begun it, the cake had continued it, the cake had brought them together; and in Eliza's retrospect now I doubted if she could find the moment when her love for John had awakened; but if with women there ever is such a moment, then, as I have before said, it was when the girl behind the counter looked across at the handsome, blushing boy, and felt stirred to help him in his stumbling attempts to be businesslike about that cake. If his youth unwittingly kindled hers, how could he or she help that? But, had he ever once known it and shown it to her during his period of bondage to Hortense, then, indeed, the flame would have turned to ice in Eliza's breast. What saved him *for* her was his blind steadfastness *against* her. That was the very thing she prized most, once it became hers; whereas, any secret swerving toward her from Hortense during his heavy hours of probation would have degraded John to nothing in Eliza's eyes. And so, making all this out by myself in the mountains after reading John's note, I ordered from the North the handsomest old china cake-dish that Aunt Carola could find, to be sent to Miss Eliza La Heu with my card. I wanted to write on the card, " *Rira bien qui rira le dernier;* " but alas! so many pleasant thoughts may never be said aloud in this world of ours. That I ordered china, instead of silver, was due to my surmise that in Kings Port — or at any rate by Mrs. Weguelin and Miss Josephine St. Michael — silver from any one not of the family would be considered vulgar; it was only a surmise, and, of course, it was precisely the sort of thing that I could not verify by asking any of them.

But (you may be asking) how on earth did all this come about? What happened in Kings Port on the day following that important swim which Hortense and John took together in the waters of the harbor?

I wish that I could tell you all that happened, but I can only tell you of the outside of things; the inside was wholly invisible and inaudible to me, although we may be sure, I think, that when the circles that widened from Hortense's plunge reached the shores of the town, there must have been in certain quarters a considerable splashing. I presume that John communicated to somebody the news of his broken engagement; for if he omitted to do so, with the wedding invitations to be out the next day, he was remiss beyond excuse, and I think this very unlikely; and I also presume (with some evidence to go on) that Hortense did not, in the somewhat critical juncture of her fortunes, allow the grass to grow under her feet — if such an expression may be used of a person who is shut up in the stateroom of a steam yacht. To me John Mayrant made no sign of any sort by word or in writing, and this is the highest proof he ever gave me of his own delicacy, and also of his reliance upon mine; for he must have been pretty sure that I had overheard those last destiny-deciding words spoken between himself and Hortense in the boat, as we reached the *Hermana's* gangway. In John's place almost any man, even Beverly Rodgers, would have either dropped a hint at the moment, or later sent me some line to the effect that the incident was, of course, "between ourselves." That would have been both permissible and practical; but there it was, the difference between John of Kings Port and us others; he was not practical when it came to something "between gentlemen," as he would have said. The finest flower of breeding blossoms above the level of the practical, and that is why you do not find it growing in the huge truck-garden of our age, save in corners where it has not yet been uprooted. John's silence to me was something that I liked very much, and he must have found that it was not misplaced.

The first external splash of the few that I have to narrate was a negative manifestation, and occurred at breakfast: Juno supposed that the wedding invitations would be out later in the day. The next splash, a somewhat louder one, was at dinner, when Juno inquired of Mrs. Trevise if she had received any wedding invitation. At tea there was very decided splashing. No invitation had come to anybody. Juno had called at five of the St. Michael houses and got in at none of them, and there was a rumor that the *Hermana* had disappeared from the harbor. So far, none of the splashing had wet me, but I now came in for a light sprinkle.

" Were you not on board that boat yesterday ? "
Juno inquired ; and to see her look at me you might
have gathered that I was suspected of sinking the
vessel.

" A most delightful occasion ! " I exclaimed, filling my face with a bright blankness.

" Isn't he awful to speak that way about Sunday ! " said the up-country bride.

This was a chance for the poetess, and she took
it. " To me," she mused, " every day seems fraught
with an equal holiness."

" But I should think," observed the Briton, " that
you could knock off a hymn better on Sundays."

All this while Juno was looking at me, and I
knew it, and therefore I ate my food in a kindly
sort of unconscious way, until she fired another
shot at me. " There is an absurd report that
somebody fell overboard."

" Dear me ! " I laughed. " So that is what it
has grown to already !   I did go out on the boat
boom, and I did drop off — but into a boat."

At this confession of mine the up-country bride
became extraordinarily arch on the subject of the
well-known hospitality of steam yachts, and for
this I was honestly grateful to her; but Juno
brooded still.   " I hope there is nothing wrong,"
she said solemnly.

Feeling that silence at this point would not be
golden, I went into it with spirit.   I told them of
our charming party, of General Rieppe's rich store
of quotations, of the strict discipline on board the
well-appointed *Hermana*, of the great beauty of
Hortense, and her evident happiness when her
lover was by her side.   This talk of mine turned

off any curiosity or suspicion which the rest of the company may have begun to entertain; but upon Juno I think it made scant impression, save causing her to set me down as an imbecile. For there was Doctor Beaugarçon when we came into the sitting-room, who told us before any one could even say "How-do-you-do," that Miss Hortense Rieppe had broken her engagement with John Mayrant, and that he had it from Mrs. Cornerly, whom he was visiting professionally. I caught the pitying look which Juno threw at me at this news, and I was happy to have acquitted myself so creditably in the manipulation of my secret: nobody asked me any more questions!

There is almost nothing else to tell you of how the splashes broke on Kings Port. Before the day when I was obliged to call in Doctor Beaugarçon's professional services (quite a sharp attack put me to bed for half a week) I found merely the following things: the *Hermana* had gone to New York, the automobiles and the Replacers had also disappeared, and people were divided on the not strikingly important question as to whether Hortense and the General had accompanied Charley on the yacht, or continued northward in an automobile, or taken the train. Gone, in any case, the whole party indubitably was, leaving, I must say, a sense of emptiness: the comedy was over, the players departed. I never heard any one, not even Juno, doubt that it was Hortense who had broken the engagement; this part of the affair was conducted by the principals with great skill. Hortense had evidently written her version to the Cornerlys, and not a word to any other

effect ever came from John's mouth, of course.
One result I had not looked for, though it was a
natural one: if the old ladies had felt indignation
at Hortense for her determination to marry John
Mayrant, this indignation was doubled by her determination not to! I fear that few of us live by
logic, even in Kings Port; and then, they had all
called upon her in that garden for nothing! The
sudden thought of this made me laugh alone in
my bed of sickness; and when I came out of it,
had such a thing been possible, I should have
liked to congratulate Miss Josephine St. Michael
on her absence from the garden occasion. I said,
however, nothing to her, or to any of the other
ladies, upon this or any subject, for I was so unlucky as to find them not at home when I paid
my round of farewell visits. Nor (to my real
distress) did I see John Mayrant again. The boy
wrote me (I received it in bed) a short, warm note
of regret, with nothing else in it save the fact that
he was leaving town, having become free from the
Custom House at last. I fancy that he ran away
for a judicious interval. Who would not?

Was there one person to whom he told the
truth before he went? Did the girl behind the
counter hear the manner in which the engagement was broken? Ah, none of us will ever
know that! But, although I could not, without
the highest impropriety, have spoken to any of
the old ladies about this business, unless they had
chosen to speak to me — and somehow I feel that
after the abrupt close of it not even Mrs. Gregory
St. Michael would have been likely to touch on
the subject with an outsider — there was nothing

whatever to forbid my indulging in a skirmish with Eliza La Heu; therefore I lunched at the Exchange on my last day.

"To the mountains?" she said, in reply to my information about my plans of travel.

"Doctor Beaugarçon says nothing else can so quickly restore me."

"Stay there for the rhododendrons, then," she bade me. "No sight more beautiful in all the South."

"Town seems deserted," I pursued. "Everybody gone."

"Oh, not everybody!"

"All the interesting people."

"Thank you."

"I meant, interesting to *you*."

I saw her decide not to be angry; and her decision changed and saved our conversation from the trashy, bantering tone which it was taking, and brought it to a pass most unexpected to both of us.

She gave me a charming and friendly smile. "Well, you, at any rate, are going away. And I am really sorry for that."

Her eyes rested upon me with perfect frankness. I was not in love with Eliza La Heu, but nearer to love than I had ever been then, and it would have been easy, very easy, to let one's self go straight onward into love. There are for a man more ways of falling into that state than romancers would have us to believe, and one of them is by an assent of the will at a certain given moment, which the heart promptly follows — just as a man in a moment decides he will espouse a cause, and soon finds himself hotly fighting for it body and soul. I could have gone out of that Exchange completely in love with Eliza La Heu; but my will did not give its assent, and I saw John Mayrant not as a rival, but as one whose happiness I greatly desired.

"Thank you," I said, "for telling me you are sorry I am going. And now, may I treat you more than ever as a friend, and tell you of a circumstance which Kings Port does not know?"

It put her on her guard. "Don't be indiscreet," she laughed.

"Isn't timely indiscretion discretion?"

"And don't be clever," she said. "Tell me what you have to say — if you're quite sure you'll not be sorry."

"Quite sure. There's no reason — now that the untruth is properly and satisfactorily established — that one person should not know that John Mayrant broke that engagement." And I told her the whole of it. "If I'm outrageous to share this secret with you," I concluded, "I can only say that I couldn't stand the unfairness any longer."

"He jumped straight in?" said Eliza.

"Oh, straight!"

"Of course," she murmured.

"And just after declaring that he wouldn't."

"Of course," she murmured again. "And the current took them right away?"

"Instantly."

"Was he very tired when you got to him?"

I answered this question and a number of others, backward and forward, until she had led me to cover the whole incident about twice-and-a-half times. Then she had a silence, and after this a reflection.

"How well they managed it!"

"Managed what?"

"The accepted version."

"Oh, yes, indeed!"

"And you and I will not spoil it for them," she declared.

As I took my final leave of her she put a flower in my buttonhole. My reflection was then, and is now, that if she already knew the truth from John himself, how well *she* managed it!

So that same night I took the lugubrious train which bore me with the grossest deliberation to the mountains; and among the mountains and their waterfalls I stayed and saw the rhododendrons, and was preparing to journey home when the invitation came from John and Eliza.

I have already said that of this wedding no word was in the papers. Kings Port by the war lost all material things, but not the others, among which precious privacy remains to her; and, O Kings Port, may you never lose your grasp of that treasure! May you never know the land where the reporter blooms, where if any joy or grief befall you, the public press rings your doorbell and demands the particulars, and if you deny it the particulars, it makes them up and says something scurrilous about you into the bargain. Therefore nothing was printed, morning or evening, about John and Eliza. Nor was the wedding service held in church to the accompaniment of nodding bonnets and gaping stragglers. No eye not tender with regard and emotion looked on while John took Eliza to his wedded wife, to live together after God's ordinance in the holy state of matrimony.

In Royal Street, not many steps from South Place, there stands a quiet house a little back, upon whose face sorrow has struck many blows, but made no deep wounds yet; no scorch from the fires of war is visible, and the rending of the earthquake does not show too plainly; but there hangs about the house a gravity that comes from seeing and suffering much, and a sweetness from having sheltered many generations of smiles and tears. The long linked chain of births and deaths here has not been broken and scattered, and the grandchildren look out of the same windows from which the grandsires gazed, whose faces now in picture frames still watch serenely the sad present from their happy past. Therefore the rooms lie in still depths of association, and from the walls, the stairs, the furniture, flows the benign influence of undispersed memories; it sheds its tempered radiance upon the old miniatures, and upon every fresh flower that comes in from the garden; it seems to pass through the open doors to and fro like a tranquil blessing; it is beyond joy and pain, because time has distilled it from both of these; it is the assembled essence of kinship and blood unity, enriched by each succeeding brood that is born, is married, is fruitful in its turn, and dies remembered; only the balm of faith is stronger to sustain and heal, for that comes from heaven, while it is earth that gives us this; and the sacred cup

There hangs about the house a gravity . . . and a sweetness

of it which our native land once held is almost empty.

Amid this influence John and Eliza were made

one, and the faces of the older generations grew soft beneath it, and pensive eyes became lustrous, and into pale cheeks the rosy tint came like an echo faintly back for a short hour. They made so little sound in their quiet happiness of congratulation that it might have been a dream; and they were so few that the house with the sense of its memories was not lost with the movement and crowding, but seemed still to preside over the whole, and send down its benediction.

When it was my turn to shake the hands of bride and groom, John asked : —

" What did your friend do with your advice ? "

And I replied, " He has taken it."

" Perhaps not that," John returned, " but you must have helped him to see his way."

When the bride came to cut the cake, she called me to her and fulfilled her promise.

" You have always liked my baking," she said.

" Then you made it after all," I answered.

" I would not have been married without doing so," she declared sweetly.

When the time came for them to go away, they were surrounded with affectionate God-speeds ; but Miss Josephine St. Michael waited to be the last, standing a little apart, her severe and chiselled face turned aside, and seeming to watch a mocking-bird that was perched in his cage at a window halfway up the stairs.

" He is usually not so silent," Miss Josephine said to me. " I suppose we are too many visitors for him."

Then I saw that the old lady, beneath her severity, was deeply moved ; and almost at once

John and Eliza came down the stairs. Miss Josephine took each of them to her heart, but she did not trust herself to speak; and a single tear rolled down her face, as the boy and girl continued to the hall-door. There Daddy Ben stood, and John's gay good-by to him was the last word that I heard the bridegroom say. While we all stood silently watching them as they drove away from the tall iron gate, the mocking-bird on the staircase broke into melodious ripples of song.

XXIII

POOR AUNT CAROLA!

AND now here goes my language back into the small-clothes that it wore at the beginning of all, when I told you something of that colonial society, the Selected Salic Scions, dear to the heart of my Aunt. It were beyond my compass to approach this august body of men and women with the respect that is its due, did I attire myself in that modern garment which, in the phrase of the vulgar, is denoted *pants*.

You will scarce have forgot, I must suppose, the importance set by my Aunt Carola upon the establishing of the Scions in new territories, wherever such persons as were both qualified by their descent and in themselves worthy, should be found; and you will remember that I was bidden by her to look in South Carolina for members of the Bombo connection which she was inclined to suspect existed in that state. My neglect to make this inquiry for my kind Aunt now smote me sharply when all seemed too late. John May-rant had spoken of Kill-devil Bombo, the very personage through whom lay Aunt Carola's claim to kingly lineage, and I had let John Mayrant go away upon his honeymoon without ever question-ing him upon this subject. As I looked back upon the ease with which I might have settled

the matter, and forward to my return empty-
handed to the generous relative to whom I owed
this agreeable experience of travel, I felt guilty
indeed. I wrote a letter to follow John Mayrant
into whatever retreat of bliss he had betaken himself to, and I begged him earnestly to write me at
his early convenience all that he might know of
Bombos in South Carolina. Consequently, I was
able, on reaching home, to meet Aunt Carola with
some sort of countenance, and to assure her that
I expected presently to be furnished with authentic and valuable particulars.

I now learned that the Selected Salic Scions
had greatly increased in numbers during my short
absence. It appeared that the origin of the whole
movement had sprung from a needy but ingenious
youth in some manufacturing town of New England. This lad had a cousin, who had amassed
from nothing a noble fortune by inventing one
day a speedy and convenient fashion of opening
beer bottles; and this cousin's achievement had
set him to looking about him. He soon discovered
that in our great republic everywhere there were
living hundreds and thousands of men and women
who were utterly unaware that they were descended from kings. Borrowing a little money
to float him, he set up *The American Almanach
de Gotha* and began (for the minimum sum of
fifty dollars a pedigree) to reveal to these eager
people the chain of links that connected them with
royalty. Thus, in a period of time the brevity of
which is incredible, this young man passed from
complete indigence to a wife and four automobiles,
or an automobile and four wives — I don't remem-

ber which he had the four of. There was so
much royal blood about that it had spilled into
several rival organizations, each bitterly warring
with the other; but my Aunt assured me that her
society was the only one that any respectable
person belonged to.

I am minded to announce a rule of discreet
conduct: Never read aloud any letter that you
have not first read to yourself. Had I observed
this rule — but listen: —

It so happened that Aunt Carola was at luncheon with us when the postman brought John
Mayrant's answer to my inquiry, and at the sight
of his handwriting I thoughtlessly exclaimed to
my Aunt that here at last we had all there was
to be known concerning the Bombos in South
Carolina; with this I tore open the missive and
embarked upon a reading of it for the edification
of all present. I pass over the beginning of John's
communication, because it was merely the observations of a man upon his honeymoon, and was
confined to laudatory accounts of scenery and
weather, and the beauty of all life when once one
saw it with his eyes truly opened.

"No Bombos ever came to Carolina," he now
continued, "that I know of, or that Aunt Josephine
knows of, which is more to the point. Aunt Josephine has copied me a passage from the writings
of William Byrd, Esq., of Westover, Virginia, in
which mention is made, not of the family, but of a
rum punch which seems to have been concocted
first by Admiral Bombo, from a New England
brand of rum so very deadly that it was not in-
aptly styled 'kill-devil' by the early planters of

the colony.   That the punch drifted to Carolina
and still survives there, you have reason to know.
Therefore if any remote ancestors of yours con-
tracted an alliance with Kill-devil Bombo, I can
imagine no resulting offspring of such union but
a series of severe attacks of delir—"

"*What?*" interrupted Aunt Carola, at this
point, in her most formidable voice.   "What's
that stuff you're reading, Augustus?"

I shook in my shoes.   "Why, Aunt, it's
John—"

"Not another word, sir!   And never let me
hear his name again.   To think—to think—"
But here Aunt Carola's face grew extremely red,
and she choked so decidedly that Uncle Andrew
poured her a glass of water.

The rest of our luncheon was conducted with
remarkable solemnity.

As we were rising from table, my Aunt said:—

"It was high time, Augustus, that you came
home.   You seem to have got into very strange
company down there."

This was the last reference to the Bombos that
my Aunt ever made in my hearing.   Of course it
is preposterous to suppose that she traces her
descent from a king through a mere bowl of
punch, and her being still the president of the
Selected Salic Scions is proof irrefutable that her
claim rests upon a more solid foundation.

XXIV

POST SCRIPTUM

I THINK that John Mayrant, Jr., is going to look like his mother. I was very glad to be present when he was christened, and at this ceremony I did not feel as I had felt the year before at the wedding; for then I had known well enough that if the old ladies found any blemish on that occasion, it was my being there! To them I must remain forever a "Yankee," a wall perfectly imaginary and perfectly real between us; and the fact that young John could take any other view of me, was to them a sign of that "radical" tendency in him which they were able to forgive solely because he was of the younger generation, and didn't know any better.

And with these thoughts in my mind, and remembering a certain very grave talk I had once held with Eliza in the Exchange about the North and the South, in which it was my good fortune to make her see that there is on our soil nowadays such a being as an American, who feels, wherever he goes in our native land, that it is all his, and that he belongs everywhere to it, I looked at the little John Mayrant, and then I said to his mother: —

"And will you teach him 'Dixie' and 'Yankee Doodle' as well?"

But Eliza smiled at me with friendly, inscrutable eyes.

"Oh," said John, "you mustn't ask too much of the ladies. I'll see to all that."

Perhaps he will. And an education at Harvard College need not cause the boy to forget his race, or his name, or his traditions, but only to value them more, as they should be valued. And the way that they should be valued is this: that the boy in thinking of them should say to himself, "I am proud of my ancestors; let my life make them proud of me."

But, in any case, is it not pleasant to think of the boy being brought up by Eliza, and not by Hortense?

And so my portrait of Kings Port is finished. That the likeness is not perfect, I am only too sensible. No painter that I have heard of ever satisfies the whole family. But, should any of the St. Michaels see this picture, I trust they may observe that if some of the touches are faulty, true admiration and love of his subject animated the artist's hand; and if Miss Josephine St. Michael should be pleased with any of it, I could wish that she might indicate this by sending me a Lady Baltimore; we have no cake here that approaches it.

OWEN WISTER (1860–1938) was a native of Germantown, Pennsylvania. His maternal grandparents were Pierce Butler, a well-to-do Georgia planter, and Fanny Kemble, the Shakespearean actress and author of the *Journal of Residence on a Georgian Plantation in 1838–1839*. A Harvard classmate and friend of Theodore Roosevelt, in his adult life he practiced law in Philadelphia. A prolific writer, he was the author of short stories and novels, of which *The Virginian* (1902) is the best known. *Lady Baltimore* was published in 1906.

THOMAS FLEMING lived for many years in the Low Country of South Carolina. He graduated from the College of Charleston and received his Ph.D. in classics from the University of North Carolina. He is a poet and classical scholar, who has also written widely on literature and political ethics. He is the author of *The Politics of Human Nature* (1988) and the editor of *Chronicles: A Magazine of American Culture*.